Someone to Belong To

Melody Carlson

HARVEST HOUSE PUBLISHERS
Eugene, Oregon 97402

Cover by David Uttley Design, Sisters, Oregon

Map illustration by Jan Cieloha, Springfield, Oregon

SOMEONE TO BELONG TO
Copyright © 2001 by Melody Carlson
Published by Harvest House Publishers
Eugene, Oregon 97402

Library of Congress Cataloging-in-Publication Data

Carlson, Melody.
   Someone to belong to/ Melody Carlson.
      p. cm. — (Whispering pines series)
   ISBN 0-7369-0064-0
   1. Women newspaper editors—Fiction. 2. Real estate development—Fiction.
     3. Oregon—Fiction. I. Title.
   PS3553.A73257 S66 2001
   813'.54—dc21   00-061404

Printed in the United States of America.

01 02 03 04 05 06 07 08 09 10 / BC-BG / 10 9 8 7 6 5 4 3 2 1

To Lucas Andrew Carlson
Love always,
Mom

One

Word of Maggie and Jed's engagement spread through town faster than a change of mountain weather, so that for the next few days Maggie could hardly go anywhere without someone mentioning it. Even after it felt like old news, she was met by Rich from the Eagle Tavern, who stopped her in front of the post office to offer his congratulations.

"Ol' Jed sure didn't waste any time, did he?" He sighed and then shook his head, though she knew it was only for dramatic effect. "Never even gave the rest of us half a chance."

She laughed, then patted him on the arm in a mock-consolatory way. "Well, I guess some things are just meant to be."

"By the way, Maggie," he added as he held the door open for her, "I've been meaning to tell you that I never did sign that businessmen's petition supporting TS Development."

She studied him curiously, unsure of why he wanted her to know. "Thanks for telling me, Rich. I appreciate hearing it. I tried not to take that whole business too seriously last year. I figured once the snow came along things would settle down around here."

"Looks like you were right." He pulled down his hat and headed back out into the icy wind.

She smiled to herself as she dropped her letters in the mail. How she longed to tell Rich and anyone else interested about the big surprise TS Development would soon receive! But the deal wasn't completely sealed yet. And even if it was, they had all agreed to keep the whole thing under wraps until just the right time. So far, Gavin's plan had gone even better than expected. Stan Williams had been here for two days, and he'd been absolutely delighted with the town and recreational area in general, but when he saw Clyde's beautiful parcel of property just down the road from Maggie's house, he didn't even bother to conceal his pleasure. It seemed the partnership was meant to be, and tonight they would all meet at the hotel to discuss the whole thing over dinner.

She crossed the street over to Jed's shop, stepping over a pile of freshly plowed snow next to the curb. She'd spotted his pickup just moments ago on her way to the post office and wanted to make sure she caught him before he headed back home to his workshop. He'd been putting in long hours lately trying to fill furniture orders and remodel his house as well as work on the building that would one day contain the new church. She and Leah had both grown a little concerned that he might be overdoing it.

"Hey there," called Maggie as she spied him placing what looked like a newly made pine table against the back wall of his shop. "Caught you!"

He walked over to her and grinned. "And I'm glad you did!" He swooped her up into a big hug. "Why don't you pop in and catch me more often?"

"Guess I'd better. It might be the only way I ever get to see you!"

He looked down into her eyes. "Hmm...maybe I have been burning the midnight oil lately. But there's so much to get done these days, and now that you and I are on track I feel strangely energized."

"I know what you mean. I think love does that to you."

"Hey, you love birds," called Leah as she came in the front door. "I'm back from lunch, so you guys can go finish making out in the back room if you want to."

Jed laughed. "Thanks, Leah. We might just do that."

Maggie gently extracted herself from his embrace. "Actually, I stopped by to see if I could talk you into joining Clyde and Gavin and me for dinner tonight. Remember I told you we're meeting with Stan and his family at the hotel?"

He frowned. "You know I'm willing to do almost anything for you, Maggie, but I honestly think I'd just be extra baggage. And I've got so much work to do right now."

She tried to hide her disappointment. "I know. And I really do understand, but I think your opinion would be helpful—you know a lot about building and design. And... I mostly just wanted to see you myself."

"How about if I promise that we'll do something soon—just the two of us?" He looked at her hopefully. "Wouldn't that be more fun anyway?"

"Of course. But I also want to make sure you're not working too hard, Jed." She glanced at Leah for support.

"Yeah, Dad," said Leah, stepping up with that exaggerated swagger that seems to come only with adolescence. Maggie smiled—she loved that Leah had taken to calling Jed "Dad" lately. And he seemed to like it even more. "Yeah," she continued, hands on hips, "just the other day, Maggie and I were discussing how we think you're working way too hard. It's not healthy. *And* we mean to put a stop to it."

He grew thoughtful, then slowly nodded. "You're probably right."

Maggie blinked. "You mean, you agree with us so easily? Just like that? We expected a little more struggle."

"To tell you the truth," he looked from one to the other, "I've been thinking about hiring an apprentice to help me out some. I've easily got enough work for two people right now, and the orders just keep coming—"

"I know, Dad. I had a lady call just this morning who wants to do a whole room in rustic birch. I think she wanted a dozen different pieces, all totaled."

"That settles it. Leah, can you call the newspapers and place a classified ad for an apprentice?"

Leah glanced at Maggie, perhaps a small plea for help, and she just nodded as if to reassure. "Sure, Dad," Leah answered with confidence. "I'll get on it first thing."

Jed turned to Maggie. "So, have you had lunch yet? If I'm getting some help, I might be able to afford the time to get a quick bite to eat."

She seized his arm. "It's a date, Mr. Whitewater." Then winking at Leah she said, "And I promise to have him back in—" she glanced at her watch. "Oh, maybe by the end of the day, at the very latest."

The deli was crowded, and Rosa looked pleased but busy. She just waved to them from the kitchen while Sierra took their order. "I'll bet Spencer is up on the mountain right now," she said glumly.

Maggie nodded. "Yeah, he talked his grandma into taking him up. But I thought you were supposed to be up there today too."

Sierra rolled her eyes. "Cara called in sick this morning, so guess who gets to fill in for her?"

"That's too bad," said Jed kindly. "I know how Leah wishes she could get in more snowboarding too, but the alternative wouldn't be so hot either."

"Yeah, it's always feast or famine." Sierra handed them their drinks. "Just as long as I don't hear about Cara being up on the mountain today."

"That'd be pretty low-down." Maggie tried not to chuckle as they made their way to the only empty table.

"When do Scott and Chloe get back from their honeymoon?" asked Jed as he pulled a chair out for her. She still wasn't completely used to his courteous, albeit slightly old-fashioned, manners. She remembered that Phil had always been pretty casual about such niceties. But Jed seemed to take the little things seriously.

She sat down. "I think they get back next week." She smiled dreamily. "Maui must be awfully nice this time of year."

"It sure was generous of Chloe's parents to foot the bill for their trip at the last minute like that," he commented as he stirred his coffee.

"Yeah, Scott was pretty shocked. He'd planned to keep everything local since their finances were fairly well stretched just by the wedding. But I'm sure her folks felt guilty about not helping out with the whole thing. I think it was simply their way of apologizing for being such poor sports at the beginning."

He laughed. "I'm glad we're old enough that we won't have to put up with all that kind of nonsense for our wedding."

"Yes, it is a relief, isn't it." She paused as Sierra placed their order on the table, then Jed said a brief blessing. "By the way, Jed, everyone's been asking me if we've set a date yet..."

He nodded. "I know, I've been getting the same drill. I suppose we should talk about it. What are you thinking?"

She picked up her spoon and thought for a moment. "I'm not really sure. I mean, on the one hand, I've had moments when I think we should just do it right away, but then I consider how busy we both are. And then on the other hand, I sometimes think we should just wait and give it lots of time."

"I know exactly what you mean."

She looked into his eyes, suddenly feeling self-conscious. "And then I think...a spring wedding has always appealed to me."

His brows lifted. "Spring?"

She nodded.

"As in this *coming* spring?"

"Well, I suppose we could wait until spring of *next* year." She tried to conceal how she felt slightly offended by his reaction.

"No way. I don't want to wait *that* long. I guess when you said *spring* it just sounded so close, like next week or something." He chuckled. "You know how it can be with someone who's been a bachelor as long as I have."

She smiled. "Yes, I'll try to be patient. And if spring feels too soon—"

"No, actually I think spring might be just right." Then he grinned knowingly. "But has anyone told you when spring actually comes to Pine Mountain?"

She shook her head.

"We don't usually see much sign of spring until around May."

"May sounds perfect."

"Then it's settled?"

She looked into his eyes. "Is it?"

He reached across the table and took her left hand in his, gently fingering the shiny new ring on her finger. "I just hope I can wait that long."

She felt her cheeks grow warm. "Good thing we've both got a lot of things to keep us busy then, isn't it?"

✺

After lunch Maggie finished her Saturday errands, then stopped by the fitness center for a quick workout. As usual, the place was busy, but Cherise took time to pull Maggie aside before she left. "It's all finished upstairs," she announced with pride. "Want to come up and see?"

"Sure, I'd love to if you can spare the time."

Cherise glanced around the workout area as if taking a quick inventory. "Everything seems to be under control down here." As they walked up the steps she explained how she hoped to be able to hire a helper in a month or two.

"Things must be going well then."

"Yeah. Greg always used to say how this place was nothing more than an expensive hobby and tax deduction. But he was wrong. I can really make a living off it." She stopped at the top of the stairs and waved her arms in a flourish. "Well, here it is in all its glory!"

Maggie looked around. "Cherise, it's absolutely fantastic. Even better than before, and I thought it looked good then. That kitchenette is adorable—I love all those bright-colored tiles."

"Still look like L.A.?" Cherise's eyes sparkled.

"You bet. Hey, can I plan your housewarming now?"

"You'd really do that for me?"

"Of course. Why not?"

Cherise shook her head. "Oh, I just remember how Greg was always so down on you—acting like you really didn't give a hoot about someone like me."

Maggie waved her hand. "Well, Greg was all wet about a lot of things."

Cherise laughed. "He sure was!"

Maggie instantly felt bad. "I'm sorry, I don't mean to suggest that you guys can't work this out or any—"

"Don't worry, Maggie. I know what you mean. But, believe me, Greg's made it pretty clear that he's thrilled to have me out of the picture. I think especially now that he's so sure he's going to be some big ol' millionaire with his land deals."

Maggie smiled. "Well, at least you seem happy."

Cherise spun around in her pretty little loft apartment. "Oh, I am!" Then she turned to Maggie with a more serious look. "And you know how I've been going to church real regular like? Well, I really do like the way Michael preaches. I never heard anyone talk about God like that before. He makes it so real and personal that I've actually started praying myself. Can you believe that?"

"Sure. And I think it's great."

"Man, wouldn't Greg be shocked about that!"

Maggie just nodded, thinking to herself that Greg was

going to be shocked about a number of things before too long. She glanced up at the retro-style clock on the wall. "Oh, I had better get going, Cherise. But thanks for showing me around—you've done an incredible job with this place. And I'll get back to you about the housewarming dates. Because I *really* do want to do it."

Cherise threw her arms around Maggie. "You're such a good friend!"

Two

"*H*ey there, Maggie," called Clyde, waving to her anxiously.

She shook the snow off her coat as she stepped into the hotel lobby. "Am I late?"

"No, Stan and his womenfolk are still upstairs. But come on in here and listen to what Gavin just told me."

She hung her coat on a rack, then joined the two of them in the waiting area. "What's up?"

Gavin chuckled. "Well, I was just telling Uncle Clyde how I ran into Greg at Dolly's Diner today. I'd taken Stan and his family up to hit the slopes, which they were suitably impressed with, I might add—"

"Come on," urged Clyde. "Get on with the good stuff."

Gavin nodded. "Anyway, Greg asked me to sit down and have lunch with him. So I figured, why not, who knows, maybe I'll hear what TS Development is up to these days—not that too much is happening after the snafu with the wetlands issue. Sounds like it's pretty much at a standstill, although Greg swears Colin Byers' attorneys are going to work it all out before spring. Anyway, Greg starts talking all friendly and nice, acting like we've never had any rift in our friendship at all. And it starts looking like he's trying to win me over into enemy camp. Then he starts going on about

15

how we used to be such good buddies and all—guess he forgot how he ditched me when I was down and out last summer. The next thing I know, he's telling me about how I can still get in on the ground floor of his development and make some big money. He knows Clyde here's just loaded, and maybe I can talk him into getting involved too, and then he says, real good-old-boy-like, how this newspaper really needs to support development like this, if only for the sake of the town. Then he asks if I can't do something about our editor's position on the whole thing—"

Maggie groaned. "Yeah, I'm sure he'd love it if the two of you would run me out of town."

Clyde slapped his knee. "Don't it just beat all, Maggie? Greg sidling up to our Gavin here, thinking he's gonna get him and me involved in *his* half-baked schemes. And all the while we're closing in on our own sweet deal that's gonna totally upset his little applecart entirely." He let out a loud whoop.

Maggie glanced up the stairs, worried that Stan and his family might think their potential business partner was going slightly senile, then she patted Clyde on the shoulder. "Okay, now take it easy, Clyde. And before you start planning your big victory celebration, don't forget you haven't even signed the final papers yet. Who knows, maybe Stan's changed his mind."

"Speaking of Stan…" Gavin spoke quickly, then stood and waved to the family just coming down the stairs. "So, did you all have a good day on the slopes?" he asked as he shook Stan's hand.

"It was terrific. Nothing but powder and sunshine. And hardly any lines on the chairlifts either. Not that that won't be changing by next year."

Gavin introduced Stan's wife, Claire, and two preteen daughters to Clyde and Maggie, and then they were all led to a large round table reserved for them in a quiet corner. Maggie could see Cindy's obvious curiosity about this interesting mix of patrons as she seated them, but she raised no questions. Maggie hoped she appreciated how the newspaper had paid to put the Williams' family up in the hotel's two finest suites for three nights.

"Are you skiers or riders?" Maggie asked the girls.

"We're riders," answered Jessie, the older. "But Mom and Dad are pretty old-fashioned. They still use those silly sticks and poles."

Maggie nodded to Claire. "I'm old-fashioned too. But my fifteen-year-old son snowboards and he absolutely loves it."

They all chatted pleasantly about the community, and Claire asked Maggie very specific questions about the local schools, activities, and even churches. Maggie appreciated her keen interest and was pleased to tell her all she could, even mentioning the library that was in development and the building that was being remodeled to house the church. "Of course, there are several other denominations in town too—Episcopal, Catholic, Baptist...you know, the regulars." She thought for a moment. "But there still isn't a synagogue. My friend Elizabeth Rodgers pointed that out when she first moved here. She goes over to Byron to worship."

"Well, I expect this town will be growing steadily from here on out. And in a couple years there will probably be lots of new additions." Claire glanced over to her husband and he winked.

"Okay, I won't beat around the bush. We're very impressed with this community and the potential here. It's just the kind of place I'm willing and eager to work with." He looked over to his two girls. "You see, I refuse to develop in an area where I wouldn't be willing to live myself. And now I'm afraid my girls are going to think we should move up here for good."

"As a matter of fact," began Jessie, "can you imagine having a mountain to snowboard on just twenty minutes from where you live!" Her younger sister, Jamie, nodded in eager agreement.

Claire laughed. "It's certainly something to consider. But think about it, girls, would you really be willing to leave your school and your friends back in Arizona?"

The two girls considered this. Then Maggie spoke up. "Moving can be pretty hard on kids. My son was absolutely furious when I moved him up here last year."

"How does he like it now?" asked Stan.

"Oh, he loves it. But it took a little adjusting at first."

When dinner was over and the discussion became more business focused, Claire excused herself and the girls. Maggie walked them back to the foyer and told Claire how much she enjoyed getting acquainted. "And if you do decide to move up here, it'll be fun getting to know you even more."

"Well, whether we permanently relocate here or not, you can be sure we'll have our own unit to use for vacationing. The girls wouldn't have it any other way, I'm sure." Her daughters smiled in consensus. "So I'll look forward to seeing you again, Maggie. And now we're going up to watch a video and then turn in early. We fly out first thing in the morning."

When Maggie rejoined the guys, it sounded as if they too were wrapping it up. Everyone seemed quite pleased with all the arrangements, and Stan promised to have the final paperwork sent up the following week. "It didn't look as if you had many revisions," he said to Clyde as they stood.

"Well, my lawyer felt that it was all pretty fair and sensibly written up. I suspect the only reason he made any changes at all was just so it'd look like he was earning his money." This made them all laugh. Then everyone shook hands one last time and said goodnight.

Outside, Gavin sighed loudly. "It looks like we're on our way."

Clyde rubbed his hands together. "Can't wait until those papers are all signed and we get to make our big announcement."

"That's one story I could probably write in my sleep," said Maggie, "I've imagined it in print so many times. But maybe we should plan a ground-breaking ceremony, take some news photos, and make it a really big deal."

Clyde slapped her on the back. "I like your thinking, young lady! That way we can *really* rub those development boys' noses into it."

Maggie's brow lifted slightly. "Now, Clyde, you're not going to get all vindictive about this, are you? We don't want to gloat, do we?"

He made a face. "Well, I sure wouldn't mind gloating a little. Especially when I think of what they did to old Arnold."

"I know what you mean. But it doesn't seem right to act too smug about the whole thing."

"I s'pect you're right about that too. Truth is, I never did much care for smugness in folks." He looked at her. "But can we at least throw a party?"

She laughed. "Why not!"

➢

When Maggie walked into the office on Monday, Abigail gave her a message to return a call to Jeanette Reinhart.

"Did she say what it was about?" asked Maggie.

"No, but she sounded pretty low. My guess is the lawyer told her the case for regaining the old Westerly property is hopeless."

"Well, that's what we all suspected anyway. But I'll give her a call and see what's up." Maggie set her briefcase down on her desk and sank into her chair. Just thinking about Jeanette and the tangled mess of the deceased Arnold Westerly's property and TS Development made her feel tired. She picked up the porcelain figurine the old man had sent her just before his death, then dialed Jeanette's number.

"Thanks for calling back so quickly, Maggie," began Jeanette in a flat voice. "I wish I could tell you something a bit more encouraging, but our family attorney said that even with those audiotapes you sent, he can't make much of a case out of this whole thing. He says it's a waste of our time and money."

"I'm sorry," said Maggie. "We were afraid that would be the case, but we were hoping."

"Yeah, and the timing for finding this out couldn't have been any worse as far as I'm concerned…"

"Why's that?"

After a loud sigh and a long pause Jeanette continued. "I just found out my husband's leaving me."

"Oh, Jeanette, I'm so sorry." She didn't know what to say.

"Yeah, I guess I'm not surprised. I'd been suspecting he and his secretary were involved with more than just business for a long time. But it seemed so silly to think that…you know, sort of predictable and obvious…I just didn't think it was really possible. But go figure, huh?"

"I guess you should never say never."

Another long sigh. "So anyway, when I first heard my husband's little bombshell I suddenly just wanted to *go home*—you know what I mean? But not to my own home which, of course, belongs to my husband too. And I wasn't even thinking about my parents' house, which was sold long ago. I wanted to go back to Grandma and Grandpa's house in Pine Mountain. Back to the farm. And then later on, that same day, the lawyer called, and I realized even that dream was entirely hopeless."

"I'm sorry, Jeanette."

"Have they torn down any of the old buildings yet?"

"No. This whole thing about the wetlands controversy has put the brakes on everything, at least for the time being. But that's not stopping Greg from telling everyone that their developer, Colin Byers, is getting it all worked out. If I were him, I wouldn't be too sure." She paused, longing to give this poor woman something hopeful to hang onto, but she was committed to their pact to keep news of the latest development completely silent until it was written in stone.

"And...well, I can't say anything too specific, Jeanette, but there's another little obstacle coming their way too."

"Really?" Jeanette's voice perked up ever so slightly.

"Sorry, I can't give out any details yet."

"Well, it's probably not going to make any difference in the long run." Her voice had gone flat again. "From what I hear, once these things start, there's no stopping them. Only delays. What's the use?"

"Well, you never know, Jeanette. Some obstacles are bigger than others..."

"I wish it were true. Oh, I know I'll never get the property back, but if only the farm could continue. That, at least, would be satisfying—just for Grandpa's sake."

"Well, this little obstacle should all be out in the open in just a few days. And I promise I'll call you as soon as we know anything for absolute certain."

"Thanks, Maggie. I appreciate you taking the time to talk to me. I still remember how rude I was to you when we first met—"

"Just forget about that. It was understandable under the circumstances. And, Jeanette, one more thing...I know this might not be of much help to you, but when I lost my husband a few years ago, and I know my circumstances were completely different, I started leaning on God like I'd never done before. And that's probably the only thing that got me through it all."

"Well, right now I'm not even sure that I believe in God anymore. Although Grandpa and Grandma taught me differently. But I'll keep it in mind. Thanks, Maggie, for everything."

⟨⟩

"Hey, Maggie," said Leah as she sliced tomatoes for a green salad. "We might not even need that ad you helped me write the other day."

She dropped the pasta into the boiling water and turned. "You don't mean Jed's changed his mind about getting himself an apprentice already? Why, he's going to work himself to—"

"No, that's not it. But, you see, this guy came into the shop today. And he was ogling all of Jed's pieces and going over ever single thing and saying, 'Man, this guy is good...he really knows his stuff...' and things like that. And so I asked him if I could help, and he said no, he couldn't afford to actually buy anything, but he just came in to see how everything was put together and examine the craftsmanship. Then I asked him if he worked in wood too." She held up her paring knife. "Bingo! The guy said he was still just learning woodworking, but that he hoped someday to be as good as Jed. Then I mentioned the apprentice position, and, man, you should've seen his eyes light up like I'd offered him a million bucks!"

"Oh, Leah, that's great. But did he seem legit? I mean, I hope he's not some wacko looking for a free ride or anything. I'd sure hate to see Jed get involved with the wrong person right now when he's already so swamped with work."

"I know exactly what you mean. So, I asked him a few more fairly direct questions. And he sounded like he was totally serious. He lives in the valley right now, but he comes over here to snowboard on weekends. He'd taken an extra day off today just to have a look around town. He said he quit college after two years because he really wanted to work with his hands. And he's been working for a cabinetmaker for the last six months, but he says he gets bored because everything is always the same. He said he wants to do something more creative."

"Oh, Leah, he does sound perfect. Have you told Jed yet?"

"Better than that. I set up an appointment. The guy—his name is Taylor—went out to Dad's. He might still be there, having an interview. Naturally, I know it's Dad's decision and everything. He might even want to wait and see if anyone else responds to the ads that come out tomorrow, one in Byron and then Wednesday in the *Pine Cone*, though I can't imagine who in Pine Mountain would make a good apprentice. At least not as good as Taylor anyway." The way Leah said his name caught Maggie's attention.

"So, about how old is Taylor?" She turned back to the boiling pot and gave the pasta a casual stir.

"Oh, early twenties, I'd guess..."

Maggie turned back around. "And did he seem pretty nice to you?"

Leah looked slightly irritated. "Well, of course he seemed nice. And before you ask me, I'll just tell you, he wasn't too difficult to look at either!" Then she broke out into a big grin. "Tall, curly brown hair, hazel eyes..."

Maggie giggled. "Well, hopefully Jed isn't aware of how you feel. Or else the poor kid probably won't have half a chance."

Leah's brows shot up. "Why not? What do you mean?"

"Oh, I'm just sort of kidding, mostly. But you know how dads can be about their little girls when it comes to *men*..."

She smiled. "Gee, that's kind of sweet, isn't it? I mean, it's still strange to think that I have a dad like that, someone who actually cares."

"Of course he cares," said Audrey as she stepped into the kitchen and began rolling up her sleeves to help. "Now tell me what exactly it is we're talking about."

The story of the remarkable young Taylor was replayed for Audrey, but Maggie could tell that something about it bothered her mother just slightly. Still, she thought it better not to ask while Leah was around and make too much of the whole thing. Who knew whether Jed would even hire the boy or not?

"Oh, yeah!" exclaimed Leah. "I can't believe I almost forgot. Something else totally weird happened today." She stopped tossing the salad and turned to Maggie. "And *you're* not going to believe this!"

"What?" asked Maggie.

Leah's dark eyes grew wide as she began to tell the next story. "Well, this lady came into the shop just before closing. I've never seen her before, but she just struck up a conversation like she knew Jed and half the other people in town as well, and I figured she was just someone from Pine Mountain I hadn't met. But then again, she didn't really look like a local—"

"What *did* she look like then?" asked Audrey as she sliced some French bread. "And how can you tell the difference?"

"Well, she was dressed nice. Sort of like an executive or some important business woman. She had on this really good-looking tan suede suit, and her shoes and purse matched. Her reddish hair was cut into a very chic style. She was kind of glamorous and pretty, especially for an *older* woman."

Maggie and Audrey exchanged looks. "How old would that be?" asked Maggie, knowing she was setting herself up.

"Oh, you know, about your age."

Audrey chuckled. "That old, eh?"

"Do you suppose she's someone from a big store, maybe wanting to consign furniture?" asked Maggie hopefully. "If Jed gets a new apprentice, he'll be able to take on some more accounts.

"No." Leah continued mysteriously. "She told me she was an old friend of Jed's!"

Maggie felt a small twinge just then, but wasn't exactly sure what it meant. "*And?*" She gave the bubbling pot another stir. "Is that all there is to your story, Leah?"

"No. Here's the really weird part. When I told her I was Jed's daughter, she acted shocked, like she couldn't believe it. Then she came up really close and just studied me as though I was some sort of science specimen or something. And then she said, 'Well, of course, I should have noticed it right off.' Then she looked me right in the eye and told me how she used to be *Jed's old high-school sweetheart!*" Leah paused for what seemed dramatic effect. "Then she just laughed and said that she should've known that Jed would be married by now."

"And then what did you say?" asked Audrey, no longer cutting bread and appearing almost as curious as Maggie felt.

"Well, I said, 'No, Jed never did marry...' but before I could even finish my sentence, she cried out, 'Oh, I knew it! He said he would always love me!'"

Maggie gasped. She wished she hadn't, but the sound just slipped out before she could stop it. Then she forced herself to laugh. "You're kidding. This is so incredible, Leah. *Then* what did you say to her?"

"I felt kind of embarrassed, most of all for her, I guess. Of course, I told her right away about how you guys are engaged and how happy Jed is, and I kind of went on and on about how great you are, Maggie."

Maggie felt her eyes grow misty. Then she marched across the kitchen and gave Leah a big hug. "Have I ever told you how much I love you?"

Leah grinned. "Yeah, lots of times."

"Hey," said Spencer from the doorway. "What's going on in here, some kind of love-in or something?"

"Love-in?" exclaimed Maggie. "Where did you pick up an old hippie term like that?"

"We were talking about the sixties and seventies in my social studies class."

Audrey laughed. "Your mom was just thanking Leah for defending her position."

"Her position?" Spencer looked confused now.

Maggie waved her hand. "Oh, not really. But Leah was telling us how one of Jed's old girlfriends came into the shop today. And how she told her that Jed's engaged."

"And hopefully she told her to hit the road too," said Spencer as he snitched a slice of bread. "Any chance of getting some dinner tonight? Or are you guys just going to continue your love-in?"

"Maybe you could go set the table," suggested Maggie as she handed him a stack of plates. After he was gone she turned back to Leah. "Did this woman give you her name?"

"Yeah. It's Amber something or other. She said Jed wouldn't recognize her married name, but she was divorced now anyway."

"And did she say *why* she was in town?" asked Audrey with blatant suspicion interwoven between each word.

"Probably looking for her old lover boy, Jed Whitewater," said Spencer as he came back in for the silverware.

"Actually..." Leah nodded to him with raised brows. "I think Spence is right on the money."

"Well, did you give her Jed's number?" asked Maggie, hoping she sounded unconcerned and casual about the whole thing. And why shouldn't she? "I'm sure he'd like to see her after all these years. It's only natural."

"I wasn't sure what to do. So I explained to Amber that I never give out his home phone number without his permission, and that I knew he was interviewing someone for an apprenticeship this afternoon. Then she said it was okay, and that she was planning to be in town for a few days anyway, taking a skiing vacation, and that she'd be staying at the hotel and could he please give her a call at his convenience."

"Do you think he will?" asked Spencer, appearing more interested than before.

"I don't know." Leah looked to Maggie. "What do you think?"

"Well, I don't know why he wouldn't want to see an old friend, especially after all these years..." Suddenly Maggie felt all three sets of eyes pinned on her. She looked at them in frustration. "Good grief, I don't know!" She threw up her hands. "It's up to Jed, isn't it? But I don't have any reason to be worried about any of this. I know that Jed loves me and the past is just the past."

Everyone seemed to relax a little after her reassuring speech. Perhaps they just needed to hear from her that she wasn't concerned. And as they ate dinner their conversation, as usual, flitted from one topic to the next. But the subject of Jed's old girlfriend, thankfully, did not resurface.

Still, Maggie knew she wasn't quite as confident as she had tried to appear. For she, perhaps better than anyone, understood that there *had* been a serious old flame in Jed's life. Someone who had somehow wounded him so deeply that he'd closed and locked the door to his heart for years. Now she wondered if this "glamorous-looking" woman might possibly be her. And, if so, what would Jed think of her return? Well, she knew she would call him right after dinner and find out. After all, they were engaged. She had every right to ask him. And besides, he had promised to tell her the whole story someday anyway. What with all the excitement of their recent engagement, she'd nearly forgotten. Until now that is.

But then again, she wondered as they began to clear the table, perhaps she should wait for him to come to her and tell her all about the whole thing. She didn't want to come across as being distrustful of him, or to appear as if she were questioning his commitment to her. Because she really wasn't suspicious of anything. Not really. At least not of Jed.

As far as this Amber person went...well, she just wasn't entirely sure.

Three

aggie refrained from calling Jed by busying herself with her slowly growing novel, now on chapter 3. But after spending several hours to create only two pages of text, she decided to call it a night. The phone rang just as she climbed into bed. She grabbed the receiver on the first ring, hoping desperately that it was Jed.

"Sorry to call so late," he apologized.

"It's okay. I'm always so glad to hear your voice that you could call me at three in the morning and I wouldn't complain. Well, not much anyway."

"I'd like to hear your voice at three in the morning."

She smiled. "You will someday."

"Mmm…Can't wait."

"I heard you interviewed a potential apprentice today."

"Yeah, did Leah tell you about Taylor?"

"She seemed pretty impressed."

"I was too. Actually, that's why I'm calling so late. He just left."

"You're kidding! He's got a late-night ride ahead of him."

"Yeah, that's what I said. But he didn't seem to mind. Especially since he's only going home to give his notice, then coming back here as soon as possible to come work for me."

"Oh, Jed, that's wonderful! So he's really the right guy after all?"

"Sure seems like it. And he's taking a little cut in pay to come work for me too."

"So he must think it's worthwhile to work with a master craftsman like yourself."

He laughed. "Funny, Taylor said almost the same thing. But I'm not sure where you people get these crazy ideas."

"Oh, Jed, you're so humble. It's one of the many, many things I love about you." She could hear him yawning now. "And before I put you to sleep with my fervent praise and adoration, maybe I should just tell you goodnight."

"But then I won't get to hear your sweet voice anymore."

"You can still dream about me."

"Mmm…Yeah, I guess I can…and it has been a rather long day…"

She imagined him in his big four-poster log bed and smiled to herself. "Yes, as much as I hate to hang up, I think you need to be a smart boy and go to sleep."

"I think you're right. I love you, Maggie."

"I love you, Jed."

They both hung up and she sighed deeply, certain she had nothing to worry about with this old girlfriend, Amber Whatever-her-name-was. And she was glad she hadn't mentioned her to him. Sure, this redheaded woman may have broken Jed's heart long, long ago, but Maggie felt she should thank her for it. For it was probably due to Jed's old heartache that he had remained single all these years, just waiting for the right woman to come along. Once again, Maggie thanked God for his amazing timing as she drifted off to sleep.

∾

By midday Tuesday, Clyde had signed and returned the final paperwork for the development agreement with Stan

Williams' company. He and Gavin came into Maggie's office with a bottle of sparkling cider to celebrate.

"I'd have brought the real thing," he said as he closed the door behind him, "but I don't want to be responsible for knocking Gavin off the wagon. Besides, I think this tastes better anyway."

Gavin set out paper cups in a row on her desk.

"Can I call in Abigail?" asked Maggie.

Clyde looked at Gavin. "Well, we're still keeping the whole thing quiet until Stan has everything sitting on his desk—and maybe until that little recision period safely passes. I want to play my hand close to my chest just to be safe."

"But I think we can trust Abigail," said Gavin generously.

Clyde smiled at him. "You bet we can."

Maggie went out and got her, quickly explaining what was going on and the need for absolute secrecy as they walked back into her office.

"Well, I'll be!" exclaimed Abigail. "Is it really true?"

Clyde handed her and Maggie each a full paper cup and grinned. "Yep! We beat those development boys at their own crooked game. Only we played it straight." He raised his cup. "And now let's toast to the success of Whispering Pines."

"Whispering Pines?" Gavin looked curious.

Clyde nodded firmly. "Yep, that's the name of our new community."

"To Whispering Pines," repeated Abigail as they all raised their cups in agreement.

"Whispering Pines," repeated Maggie as they all sipped. "That's beautiful, Clyde. Who came up with that name?"

"My sweet wife, God bless her."

Everyone turned to look at him. It was the first time Maggie had ever heard him mention the wife who'd passed away more than forty years earlier.

Clyde sighed, his eyes in a faraway place. "Olivia used to call that stand of old ponderosa pine trees her 'whispering pines.' She said if we ever wanted to get fancy and give the place a proper name, we'd call it that—Whispering Pines. I'd almost forgotten all about it, but when I was up there the other day with the surveyor and the wind was just a gently blowing, I'll be durned if I didn't hear them pines a whispering to me too. And it made me think of my dear Olivia."

"I can barely remember Aunt Olivia," said Gavin with a smile. "But all my memories of her are good. She was a real sweet lady, Uncle Clyde."

He nodded. "That she was." Then his eyes flashed as if he had just remembered something else. "And now that I think of it, I recall she was quite fond of Mrs. Westerly too. I'd almost forgotten. Now, what was the first name of old Arnold's wife?"

"Nellie?" Maggie offered.

"That's right. Nellie. My Olivia and Nellie got to be pretty good friends there at the end. Nellie came out a lot when Olivia was sick. She was real motherly to her. I can't believe how I'd almost forgotten that. But it's the unhappy days we tend to wipe from our memories, isn't it."

Abigail nodded. "Well, then I think your Olivia would be very happy to know what you've done for her dear friend, Clyde."

"Who knows?" said Maggie. "Perhaps all three of them are up there right now looking down on us and celebrating this whole thing too."

"You think so?" Clyde didn't look too convinced. "I've never been all that sure of that heaven and afterlife stuff myself."

"Well, you might want to give it some thought, Uncle Clyde," offered Gavin. "I know I have. That Michael Abundi has got me thinking about all kinds of things concerning God these days."

Clyde chuckled. "Yeah, well I'm not getting any younger. Maybe I'll have to go talk to that young man myself someday. Who knows, maybe you can teach an old dog a few new tricks."

"Speaking of old dogs," said Abigail, "how soon until we can let this cat out of the bag?"

Clyde scratched his head. "Good question. Well, how about if we tentatively set the ground-breaking ceremony for, let's say, one week from today."

"That sounds good," agreed Maggie. "That way we can cover it in the paper the following day. And Scott will be back by then to take photos."

"But how will we let everyone know about it?" asked Abigail. "Don't you want to have a big crowd present? Make a heyday out of it?"

"The business association has a meeting scheduled next Monday night," offered Maggie. "I wasn't planning on going myself after certain people made it pretty clear that it might be time for me to step aside from the association."

"That's nonsense," said Abigail. "You all but started that whole thing up in the first place."

Maggie firmly shook her head. "No, I think it's time for me to step down. But perhaps Gavin should go." She looked at him. "Since you're one of the developers of Whispering Pines, wouldn't that qualify you as a local businessman?"

"I suppose so."

"Of course it would," agreed Clyde.

"And you own the newspaper, Clyde." Abigail nudged him with her elbow. "That makes you a businessman. No reason you shouldn't go too."

Clyde considered this. "Maybe, but I'd like Gavin to make the announcement."

Maggie studied the old man for a moment, amazed at how much he'd softened toward his nephew in the last couple months. Then she smiled at Gavin. "Do you want to do that, Gavin?" she asked.

He grinned. "You bet I do. I can't wait to see Greg's and Rick's faces when they hear about this whole thing. And it's certain they'll be there trying to win support for their little venture. Maybe I should just wait until the very end of the meeting. Then I can casually toss out my little invitation and be on my way before anyone can ask any questions."

Clyde clapped his hands together. "That does it! I've made up my mind I'm going too. Why, I wouldn't miss this for all the tea in China! How about you, Maggie girl?"

She thought for a moment. "Actually, I should probably be on hand to report on the meeting. Scott'll just barely be back by then..." She glanced at Abigail. "So, how about you? Any excuse you can think of to come along and enjoy the fun?"

Abigail chuckled. "Shoot, I don't need an excuse. I'll come simply because I want to. I'll sit with Clara and Lou and no one'll be the wiser."

"Okay, now, everyone remember," Clyde grew more serious. "Mum's the word until then. You all know how news spreads through this town."

Everyone agreed and then returned to their normal work. Maggie had started to realize just how much she missed Scott last week when they'd printed their first edition of the New Year. At least he'd had a few things nearly ready for print before the wedding and subsequent honeymoon. But without his contributions this week, the paper looked thinner than ever. If not for several large ad spaces, sold by Gavin, and a couple of AP human interest stories, it would be pitiful. She wondered if Scott might not be deserving a raise before too long. Well, she consoled herself, at least next week's paper would have some good local stories. The front page would be filled with news of Whispering Pines, and Scott could be sure to get some good photos of the ground-breaking ceremony.

"Someone's here to see you, Maggie," came Abigail's voice over the intercom. "A Ms. Feldman."

Maggie frowned up from her desk. It was cluttered with work that needed to be finished before she went home in order to get the paper to bed in time. "I don't know a Ms. Feldman, Abigail. And I'm awfully busy right now."

"Would you like me to take a message?"

Maggie considered this, but curiosity overcame her. Perhaps this had something to do with TS Development or the wetlands issues. And, who knew, perhaps it would provide another much-needed story to fatten the paper. "No, Abigail, ask her to wait, and I'll be out in a moment to see what this is about."

When she stepped into the main office a few minutes later, she saw an attractive woman dressed in the kind of outdoor clothing that appeared to have come straight off the cover of the L.L. Bean catalog, and so new, Maggie felt certain these clothes had never seen the real outdoors. She smiled as she extended her hand. "Hello, I'm Maggie Carpenter."

The woman removed a neat felt hat and shook out her short auburn hair. "Hi. I'm sorry to intrude on you like this, Maggie. I'm Amber Feldman, and I know we haven't met, but I've been just dying to make your acquaintance."

Maggie slowly released the woman's hand and stepped back to lean against the front counter. She now knew exactly who this was, and Leah had been right—she was a very attractive woman. "Well, here I am. What can I do for you, Ms. Feldman?"

"Oh, please call me Amber. I know this must sound so silly, but you see, I used to be a good friend of Jed's. I'm in town for the week, and when I heard about you, well, I just thought to myself—I *must* meet her! And then I hoped perhaps we could all get together for drinks and laughs or something."

"Oh, yes," said Maggie, forcing her lips into what she hoped appeared a sincere smile. "Jed's daughter, Leah, mentioned that you stopped by the shop yesterday. Have you been able to catch up with him yet?"

Amber laughed. "No. I'm halfway tempted to drive up to his old place, but I'm afraid I might get lost—it's been so long, you know. Leah said she gave Jed my message, but I've been in the hotel all morning long, and he hasn't called yet."

She made a pouting expression, then smiled again. "Do you think he's avoiding me on purpose?"

Just then Gavin walked in the front door and paused, taking a long look at Amber as if he faintly recalled her face but couldn't quite put it all together.

Amber beat him to the punch. "Why, if I'm not mistaken, you must be Gavin Barnes!" She stuck out her hand. "Don't you remember me? From back in high-school days?"

"Amber McLeer!" He smiled. "You've hardly changed at all."

She shook her head. "Hair's shorter and more wrinkles, not to mention several other casualties of aging."

"Hey, we missed you at our twentieth reunion."

"I know, I would've loved to have been there, but we were out of the country at the time. Maybe I'll make the thirtieth. You know, it's coming up before long. Can you believe it? When did we get so old? I sure don't feel much different than I did back then."

"You don't look much different either." Then Gavin shook his head. "But I suppose it's true we are getting up there."

Maggie made a move, considering returning to her office as it seemed they were doing just fine without her. But then Gavin turned to her.

"It looks like you two have already met then. Amber, did you know that Jed and Maggie were recently engaged?"

"Actually, I have heard the news. And I just wanted to see with my very own eyes the woman who'd finally captured dear old Jed's heart. Congratulations, Maggie. Have you set a date yet?"

Thankful that she and Jed had already had that conversation, Maggie answered with an air of confidence, "Yes. We haven't really told anyone, but we plan to tie the knot in May. We think a spring wedding might be nice."

"Well, I'm very happy for you both." Amber glanced back to Gavin. "I was just saying to Maggie that perhaps we could all go out for old time's sake tonight. Why don't you join us, Gavin? We could make it a foursome."

Gavin looked to Maggie. "Well, I don't really know…"

"Actually…" Maggie looked at her watch and saw that it was nearly four now. "I was just about to say that tonight won't work for me. I'm short a writer, and I've got to get this paper ready, and—"

"How about this?" interrupted Gavin. "Maybe Amber would like to join me for dinner tonight. And then perhaps you and Jed could get together with her another time when you're not under a deadline crunch."

Maggie smiled. "I guess that's up to Amber, but it would work better for me. Will you be around for a day or two?"

"Yes, I'll be here until the weekend." She turned to Gavin. "And I think I'll take you up on that offer. Who knows, maybe Jed can still join us too." She turned back to Maggie. "So nice to meet you. I'm sorry to have taken up your time."

Maggie felt dismissed. "Well, okay, then, I had better get back to it. Nice meeting you, Amber. Hope to see you again."

"I'm sure you will."

Maggie went back to her office and wondered how she'd be able to concentrate enough to finish her work now. Would Jed agree to have dinner with Amber and Gavin? She didn't really think so. But then again, why shouldn't he? And why did it even bother her? Grow up, Margaret LeAnn, she scolded herself.

Finally, her mind back on the paper, she spent several grueling hours getting everything arranged and ready for the next day's printing. When she finally locked the front door, it was almost nine and she was famished. She glanced over to the hotel, tempted to go by and see if she could spy Amber and Gavin still visiting after dinner. She wondered if she would also see Jed, although she hoped not. But then she thought better of it and using the side street to purposely avoid Main, she went straight home, hoping her mother had saved her some dinner.

At home, Leah and Spencer were engrossed in some new TV game show, and Audrey had already turned in. Maggie found leftovers in the refrigerator and hungrily sat down to eat in the kitchen without even warming up the plate.

"Gross, Mom," said Spencer. "How can you stand to eat that stuff cold?"

She looked at her dinner and grinned sheepishly. "Actually, I was so starved I didn't even notice. Besides, Grandma's lasagna is good in almost any form."

"I s'pose. But how come you're so hungry?"

"Working late." She shoveled in another bite.

"But Leah said you were having dinner with Jed tonight."

Maggie's fork stopped in the air. "Huh?"

Just then Leah stepped into the kitchen to put a glass in the dishwasher. "Hey, Mag." She looked down at the half-empty plate. "Why are you eating again?"

"Again?"

"Yeah, Dad said you guys were all having dinner together at the hotel." Leah laughed. "What happened? Didn't you get enough to eat? Or did that Amber chick make you lose your appetite altogether?"

Maggie shook her head. "I've been working on the paper all night. I haven't eaten since I had yogurt and an apple at noon."

"Weird." Leah shook her head. "Dad called this afternoon about something else, and told me you guys were all getting together at the hotel for dinner tonight."

"Hmm..." Maggie wiped her mouth with a paper napkin. "Well, Amber did stop by to invite me out this evening, but I explained to her that I had too much work to do and couldn't go."

Leah frowned. "Does that mean Dad had dinner with Amber alone?"

Maggie shook her head. "No, I think Gavin joined them."

"Whew," said Spencer. "That's a good thing."

Maggie looked curiously at her son. "What do you mean by that?"

"Well, you don't want Jed and that old girlfriend eating dinner alone, do you?"

She made herself laugh. "It's no big deal, Spence. They're just old friends. They probably have lots of catching up to do."

He rolled his eyes. "Don't be so naive, Mom."

This time she laughed for real. "I know I can trust Jed, Spencer."

"I'm not talking about Jed, Mom." He glanced over to Leah. "Don't you remember how Leah said this woman looked pretty hot for an old chick?"

Now Maggie laughed even harder. "Well, I'll admit she was quite attractive 'for an old chick.' But so are lots of other women, honey. You know that Jed and I love each other. And we're getting married, remember?"

Finally he nodded. "Yeah, I guess so. But just the same, if I were you I wouldn't trust this other woman. You just never know about these things, Mom."

She pretended to take his advice seriously. "Okay, Spence. I'll keep that in mind. In fact, if it makes you two feel any better, I'll call Jed as soon as I finish eating."

"Good thinking." He poured himself a glass of juice. "I mean, don't kid yourself. Jed's a pretty good catch. That Amber lady probably wants him back."

Four

aggie puttered around for a while before she finally forced herself to sit down and dial Jed's number. It was already past ten, and she really didn't want to put it off any longer. After several rings, Michael answered in a sleepy voice.

"Oh, I'm sorry, Michael. This is Maggie. Did I wake you?"

"It is okay, Maggie. I am awake now. What is wrong?"

"Oh, nothing's wrong. I just called to talk to Jed. Has he already gone to bed too? Don't bother him if he's asleep."

"No. I do not think he is home yet. I am looking outside I do not see his truck here and the light is still on."

"Oh…"

"Is everything okay, Maggie?"

"Yes, of course. I just wanted to talk to him. No big deal, Michael. You go back to bed and I'm sorry—"

"But did you not talk to Jed at dinner tonight, Maggie?"

Maggie pressed her lips together. "I wasn't able to join them for dinner, Michael. I had to work late at the paper."

"Oh." He paused. "Do you think Jed is all right? Do you suppose his truck slid on the icy road like when Leah got stuck?"

This thought sent a shudder down her spine. "Oh, no, I'm sure nothing's wrong, Michael. I'll bet that Gavin and Jed and Amber are just remembering their old school days and lost track of the time."

Michael laughed. "Oh, yes. I have done that before with my good friends back in my village. Sometimes we all sit around the fire until almost the next day remembering the things we did as boys."

"Do you miss your home in New Guinea, Michael?"

"Yes. I miss my good friends there. But I believe my home is wherever God sends me, Maggie. As long as God is with me, I am at home. And now you and Jed and Barbara and so many others are my dear friends."

"I'm so glad you came to us, Michael. I didn't get a chance to tell you Sunday how much I enjoyed your sermon."

"Oh, you must give that credit to God, Maggie. For if I say anything that touches your heart, it is God who is doing the actual speaking. I am only his instrument." He paused. "It is a lot like this telephone here. We are having a good conversation, Maggie, but you would not say to the telephone, 'Oh, you are doing such a good job, Mr. Telephone.' Now would you?"

This made her laugh. "No, I suppose I wouldn't. You explain things so well—" She caught herself. "God uses you to make things so clear, Michael. I'm thankful to God for you."

"Ah, now that is what I like to hear, Maggie."

"I'll let you get back to sleep."

"Shall I tell Jed you called?"

"No, I'll talk to him tomorrow. Good night."

"God bless you!"

ᴥ

Maggie tried to call Jed the next morning, but only got the answering machine. She left a brief message asking him to call, and then she hung up. Leaning back into her chair, she rhythmically thumped her pencil on her desk and wondered what she should do besides wait for Jed to get back to her. She hadn't seen Gavin yet, but that wasn't unusual because he did much of his work outside of the office. She was dying to know how things had gone last night. She knew she could call him on his cell phone, but she didn't want to appear overly curious. No, she would just wait. For a moment she tried to put herself in Jed's shoes. This whole surprise of the old girlfriend coming back to town must be somewhat shocking to him. What was he thinking? How did he feel? Did it bring back unhappy memories? Oh, how she longed to know!

She worked until half past twelve, hoping that Jed might get her message and call back. But finally she gave up and went to the fitness center. On her way over, she remembered her promise to give Cherise a housewarming. She'd penciled in Saturday night on her own calendar, but hadn't had time to confirm it with Cherise or anyone else for that matter. Cherise had already made it clear she had very few friends in town besides her regulars at the fitness center. Maggie suspected this had more to do with Greg than Cherise and hoped it would begin to change.

"Hey, Maggie," chirped Cherise. "I was hoping to see you today."

Maggie smiled. "Say, how does Saturday night sound for a little housewarming?"

Cherise beamed. "Sounds great!"

"Good, let's plan on it then. I thought maybe from seven to nine—sort of open-ended so people can come and go as they please."

"Yeah, that is if anyone really wants to come."

"Of course they will! It'll be lots of fun. Just wait and see."

"Okay, I'll trust you on this." She pointed to the free stepper machine. "I'll save that for you while you dress down."

Just as Maggie came out of the dressing room, she noticed Amber Feldman walking up to the front counter to talk to Cherise.

"Hello, Maggie," called Amber as Maggie walked toward the stepper. "I thought I'd see if I could schedule a little workout myself. This looks like an absolutely great place."

"It is," said Maggie, smiling at Cherise. "And this is the owner, Cherise Snider."

Amber shook her hand. "Are you related to Greg Snider?"

Cherise rolled her eyes. "He was my husband, but we're separated now."

Amber laughed. "Well, join the club. I just divorced my husband last year. That was after twenty years of pure—"

"I'll see you," called Maggie as she slipped over to the machine. She didn't want to be rude, but she had no desire to stand there and listen to Amber's marriage woes. And she really didn't wish to speak with Amber before she'd had a chance to talk to Jed first. She finished a rushed workout, then hurried back over to the newspaper, checking her phone for messages. But still Jed hadn't called.

By the end of the day, Gavin stopped by to tell her about a full page ad the hardware store wanted to purchase for a January clearance sale. "Looks like they haven't given us up after all." He smiled with satisfaction.

"Great work, Gavin." She chuckled. "Can you imagine them running an ad like this in Randy Ebbert's little three-page flyer he calls a newspaper?"

"Yeah, I don't think we need to be too worried about the competition just now." He paused. "Say, Maggie, have you talked to Jed today?"

She shook her head and fiddled with a small stack of papers on her desk. "No. I realize he's really busy right now, trying to fill all those orders, not to mention working on his house and the church…"

"Yeah, he said last night that he's so overwhelmed with work he'd actually hired an apprentice."

"I can't wait for Taylor to get here." She felt relieved to be able to sound as if she was somewhat involved in Jed's life. Just to be able to actually drop the name of the new helper seemed important right now.

"Isn't it great that he's able to leave his other job so soon and start this weekend?"

Maggie looked up, but she tried to mask her surprise. This was something she hadn't heard yet. "Hmm, I wonder where Taylor will stay?"

"Well, sounds like he'll be staying out at Jed's."

"But what about Michael?"

"I guess Michael's been wanting to move into town. And Barbara Harris just signed the lease on a small house that's within walking distance of the church. Do you know the old Phillips' house?"

Maggie stared up at him, no longer bothering to hide her astonishment. "Good grief, Gavin Barnes, *you* should be a reporter! You know lots more about what's going on in this town than I do!"

He laughed. "Well, you've just been working too hard, Maggie. You need to slow down and get out more."

"I guess so." She fiddled with a pencil, rocking it back and forth between her fingers. "Speaking of getting out, how did it go last night?"

"Okay, I guess. It felt pretty awkward at first. I felt sorry for Jed. It's too bad you weren't there, Maggie. We mostly made small talk. Amber told us about her job and all the places she's traveled to. Then after about an hour, we called it a night."

"Really? Only an hour?"

"Yeah, we kind of ran out of things to talk about. Jed was being quiet. I think he felt pretty uncomfortable. Can't say as I blame him..."

"Did he and Amber go together for a long time in high school?"

"Jed hasn't told you about any of this?"

She shook her head. "Not really."

"Well, some things are probably better left unsaid. I doubt that I'd tell my fiancée about all my past loves. Not much purpose to that."

"So...you would consider Amber one of Jed's past loves?"

He looked at her carefully, then spoke. "I would've considered Amber the love of his life. That is until you came along, Maggie. I'm fairly certain that you've changed all that."

"I sure hope so." She set the pencil down. "Did Amber break Jed's heart back in high school?"

He shrugged. "To tell you the truth, I don't really know exactly what happened because they were still going together when my mom and I moved back east. But I guess I always expected that Amber and Jed would get married and live happily ever after."

"But they didn't..."

"The next time I met up with Jed again was by chance when we were both in Phoenix. He'd just gotten back from Vietnam, and I almost didn't recognize him. He was pretty messed up then." He frowned. "I'm sorry, Maggie. I probably shouldn't be saying any of this."

"It's okay. Jed's already told me about those days. He's not proud of his past, but he doesn't try to hide it either."

"Well, I can sure understand that from my own personal experience. He was lucky that he straightened himself up a whole lot sooner than I did. So I suppose you know how he was using and drinking pretty heavily back then, which was pretty surprising to me, since Jed had always been as straight as a stick about that stuff before. But what really got my attention was how he'd become so angry. It seemed as though he was mad at everyone. He'd never been like that before—even if he'd had good reason. But, man, was he ever bitter. I figured it had to do with Nam. A lot of guys were like that in those days. But I remember I asked him once what had become of Amber, and he flipped out and called her every name in the book. I think I touched a sore spot."

"You probably had."

"I didn't really see him much after that—until we both ended up here, that is. And we didn't talk much then, although Jed wasn't unfriendly to me. But I was still pretty messed up, and he was walking the straight and narrow. But he never treated me poorly during all that time. Even when my supposed friends like Greg turned on me, Jed was never like that. He's a good guy, Maggie."

She smiled. "I know. I just wish I knew what he was thinking right now."

"Why don't you ask him?"

She sighed. "Yeah. I think I'd better." Then she noticed the note she'd made about Cherise's housewarming. "Hey, Gavin, I'm helping with a housewarming for Cherise Snider—she's all set in her new apartment above the fitness center. Do you have any plans for this Saturday night?"

He grinned. "No. And for the record, I've always liked Cherise. She's never gotten a fair shake in this town, and Greg's always treated her like a dog." He shook his head. "No, I take that back. He treats his dog a heck of a lot better."

"I'll take that as a yes then?"

"You bet I'll be there."

Maggie called the other few names on her list: the Galloways, a few people from church, Buckie and Kate, and then she finally dialed Jed's number again, thinking she'd probably just leave him a message. To her surprise, he answered.

"You mean this is really you and not your machine?" she said dumbly.

"How are you doing, Maggie?"

She closed her eyes. "I've been better."

"What's wrong?"

"Oh, I don't know...Actually, I was thinking of asking you the same thing."

"I missed you at dinner last night."

"Didn't Amber tell you I had to work?"

"Well, not until I got there. And then it was too late."

"I'm sorry. Do you want to talk about it?" She waited during a long pause, then finally she spoke again. "Are you okay, Jed?"

"Yeah. It's just that seeing her again has dredged up a lot of old feelings—feelings that I'd just as soon forget."

"Oh…" She felt her heart start to pound—the way it did after a bad dream, or if something had startled her.

He sighed. "I want to talk to you, Maggie. But I think I may need a little time to sort all this out. Can you understand that?"

"Sure." She swallowed. "It's a lot for you to take in. I tried to imagine how I'd feel if I were in your place. I'm sure it's not easy."

"Thanks, Maggie. I love you."

"I love you too, Jed." She felt her eyes grow misty. "I'm just so sorry this all had to happen, but maybe it's for the best, you know."

"Yeah. I'm sure you're right."

She changed the subject, telling him about Cherise's housewarming, and he promised to come and to tell Michael too. "Is it okay if I bring Taylor along? He'll just be getting settled in here on Saturday. It'd be a good way for him to meet a few folks."

"Oh, that'd be great. The more the merrier!"

"And thanks again, Maggie."

"For what?"

"For being so patient and understanding about all this. And for just being you."

She smiled. "I love you so much, Jed."

"I know. And it means the world to me."

Five

Scott and Chloe came home from their honeymoon the following day, and Maggie and her family were invited to a little party given by Rosa to welcome the couple's return, and then watch as they opened their wedding gifts.

"Where's Jed tonight?" asked Rosa as she handed Maggie a cup of punch. Then she slapped herself on the forehead. "Oh, my goodness, I completely forgot!"

"Forgot what?" asked Maggie, nearly spilling her drink. "Scott and Chloe don't even know!"

"Know what?" called Scott. He removed a paper bow Chloe had put in his hair and stuck it to her nose with a mischievous grin.

"The big news," said Rosa. "I forgot to tell you. It didn't happen until just after you kids left for your honeymoon."

Maggie held up her left hand and fluttered her fingers to display her diamond engagement ring.

"Oh, Maggie!" cried Chloe. "You and Jed?"

Maggie nodded.

"Congratulations!" exclaimed Scott. "Hey, Chloe, we must've started a trend."

Sam laughed. "I think it goes back a little further than you two."

"So where's the lucky guy?" asked Scott.

"He's pretty busy these days." Maggie had tried to talk him into coming, but he had gently declined. "But if you come to Cherise's housewarming on Saturday, you can congratulate him yourself."

Later on, Maggie went to join Rosa in the miniature kitchenette. "Goodness, you can barely fit two people in here at the same time," she said as she covered the leftover cake with plastic wrap.

"I know, but isn't it sweet and cozy?" Rosa put a pitcher into the tiny fridge, then turned to look at Maggie. "Speaking of cozy, how are things with you and Jed these days?"

"I'm sure you've heard about Amber by now."

Rosa nodded. "Actually, I've met her. She's been in the deli a few times. How long does she plan on staying?"

Maggie shrugged. "I thought just a few days. At least I hope so. I think this whole thing has been pretty disturbing to Jed."

"I can imagine." Rosa pressed her lips together and sadly shook her head. "Sam's told me a bit about what went on in the past. Poor Jed."

"That's right. I'll bet Sam knows the whole story."

"Well, I doubt that he knows everything. But enough to know this can't be easy for Jed."

"Please tell me, Rosa," demanded Maggie. "He's been keeping everything to himself, and I feel like I'm going to explode from the suspense. Just what exactly happened between those two?"

Rosa glanced at the noisy group laughing and joking and still sitting shoulder to shoulder in the living room, and then back to Maggie. "How about if I give you the condensed version?"

"Sure, I don't want it to take all night."

"Okay. Well, Sam said that Jed and Amber went together all through high school. Apparently Amber was outgoing, popular, pretty—all that. But for some reason, she set her sights on Jed, who had always been a little on the outside of things. But it sounds like it was the best thing that ever could've happened to him. Until then he'd been fairly quiet and reserved, but Amber managed to draw him out. Before long, he started participating in sports and was doing better in school. And he even began to have more friends. Sam said he seemed really happy back then. After graduation, even though Amber went away to college, she and Jed were still going together. But not long after that he was drafted. Sam said that while Jed was over in Vietnam, he got a letter from Amber telling him she was engaged to another guy."

Maggie groaned. "You mean a Dear John letter?"

"Yeah, something like that. It broke his heart. After that, Sam says, he took all kinds of risks and didn't expect to make it back home alive—you know, lots of boys didn't make it. Anyway, he did manage to survive all that and come back home. But then he tried to throw away his life all over again. Sam said it nearly broke his father's heart too."

Maggie nodded sadly. "I think I know the rest of the story, Rosa. And I suppose it's all pretty much what I'd imagined with Amber. But I just can't understand why she's come back now; I mean, after all this time. And why does she insist on hanging around all week? Surely she needs to get back to her job or something."

Rosa shook her head. "I don't know. Maybe she thinks, after all these years, that she still..."

"Wants him back?"

"It seems possible. Jed's an awfully sweet guy."

"Believe me, I know." Maggie looked down at the dish-towel twisted in her hands. "That's what worries me."

"But he loves *you*, Maggie!" Rosa grasped her arm and gave her a gentle shake. "I know he does! I've seen it in his eyes again and again."

"Thanks, Rosa." She unwound the towel and placed it next to the sink. "And I really do believe he loves me. But it's so hard watching him go through all of this suffering and everything, and he's so quiet about it. I just wish that Amber would go away and leave us alone for good."

Rosa gave her a hug. "Don't worry. It's going to be okay."

⌒

On Friday afternoon, Amber called at the newspaper and asked Maggie if she and Jed would join her for dinner that night. "Jed told me that he would come if you would come," pleaded Amber, sounding a bit like a fifth-grade girl Maggie had once known but never liked.

"I don't know…" she paused, wondering if there was some easy way to gracefully escape this. But then, it hit her—this might be her only chance to see what this woman was really and truly like, and to observe Jed's reaction to her. "Sure, Amber. I don't see why not. I'd like to get to know you better before you leave."

"You would?" She sounded dumbfounded.

"Of course. I know you were once a big part of Jed's life. And that's important to me. I'd be glad to come tonight."

"Oh, thank you, Maggie. How does seven sound?"

"Sounds perfect. Shall I let Jed know?"

"No, I'll take care of that. Thanks again." And then she hung up. Maggie set the receiver down, instantly wishing she'd insisted on letting Jed know. But, then, what did it matter? They would simply meet, eat, chat, and Amber would be gone the next day or so. End of story.

"Excuse me, Maggie," called Abigail. "But do you have a minute so I can run the plans for the ground-breaking ceremony by you?"

"Sure, and while you're at it, call Scott in here. I want to bring him up to date about all this."

"And swear him to secrecy?"

"That's right."

The three met briefly, and Maggie told Scott the good news. They also discussed the kind of shots he should get.

"I won't tell Chloe or my parents," he promised. "And

believe me, keeping things from my wife isn't easy. But this is just the greatest story! I can't wait to see Greg's and Rick's expressions when they hear the news. Sure you don't want a candid shot of them at the meeting?"

Maggie laughed. "Truthfully, I'd love it. But I just recently got on Clyde's case about not gloating. I had better listen to my own advice."

It looked as if Abigail had all the details for the celebration worked out. And even Stan Williams planned to show up for the day.

"How about calling in the Byron paper?" asked Scott.

"Way ahead of you." Maggie grinned.

"Maggie already put together a press release," explained Abigail. "I'll send it out just before closing on Monday afternoon—a couple hours before Gavin announces the groundbreaking at the business association meeting."

"All right!" Scott gave them both a high five.

"And I'm calling it a day," said Maggie as she shut off her computer.

"Good for you," said Abigail. "You've been working too hard lately."

Maggie smiled at Scott. "Yes, I've been missing my right-hand man. In fact, I wouldn't wait too long before I hit up the boss for a raise if I were you, Scott!"

He grinned. "Shall I put it in writing?"

"You're a writer, aren't you?"

"Gotcha." He gave her a thumb's up. "Thanks, Maggie."

✧

The sky was leaden as she drove home. It looked as though more snow was on the way. She'd heard a couple of townsfolk complaining at the deli today, which seemed ironic in light of how they'd been longing for it just over a month ago. But she still wasn't tired of it yet. And she didn't mind sweeping it from her porch or shoveling it from the walkway. To her it was still fresh and new and wonderful.

Maybe next year she'd see it differently, but she didn't think so. Where would she be next year, she wondered, as she pulled into her own driveway. Would she be living at Jed's? The idea appealed to her. But at the same time, she wasn't eager to give up this house. Maybe, like Michael had said just last Sunday, God would make it all clear when the time came. Surely there was no use in looking for trouble tomorrow when there was usually enough for today.

She walked through the house. No one was home. Not even Audrey, who'd said she was going to spend the day doing some planning at the building that would house the town's library by spring or summer. Maggie was so glad her mother had finally found something to occupy her time besides taking care of them. Not that she minded all of Audrey's help. Where would she have been without it?

Maggie went into her room and kicked off her shoes, deciding to indulge herself in a nice, long, hot bath and a little pampering before dinner. Maybe she'd even take a short nap. There was no denying she wanted to be at her very best this evening. And, of course, she wanted to look great too! She studied her reflection in the mirror. Her hair, as usual, was trimmed bluntly below her shoulders. She thought about Amber's short, neat haircut and how it looked so stylish. But she knew Jed liked her long, dark tresses. Maybe tonight she'd let them hang loosely over her shoulders. Amber, though older than Maggie, was the same age as Jed, and other than a few tiny lines around her eyes, hid her age very well. Maggie wondered if she may have had a facelift.

"Don't be so petty!" she chided herself as she went to examine her closet. What could she wear? She wanted to dress for Jed, but also felt the need to impress Amber—and again reprimanded herself for her silliness. "You're making way too much of this, Margaret LeAnn!"

Finally she selected an outfit her mother had given her for Christmas. Audrey had specifically said that she thought it looked like a good "date dress" for going out with Jed.

Maggie remembered how she'd rolled her eyes. She and Jed had still been patching things up at the time. But now she thought it would be just right. It was a well-cut, two-piece dress in a dove gray suede. Audrey said she'd gotten it at a greatly reduced price, but Maggie was sure that even then it couldn't have come cheap. She already knew it fit perfectly, and Audrey had commented on how lovely it looked with Maggie's gray eyes. Maggie hoped she wasn't just saying that.

A few hours later she walked into the hotel feeling refreshed and invigorated. She was ready for this. Maggie shook the snow off her coat and hung it on a nearby rack, then glanced around the semi-crowded room to spy Amber already seated near the fireplace. She stood and waved to Maggie. "Come and sit down," she said warmly. "Jed's not here yet, but we can chat while we wait."

"Thanks. I'm a little early, but with it snowing like this, I always give myself extra time. I'm from California, you know, and I'm still not completely used to this winter driving."

Amber smiled. "Well, I grew up here and learned to drive in all this stuff, and yet I'm not very comfortable with it myself."

"How long has it been since you've been back?"

Amber waved her hand. "Ages. Since high school, I guess. Too long."

"Do your parents live around here?"

"My dad moved away as soon as I left for college. The only reason he stayed on at all was because I insisted. My mom was the only reason he ever agreed to live here in the first place. She'd grown up in Pine Mountain and loved it. But she died when I was fifteen. And my dad died a couple years ago."

"I'm sorry. Do you have brothers or sisters?"

"Just me. I suppose that's why Dad gave in so easily back then, allowing me to finish high school here. I was rather spoiled. Anyway, that's what my ex-husband always said."

"Do you have children?"

She shook her head. "Not for lack of trying. I think I've been to every professional between Seattle and L.A. I finally gave up when I hit forty and decided to completely throw myself into my career—not that it's been so fulfilling working in international sales. But it was great to show Ben, my ex, that I could make just as much money as he. And, of course, the travel was fun." She smiled brightly, then waved. "And here comes our man of the hour!"

Maggie looked over to see Jed approaching. Amber had already risen, moved toward him, and was now cheerfully shaking his hand. He looked slightly flustered beneath what seemed a thin veneer of gracious manners. He had on the charcoal-colored turtleneck and sports coat he'd worn to Scott and Chloe's wedding—the night he'd proposed. Somehow that small thing warmed her heart, and trying not to feel like second fiddle, she stood to welcome him too.

He leaned over and kissed her on the cheek. "Hi, Maggie." She blushed just slightly. He didn't usually display much physical affection in public. Not that she minded it, especially tonight. Then they sat down, Maggie and Amber facing one another with Jed in the middle.

"Did you have another long day?" asked Maggie.

He nodded. "I'm trying to get some things all lined up and ready for Taylor to work on when he gets here."

"Is that the new apprentice?" asked Amber.

"Yes, and as glad as I am to have help, it takes a little time to figure out exactly what he's going to do."

"I know exactly what you mean," said Amber. "I had to hire an assistant a few years ago because I was so swamped, and I swear it took more time to train her than it was worth."

"But hopefully it got better over time?" Maggie interjected, trying gracefully to squeeze back into the conversation.

"Yes, I suppose. But the girl was a little bit of an airhead. I finally had to let her go completely."

"Well, Taylor seems to have a good head on his shoulders." Jed looked at Maggie. "So how's everything at the paper?"

"Great. Scott's back now, which will lighten my load considerably."

"Sounds like you both might be able to have some spare time now," observed Amber. "I hate to think of you people over here in beautiful Pine Mountain just working your fingers to the bone and not taking any time to enjoy all there is to do and see around here."

"Did you get in much skiing this week?" asked Jed.

She nodded smugly. "I sure did. And it was wonderful. Hardly any lines, fresh powder. Why, a girl could get used to this."

Maggie hoped Amber wouldn't. Just then the waitress came to take their order.

"And the food in this hotel," continued Amber "is incredible. I never dreamed little Pine Mountain could offer such fine cuisine."

"Yes, there's probably a lot about Pine Mountain that people don't know." Jed sipped his water, and Maggie wondered what he meant by that.

"Well, it's a town that's certainly coming into her own." She smiled. "And I'm sure my parents would've been surprised to see how much it's changed. Don't you think so too, Jed?"

He nodded to Maggie. "A lot of the recent changes have been helped along by Maggie here, and all her hard work at the paper."

"I'm so anxious to hear more about you, Maggie," said Amber. "What brought you to Pine Mountain?"

Maggie felt relieved to relay the story. It seemed to give Jed a chance to catch his breath. She could tell by his face that this was hard on him; she suddenly wished the dinner would just end, and that she and Jed could just escape somewhere, anywhere, and talk privately.

"That's amazing," said Amber as their salads were served. "And you haven't missed city life at all?"

"Not at all. I'm perfectly happy here." She turned to Jed and smiled into his eyes. "And nothing could entice me to leave now, not ever."

Jed said a quick blessing, and the table grew quiet for a moment as they began to eat. Then Amber spoke in a more subdued tone. "Sometimes I wonder why I ever left this place myself."

Jed looked up, and Maggie felt a bite of lettuce sticking in her throat. She reached for her water and took a big gulp.

"What do you mean?" he asked in a flat voice.

Amber just shrugged. "Oh, I don't know really. But sometimes I wonder why I ever left. I know I had promised Dad if he let me finish high school here that I'd go wherever he wanted me to for college. But I made that promise when I was so young. What did I know?" Her fork played with the salad before her.

Maggie considered jumping in and changing the subject for Jed's sake, but she stopped herself. Perhaps there were things that needed saying here tonight. Why should she prevent it?

"And what if you'd stayed, Amber?" Jed's voice was firm. "Would you have ever been happy in this little one-horse town?"

She lowered her eyes, diverting her gaze from his. "I might have."

What is going on here? wondered Maggie frantically. But her lips remained tightly closed, her eyes fixed on Jed, trying to read him, but without success. His face looked completely blank. What was he feeling?

He turned then to look at Maggie. A long look, full of reassurance. She heard him speak in a slow, deliberate voice. "You know, Amber, we all have a past history at this table. Maggie was married to a man she thought she'd love forever. But then he was killed and taken from her. And she had to move on. You were married for years, I assume happily, but now you're divorced. I remained single dealing with my own issues and personal struggles. Then finally I found God and things changed. And Maggie came into my life just when I was ready for her. There's a lot of water that's gone under these bridges. But what's past is past. I see no point in bringing it all up again."

Maggie wanted to jump up and kiss him, or at the very least, clap her hands with joy. But somehow she managed to just sit there smiling demurely.

"I think you're right, Jed," she finally said, simply to break the thickness of silence. "So much has happened in all our lives. Some of it is unexplainable. I never would've guessed five years ago that I'd be sitting here right now."

"Me neither," said Amber, then she laughed lightly. "But I'm glad I am. I'm glad I came back home." She turned to Jed, her eyes overly bright. "And I'm glad I got to see you and talk to you again. I really am. And something you said the other night, and then again tonight, *really* interests me."

"What's that?"

"You mentioned God."

He nodded, his brows just slightly puzzled by this. "That's right."

"You mentioned God in what sounds like a very personal way. Like God might be real to you, Jed. Is that true?"

"That's true. God is very real to me, Amber. God saved my life when I was busy trying to throw it all away."

Though she just nodded, Maggie saw her swallow hard and could see the tears building in her eyes. Did Jed see them too? Finally, Amber spoke again, her voice slightly stiff and formal now. "I guess I just never thought of you as a particularly religious person, Jed."

"I never was. Not until a few years ago."

She shook her head. "Well, I suppose I don't believe in God. Or if there is a God, I don't think he cares very much about me."

Jed reached over and placed his hand on her arm. "Amber, I used to think that same thing too. But it's not true."

Amber looked directly into his eyes. "Really? Of all people, Jed, I think I could believe *you*. But how can you be so sure? How do you really know?"

Maggie suddenly felt uncomfortable, and worse than that—invisible. She chided herself for the little wave of jealousy that rose within her, telling herself that this conversation was valuable, important. Good grief, Amber seemed to be searching for God!

"It's hard to explain. It's not something you know or even completely understand in your head; it's something you believe in your heart. It takes faith. But God can even give you faith."

"How, Jed?" Amber's features tightened a little. "How can he give faith? And if he can do that, why hasn't he done it for me already?"

He smiled. "Have you ever asked him? Maybe he's just waiting for you to come to him and ask."

She seemed to consider this, then she sighed deeply. "I don't know. I've tried to pray before, but it never seemed to do any good."

"Maybe it's just God's timing," offered Maggie, wanting to be a part of the conversation again. "I know I never fully experienced God until I was so angry and hopeless that I cried out in complete frustration."

Just then their entrees were served, and Amber changed the subject to some of the local changes she'd noticed in town. Then somehow, and to Maggie's guilt-ridden relief, they made it through the entire meal just making small talk. But after their last cup of coffee, Jed grew more serious.

"Amber, I sense that you're searching for something," he said quietly. "But I think what you're really looking for is God."

Her brow furrowed slightly. "It's possible."

"And I want to encourage you to keep looking," he said. "Keep seeking. And don't be afraid to question God. He can't be intimidated, you know."

Maggie smiled. "No, he can't. I'll personally guarantee it. When I was so upset about Phil's death, I used to rant and rave against God as if he were the enemy. And he never once threw a bolt of lightning at me."

Amber sighed and refolded her napkin. "Really? Well, I suppose you two have given me something to think about anyway."

"Will you be leaving tomorrow then?" asked Jed.

She shrugged. "I thought so last week. But right now, I'm not so sure. And Cherise at the fitness center invited me to some little get-together at her place tomorrow night. So I might stick around a little longer."

Good nights were said, then Jed helped Maggie into her coat and walked outside with her, slipping his arm snugly around her waist as they stepped into the freshly fallen snow. "Mmm, I've missed you," he whispered into her ear.

She smiled up into his face. "Really?"

He nodded. "I'm sorry this whole thing with Amber came up. I have to admit it kind of threw me for a loop."

"I understand. And I think you handled everything very well."

"You really think so?"

"Totally. I was so impressed with what you told her about the past being the past. It was the perfect way to tell her—" Maggie stopped herself.

"That it's over?"

"I guess that's what I was thinking." She peered into his eyes. "It *is* over, isn't it, Jed?"

"Maggie, I love you so much. I'll never stop loving you. You are like the other half of me that was missing for so many years."

She felt her eyes grow misty. "I love you too, Jed."

He sealed her words with a kiss, and then walked her to her car. "And I promised to tell you about the whole thing, didn't I?"

"You did."

He glanced down the street. "No handy coffee shop to duck into."

"My house isn't too far away, you know." She smiled. "Leah was driving Spence and Daniel to see the home game tonight. And I'll bet Mom's all tucked into her little house by now."

"I'll meet you there in five minutes," he promised as he helped her into her car.

Six

I've already heard the nutshell version," Maggie said as she set a tray of cocoa mugs and homemade gingersnap cookies on an end table in the library. She smiled when she saw that Jed had already started a fire that was just beginning to crackle nicely. "Rosa told me Sam's version of how you and Amber met in high school and went steady for a few years."

"Three years." He leaned back into the couch with his arms folded behind his head, his gaze fixed on the ceiling. "And back then three years felt like a lifetime."

Maggie pulled up an ottoman and sat down close to Jed, resting her elbows on her knees and studying him with both affection and curiosity. "I know what you mean. I can remember how everything felt so important and momentous and like it would last forever back in my high-school days."

"Yeah, I thought Amber and I would always be together back then." He sighed and reached for a mug of hot cocoa, then looked directly into Maggie's eyes. "But believe me, I'm sure glad I waited for you."

She smiled up at him, then sipped her cocoa. Part of her wanted to sweep the whole Amber thing beneath the rug and pretend like it'd never happened, yet another part felt she needed to hear the story, in full. "How do you feel, now—I mean, seeing her again? Does it stir up any of those old feel-ings?"

He shook his head. "No, not like that. She seems like a completely different person to me. Nothing like I remember her. But I suppose seeing her did stir up some feelings at first." He took another slow sip. "Mostly it was feelings of anger and old bitterness rising up in me, things I thought I'd put behind long ago. But now it seems I need to forgive her all over again."

"And have you?"

"I think so. At least as much as I know how to do at the moment." He reached over and stroked Maggie's hair. "Did I tell you how pretty you look tonight?"

"Are you changing the subject?"

"No. I just got distracted for a moment." His brows drew together slightly. "And as far as Amber goes, I suppose it was a good thing she came along after all. I think it's given me a chance to put some closure on that whole episode of my life. Even though I thought it was all over and done, I apparently still had some old feelings I need to put to rest. But I honestly think I've done that now. Still, I'd be lying if I said I wasn't eager to see her go."

"Why's that?"

"Oh, I don't know. I suppose it just makes me uncom-fortable having her around."

"Are you worried you might be attracted to her?"

He looked directly into her eyes, then grinned a little slyly. "Not while you're around."

She made a face. "But what if I'm *not* around?"

This seemed to disturb him a bit. "Why? Are you plan-ning on leaving?"

She firmly shook her head. "No. But I think you know what I mean."

"Do you mean, would it tempt me away from you to have Amber hanging around all the time?"

She shrugged. "Maybe..."

"Like I already said, Maggie, my one and only love, Amber is a totally different person to me now—a complete stranger, really. Honestly, there's no attraction at all. I have nothing in common with her other than some old adolescent memories. I'm not saying she's not a decent person—I think she probably is. But at the same time, I don't think her life has been all that happy."

"I know. She seems really sad beneath that cheerful exterior. I do wonder if she might really be seeking God like you suggested at dinner tonight. I know I'll be praying for her now."

"So will I."

Just then Leah and Spencer came home and the house was quickly filled with a lively recount of the basketball game going into overtime and how Pine Mountain pulled it off by one point in the final second.

"It was so cool," said Spencer. "I sure hope I make the team next year."

"We should put up a hoop in the barn," suggested Jed. "We could shoot around a little, get you into shape."

"That'd be great. And by the way," Spencer pointed his finger accusingly at Jed, "I saw a picture of you from your old high-school days. I never would've recognized it myself, but Sierra pointed it out the other day. Her dad's in it too."

Jed rolled his eyes. "You mean they still have all that old stuff in the trophy case next to the gym?"

Leah nodded. "Spencer showed it to me tonight. It was funny seeing you guys as kids. Man, was your hair short! And those uniforms and the shoes you guys wore back then were pretty hilarious. But why didn't you ever tell me how your team won the state tournament in basketball, Dad?"

Jed laughed. "Well, somehow that's not something that just comes up in everyday conversation. At least not after all these light years have passed."

"I'll bet you have a high-school annual hidden away somewhere," suggested Maggie. "Maybe Leah would like to see it."

"Yeah!" Leah winked at Maggie. "And I bet I'm not the only one."

Maggie smiled, then said in a mock-hushed tone, "Maybe you can sneak it over here and I'll have a look too."

"Sounds like they're ganging up against me," Jed said to Spencer. "Guess I'd better get out of here while the getting's good."

"Oh, Dad, don't be such a chicken."

He laughed and hugged Leah goodbye. "Hey, don't forget our apprentice is arriving in town tomorrow. He'll be stopping by the shop around noon. See you then."

Maggie walked Jed to the porch, lingering for a good-night kiss. "Don't you forget that you promised me you'd make it to Cherise's housewarming tomorrow night."

"And it's okay to bring Taylor?"

"You bet. The more the merrier. Cherise is jazzed about this whole thing."

"Okay, see you then."

∽

Maggie went over to Cherise's an hour before the party to start setting things up. Audrey had helped her prepare several trays of appetizers and things, and would come later with Leah.

"This food looks delicious," gushed Cherise. "And there's so much of it. Do you really think anyone will come?"

Maggie laughed. "Of course. I can think of a dozen people right offhand."

Cherise's eyes sparkled. "It's so great to have friends. All those years with Greg, it was only *his* friends who came over, and then he expected me to wait on them. And if, heaven forbid, I should ever invite a girlfriend over, Greg would make her feel so uncomfortable that she'd never come again."

"That's too bad." Maggie carefully filled the punchbowl, then turned to face her. "Do you really think it's all over between you and Greg?"

"Oh, yeah." Cherise waved her hand. "Greg said the divorce will be final in just a few weeks."

Before Maggie could say anything, they heard a man's voice on the stairs. "Hey, the sign on the front door says to come on up."

"That sounds like Gavin," said Maggie.

Cherise went over to the stairway to greet him. "Come on in, Gavin. Thanks for coming over."

He handed her a bouquet of flowers with a smile, and then he looked around the room. "This place looks fantastic, Cherise. Did you do this yourself?"

"Well, I didn't do the actual remodeling, but I did all the decorating." She looked around the loft with pride. She had lit colorful candles here and there and the overall effect was cheerful and fun and bright.

"Very uptown, Cherise. I like it."

She hung up his coat and went to the stairway to greet other guests who were just beginning to arrive.

"Have you ever seen the inside of Greg's house?" Gavin whispered to Maggie as she arranged the flowers in a sleek new vase.

"No, but Cherise told me it was pretty boring."

"Yeah. Really dark and somber." He glanced around. "This is much better."

Maggie looked over to see Cherise giving an impromptu tour of her apartment, and mixed in with the familiar crowd of friends was Amber Feldman.

"I thought Amber would be gone by now," Gavin said quietly, almost as if sensing Maggie's feelings.

"I guess she didn't want to miss Cherise's little get-together. You know, she's been working out at the fitness center a bit this week."

He nodded, then went over to join the larger group while Maggie continued with her last-minute preparations in the kitchen.

Soon her mother and the kids arrived. And not long afterward, Jed showed up with his new apprentice. Taylor was introduced around and seemed to immediately fit right into the group, visiting congenially with everyone. Maggie engaged in a short but friendly conversation with Amber, then spent the rest of her time helping to keep the party running smoothly. She noticed Amber staying fairly close to Jed as he navigated the room, visiting with friends, but Maggie told herself it was nothing and by tomorrow this woman would surely be gone, hopefully for good.

"Amber certainly seems to stick to Jed," commented Audrey as she helped Maggie rinse punch glasses.

Maggie shrugged. "Well, I don't think she knows that many people here."

"Then why did she come to the party?"

"She's been coming to the fitness center, and Cherise invited her."

"Oh." Audrey set a glass in the dishwasher. "Well, if it's any consolation, Jed seems to be trying to keep her at a distance. You know me, I watch for these kinds of little nuances."

Maggie laughed. "I suppose if you hadn't become a counselor, you could've made it as a private eye."

"And as long as I'm disclosing my sleuthing information, I might as well tell you that I think Leah's got her eye on Taylor."

Maggie smiled. "Big surprise there, Mom. I suspected that right from the moment she told me about him. Which reminds me, you had expressed some concern on that account."

"I just don't want to see Leah getting stuck here. Not that Pine Mountain isn't a wonderful place, mind you. But I'd like her to continue her schooling and explore all her options before she settles down."

"I know what you mean. But isn't it more important that Leah does what she wants?"

"Does any eighteen- almost nineteen-year-old really know what they want?"

"Good point. Maybe they think they do, but things have a way of changing, don't they?"

"Yes. Consider Cherise. You said she'd been in love with Greg since adolescence, but I think she just never got a chance to grow up and have some independence."

"You may be right. But at least she's doing it now." Maggie looked at her mom. "How about you? Wasn't that how your life went?"

Audrey sighed. "Yes. And I don't wish that upon anyone. Especially someone as dear as our Leah."

"Well then, we'll just have to very gently and carefully see if we can encourage her to consider all the options."

"Yes, I was thinking perhaps she could sign up for some classes at the community college in Byron for spring term."

"How about if I suggest this to Jed?"

"Sounds like the best way to go."

Maggie glanced over to where her own son was clowning around with Sierra. "Now, speaking of adolescent romance, what about those two?"

Audrey chuckled. "Well, fortunately for you, Spencer has lots of competition where Sierra's concerned. That girl attracts boys like bees to honey. And Rosa says Sierra's determined not to go steady with any single boy right now, including Spence. I think she's enjoying the attention of the multitudes."

"Well, Sierra's got her head on straight. And I'm glad she and Spencer are such good friends."

As the party drew to a close, Maggie went over to join Jed. Taylor had already gone home, giving Michael a ride too. But Amber was still there, and still right at Jed's side, but at least she appeared to be saying good night.

She turned to Maggie. "This was such fun. Do you know how lucky you all are to live in a small town with such delightful friends all around you?"

"Oh, I'm sure you must have all sorts of friends and social events to keep you busy in the city." Maggie linked her arm into Jed's and gave him a squeeze.

"Not really. Not like you'd think. Sometimes it can get kind of lonely around all those people."

Suddenly Maggie felt guilty, almost as if she were being smug. "Yes, now that you mention it, I can remember that same feeling down in L.A. Sometimes it felt kind of like being lost in the crowd."

Amber looked right into Maggie's eyes. "That's it. *Exactly!*"

Just then Gavin and Cherise, the only remaining people in the apartment, came over to join the trio. "Maggie, this was great!" gushed Cherise. "Thanks so much for putting it all together. And Gavin even helped me finish up in the kitchen just now."

Amber patted Gavin on the back. "Whoever would've guessed that you would one day grow up to be such a nice guy."

He laughed. "Actually, until just recently I'd been a dirty, rotten scoundrel—at least that's how my uncle used to put it."

"Well, he's sure not saying that anymore," said Maggie. She stopped herself just short of mentioning how proud Clyde would be of Gavin in the next few days when news of their land development deal broke.

"Yeah, I finally got smart and cleaned up my act."

"Good for you," said Amber. "Now that's a tale I'd be interested in hearing more about."

He smiled. "Well, I'm an open book these days. Ask me whatever you want to know, and I'll be happy to tell you all about it."

"Do you want to walk me back to the hotel?" she asked. "Maybe we could rustle up a cup of coffee..."

Gavin briefly glanced over to Cherise, then to Maggie and Jed, and then finally said, "Sure, Amber. That sounds great. I'll get our coats."

Maggie wondered if he was doing this for her benefit. But whatever the case, it seemed a kind gesture. Goodbyes were exchanged, and Cherise once again thanked everyone for coming, then Jed walked Maggie to her car.

"That was good of Gavin to go with Amber," commented Maggie as Jed opened her car door.

"Well, I'm sure Gavin doesn't consider it any big sacrifice."

Maggie felt slightly defensive. "I wasn't suggesting that he did. I just thought it was especially kind of him."

Jed looked down at Maggie, his face a series of shadows in the overhead streetlight. "Do you think it's possible that Gavin might be having coffee with Amber for his own sake—not just to do you a personal favor?"

"I'm sure that's possible." She studied his face, wondering what he meant. "Does that bother you, Jed?"

He seemed to consider this, then finally spoke. "It doesn't make me jealous, if that's what you're thinking, not of Gavin or Amber. But it does make me a little concerned because, to tell the truth, I'd hate to see something developing between those two."

"Why?" Suddenly Maggie felt defensive of Gavin. "Do you think Gavin's not good enough for her?"

"That's not it."

"Because Gavin has really changed, Jed. Even Clyde is amazed. He's like a new man since he quit drinking. And I think it's very nice of him to spend time with Amber—and to share his story with her."

"Well, I just hope that's all he shares."

"What do you mean?" She could feel herself growing irritated.

He cupped her face in his hands. "You're taking me all wrong, Maggie."

"Then could you please explain?"

"I just don't want Amber to have any excuse to come back around here again. You know, I want a clean break, so long, farewell, adios. It makes me feel uncomfortable when she's so close by, like maybe she expects something from me. Something I don't have for her."

Maggie softened. "Oh, now I think I understand."

"Good." He kissed her soundly. "How about if we don't talk about Amber and Gavin anymore."

"What were we talking about?"

"I haven't the slightest..."

Seven

To Maggie's surprise, Amber was in church the following day, sitting directly in front of Maggie and her family. Afterward, attempting to be polite, Maggie greeted her. And then Amber somewhat apologetically explained that Michael had invited her last night to come visit their service, and how she hadn't minded delaying her return in order to hear this interesting young man speak.

"We've sure enjoyed him," said Maggie, wondering at the same time if Amber was ever going to go home.

"You know, I used to be pretty good friends with Steven Harris," Amber said as she and Maggie walked toward the door together. "Steven was quite the rebel in high school. I never would've guessed back then that he would've become a missionary, of all things."

"Of course," said Maggie, suddenly remembering Amber's old roots in town. "It makes perfect sense that you knew Steven. He was a good friend to Jed. Have you seen his mother since you've been in town?"

"Yes, I ran into Barbara at the hotel a couple days ago. Believe it or not, she doesn't look that much different from back in my high-school days—just older, of course. I really like her, and we spoke for quite a little bit. I was so saddened to hear of Steven's death." She shook her head. "I'd had no idea."

"No, you wouldn't."

"So much has happened over the years..."

"Yes, life moves on, doesn't it?" Maggie really wanted to ask when Amber planned to move on, but knew she couldn't be so rude.

Amber sighed. "Yes, but being here has been like going down memory lane." She glanced around the slowly emptying room. "I almost feel as though I have more friends in Pine Mountain than I do back home."

"I know that's how it has become with me." Maggie considered her old life down in L.A. with almost disbelief. "I haven't even been here a year, and yet this place has truly become my home."

Suddenly Amber brightened. "Yes! That's just how I feel too. And somehow, hearing your words just clinches it for me now, Maggie. I mean, Pine Mountain was my home during the very best years of my life. Why shouldn't it be my home for the remainder?"

Maggie felt as though she'd stepped on a land mine. "Do you mean that you plan to actually *live* here?"

"Yes! Isn't it exciting?" Amber's eyes burned brightly. "I'm not leaving after all. I've come home to stay, Maggie!"

"But what about your job in the city?"

Amber waved her hand. "Oh, I've been considering early retirement anyway. And I still own a house in town—my parents' old home. It's been a rental off and on over the years, not very profitable, but I could just never bring myself to sever that last tie and sell it. And it just happens to be vacant right now." She glanced at her watch. "Goodness, I have so much to do! I'd better get going, but I'll see you later, Maggie. Thanks so much for helping me figure this thing out."

Maggie just stared as Amber dashed out the door. *Thanks?*

"Did you just tell Amber goodbye?" asked Jed, looking curiously at her face.

"I think I just told her hello."

"Huh?"

"Amber has decided to *stay* in Pine Mountain. Indefinitely, I think."

He ran his hand over his chin, then shook his head. "I was afraid this might happen."

She forced a smile to her lips. "What's the matter, Jed Whitewater? You afraid this town isn't big enough for the both of you?"

He chuckled. "Well, I don't plan to meet her at high noon, if that's what you mean."

"You've made yourself perfectly clear to her, haven't you?" She studied his eyes for any sign of hesitation. "You've told her there's no chance—"

"You heard me say it, Maggie. And I'd told her before that too."

"Well then, we should have nothing to worry about. Right?"

He nodded. But something in his expression didn't quite convince her. Not that she thought he'd be attracted to Amber, but she sensed he still wasn't comfortable with the whole situation. And that was understandable.

∽

All day Monday the newspaper office was energized with activities related to the ground-breaking ceremony planned for the following day. Maggie felt thankful for the preoccupation, for it distracted her mind from wondering exactly why Amber had decided to relocate her life back to Pine Mountain. She'd already questioned Gavin about whether he'd possibly given her any reason to stay, but he'd guaranteed her that their conversation had only been about how he'd quit drinking and finally turned to God for help.

"I'm as surprised as you are," he told her. Then he added, "Do you think she understands that it's really over with between her and Jed?" Maggie told him what Jed had said and left it at that.

Later in the afternoon, Maggie called Jed at his workshop to remind him of the business association meeting.

"I'd forgotten all about it," he admitted. "I don't suppose anyone, besides you that is, would really miss me much."

"Maybe not. But then again *you* might miss out on something. Something pretty interesting too…"

"What's that?"

"Can't say." She smiled to herself.

"Are you going all mysterious just to entice me to come?"

"I do what I can."

He laughed. "All you need to do is promise to save me a seat next to you, and I'd probably drop everything to be there."

"Okay, then. I'll save you a seat. But really, Jed, I don't think you'll want to miss this one. Something good is up."

"Well, you've really got me curious now. Why don't you save two seats, and I'll bring Taylor along."

"How's it going with him?"

"Okay. He seems to catch on fast. And he's a hard worker."

"Great. I'll see you tonight."

ᔣ

Maggie sat inconspicuously near the back with Leah and Audrey. They had decided to come along after she'd hinted to them that it would get interesting. They saved two seats, and Jed and Taylor came in just as the meeting was about to begin. Rosa, acting as chair, called the meeting to order. She covered old business and gave a report on the possibility of creating a chamber of commerce. Then she handed the floor over to Elizabeth Rodgers.

"As you all know," began Elizabeth in her theatrical voice, "our little community has been besieged of late by those of an intolerant nature—those who would seek to divide and destroy. And while I know some of you are simply of a mind to ignore these incidents and wait for them to pass, I am reminded of those citizens in Nazi Germany who simply turned their heads, thinking that Hitler's words were only political rhetoric. But let me tell you, hatred and bigotry are like a cancer that, when left hidden and ignored, can begin to root and grow. And although I am not suggesting we go to all-out war against people who espouse such things as white supremacy, I am suggesting we consider an alternative route." She paused dramatically.

"And what would that be?" called out Lou Henderson.

She smiled. "Well, we have already discussed the possibility of having some sort of spring festival to promote our town during the slower part of the tourist season. But I suggest that we consider having a cultural fair of sorts. We could have food booths featuring different kinds of ethnic cuisine. And perhaps we could invite people of varying cultures to participate with crafts and music. It would be a celebration of our ethnic diversity." She looked around the room. "For although our town's population is primarily Protestant white, we do have a few people of other ethnic heritage. And, certainly, many of those outside of our area, for instance, the tourists we wish to welcome to Pine Mountain, are of other ethnic backgrounds. And, dear people, don't we want *everyone* to feel welcome in our little community?"

Rosa returned to the podium and opened this suggestion for discussion. No one was surprised that, though most of the comments were enthusiastic and supportive of the idea, a few people questioned this thinking. Cal, from the secondhand store, was among the loudest.

"I just don't know," he droned on. "I'm not saying I'm opposed to people from different backgrounds. But we might be inviting all kinds of undesirables into our town. And before you know it, there'll be graffiti on every wall, the crime rate'll go up, and you can be sure our taxes will go up right along with it—"

"That's nonsense," said Clyde, glancing impatiently at his pocket watch as he stood. Maggie knew he was anxious for this meeting to come to an end. "Everyone here knows I'm an old-timer and can sometimes be set in my ways. But I say we live in a constantly changing world. And to survive we need to welcome the new. Besides, our country has always been a melting pot for all kinds of folks from all over the world. Why, all of our ancestors came from someplace else to start with." He looked over to Jed. "Well, 'cepting for maybe Jed here. But what I mean to say is, we need to be like one big family—accepting our differences. And if Elizabeth's idea can help us do that, then I say all the better. I move we put this thing to a vote and settle it tonight." He looked around the room. "Do I hear a second?"

Lou Henderson stood up. "I second!"

Maggie wrote furiously, wishing she'd brought along her pocket recorder. The vote was a landslide in favor of the Cultural Celebration, with a small number abstaining, and not one single "nay," including Cal. Elizabeth rose to eloquently thank everyone, and she even offered to head up the committee if the group liked.

Finally, just as Rosa was calling the meeting to an end, Gavin stood and asked if he could make a brief announcement that concerned the entire business community.

"Come on up," said Rosa.

"Thanks, everyone. I know you're all eager to get home, so I'll keep this short and sweet." Gavin's eyes scanned the room, and Maggie felt certain he paused a split second longer on Greg and Rick, who were sitting near the front. "I have some great news for the whole town. First off, we want to invite all of you out to the old Barnes' homestead out on Bear Creek Road. Just go on past Maggie's house and you'll see a crowd of us all gathered on the west side of the road.

You see, we're going out there to celebrate the birth of a brand-new land development. We've got two hundred acres of prime mountain-view real estate to develop, and we're inviting everyone in town to attend the ground-breaking ceremony of Whispering Pines. It's guaranteed to be the finest style of community living in the Pacific Northwest. So, come on out tomorrow at four o'clock, and we'll share all the details with everyone who wants to hear. And then afterward, a small reception will follow right here in town at the newspaper office." Gavin quickly made his way from the podium as people began to murmur and chat, many of them glancing toward Rick and Greg with raised brows.

"I think that's it. Goodnight, everyone," called Rosa as Gavin and Clyde slipped out the side door.

"Looks like the fun's just beginning," said Jed wryly.

Maggie looked over to see Greg's face tighten into a dark scowl, and Rick was whispering something in his ear. Clearly agitated, both men pushed their way through the crowd, ignoring comments and questions. She hoped they weren't taking off after Clyde and Gavin. Surely they wouldn't resort to some sort of violence. She glanced up at Jed. "They wouldn't confront Clyde and Gavin right now, do you think?"

His eyes sparked. "You never know with those two. And they've been hit right where it hurts. Excuse me, Maggie." He hurried over to Sam with Taylor at his heels and they quickly gathered a couple more reliable men and exited the room.

"You think there's going to be trouble?" asked Audrey with alarm. "Suddenly I feel like I'm in the middle of an old western."

Maggie forced a laugh. "I seriously doubt Rick and Greg would do anything too stupid. It would only get them into trouble. But I'd hate to see Clyde hurt in any way, or Gavin for that matter."

It seemed everyone in the room sensed trouble, and the crowd broke up and gathered outside in the dimly lit parking lot. As they walked, Maggie could hear Greg's raised voice, yelling at Gavin as if he'd personally betrayed him.

"—and I thought you were my friend! But you're nothing but a—"

"Why don't you guys go on home now and cool off a little," came Jed's voice, loud enough to be heard but even and calm.

"Why don't you stay outta this!" yelled Rick.

"Yeah, Jed! This isn't your business." Greg was right in front of Gavin now, directly below the streetlight, his face livid with anger. "This is between me and the Barneses here."

"Greg!" came Sam's voice more firmly. "You and Rick need to go home right now. You're upset, and though we can all understand—"

"*You* understand?" Greg nearly screamed. "Don't tell me you understand, Sam Galloway, 'cause you don't! I've sunk every cent I have and then some into Pine Mountain Estates. And you expect me to just quietly sit by while someone else tries to move in and steal it from me?"

"No one is stealing anything, Greg." Jed stepped closer and spoke calmly.

"Says you!" yelled Rick.

Clyde had remained quiet until now. Maggie could tell by his face that he wasn't much bothered by this little display. "You boys have been all over my paper for not being more supportive of growth and development in this town," he said matter-of-factly, "and so now here we are getting involved in the game, and you fellars go and throw a regular tizzy fit."

For a moment, everyone was silent. But even in the dim light, Maggie could see the veins protruding on Greg's neck. And both men's fists were tightly clenched. "It's one thing to support development," snarled Greg, "and it's something else entirely when you slip in the side door and try to steal the whole show!"

"That's right!" shouted Rick. "You guys are nothing but a couple of sidewinders."

"Watch who you go calling a sidewinder," warned Clyde in a calm but stern voice. "Everyone in town knows you boys all but stole old Arnold Westerly's land."

"I'm sick to death of hearing that!" yelled Greg, stepping up to Clyde now, his chest puffed out in anger, his fists starting to raise. "And I don't even care if you are an old man."

"Take it easy, Greg," calmed Jed, nudging his way between them. "Fighting will get you nowhere. And you're way outnumbered anyway."

Sam held up his cell phone. "Listen, Greg and Rick, if you don't clear outta here right now, I'm calling in the sheriff."

"Go ahead and call him!" Greg spat. "Warner and I are good buddies."

"Yeah," agreed Rick. "No law against having us a little discussion in the parking lot."

"Not as long as you keep it under control," said Jed, "and as long as both parties want to participate." He looked over to Gavin. "Are you and Clyde wanting to continue this discussion with Greg and Rick here?"

Gavin shook his head. "I have nothing more to say to these guys."

"I'd like to tell 'em a couple more things," grunted Clyde, "but it's getting cold out here, and I don't have my huntin' coat on." He looked Greg right in the eye, then smiled. "But if you boys want to schedule you a civilized conversation, you just give Abigail a call, and we'll see what can be done to accommodate you."

"And if you want to hear more about Whispering Pines," added Gavin, "you're welcome to attend the groundbreaking ceremony tomorrow—as long as you can control yourselves."

"And with that, we will bid you all goodnight." Clyde tipped his hat and the two walked over to Gavin's car while the small crowd of onlookers burst into enthusiastic applause.

Greg and Rick made a move to follow them, but Sam and Jed blocked their way.

Sam's brows knit together as he spoke. "Warner may be a friend of yours, Greg, but he's also the enforcer of the law around here, and not the only one. And if he wants to put his job at risk, we can always get him replaced easily enough. But I don't think he wants to do that. Do you? Maybe we should go discuss it with him right now."

"Go discuss whatever you like," growled Greg, then he turned to Rick. "We've had enough of their talk." The two stormed off toward one of their big new pickups, and the crowd began to quickly dissipate.

Maggie and Rosa joined Sam, Jed, and a few others.

"Do you think they'll try anything stupid?" asked Rosa with wide eyes.

"I doubt it." Sam put his arm around her.

"But I'm worried about Clyde being all alone in his cabin tonight," said Maggie.

"If old Clyde can defend himself against a grizzly bear," said Jed, "I think he can handle those two buffoons." Then he grew more sober and turned to Sam. "But maybe we should go on out there, just to be sure—"

"Yeah, I'm thinking the same thing."

"Take some others with you," suggested Maggie.

"Yes," agreed Rosa. "And phone the sheriff just to tell him what's up."

"We've already done that," called Audrey as she and Elizabeth hurried toward them.

"Yes," gasped Elizabeth. "We went back inside and called on my cell phone. He should be here any minute now. I've found it's always better to be safe than sorry."

"This whole thing will probably blow over in an hour or two," assured Sam.

Maggie shivered. "Well, it doesn't do any good to stand around and freeze to death. Can we give you a ride, Rosa?"

"Sure." She looked up at Sam. "You be careful."

Maggie followed her lead. "You too, Jed."

They reassured them that everything would be fine. And just then the sheriff's jeep came down the street with lights flashing.

"Well, it's not every day you get to see something like this in Pine Mountain," said Rosa.

Taylor, who had remained silent during this whole thing, finally spoke up. "And here I thought I had moved to this quiet, little, peaceful town."

Everyone laughed.

Eight

The ground-breaking ceremony went off without a hitch, other than a little difficulty with planting a shovel in partially frozen sod. Both Stan Williams and Clyde made speeches, keeping them short due to the cold weather. And they hurried to bring it to a close as it looked like a new storm was coming in. To everyone's relief, Greg and Rick stayed away from the celebration altogether. Maggie had already learned that no new trouble had developed after their fiery display of emotions in the parking lot the night before, but Gavin had spent the night out at Clyde's just to be safe.

Now, back in the warmth of the newspaper office, a couple dozen business people snacked and chatted happily. Some even showed serious interest in the possibility of investing in building lots.

"I can almost guarantee you a fifty percent equity growth after five years," said Stan to the Hendersons. "But I never put anything like that in writing because you never know what might happen. Just the same, most of the lots in my developments have gone up far more than that."

"Well, I always figure land and antiques are a safe investment," said Clara. "They can only become more scarce over time, which I realize makes them increase in value."

"Sounds like you know what you're talking about." Stan nodded toward Gavin. "He's your man, should you decide you want in on the ground floor."

The front door opened again, and Amber Feldman walked in, tentatively looking around the mixed group. Maggie went over to greet her, curious if she were here for the celebration or something else. "Hi, Amber, how are you doing?"

"Okay, I guess. I'd meant to attend the ground-breaking ceremony earlier, but I got waylaid. Anyway, I thought I'd stop by here to say hello."

"Make yourself at home." Maggie held out a tray of cheese and crackers. "And there are hot drinks over there."

"Actually, I wanted to speak to someone about purchasing some land."

Maggie smiled toward Gavin, who was coming their way. "There's your guy. At least one of them."

Gavin greeted them and shook Amber's hand. "Did I hear you mention some interest in land?"

She smiled brightly. "Yes. Shall I make an appointment with you?"

Feeling her job was done, Maggie moved across the room to where the Jordans, from the hotel, were chatting with Buckie and Kate. She held out the tray to them.

"Thanks, Mag," said Buckie. "This development is such great news. What with all the problems out at Greg and Rick's place, I'd almost given up all hope of seeing any growth of this kind around Pine Mountain."

"Well, you never know what's around the corner." Maggie set the tray on the counter.

"I'm sure glad I didn't invest in Pine Mountain Estates," said Brian Jordan. "And I was looking into it too."

"See," said Cindy, "it pays not to be too hasty sometimes."

"Say, Maggie." Buckie gently elbowed her. "Have you guys been planning this little scheme for a while? Is that why you gave Snider and Tanner all that flack in your paper last fall?"

"No! Of course not, Buckie."

"Well, it seems to me that all those troubles with wet-lands and whatnot didn't hurt old Clyde and Gavin's plans any."

"Buckie, if you're insinuating we did anything unethical at the paper—"

"No, no." He laughed. "You know me, Maggie. Don't take it wrong. I just like to call it how I see it."

"Well, you're seeing it all wrong."

"Don't listen to him, Maggie," soothed Kate. "He tends to let his mouth run away with him from time to time." She smiled at Buckie. "It's just one of his endearing little qualities."

Maggie was glad Kate thought so, because she sure didn't. "And just so you'll know, Buckie, the plan for developing Whispering Pines didn't come up until just before Christmas. It was Gavin's idea, really. He was thoroughly irked over what had happened to old Arnold Westerly's property." Suddenly she thought of the old man's grand-daughter, Jeanette. "If you'll excuse me, I just remembered I have an important call to make."

Maggie worked her way through the crowd and into her office, closing the door and leaving most of the sound behind her. She quickly found and dialed Jeanette's number, anxious to share the good news.

"Oh, Jeanette!" she exclaimed. "I'm so glad I caught you. How are you doing?"

"All right, I suppose. But I kind of go up and down like a teeter-totter. One day, I think that being single might be really great. And the next day, I feel like completely giving up on everything and just pulling the trigger."

"Oh, don't give up, Jeanette."

"Well, I'm trying to hold on. And I've even taken your advice and tried to pray. But usually it just feels like I'm talking to myself or to the ceiling."

"I know, I used to feel that way sometimes. But you just have to keep pressing on. In time you'll see a difference." She paused. "And now, I have some fairly encouraging news."

"About Grandpa's farm? Can it be saved?"

"Well, I'm not totally sure about that. But let me explain." She then told Jeanette all about the Whispering Pines development, barely pausing for a breath between sentences.

"Wow, that's great! Do you think it might possibly shut down TS Development for good?"

"It sure looks like it could. You should've seen how mad Greg and Rick were last night. On the other hand, maybe it's good that you didn't. It wasn't pretty. But I think it's starting to blow over now."

"And last I heard they still hadn't leveled the old house or any of the farm buildings. Is that so?"

"Yes, I think everything's been put on hold."

"Do you suppose they'll have any interest in selling it back?"

"I don't know why not. I can't imagine how they'd seriously think they can make a go of it now. But you might be wise to give them a little time, Jeanette. I'd think the more worried they get, the better their price might be."

"Yes. Maybe I should just indicate a little interest, so they don't end up dumping it on someone else, but then I could just step back and bide my time." She laughed nervously.

"Good idea."

"Of course, who am I fooling?" Her voice fell flat. "I can't afford to buy that place. And with my new single status, I'll never qualify for much of a loan."

"Do you think you could get all your family together on this? Get them all to chip in somehow for a joint ownership?"

"Boy, I don't know. But I suppose it's worth a shot, for Grandpa's sake."

"You might invite them all to listen to that tape I sent you. Remember how your grandfather talks about his farm, and the importance of keeping it all intact."

"Good plan. I might just try that. Thanks for telling me about this, Maggie. Believe me, it's the best news I've heard in ages."

Maggie hung up and started to straighten her desk when she heard a knock at the door. "Come on in," she called.

"Sorry to bother you," said Amber as she stepped in.

"No bother. I was just tidying up. If I let it get bad in here, Abigail comes in like a tornado, and I can't find anything for days. Want to sit?"

"Sure, thanks." Amber sank into a chair and sighed deeply.

"Everything okay?" Maggie studied her carefully, noticing for the first time the shadows beneath her eyes. "You look a little worn out."

Amber waved her hand. "I've probably been trying to do too much, that's all."

Maggie plunked a pen into her pencil cup and leaned back into her chair. "I know just what you mean. So, what can I do for you, Amber? Or did you just want to chat?"

Amber leaned forward. "I need a friend, Maggie. I...I don't think it can be Jed—and I know this must sound rather strange—but I was wondering if it could be you?"

Maggie blinked. "Well, of course I'm your friend, Amber. Why wouldn't I be?"

Amber laughed. "I can think of one pretty good reason."

"Jed?"

She nodded. "I wouldn't blame you a bit. I'm sure I'd be crazy with jealously if I was in your shoes. In fact, to tell the truth, I was. At first."

"But you're not now?"

"No. I've watched Jed's face when he talks about you. I've seen his eyes when he looks at you. I've even asked other people around town. And it seems pretty clear to everyone that Jed's hooked on you, Maggie. And he's hooked good."

Maggie didn't care much for that metaphor, but tried to receive it as a compliment. "And that doesn't bother you?"

"Of course it bothers me. I was absolutely furious when I first got here and found out. I wanted to challenge you to a knock-down, drag-out fight. I wanted to pull your hair and scratch out your eyes."

Maggie stiffened a little in her chair.

"Sorry." Amber laughed lightly. "You'll have to get used to me. I tend to speak my mind without always considering how it might sound to others. But the truth is, I was very upset to learn that after Jed had remained single all those years, I only just missed him by a matter of weeks."

"We only got engaged on New Year's Eve, but Jed and I have been seeing each other longer—"

"Oh, I know, Maggie. I'm just being melodramatic."

"So, if we're being completely frank and honest here, you won't mind if I ask you what made you come to Pine Mountain in the first place. Was it for Jed?"

"No. I was feeling homesick. Suddenly I wanted to return to the good ol' days, back to when life was simple, and I was young and optimistic, and all things seemed possible."

"But you did look up Jed as soon as you—"

"Of course, when I got into town he was the first person I thought of." She ran a hand through her short hair. "Oh Maggie, what Jed and I had was so magical. I sometimes still wonder what happened to destroy it all so many years ago."

"What did happen, Amber?"

"It's a long story…"

Maggie glanced at her watch. It was already half past five, but somehow this seemed important. "That's okay. I've got time."

Amber smiled. "Well, then so do I. And if you're going to be my friend, and I hope you are, you should probably hear the whole thing. Can I buy you dinner at the hotel tonight? Or do you have plans with a certain Mr. Whitewater?"

"No, we don't have plans. He took time off to attend the ground-breaking ceremony, and then he wanted to go home and work tonight." She considered Amber's offer. "I'd like to have dinner with you. Let me call and let my family know what's up, and then how about if I meet you there. Say six?"

ᕋ

Though the hotel was fairly busy, Amber and Maggie were quickly seated near a window.

"I just love seeing it snow," said Amber as she glanced outside to look at the tumbling flakes illuminated in the nearby streetlight. "In the city we got mostly rain, and when it did snow, it just made a great big slushy mess. I used to long for a good old Pine Mountain winter with clean air and crispy snow crunching underfoot."

"But you never came back?"

Amber shook her head. "Not because I didn't want to."

"What happened?"

Amber got a faraway look in her eyes. "Well, it seems the only place to start is at the beginning." She smiled. "No, I won't start with my birth."

"Go ahead, if you want. I'm a writer, I like those kinds of details." She set her menu aside and focused on Amber. "And I like listening to people's stories."

Her eyes lit up. "You do? Then it's certain you and I must become friends, because I'm always looking for someone to listen to my stories. My ex used to be good at it. But it seemed, toward the end, the only one he ever really listened to anymore was himself."

The waitress came over and took their order, then Amber began. "My mother got cancer when I was twelve. Throughout junior high all I ever did was worry about her. I went to school, then came home to be with her. I don't recall going to one single social function during that whole time. Oh, I loved my mother dearly, and I don't regret a single moment that I spent with her. I suppose the reason I stayed so close to home was because I was afraid I might lose her. My father and I had never been close. He was of the old school, you know. He worked to provide a good living and then expected to come home to a clean house and dinner on the table. That was it. No questions asked."

"I had a father like that too."

"I knew we had some things in common—besides Jed, that is. Anyway, my mother's cancer was what they called untreatable—that was back in the days when they simply diagnosed, then sent you home to die."

"That must've been hard."

"It was. I tried to be nurse and housekeeper, everything. I thought if I did it well enough, she might actually live. But she didn't. She died the spring I turned fifteen. My father never showed it, but I know he missed her a lot. He just kept it all to himself. I never saw him cry once."

"Men used to be so afraid to show their emotions."

"But my father was always good to me. I never wanted for anything. When fall came and I started high school, I felt like a newcomer. Oh, sure, I knew all the kids and they knew me. But it felt like I didn't quite fit in. Just the same, I threw myself into every activity I could find. I think part of me wanted to be so busy that I wouldn't miss my mom. And another part was determined to make up for the lost years in junior high. To my surprise, I became quite popular. Maybe it was because of my big mouth. But before I knew it, I was being nominated for all sorts of things. I made cheerleader, and I felt sort of like Cinderella. My dad was proud of me, and that meant a lot. But all the while, I still felt like an outsider."

Amber paused while the waitress set down their meals.

"I think most kids feel that way at one time or another during adolescence," said Maggie. "But they usually just keep it to themselves."

"You could be right. Anyway, Jed and I were in an art class together. I'd watch him from across the room. I'd known him since grade school, and I had always admired how he seemed to have this quiet confidence about him. Some kids were really mean to him back then, you know, picking on the one who's different. But Jed always seemed somehow above them. He didn't ever let it get to him, at least not that you could see. In art class, I noticed right off that he really had talent. And so I started talking to him about his work. You know, with me and my big mouth, I just forced my way into his quiet little world. I asked him to help me with my art projects, and then I asked him about other things. Anything to get him to talk to me. And it wasn't long until we became friends. Good friends."

Maggie set down her fork and smiled. "I can imagine that. It sounds like Jed."

"We actually had a lot in common. His mother had died a few years earlier. And he felt like an outsider too. By that spring we were going out. It was the first time either of us had dated."

"And was your father okay with this?" Maggie imagined her own father back in those days. He'd have protested a relationship with anyone even slightly different from their stodgy white, middle-class background.

"No. He was pretty upset at first. He wanted to move me as far from Jed Whitewater as possible. But I threw a complete fit. I told him I'd run away, or kill myself, or something equally drastic. I think I scared him. And who knows, I might have done something crazy...after all, I was sixteen and it was the sixties. But I knew that I really needed Jed right then, and I refused to give him up. Dad finally agreed to stay here in town until I graduated. But that was also on the condition that I would remain in the honor society and keep up all the activities I had been involved in, as well as keep house for him. I'm sure he thought if he kept me busy enough, I'd have no time left for romance. Or if romance took over, I'd fail at all those other things. But somehow I managed to do it all and have it all."

Maggie could imagine Amber as a feisty teenager. "You must've had a lot of drive. That's quite a bit for a high-school kid to take on and succeed at."

"Well, I was pretty determined. And I've always been a fairly energetic person." She paused. "Although, I am slowing down a bit these days."

"I think we all are. I know I can't do the same things I did in my twenties. Time catches up with us whether we like it or not. But I sort of look forward to a slower pace in the upcoming years. I don't think I'll mind growing old gracefully."

Amber considered this. "I suppose...anyway, Jed and I went out all during high school. We only broke up a couple times. Over silly things—I can't even remember what anymore. But we always got back together. During those years, I encouraged him to get more involved with activities at school and to go out for sports. And he really seemed to enjoy it."

Maggie nodded. "I know. Sam Galloway says that Jed became quite popular and actually had a good time in high school, greatly due to you."

"Oh, I don't know about that. Jed already had what it takes. But I suppose he did need someone to prod him along and encourage him. His dad tried to stay out of the picture mostly. Even if he came to one of Jed's games, he'd sit way in the back of the bleachers and leave the instant the last buzzer rang. But I'd always try to go up and talk to him. I know it embarrassed him a little, at first, because he was such a quiet man. But he seemed to enjoy it more as time went on. I always liked Mr. Whitewater. He was a truly good soul and a gentleman too."

"That's not surprising, when you consider his son."

"So, high school was coming to an end. And my dad reminded me of my promise to move away and go to college. I tried to get out of it at first. But I finally gave in, picking the closest college my dad would agree on. It was only three hours away. I tried and tried to convince Jed that he should come and go to college too. But he said he had to wait until the following year; he felt he had to earn some money first, although I was certain he could have gotten good scholarships or financial aid if he'd really wanted to. So, off I went to college. We wrote each other almost daily, at first. But the next thing I knew Jed was drafted into the service. They did that stupid lottery thing back then where birthdays were picked, and Jed's birthday was number one. *Number one!* Can you believe it?"

"I never knew that. Poor Jed. He must've felt horrible."

"Well, he never tried to get out of it. I saw guys at college doing everything possible to avoid Vietnam, but not Jed. No, he had some strange sense of duty. He just went. I was pretty mad right at first, because I thought if he'd only started college like I'd wanted him to, or if he'd told the draft board that he was the only son in his family he might have been excused. I mean, there were ways to get around being sent into the thick of that stupid war. But good ol' Jed, he never said a single thing. Like a lamb being led to slaughter, he just closed his mouth and went."

"He has a strong sense of duty and pride."

Amber paused long enough to take a bite of her barely touched meal, and Maggie tried to carry the conversation for a while, giving her new friend a chance to eat. But she didn't seem hungry, and before long she was continuing her saga.

"I'm sure you've heard by now about the letter I sent him." She shook her head and rolled her eyes. "I still can't believe I did that. But what can I say? That I was young and naive? Or maybe I really did want it to be over with. I don't know…I don't really understand it even now. But, you see, Jed hadn't written to me for months, at least I think it was months. And every single day I'd go look in my mailbox, hoping and praying to hear from him. And *nothing*—not a word. I was so consumed with worry for him. I'd watch the news every night and see—" She closed her eyes and grimaced. "Well, you know what I mean, although you were probably too young to pay much attention to it. But it was just awful. I kept imagining Jed all shot up and crippled or blown to pieces. I became absolutely certain I was going to lose him, just like I'd lost my mom. It was almost making me crazy. My dad even wanted me to see a psychiatrist. I could hardly eat anything, and I chewed my fingernails down to raw skin."

"It must've been horrible for you, Amber. I'd heard about how awful it was for Jed. But I never even considered what you might have gone through. All that not knowing must've been torture."

"It was. And there was this guy in a couple of my classes. Ben Feldman. He felt sorry for me and decided to try to draw me out, sort of like what I'd done for Jed. He would bug me and bug me just to go out and have a cup of coffee with him. Well, finally, on a really discouraging day, I agreed, but I made it clear I had a boyfriend over in Vietnam. Ben was real understanding, and he just let me go on and on about Jed, how I missed him, how I was so worried, how my dad didn't care. I sat there in the coffee house just crying my eyes out. And that's when we became friends. Over time, Ben convinced me that if Jed really cared for me, he would write. So, Ben and I started dating. I didn't call them dates back then, but they were. Before I knew it, I started to love Ben and the security he offered me. And there was no doubt that he loved me. Of course my dad was thrilled, even though Ben was Jewish! Well, Ben still had a year before he graduated, but I think Dad pushed him into proposing. Then Dad helped us get into our first apartment and continued paying my tuition and everything. I think it was all part of his big plan to keep Jed and me apart permanently."

Maggie exhaled slowly. "And so that's why you wrote that letter."

"I cried when I wrote those words, Maggie. I sobbed and sobbed. It was the hardest thing I'd ever written. The truth is, I was deeply hurt by his silence. But on the other hand, I didn't know *what* had happened. I wondered if there was a reason. Or if he'd been injured, although when I finally contacted his dad, he said he'd heard from him and showed no reason for undue concern. I felt fairly certain my letter would hurt him, but I don't think I cared by then because I was so hurt. I was young and stupid, and I let Ben and Dad influence me. Although, I don't blame them. It was my own choice, my own fault."

Maggie felt a lump growing in her throat, partly for herself and partly for Amber. "It's so sad, Amber. Have you ever told Jed all of this?"

Amber tried to laugh, but it came out sounding more like a hiccup. "Oh, no. I couldn't possibly. I've told him bits and pieces and how I'm so sorry and all. But, like Jed says, the past is the past. It's over, and we need to let it rest." She reached over and patted Maggie's hand. "I have no intention of trying to come between you two." She smiled sadly. "As if I'd even have a chance. But I had hoped that Jed might accept me as his friend once again. For some reason that would mean so much to me…"

"I don't see any reason why he shouldn't." At least she hoped not. "I think it was just unsettling for him to see you again. It stirred up some unpleasant feelings. And perhaps he's trying to be protective of me too. But now that you plan to stay in town, maybe in time Jed will come around."

"Maybe, in time…"

Maggie looked right into Amber's eyes. They were a curious but pretty mix of green and blue and gold. "Thanks so much for sharing this with me, Amber."

"I feel like I just dumped on you."

"No, not at all. It helps me to understand things better. I had no idea."

"Well, I figured if you and I are to be friends, Maggie…and I really hope we can be. I need a good friend."

"I feel certain we'll become very good friends." Maggie set down her coffee cup. "I just hope our friendship doesn't make Jed feel threatened. But I think he'll understand."

"I sure hope so. Even if Jed never forgives me for the past hurts, it means a lot to me that you do."

"Jed has already forgiven you, Amber. He's told me so. Although, I've found in my own experience that forgiveness is usually an ongoing process. It doesn't always happen in one easy session."

"Yes, I'm sure you're right."

"And Jed may just need to work out some of those old hurts he's kept buried for all those years." Maggie smiled. "Which reminds me of something. I was always going to thank you, Amber."

"Thank me? Whatever for?"

"Well, in a way, it's greatly due to you that Jed and I are together now."

"How's that?"

"You know I was married all those years and then my husband died. Well, Jed could've easily married—many times over, I'm sure. But because he hadn't gotten over his broken heart, he had remained single, and he was still available when I got to Pine Mountain."

"Oh, I see. Well then, I'm glad I could be of service."

They both laughed.

"Actually, I think God has something to do with it too."

Amber seemed to consider these words. "You people around here sure seem to talk about God a lot. I've never heard anything quite like it. You make it sound as if he's a real person or something."

Maggie smiled. "That's because he is. He's a very real part of our lives."

"It seems that he is. I suppose that's a big part of the reason that I want to stay on in Pine Mountain. I want to find out more about this, and I want to hear more of what Michael Abundi has to say. I need to know whether this is really real or just wishful thinking."

"I can hardly believe I'm saying this now, Amber, but I'm really glad you decided to stay on too. And I do look forward to knowing you better." She frowned slightly. "I guess I'm just not sure what Jed's going to think about all this—I mean what you told me tonight."

"I suppose you don't have to tell him."

"I don't like to keep anything from him."

"No, of course not. Maybe just tell him as much as you think he needs to hear. I'm not sure that I want him to know all about that stuff in college and how I was so worried. I really don't want to make him feel bad. Like he said, it's all water under the bridge now. But if he could only come to understand just how sorry I am and how I really never meant to hurt him…"

"Jed can be somewhat stubborn at times. But I want to help him to understand your side of things and what you suffered. Naturally, I won't go into everything. But I want him to hear some of this. I think he needs to, for his own sake."

"You may be right. It might help him to get some closure on this whole thing. And perhaps in time we can all just forget about it completely."

Maggie nodded hopefully, but she wasn't so sure. Despite her earlier reservations, she really liked Amber now. She could clearly see and understand her side of the story. Perhaps that's what worried her most.

Nine

During the following week, Maggie didn't see much of Jed. Getting Taylor up and running required a lot of his time and energy, and it seemed new orders for furniture continued to come in on almost a daily basis. A good problem, really, but one that Maggie hoped would become more manageable in the future. In the meantime, she stayed busy at the newspaper. Due to the workload and the possibility of two editions a week, she was considering hiring another writer.

By the end of the week, Jed called Maggie, apologizing profusely for being somewhat unavailable and preoccupied. Then he invited her to dinner at his place for what he promised would be a special surprise.

On Saturday, Maggie drove out to see what Jed was up to. He'd said to come to what he now called the "main house" but what she still thought of as the old church building.

She knocked on the big wooden front door and waited, then timidly opened it and called out, "Hello? Anyone home?" She stepped inside and couldn't believe her eyes. Of course, the remodeling was still in process, but the transformation was amazing. Several partition walls were already up. And a stairway to an open loft area in the rear of the building had been begun. As always, the space radiated with the warm, golden light of pine; Pine log beams, pine plank floors. And all this framing the massive window that normally showed off the spectacular mountain view.

"Sorry," called Jed as he stepped from behind a partial wall. "I didn't hear you come in."

"Oh, Jed, how have you gotten so much done?"

He smiled. "Been working night and day."

"Oh, goodness, I hope not."

"Actually, these interior walls went up pretty quick. Taylor's quite handy, and we were both feeling restless one evening."

She laughed. "As if you don't have enough to do."

"What do you think?"

"I like it. I couldn't quite imagine it when you first told me your plan. But it makes perfect sense." She nodded to the partial wall. "And that's where the kitchen will be?"

"Yes. That's one of the reasons I wanted you to come over. I'd like your opinion on a few things." He took her by the hand. "Come and see."

She stepped past the partial wall to a well-proportioned area where a temporary kitchen was set up with a microwave, old refrigerator, and several other makeshift measures. "I decided to start setting this place up for habitation," he explained as he showed her around. "Though Michael will be moving out in a week or so, it was getting a little crowded in the cabin. My plan is for Taylor to make himself at home there eventually. I'm already sleeping over here now."

"That sounds like a smart plan." She looked around the room. "I really like how this still feels open and connected to the rest of the house. That's what worried me at first. I wasn't sure how you would maintain that wonderful feeling of openness when you put up walls. But you've done it perfectly." She glanced over to the big windows, now darkened with the night. "And I wanted that view to be visible from all angles."

"It almost is. Although I think we need a few private areas." He pulled her close to him and smiled down into her eyes. "I've missed you this week, Magpie."

She nodded, relaxing in his embrace. "I know what you mean."

After a few moments, he continued the tour, showing her what he'd already done and asking her opinion on cabinets and appliances and decisions that needed to be made before he continued remodeling.

"I hope you don't feel rushed on this, Jed." She considered how she'd wanted a spring wedding and now wondered if that had put undue pressure on him. "I know you've got a lot on your plate right now."

"I'm doing this because I want to, Maggie." He gave her a gentle squeeze. "I'm as anxious as anyone to have this all done. And I like working on it in the evenings. It helps to pass the time."

She noticed the romantic arrangements he'd made by the tall river rock fireplace. The handhewn table was set for two. Several candles glowed warmly, and a fire crackled in the background. "That looks very inviting, Jed. Is there anything I can do to help?"

"No, just make yourself at home. I better go check the steaks. I'm cooking them on the gas grill outside."

"Isn't that awfully cold?"

"It's not too bad. It's pretty sheltered out on the back porch. Go ahead and look around, or sit if you like. I'll be right back."

She wandered around the house, anxious to take it all in and imagine herself living out here with Jed. The two downstairs bedrooms were neatly framed in with an already finished bathroom in between. Jed had put in the bathroom long ago to accommodate the church gatherings. She smiled to see how he was already using one of the downstairs rooms for his own bedroom. Above these rooms was the loft. She climbed the stairs and looked to see the master bedroom set back into the loft. Again the remodeling was in process, but she could imagine it finished. The front part of the loft remained open to the room below and was big enough for a small office. Jed had already told her that was to be her area for writing. She pushed open the door to the master suite, feeling slightly nosy but knowing that she was welcome to look around all she liked, and that one day she would actually live here. The room was spacious with its vaulted ceiling and large windows to the rear. A roomy master bath was already framed in, with a walk-in closet off to one side. All the amenities. She would miss her old-fashioned house a little, but she looked forward to this. And to her wedding. And to her life with Jed.

"Where are you?" he called.

"Coming!" She hurried down the stairs. "Everything looks so wonderful. I still can't imagine how you've gotten so much done."

"Actually, what you're seeing are the results of the fast part of this process. It slows down a lot when the finish work begins."

"This reminds me," she said as he seated her at the table. "I have some good news about my house."

Jed said a short blessing, then looked up. "What's your news?"

She hungrily examined the juicy steak as he placed it on her plate. "Mmm, that smells absolutely delicious. I don't know if I can concentrate on anything but eating right now."

"I slave away fixing you dinner, and now you're going to torment me?" His eyes twinkled.

She picked up her knife, then paused. "Mom wants to buy my house."

"You're kidding! But what does Audrey want with that big old place?"

"We'll both be part-owners. Mom says she really likes the idea of running a bed-and-breakfast eventually."

He nodded. "I guess that does make sense—the way she loves to cook and take care of people."

"Yes. In fact, she's already told Leah and Spence they can stay on with her as long as they like, but…" Maggie looked around the cabin still in process. "I'd like to have them out here with us. Maybe not right at first, but soon."

He smiled. "One big happy family?"

She nodded. "Spencer will be grown up before we know it. And I'm sure Leah won't be around here forever."

"Yes, we'll have to enjoy the times we have with both of them while they're still living at home."

"But I'm so glad that Mom wants the house. I really hated to see it be put up for sale. We've all worked so hard on it, and it's very dear to me. I really can envision it as a great bed-and-breakfast."

"Yes, and with Whispering Pines being developed down the street, I could imagine that Audrey might have a flourishing business on her hands."

She buttered her roll. "That's right. I hadn't even considered that."

They visited on happily, catching up on the past week. It felt so right to be here with him, to be eating in their own house together, enjoying their fire and each other's company.

"Leah mentioned that you've been spending some time with Amber." Jed refilled her water glass. "What's that all about?"

She wiped her mouth with her napkin, then looked directly into his eyes. "It's kind of a long story."

His brows lifted slightly. "A long story?"

"Well, Amber told me she needed a friend…"

"And she picked you of all people?"

She nodded. "I know it seems strange, Jed, at first. But I really do like her. I can understand why you two used to be close."

He looked down to his empty plate for a long moment. "Would you like some coffee?"

"Sure. Let me help you clear this."

She carried some dishes into the kitchen area, then watched as he made coffee. "Jed, I know this is going to be difficult for you to hear, but I'd like to tell you Amber's side of the story."

He made a moaning sound as he turned on the coffee pot. "Can't we just let it go, Maggie? Forget about it?" He turned and looked into her eyes, and she felt she could see the pain still lingering in his.

"Can *you* forget about it, Jed?" she asked softly. "Amber isn't going anywhere. You're bound to see her around town and socially. Can *you* forget there was ever anything between you two?"

He seemed to consider this. The only sound was that of the coffee gurgling and then dripping into the pot. Finally he spoke. "I don't know, Maggie. I want to forget. And when I'm with you, I feel like that part of my life belonged to someone else. But I suppose you're right. When I see Amber and speak to her, I can't always forget. I carried that hurt around for an awful long time." He slammed his fist down onto the dresser he was using for a counter, making the items on top jump. "I just don't see why she had to come back here—now, when everything is so perfect between you and me."

Maggie stepped closer, slipping her arms around his waist. "Maybe God just wanted to give you a chance to completely close that door, Jed."

He pulled her closer to him. "Maybe. But believe me, Maggie, I thought it was closed."

"Maybe this will permanently lock it."

He chuckled. "Maybe so. Okay, let me get our coffee and a little dessert that Leah picked up for me at Rosa's. Then you can tell me your story."

Maggie only told him bits and pieces of what Amber had said. But enough that she felt certain he could see it from a different angle.

He set down his empty cup and stared at her. "So, are you telling me that Amber said she didn't get any letters from me at all?"

"Well, she got letters from you before you went into the service. But after that—"

"Maggie, I wrote to her from Vietnam. Almost every day. It was like therapy for me to write. And she hardly seemed to write to me at all. And now that I think about it, she did complain about not getting my letters, but I figured it had something to do with international mail. Her letters to me were often delayed. And then finally, I got that last letter. It didn't take her long to forget about me."

Maggie blinked. "You wrote her almost every day? Jed, that would be a lot of letters. But she said she never got them. Not one."

"Maybe she's lying. Maybe she just wants to gain your sympathy." He stood and shook his head with a puzzled expression. "I don't even care what she's up to. If she needs a friend that bad—" Then he looked down at Maggie. "But *why* is she doing this to us? Do you think she wants to come between us?"

Maggie stood and took his hands. "I don't think so. I mean, she said how she could tell we belonged together and everything. I know it must seem confusing, but I honestly don't think she has any wrong motives."

"Then why?"

She shook her head. "I don't know. Maybe you should ask her."

He let go of her hands. "I don't want to. It's over, Maggie. I don't want anything to do with her."

"But maybe there's still something—"

"There's nothing." His voice was hard now. But Maggie knew it wasn't directed to her.

"Jed?" she spoke quietly.

"I'm sorry, Maggie. I didn't mean to sound so angry."

"Do you think there could be a reason Amber is bringing this up? Do you think it's so you can be completely free of her? The old memories?"

He gently took her face in his hands. "Maggie, when you came into my life, I did become free of her. Don't you believe that?"

She nodded, swallowing back the lump that was growing in her throat. "But, then, maybe it's for me, Jed. I can't help but think you had this other great love in your life. Someone it took you years—literally years—to get over. And what if it was all a mistake—" Her voice broke.

"A mistake?"

She nodded again, now with tears escaping down her cheeks. "I've been thinking about it all week, Jed. What if— what if—" Another sob escaped. "What if Amber's father had destroyed your letters—and it wasn't her fault—" She closed her eyes tightly, unable to get any more words out.

He pulled her toward him, burying her head in his chest. "Maggie, Maggie," his voice soothed over her. "Even if that was the case, I would still love *you*. I would still choose *you*."

She looked up, her eyes blurry with tears. "You would?"

He nodded. "I have."

Relief washed over her. "Oh, Jed. I'm so sorry I doubted you."

He ran his hand over her hair. "I understand. Don't worry. And if it will make you feel any better, I'll talk to Amber about this. Maybe she's the one who needs to get it all settled. Maybe she needs to understand that no matter what happened or even why, I'm in love with you. I want to marry you. I wouldn't turn back the clock even if I could."

"You wouldn't?"

He shook his head. "And I won't ask you the same question, dear, because I know it wouldn't be fair."

"Thanks." She leaned into him and felt herself completely relax. Everything was going to be okay.

She helped him to clean up in the kitchen, then they both settled back down by the fire once more. He'd placed an old couch from the cabin across from the flickering flames.

"I'm sorry to get so emotional about this whole thing," she said quietly while studying the constantly moving pattern of the firelight.

"I'm glad you care enough to get emotional. And just because I don't always show it doesn't mean I don't have some pretty strong feelings about this whole thing."

"I'm sure you do." She turned and looked at him. "And be honest with me, Jed, how does it really make you feel to think that Amber's father may have destroyed your letters?"

"Well, the thought has occurred to me before this. And it wouldn't surprise me if her father had done something like that. But for Amber to so easily write me off like that—and to fall in love with someone else so soon..." He sighed deeply. "I think it was never meant to be."

"It must've hurt."

"Oh, yeah. It hurt like heck. I suppose I held her up on some sort of pedestal back then. Even after those high-school years of being together, I was still infatuated with her, or maybe with who I thought she was. To be honest, I had convinced myself that she was almost perfect. More like a fantasy, I think."

"She had been a good friend to you, Jed. And your first love."

He nodded. "You're right. And there's no denying, I really needed her in my life back then."

"She said the same thing about you."

"I guess we were just two needy kids, falling in love before we were old enough to know better."

"Well, I told her thanks."

"For what?"

"It's selfish really..." Suddenly she didn't want to say more.

"For breaking my heart? For turning me against women and romance long enough for you to come into my life?" He laughed lightly. "I should thank her too."

Ten

Two weeks after the ground-breaking ceremony at Whispering Pines, Greg Snider and Rick Tanner paid the newspaper office a noisy and unwelcome visit. At first, Clyde and Maggie listened without comment as Greg ranted on about how their lawyer would be in touch with them regarding the unscrupulous way they had used their newspaper to line their own pockets and in essence shut down TS Development altogether.

"And thanks to you," Rick exploded, his finger pointing at Maggie, "Colin Byers has bailed—"

"Don't waste your breath," Greg interrupted hotly. "They'll hear from our lawyer soon enough." Then they turned and left, slamming the front door behind them.

"Do come again, boys," came Abigail's sweet voice from behind the counter. "It's always such a pleasure."

"Better get my attorney on the phone, Abigail," directed Clyde. "Sounds like we've stirred up the hornets' nest again."

"I think they just like being agitated," commented Maggie dryly. "Greg seems to thrive on controversy. If there wasn't something already in the works, he'd surely stir up something to get it going."

"He should run for public office," added Abigail. "He's got the wind for it."

Just then Gavin walked in. "Was that who I thought it was?" he asked as he hung up his overcoat. "I just saw the back end of a black pickup truck whipping around the corner."

Clyde nodded, his eyes narrowed. "Just when I think things are about to settle down around here, those boys have decided to sic their lawyer on us."

"What did you expect?" asked Maggie. "You didn't think they were going to take this kind of defeat lying down?"

"What're they going after now?" asked Gavin.

"They say we used the paper to run them out of business just so we could launch our own deal." Clyde ran his thumbs up and down his suspenders. "And come to think of it, I s'pect it could look that way too."

Gavin chuckled. "Well, I thought they might pull something like this. But not to worry, Uncle. I've kept a paper trail of all my dealings with Stan Williams related to the property. Everything's dated. The fact is, we didn't even start talking about Whispering Pines until long after TS Development was yesterday's news. The wetlands issues was already an established problem. And Maggie had run numerous stories before we'd ever considered the possibility of competing with them. That's easily verifiable by pulling out old editions of the paper. Greg and Rick don't have anything on us."

Clyde patted him on the back. "Good work, son. I should've figured you'd have us covered." He pulled out his pocket watch. "It's already past one, but have you had your lunch yet?"

Gavin looked pleasantly surprised. "No, I was just out selling some ad space."

"Well, this one's on me then." And the two men walked happily out the front door just like they'd been doing it for years.

"Don't it beat all," commented Abigail. "Those two are getting along so well. Who, in a million years, would've guessed?"

Maggie smiled. "I know. I'm so glad for both of them."

"Why, just a year ago, I thought Gavin's best hope for a future would be wearing a striped suit and working on a chain gang." Abigail handed her some slips of paper. "Here are your messages, dear. And your mother just called."

Maggie scanned the messages, mostly related to the paper, although one from Amber caught her eye. "Was Mom okay?" she ask absently. "Anything up?"

"She sounded fine. In fact, we started discussing a certain couple's wedding plans." Abigail smiled sheepishly. "Hope you don't mind."

Maggie laughed. "Not at all. Just keep me informed. I'd like to know what you two are thinking."

"Well, I'm thinking that time's a wasting, Maggie." She looked at the calendar. "Goodness gracious, it'll be Valentine's Day next week. And then spring's just around the corner."

Maggie glanced out the window at piles of sodden snow still heaped in along the curbsides. "You wouldn't know that by looking out there."

"You know what I mean. The fact is, you only have about three months until your big day."

"But look how quickly and easily we got Scott and Chloe hitched. And that came off all right, don't you think?"

"Of course. It was a beautiful event, but there's no reason to put all these things off until the last minute." She scrutinized Maggie closely. "Everything's going okay with you and Jed, isn't it?"

"Of course. We're great. Why?"

"Well, there's been some talk around town lately. Seems people have noticed Jed being seen with that Amber gal."

Maggie laughed. "I know all about it, Abigail. Believe me, I've encouraged it. Amber and Jed go way back. And they've had some issues to work out—some things I'd rather see them take care of *before* Jed and I get married."

"I guess that makes sense. But too much of that's not such a good thing, Maggie. I remember when my husband,

God rest his soul, ran into an old girlfriend that he'd been serious about before the war started. Next thing I know, he's having what you folks now call a midlife crisis."

"Really? How did it turn out?"

"I gave that hussy a piece of my mind, and that was the end of it."

Maggie laughed as she headed toward her office. "Well, I'm not the least bit worried about Jed, Abigail. And you shouldn't be either." She set her messages on her desk and started to pick up the phone to call her mother. But then, and probably due to Abigail's comments, she wondered why Amber had called. Just the same, it was her mother's number that she dialed.

"What's up?" she asked.

"Well, that's what I'm wondering, Maggie." Audrey paused, then continued. "You know I don't like to interfere, honey, but I've just had lunch with Elizabeth over at the hotel, and we saw Jed and Amber there."

"Oh, brother." Maggie sank into her chair and leaned back. "Why is everyone acting so paranoid and suspicious? First Abigail, now you."

"I'm sorry, dear. But Elizabeth mentioned that she'd also seen them together a few days ago, having lunch over in Byron."

"So..." She hoped to sound nonchalant and unconcerned, but at the same time felt slightly uneasy at this news. "You know, Mom, it's a free country. And I encouraged Jed to talk to Amber in the first place. There's really nothing to worry about."

"I'm sure you're right. But after hearing Elizabeth go on—you know how she can be, well, rather melodramatic about things."

"Yes, I know. But I also know Jed." Maggie felt her voice growing sharper. "And nothing whatsoever is up. But if it makes you feel any better, I'll ask him all about it and then report back to you. Okay?"

"Oh, you don't need to—"

"But I want to. And then perhaps you can set Elizabeth and anyone else for that matter straight."

"I'm sorry, dear, I didn't mean to upset you."

"I'm not upset, Mom." But she knew her voice sounded strained.

"Okay. I'll let you get back to your work then."

"Thanks." Maggie hung up. Why did she feel so irritated? Jed was only doing what she'd encouraged him to do. But why had he felt the need to take Amber to lunch in Byron? Or perhaps Elizabeth was wrong about seeing them. She disliked confronting Jed about this. She knew she would sound worried or perhaps even jealous. She picked up the message from Amber and quickly dialed her number.

"Thanks for returning my call," said Amber. "I've just gotten somewhat set up in my house, and I wanted to have a few friends over tomorrow evening. Can you come?"

Maggie bit her lip. Right now she wanted to say forget it and hang up. But besides being immature, it was completely unfair. After all, she'd only been hearing rumors. "I'm not sure, Amber. Jed and I usually do something on the—"

"It's okay. I already checked with Jed, and he said he wants to come."

"Oh." Maggie twisted the cord between her fingers. "Well, sure then. What time?"

"Sevenish. I don't have anything formal in mind. Just a casual get-together."

"Sounds good."

"Is everything okay, Maggie?"

She searched for some excuse for her edginess. "I guess I'm a little stressed out from having Greg Snider and Rick Tanner in here a little bit ago. They were in one of their usual foul moods."

"Poor Maggie. Those guys can be such stinkers."

"Say…" She tried to make her voice sound casual and unconcerned. "I hear you and Jed had lunch together today."

"Yes. Oh, Maggie, he is being such a dear since you talked to him. And I think we finally made it over that initial hump. Remember, you told me we would in time."

"Of course. No reason two reasonable people can't forgive and forget and move on." She took a breath. "And did you guys have a good chat when you had lunch over in Byron the other day?"

"Yes. I think that was our major breakthrough. Did Jed tell you all about it?"

"Not everything." Suddenly Maggie longed to slam down the receiver.

"Well, I suppose some things are best left unsaid. Right?"

"Right." She bit her lip. "Well, I have some more calls to return right now, but I'll see you tomorrow."

"Great. Can't wait."

Maggie hung up. She picked up a pencil and began to tap it rhythmically on her desk, over and over. Thoughts tumbled through her mind faster than she could catch them. Why had they needed to have lunch *twice?* Was it possible they'd met *more* than twice? She had only spoken to Jed a couple times this week, and then only briefly. She knew he was busy with so many projects, and she was trying to protect his time. But if he'd had time to meet with Amber at least twice…And why hadn't he mentioned any of this to her? And why—she slammed the pencil down, breaking the sharpened lead—did this bother her so much?

She picked up the phone, then set it down again. No, she would wait until he called her. Surely he would call this evening. Or even stop by the house. Then she would wait and see if he raised the subject of Amber himself. And if he didn't? Well, she wasn't so sure what she'd do. But she'd do something. Something mature and reasonable, of course, but something to clear the air.

Distracting herself with work, she muddled through the afternoon, thankful it was Friday. Finally it was time to go. She considered calling Jed again, considered driving out to his place. But finally she just drove home, playing the radio loud in an attempt to drown out her troubling thoughts. Perhaps this was how Jed had felt last fall when it seemed she had too many single men hanging around. Maybe she should just take a deep breath and be patient.

Daniel's car was parked by the barn. His grandfather had gotten him an older Ford Taurus shortly after Daniel's cast came off. Daniel wasn't too crazy about the car, but his grandfather had heard they were especially safe. She heard music coming from the barn and remembered that the band was trying to get some songs together for the upcoming Valentine's dance next week. And when Leah learned that Taylor played bass, she had agreed to sing with the band as long as Taylor could join them, which suited the boys just fine. Tonight would be their first time to practice all together.

She found her mother busy in the kitchen, preparing what looked like enough food to feed at least a small battalion. "What's up, Mom?"

"Oh, I thought I'd fix the kids a snack." Audrey turned and wiped her hands on a towel. "Maggie, I'm sorry I bothered you at work with that nonsense about Jed. I just feel so silly for alarming you—"

"You didn't alarm me, Mom. I probably sounded a little uptight because Greg and Rick had just been there threatening to sue the newspaper."

"Oh, good grief, I should've known something was up. You sounded unusually stressed." She held out a plate of cookies. "Just the same, I never should've troubled you with Elizabeth's overblown worries."

"No, it's okay, Mom. To be honest, I appreciated the head's up. I haven't really talked to Jed much this week. And, in a way, it's helpful to know he's spent some time with Amber."

Audrey's eyes grew troubled. "But everything's okay between you two?"

"Oh, sure. Like I said, I'm the one who'd been trying to get him to talk to her. And I'm sure he'll tell me all about it." She glanced up at the clock. "In fact, I think I'll give him a call right now. And it looks like you've got plenty of food here..."

"Of course, invite him on over. I haven't seen the boy in ages. And if he plans to be my son-in-law, I expect to see him over here on a more regular basis."

Maggie frowned. "He's been awfully busy, Mom."

"I know. But you know what they say about all work and no play…"

"Yeah, yeah…I think I've heard that one a time or two myself."

Maggie felt slightly alarmed when she got Jed's machine. She left a short cheery message inviting him for dinner, then wondered if he might possibly be with Amber again. No, she chided herself, that was ridiculous. Just the same she was half tempted to dial Amber's number to see if she was at home. "Margaret LeAnn," she scolded herself. "Don't be so paranoid."

But when he still hadn't returned her call by dinnertime, she offered to take the food out to the barn for the musicians, hoping she might glean some information of Jed's whereabouts from Leah or Taylor.

"This looks great," exclaimed Taylor. "I didn't know this gig included food too."

"Spencer's grandmother loves any excuse to cook, and she suspected you guys might work up an appetite." She set down the tray. "So are you still getting lots done over at Jed's place?"

He loaded a plate. "Yeah. It's going really well."

"Is Jed working tonight?" asked Maggie, hoping not to sound too anxious. "I just called and got his machine."

"Yeah, I think he's working over at the church building tonight," offered Leah as she began to fill a plate. "He and Michael were talking about it in the shop this afternoon. It sounds like it's really coming along."

"Poor Jed," said Maggie. "He hardly ever gives himself a break."

"Oh, he's been taking a few breaks," offered Taylor. "He's left me on my own several times now. And so far I haven't messed up anything too bad. At least not so bad that it couldn't be fixed."

"That's not what I hear," teased Leah, her eyes sparkling. "I hear that you're the wonder boy who hardly needs to be told twice how to do anything."

Taylor's cheeks reddened just slightly, and Maggie smiled to see it. "Well, I'm really glad for Jed. He needs a good right-hand man."

"Thanks," said Taylor. "I'm learning a lot from him."

Maggie returned to the house, looking over the food still remaining in the kitchen. "Hey, Mom, maybe I'll take some of this over to Jed and Michael. They're working on the church building tonight, and I bet they'd appreciate some handouts."

"Good thinking, Maggie. I was just wondering what to do with all of it."

～

Maggie drove over to the old building that would house the new church, only to find it completely dark and not a vehicle in sight. She parked in front and looked all about, but no one appeared to be around. Dismayed, she started to head back home, but then on a whim decided to swing by the house that Amber had so recently moved into, the house where she had grown up in and would host a party tomorrow night. Maggie had admired the house from the outside a couple of times. Craftsman style and solidly built, it was something Maggie might've lived in herself. As she turned up the street, she noticed lights glowing in the windows, welcoming and golden. Then Maggie took in a sharp breath as she saw a familiar red pickup parked right in front. Why was Jed at Amber's?

Not wanting to appear conspicuous by stopping or turning around, she felt there was no choice but to drive right on past the house. But she drove quickly, hoping in desperation that she hadn't been observed. Her face burned with what felt like hot humiliation. But why was that? Was she embarrassed for spying? Or was she just plain angry? She couldn't even decide which, but her heart pounded wildly as she continued driving straight toward home, futilely wishing she'd never ventured out of her house tonight.

What on earth was going on between those two anyway? Why was she blowing everything out of proportion? Or was she? Maybe something really was wrong. And if so, wasn't it her own fault for naively pushing Jed back toward his old first love in the first place? Good grief, how stupid could she have been! Wasn't it just her own two hands that had helped to ignite this unwanted flame?

Thankfully, her mother had already turned in for the night and the kids were still in the barn when Maggie slipped upstairs and fell across her bed, allowing herself the luxury of thick, heavy sobs. And some little fatalist part of her being told her that whatever must be would be, and perhaps it was just as well to get it over with now. But another part of her said to "hang on" even though it felt as if her heart had just been ripped from her chest and thrown into some deep, black abyss.

"Hang on, and believe the best of him," she told herself once again, after the tears finally subsided, only this time she spoke the words out loud, possibly to convince herself of their meaning. "Believe the best..."

And yet another voice seemed to be whispering: "But prepare for the worst."

Eleven

aggie awoke early the next morning feeling
rumpled and weary and as if she'd barely
slept. She considered going straight to Jed's
and demanding to know what was going on between him
and Amber. But instead she launched herself into a major
housecleaning spree, hoping he would soon call and explain
everything.

By midmorning he still hadn't called, and she decided to
escape her house and the questioning looks from both
Spencer and her mother by going for a workout at the fitness
center. She felt like a bundle of raw nerves and undirected
energy, and she knew she wouldn't be able to sit still and
rest. But when she reached the fitness center, the lights were
off and the closed sign was still hanging inside the door.
Besides being irritating, this seemed odd. Cherise never
closed during regular business hours unless it was an emer-
gency, and even on that rare occasion she would always leave
a handwritten explanation about why she was gone and
exactly when she'd be back. Her customers were important
to her. Confused, Maggie started to head back to her car, but
then wondered if something might be wrong. Perhaps
Cherise was ill or hurt and unable to make it downstairs. She

knew Cherise had no family here in town, so she decided to call her on her cell phone just to check.

After a few rings, Cherise answered, but her voice was quiet and flat, not at all like her usual perky self.

"Sorry to bother you," explained Maggie. "But I noticed your place was closed and I just wanted to see if everything's okay. Are you all right?"

After a slight pause, Cherise spoke. "I'm okay—um—just feeling a little sick, is all."

"Is there anything I can do?"

"No, Mag—" She paused again. "Um, but thanks—"

"Are you sure, Cherise? You really don't sound well. Can I get you anything from the store?" Maggie waited for a long pause, but Cherise didn't speak. She could tell she was still on the line, but all she heard was some muffled background noise. And then suddenly Cherise appeared at the front door, still in her bathrobe. She unlocked the door, and that's when Maggie noticed Greg was just a few steps behind her. Cherise started to say something, but he interrupted.

"Come on in, Maggie," he said loudly. "Maybe there's something you can do for Cherise after all."

Maggie started to step in, but in the same instant, sensed something was wrong. Cherise's face looked tense and blotchy, as if she'd been crying.

"What's going on here?" asked Maggie, taking a step back. But just then Greg reached out and snatched her arm, pulling her inside. Speechless, Maggie stared at him, quickly taking in his messy hair and unshaved appearance. Then she noticed a small revolver in his hand and a jolt of horror like an electric shock ran through her.

"Lock the door, Cherise, and you two get up there." He jerked his head toward the stairway. "Now! Move it!"

They did as ordered. Maggie, too frightened to speak, stumbled up the stairs with Cherise, now starting to sob, just a step ahead of her. At the top of the stairs, Cherise turned to Maggie. "I'm so sorry, Maggie. Greg saw you from upstairs—I hoped you'd leave, but when you called he made me—"

"Shut up, Cherise!" he snapped. "You both go sit on the couch." He began to pace. "I gotta figure out what I'm going to do now."

Maggie reached for Cherise's hand, and they sat down on Cherise's purple leather couch. For some reason, in light of this unexpected danger, Cherise's apartment no longer seemed bright and cheerful, but rather garish and frightening. Maggie's eyes darted around the open room, trying to think of a solution—a way to escape. Finally her eyes came back to rest on Greg, still pacing like a wild animal that had been trapped and caged. What was he doing up here? And why?

"Greg?" she began, trying to maintain a calm voice despite the violent trembling going on inside of her.

He looked at her, his eyes narrowed with anger. "What?"

"I can see you're very upset—"

"You bet I'm upset! And it's handy you showed up here, 'cause now that I think about it, this's got more to do with you than my little ex-wifie."

"I don't know what's troubling you, but—"

He leaped toward her, the gun just inches from her face. "You don't know? Well, think about it, Maggie Carpenter. Juz think real hard."

Of course, she thought, it's the land development deal. She pressed her lips together trying to think of something—anything she could say to calm him down.

"What'za matter? Can't figure it out? Let me give you a hint." With his left hand, he reached into his pocket, then pulled out the lining. It was empty. "All your interference has ruined me. I've lost every penny."

"What about the lawyer?"

He snickered. "You think I can really afford a lawyer?"

She took a deep breath, then continued slowly, soothingly. "But why the gun, Greg? This isn't like you. Surely you're not thinking of anything violent—"

He laughed a mean laugh. "Me? Be violent?" He waved the gun around. "Don'cha know I was the postmaster for quite a few years? And everyone knows juz how dangerous us postal workers can be when things don't go right."

That's when she noticed a couple of nearly empty whiskey bottles on Cherise's breakfast bar. That explained his slurred speech. She knew, from many tragic stories back at the *Times*, how guns and alcohol could prove a deadly combination, and she breathed a silent prayer, then turned to look at Cherise. Her shoulders sagged forward and her features seemed to hang on her face as if she had suddenly grown very, very old.

"How long have you been here, Greg?" asked Maggie. What she really wanted to know was when he had done all his drinking. Perhaps if she distracted him with talking long enough, he would begin to sober up and reconsider whatever it was he had come here to do.

He shrugged, but continued pacing, his eyes still fixed on the two of them on the couch. "I dunno. Laz night some time. When was it, Cherise baby doll?"

She looked up, her eyes cloudy and sad. "He came over about midnight last night." She stared up at him and continued talking in a flat voice, slowly and carefully, as if just waiting for him to shush her up again. "He knocked on the door and woke me up. I went to see what was wrong. He asked if he could come in. He said he needed to talk to someone. I suggested he wait until morning, and he pulled out that gun." She paused, watching him carefully. "He told me he was going to kill himself, and he thought I'd like to watch him do it."

Maggie shuddered.

"Thaz right!" he yelled. Then he pointed the gun at his head, his elbow pointing toward the ceiling. Maggie closed her eyes, praying silently and desperately. But he just continued to talk, now in a singsong sort of voice. "Then I got me to thinking. A thinking and drinking. A drinking and thinking."

Maggie looked at him with the gun at his head, too terrified to even speak.

"And I thought, hey, whaz a matter, Greg, ol' buddy o' mine? Why, you don't have to do this all by yourself. Why not juz take the little woman here along with you so you won't be lonely?" And now he slowly straightened out his arm and pointed the gun directly at Cherise.

"Greg," began Maggie, trying to sound calm. "I don't really think you want to hurt Cherise. She has never done a single thing to hurt you, not ever."

His eyes moved from Cherise to Maggie, and the aim of his gun went with it. "You're right about that, Maggie. Poor little Cherise hasn't done nothing. But you sure have."

She swallowed hard, but looked evenly back at him. "Greg, I don't think you really want to murder anyone. Do you?"

He seemed to consider this for a moment, then returned to his pacing, the gun still loosely aimed in their direction. Maggie closed her eyes and tried to think. She still had her cell phone in her gym bag, but it made beeping noises when in use, and she didn't want to set him off. No, there must be some way to reason with him. Greg might be a lot of things, but she didn't think he was a murderer. At least...she hoped not.

For a long time he paced, and she wondered why he didn't get tired. But during this time she continued to pray. She begged God to send someone to rescue them or to make Greg change his mind. She asked God to spare their lives. Even Greg's.

Finally he came over and sat down in the club chair right across from them, the gun still firmly grasped in his hand, but now resting on his knee, yet still pointed in their direction.

"Greg, you look worn out. Can I make you some coffee or something?"

He seemed to consider this. Then glancing at Cherise and back to Maggie, he finally said, "Okay, you go in there and make some coffee. But if you try anything, I swear, first Cherise gets it, then you, then me."

Maggie slowly stood. She glanced at her nylon sports bag still down at her feet.

"And leave that bag here." He kicked it away from her with the toe of his boot, and it slid across the hardwood floor.

She slowly moved toward the kitchen, afraid with each step that she would hear a gunshot blast ring out. She thought about Spencer and how badly something like this would hurt him. Somehow God had to save her from this, if only for her son's sake. She continued to pray silently as she filled the glass carafe with water and searched out the coffee and filters. "Can I get you some juice or anything?" she asked.

"Sure, why not," he called out in a sassy tone. "No sense in leaving this world on an empty stomach."

As if in slow motion she sliced some bagels and poured orange juice and even found napkins, then arranged all these on a colorful tray. Finally, she carried it back to where Greg and Cherise were still sitting. Cherise looked up at Maggie with such a pleading look that Maggie felt tears fill her own eyes as she set the tray on the low coffee table between them and Greg.

"Looks good, Maggie," commented Greg, reaching for a cup of coffee. "Who would'a thought a tough, liberated newspaper woman like yourself could find her way around a kitchen?"

Maggie handed Cherise a glass of juice, then sat down and looked evenly at Greg. "Actually, I used to consider myself just an ordinary mom and housewife, Greg." She kept her tone congenial, as if talking to a new friend she'd just met at the coffee shop. She told him all about when she got married and when they got their first house, and how she loved taking care of Spencer and growing her own flowers. And she told him about how her writing career was put on hold while she did ordinary things like take Spencer to preschool and swimming lessons and cub scouts and how she used to love to bake pies.

"Those were good days," she said almost dreamily, "and I guess I thought they would go on forever." She looked at Greg to see if he was still listening to her random ramblings. To her surprise, he seemed slightly interested. "But then when Spencer was only twelve, my husband was shot and killed. And that's when my whole happy little life just turned totally upside down."

Greg's brows drew together, but not in an angry way, more as if he was puzzled by this. "Who shot your husband?" he asked.

"Just a kid on the street. They'd never even met. Phil was a cop. He was trying to rescue a girl who was in danger—a gang-related sort of thing. And this kid pulled out a gun and shot him. He died almost immediately." She felt tears slipping down her cheeks now, and Cherise reached over and placed her hand on Maggie's arm.

"I didn't know about all that, Maggie," she whispered. "I'm so sorry."

They all sat there in silence for what seemed a very long time. But when Maggie looked up at the clock in the kitchen, it was barely past one. She wondered if Spencer or her mom would begin to miss her at all. Since she'd been there, the phone had rung numerous times, but the answering machine was on automatic answer, with the sound turned down low, so they heard nothing but it clicking off again. Maggie considered Jed. And suddenly her feelings of worry about him and Amber seemed foolish and minor. Everything seemed minor compared to this day.

She looked back at Greg. His eyelids drooped some as if he might be becoming sleepy. "Greg," she tried again, "don't you want to forget about all this and just get some rest?"

He looked right at her, almost as if he wanted to say yes. But then he shook his head. "There'll be plenty of time for rest when I'm finished here."

Maggie sighed deeply. "You know, I'm not so worried about myself, Greg, although it would be incredibly sad for Spencer if both his parents were shot." She tried not to think about that. "I'm pretty sure about where I'm going after this life on earth is over." She turned and looked at Cherise. "And I think you are too, Cherise. Aren't you?"

Cherise's chin lifted just slightly. "Yes." She nodded. "I've been getting my life right with God."

Greg cocked his head slightly to one side as if confused. "What'r'ya talking about, Cherise? You've never been a religious person in your entire life."

She nodded again. "I know. But recently I've been going to hear Michael Abundi preach. And everything he says makes a lot of sense to me. And so I gave my life over to God a while back."

"I don't believe it!" Greg sat his cup down on the tray with a thump, then stood up again. "You getting religion! Now, don't that beat all."

"It's not exactly *religion*, Greg," Cherise gently corrected him. "It's more about realizing that God is real. And that he really loves you no matter what you've done or where you've been. Michael says there's nothing we can really do to please God except to come and put our lives right into his hands."

Greg began pacing again. He looked even more agitated, and that didn't seem a good sign. The phone rang again, and once again they all just waited in silence until the machine shut off. Then Greg paced some more. Maggie continued to pray silently, and she sensed that Cherise was joining in with her now. But after a while, Cherise slumped limply against Maggie's shoulder, and Maggie could tell the exhausted woman had fallen sound asleep. Maggie slowly leaned back into the couch too, careful not to disturb Cherise as she did so. Then she closed her eyes too, suddenly longing for sleep—anything to escape this frightening yet unending scenario. How long could Greg possibly last? How would this all end? After a few moments, she heard him sit down again.

When Maggie finally opened her eyes again, it was very quiet in the room. Greg was back in the chair across from them, only this time his head was leaning forward with his chin on his chest. The gun was hanging loosely from his relaxed fingertips. And from the sound of his even breathing, Maggie suspected that he too had fallen asleep.

Her heart began to pound furiously as she considered how she might possibly get across the coffee table and somehow remove the gun without making the slightest noise and awakening him. But what if she startled him before reaching the gun? Who knew what he might do in a flash of anger? Perhaps it was safer to just wait it out. Maybe after a good rest, he would reconsider this whole thing and simply let them go. But then again, maybe not. Who knew?

Silently and fervently, she pleaded with God to lead her, to show her what she was to do, and to protect them. Most of all she prayed for the courage to do what she now felt must be done. Greg continued breathing deeply and evenly, and without making a sound, she gently nudged Cherise, placing her index finger over her own lips to signal quiet. Then she nodded toward Greg and pointed to the gun in his right hand. And Cherise seemed to understand.

Because Maggie was on the gun side, she knew she'd have to be the one to go for the weapon, and perhaps that was best as Cherise seemed weary and worn down. Hopefully, she would help in whatever way she could, possibly by restraining Greg should he awaken too soon. Maggie silently pointed to herself and over to Greg's gun, just to be absolutely certain that Cherise completely understood what almost seemed an impossible plan. And Cherise just barely nodded her chin, but her eyes locked with Maggie's as if to signal total agreement and cooperation.

Almost without breathing, Maggie began to silently rise to her feet, and then with speed she never knew she possessed, she moved gracefully toward the gun, firmly grasping it then whipping it out of Greg's hand in one swift motion. By the time he realized what had happened, Cherise was behind his chair, holding onto his shirt collar and restraining him from rising. Then Maggie firmly held the gun and pointed it directly at him. She knew she didn't want to kill him, but thought she might go for a leg if he tried anything.

"Don't move, Greg," she said in a surprisingly even voice. "I know how to use a gun. Remember, my husband was a cop. Cherise, get on the phone. *Quick!*"

Greg just studied her without saying a word. She wondered if perhaps he was actually relieved by this little change of events. Then finally he spoke. "Well, as usual, you win, Maggie Carpenter."

For some reason this made her feel sad. "Greg, this isn't about winning. We just wanted to keep you from doing something you would later deeply regret."

He shrugged, then spoke quietly. "I don't think I really would've done it."

She thought for a moment. "I don't think you would've either. But we had no way of knowing, did we? And you've scared us badly. Do you understand that what you did today was very, very wrong? You need help, Greg. Serious help."

He made a half smile as the cry of a nearby siren sounded. "Looks like I'm going to get it too."

Within moments, the sheriff and deputy arrived. The sheriff removed the gun from Maggie's now-shaking hand, and Greg was read his rights, then cuffed and removed from the premises. Maggie and Cherise hugged each other in ecstatic relief, both crying as they realized how narrowly they had escaped a very real danger.

"You did it, Maggie," gasped Cherise. "You saved me."

"We *both* did it, Cherise." She wiped the tears from her face and sighed. "And God helped us do it."

"I know," agreed Cherise with wide eyes. "I could tell you were praying, and that's when I really started praying too."

Soon the state police arrived as backup, and then the women were questioned extensively about their ordeal, both filling out and signing affidavits. Finally Maggie took a moment to call home and let them know she was okay without mentioning anything of what had transpired in the last few hours.

"I just figured you went out shopping," said Audrey just as calm as you please. "You seemed pretty restless this morning. By the way, Jed called. He wants to take you to dinner before you go to some function at Amber's house tonight. You'd better give him a call to confirm it."

Maggie hung up then turned to Cherise. "It's funny how the world just keeps right on turning even when you're right in the midst of the most frightening crisis of your entire life!"

Cherise put an arm around Maggie's shoulders. "But just wait until everyone hears about this. It'll be the talk of the town for weeks to come. And you shouldn't have any difficulty making this into one sizzling hot story for the front page of next week's newspaper."

Maggie frowned. "Despite everything, I do feel kind of sorry for Greg."

Cherise considered this. "I know what you mean. And maybe, when I get done being really, really angry at him for putting me through all this, well, maybe by then I'll feel sorry for him too."

"It was a desperate thing for him to do, Cherise."

"I know. I told the sheriff they'd better keep a close eye on him in jail."

"I did too. I'm sure he's still suicidal."

"Poor Greg. I always knew he had this sort of crazy and unpredictable side to him, but I never dreamed he'd try anything as nuts as this."

Maggie shook her head sadly. "I think we should both really be praying for him."

"Maybe we could ask Michael to pay him a visit," suggested Cherise, her perennial optimism rising to the occasion again. "Maybe Greg will be ready to listen now."

"That's a good idea. It sure couldn't hurt." Maggie glanced at the clock. It was almost four now. "I better go. Are you going to be okay by yourself? You could come home with me, if you like."

Cherise glanced around her little apartment, then shook her head. "Thanks, Maggie, but I'll be just fine now that

Greg's safely locked away. And I was going over to that thing at Amber's tonight anyway. Will you be there too?"

"I think so." Maggie remembered all the questions she'd wanted to ask Jed earlier. And although they seemed much less important than last night, she knew she needed to hear the answers just the same. "You take care now, Cherise, and get some rest," she said. She felt reluctant to leave. They'd been through so much together in just a few short hours.

"You know, you're my hero, Maggie," said Cherise as she hugged her once again.

Maggie laughed. "Well, like Michael would say: Let's give God the credit since he's the one who did the miracle here today."

"Well, I'm sure glad he sent you along to help then."

"So am I," replied Maggie. And she truly meant it. She didn't even want to think about what she could've been writing in next week's paper if she hadn't stopped by today.

Twelve

aggie went home and told Audrey and Spencer about all she'd just gone through over at Cherise's, and for their sake she tried to play it down. But as she answered their incredulous questions, even she found it hard to believe that Greg had really snapped and stepped over the line like that.

"Man!" exclaimed Spencer after he gave her a long hug filled with sweet relief. "I'm so glad you're okay, Mom. I mean, I always knew Greg Snider was nuts, but I didn't realize he was psychotic too."

"He must have felt totally hopeless to resort to such extreme measures," said Audrey as she placed another half sandwich on Maggie's plate. "What an absolutely desperate cry for help. How shocking!"

"He'd had quite a bit to drink too." Maggie shook her head, wishing she could wipe her memory clean of the whole thing.

"That might have been a good thing. Maybe that's what made him so sleepy in the end," said Audrey.

"Well, like I already said, I truly believe God had something to do with him falling asleep too. It was just so amazing. I still feel like it was only a dream."

"You must be in shock," said Audrey soothingly. "Goodness, I wonder how poor Cherise is doing. Do you think she'll be okay by herself? I'm sure she must've been scared half to death."

"She seemed fine when I left her. Hopefully she's taking a nap now. But she's pretty resilient. Once it was all over, and Greg was securely locked up, she became her same happy self again."

"And what about you?" asked Audrey, her brow creased with concern. "Are you sure you're okay? That was quite an ordeal."

Maggie shrugged, then set her empty plate and cup aside. "I think I'm just fine. But to be perfectly honest, I do feel sort of guilty. Like Greg said, it's partly my fault that he lost everything in TS Development."

"Aw, Mom," groaned Spencer. "When are you gonna stop trying to blame yourself for every nut case who walks the streets?"

She looked at him. "Do I really do that?"

"He makes a good point, Maggie. You do have a tendency to take a lot on your shoulders. And I don't think God wants you to do that. Besides, think about all that Greg and Rick were doing in that sleazy development project of theirs. It's certainly not *your* fault they were choosing to do what everyone else could see was wrong. All you did was bring their deceitful ways to light."

"Yeah," agreed Spencer. "That's your job, Mom. That's what Clyde pays you to do. To find out the truth and then write about it. You can't blame yourself for Greg's stupid problems."

She smiled at both of them. "Thanks, I needed to hear that just now."

"You look beat, dear." Audrey patted her on the arm. "If you're still planning on going out with Jed tonight, I think you should take a nap, young lady."

Maggie smiled. "You're right, Mom. I'll give him a call, then get some rest."

"Can I call Daniel and Sierra and tell them about all this?" asked Spencer eagerly. "And Leah when she gets home?"

"Sure, tell anyone you like. Remember this is Pine Mountain. It'll all be old news before bedtime. And ancient history by the time next week's edition comes out."

"Well, you'll just have to save some of the juicier details for the paper," said Audrey with a wink. "Now, go take a nap."

Maggie left a message on Jed's machine, then took a quick shower and fell into bed exhausted. When she awoke her room was dark and her clock told her it was almost seven. She crept out of bed and opened the door into the hallway to hear voices talking quietly below. It sounded as if Jed's was one of them. She quickly but carefully dressed, then went downstairs to see what was up.

"There she is!" exclaimed Spencer as she entered the library. "The woman of the hour."

Maggie laughed nervously. "What do you mean?"

"We just told Jed the whole story of how you rescued Cherise by tackling Greg and taking his gun."

She waved her hand in dismissal. "There you go, already blowing the story way out of proportion. I didn't *tackle* Greg—"

Jed moved toward her and took her hands in his and pulled her toward him. "I can't believe it, Maggie. You were in such danger."

She forced a smile. "God was watching out for us."

"No doubt. But it's an incredible story. I can't believe Greg could go that far. To attempt murder, suicide...it's just too much."

"I don't know if you'd call it an attempt. He never actually shot the gun. The police called it a hostage situation."

"But surely they won't let him out of jail."

"Oh, no. I don't think so. Actually, right now, I think Greg is more dangerous to himself than anyone else. He could really use our prayers."

Leah stepped up and hugged her. "That is so cool, Maggie. I mean, here you are, nearly killed by a madman today, and now you're telling us to pray for him."

She smiled at Leah, then turned to Jed. "And Cherise and I were hoping that perhaps Michael could pay Greg a visit. We tried to share a little about God, but we think he might be more open now."

Jed glanced at his watch. "We'll see Michael tonight." He paused. "That is if you're sure you still want to go. You've been through so much today. Maybe we should just stay in and let you rest."

She considered this along with her earlier concerns about the situation with Jed and Amber, then firmly shook her head. "No, I'm fine. Really. I want to go."

"But should you have something to eat first?"

"I'm okay. My mommy made me eat something before she sent me upstairs to take my nap." She gave her mother a childish grin.

"Good for you, Audrey," said Jed. "Well then, I guess we should be going."

⌐

Maggie sat quietly in Jed's pickup as he drove toward town. She searched her brain for some graceful way to bring up the questions that were still troubling her about Amber and Jed, yet nothing seemed to sound quite right. Just the same, she was determined to clear the air before they reached Amber's house. Just as Jed turned onto Main Street, she began to speak.

"Amber told me that you two have worked out all your differences." It wasn't what she really wanted to say, but it was a good lead, and she felt compelled to get this conversation flowing.

"Yes. You should be proud of me, Maggie." He turned and smiled.

Now this threw her. *Proud?* That was an emotion that hadn't occurred to her. "How long did it take to get it all worked out?"

He paused as if thinking. "Well, first we met for lunch. I really didn't want to, but she called and pleaded with me. Trying to get out of it, I told her I had to go pick up some tools and things in Byron, but if she wanted to meet me over there, I promised to give her about an hour of my time, but not a minute more." He chuckled. "I'm surprised she even agreed since I really wasn't very nice about it."

"But you did meet?"

"Yeah. And by the time an hour was up, I felt like we'd covered just about everything. And in my mind, that was it, end of story."

"But then you met again?"

He nodded, slowing down before he got to Amber's street. Then he pulled off to the side and put the truck into park, the engine still running. He turned to face Maggie. "You're not worried about this, are you?"

She wanted to be totally honest, yet without sounding suspicious or distrustful. "Well, I'd heard that you two had been seen together around town. And you know I haven't really talked with you much this week, and..."

He reached over and took her hand. "Oh, my sweet Maggie, I'm sorry. I never considered this from your perspective. Well, let me put your mind completely at rest. Yes, you're right, I was in town the other day, dropping off some small pieces at the store. And I ran into Amber when I came out. She seemed pretty upset about something, and I asked if she was okay. She started to cry, and then asked if I had time to talk. I told her sure, that I was about to grab a couple sandwiches at the deli to take back for Taylor and me. So she came along. We sat and talked for, I'd guess, about twenty minutes."

"And did you help her get over whatever was bothering her?" Maggie really wanted to ask what it was that had upset her. She suspected it was that Jed had been brushing her off, but didn't want to say as much.

"Well, I don't know if I really helped her. But I did listen."

She couldn't stop the next words. "What was she upset about, Jed?"

He pressed his lips together for a long moment without answering, then finally he spoke. "I can't really say, Maggie."

That wasn't good enough. "Was it about you and her?"

"Oh, no." He turned and looked into her eyes. "Nothing like that at all. The problem is, she asked me not to tell anyone about it. And I told her she could trust me with it."

She studied him carefully. Somewhere deep inside of her, she knew he was telling her the truth. In her heart, she knew without a doubt that he loved her, and yet her mind was still slightly troubled.

"Can you trust me too, Maggie?"

"I think so. But I do have one more question, Jed. And I need a completely honest answer. Okay?"

"Shoot away."

"Well, last night, I heard that you and Michael were working over at the church. My mother had made this huge dinner, so I brought a basket of food over to share with you guys…but no one was there."

"That was so thoughtful of you, Maggie."

She nodded. "But on my way back home, I…happened to go down Amber's street, and I saw your truck there."

"And you thought…"

Her head dropped down. "I didn't know what to think, Jed. But can you understand why I was disturbed by this and, well, by everything else I'd heard this week?" She tried to swallow against the lump that was steadily growing in her throat.

"My poor Maggie. You've really been through the emotional wringer lately." He leaned over and lightly kissed her on the forehead. "Well, let me put your mind completely at rest, okay?"

"*Please.*"

"Last night, I *was* with Michael, working on the church just like you thought. We were framing in the walls where the restrooms will go. And as we were working, I told him a little about what Amber had told me. I figured since he was a pastor, well, I knew I could trust him with what Amber had shared with me." He paused and looked at her. "Not that I can't trust you, Maggie. I didn't mean that—"

"It's okay. I think I understand what you're saying. So, anyway?"

"Anyway, I told Michael about it, and all of a sudden he just stopped working and said he thought we needed to go over to Amber's house and pray for her."

Maggie blinked. "Pray for her?"

"Yeah. It seemed kind of strange to me too. But you know how Michael can be about these things. It's as if God is leading him. And who am I to question? So I said, 'Sure why not?' Besides, I figured if Amber didn't want to be prayed for, she'd certainly tell us."

"And did she?"

"Want to be prayed for?"

"Yes." She was curious now. "What did she say?"

Jed sighed. "Actually, she *didn't* want to be prayed for. So Michael asked if we could just sit and visit with her for a while."

"And that's what you did?"

Jed nodded. "Yes. We stayed about an hour, I suppose, between eight and nine. That's probably when you drove by."

"And last night, when I called you at home?" asked Maggie.

"I was working in my shop until well after midnight. When I went into the house, I got your message, but it was too late to return your call. And when I called today, you were already gone. Being held up by a crazed gunman, as it turned out." He reached over and pulled her into his arms.

"I'm so thankful you're okay, Maggie. I don't know what I would've done if Greg had shot you or harmed you. And if he hadn't killed himself, I'm not sure that I wouldn't have finished him off and then spent the rest of my life in prison being completely miserable."

"Oh, Jed. Don't say that. Poor Greg, he's got enough troubles right now."

"I know, and I do feel a little sorry for him. But still it makes me furious to think what he put you through today." He reached over and ran his hand down her cheek. "And I suppose I'm mad at myself too."

"For what?"

"For what I put you through. I'm sorry you had to think something was going on with Amber and me. Don't ever think that, Maggie."

She nodded soberly. "I won't. I really do trust you, Jed. But…there were just so many things to make me wonder…"

"I know. And from now on if you have any concerns about us, just come straight to me. Okay?"

"I promise, I will."

"And right now, Amber does need a few good friends around her. She considers you to be one of them, Maggie. And me too, I'm afraid. And I think she's starting to trust Michael more too. But if it troubles you for me to spend time with her, I'm sure she'll understand. She knows there's no possibility for romance between us. I've made it completely clear. And, to be perfectly honest, I don't think she's even looking for that."

Maggie smiled. "Well, speaking of friends, we better get over there. We're already running late, and I don't want her to think we're not coming."

"You're a real trooper. I love that about you."

ᴏ

Gavin and Michael and several others were already seated in the living room at Amber's house, all being held spellbound it seemed by Cherise as she rehashed the day's strange events.

"And there she is," called out Cherise as she spotted Maggie and Jed removing their coats in the entryway. "My hero!"

Everyone laughed and clapped, and Maggie tried to play it down, but it seemed no one wanted to talk of anything else.

"Poor Greg," said Gavin to Maggie, who'd been trying to lay low in the kitchen for a few minutes. "If I'd known he was so close to losing it like that, I never would've told him about my paper trail with the Whispering Pines development. But I just figured I might as well save him some unnecessary legal fees."

"Maybe that was the final straw for him." She considered this possibility as she poured herself a cup of tea. "But, like I've been told by my family, we can't blame ourselves for what happened, Gavin. Those were Greg's choices right from the beginning. He got in over his head, and he just kept going deeper and deeper down."

"I know. But it is pretty sad."

"It is."

"Finding everything you need in here?" asked Amber as she came into the kitchen to refill a platter of crackers and cheese.

"Yes, thanks," said Maggie. "This herbal tea is wonderful. I'll have to write down the name."

"I'm so glad you still came despite your ordeal today," said Amber, handing her a couple of unused tea bags. "Take these home with you, then you won't have to write down the name. You know, once I heard about all that happened to you and Cherise today, I would've understood completely if you'd wanted to stay home tonight."

"Jed suggested we stay in, but I did want to see your place, Amber. And you too."

Amber smiled. "Well, I really do appreciate you coming."

"And I love the style of this house. It seems you have a real knack for decorating too. Your area carpets are beautiful against these wood floors."

"Thanks, Maggie." Amber looked around. "Actually, all this is from my other home back in the city. But it seems to go pretty well in here too. Mostly I just unpacked. It's good to have my familiar things all around me. And it's also good to have people over. It makes me feel almost at home."

"There you are," said Jed as he spotted Maggie leaning against the counter. He walked over and slipped his arm around her waist. "I was hoping you hadn't been abducted by another crazed maniac."

Gavin laughed. "Yeah, Rick's still on the loose. You never know what he might pull."

Maggie gently punched him in the arm. "That's not nice, Gavin. I imagine Rick is feeling pretty bad about all this by now."

"Do you think he even knows?" asked Jed.

Cherise popped her head in through the pass-through in the kitchen wall. "Did I hear someone mention Rick's name?" she asked.

"Yeah," said Gavin. "Does he know about Greg yet?"

Cherise's head disappeared and then she came around the corner. "Yes he does. He called me just before I came over. And he sounded pretty shocked. He just kept saying, 'I don't believe it...I don't believe it...' I felt kind of bad for him. He's got a lot of stuff to sort through right now, and Greg's not going to be much help."

"What a mess," said Amber. "But lucky for you two, you're both alive and able to talk about it."

By the end of the evening, Maggie was glad that she'd come. Mostly she was relieved to have things settled between her and Jed. But talking about the events of the day had felt like a form of therapy too. And by the time Jed drove her home, the whole episode at Cherise's seemed like a really bad movie she'd seen but couldn't quite remember.

"I'll bet you're tired," he said as he pulled into her driveway.

She nodded sleepily. "I guess so."

"I just want to make sure about one thing before I tell you goodnight."

"What's that?"

"I want to make sure you're really okay about that stuff between Amber and me. I don't want you worrying about it, not even a little."

She turned and looked at him, his face illuminated by the light from her front porch. "Jed, I really do trust you. Even when I was in the thick of wondering what was going on, I kept telling myself to believe the best. If you say there's nothing to be concerned about, that's the end of it."

"And if you start feeling worried, you'll come directly to me?"

"You bet, I will."

"Good." He kissed her.

"And one more thing," said Maggie.

"Uh-huh?"

"If you discover you really do love Amber instead of me, will you make sure you come directly to me and tell me?"

"Oh, Maggie!" He threw back his head and laughed. "First of all, that will never, ever happen. But, yes, I promise if I ever fall out of love with you, you'll be the first one to know."

"Thank you." She smiled smugly, then snuggled back into his arms.

"You know, Maggie, for such a beautiful, intelligent, creative, and absolutely delightful woman, you can be somewhat insecure sometimes."

And for that she punched him, but ever so gently.

Thirteen

*I*t came as no surprise that Greg Snider was the talk of the town for most of the following week. After the first day of ceaseless questioning by everyone from Dolly at the diner to Elizabeth Rodgers, who made a special trip to the newspaper to hear it herself, Maggie decided to lay low until the community settled down about the whole thing. She had asked Scott to write the news report, agreeing to only a short interview herself, although he could talk to Cherise for as long as they both liked. And she made him promise not to sensationalize it or make any unnecessary implications. She was pleased when the story was done to see that Scott had handled the whole thing in a very professional manner, answering every imaginable question in a thorough yet dignified way. Maggie hoped this would be the end of it, and that the town would be satisfied and move on to the next piece of gossip, whatever that might turn out to be.

Michael had tried to visit Greg in jail twice, but he refused to see anyone except his lawyer. According to Cherise, he was depressed and remained on a round-the-clock suicide watch. The Sunday following the incident, Michael had encouraged their congregation to commit to pray for Greg, not only on that day but for the next several weeks as well. Maggie kept a note on her desk to remind her. She hadn't seen Rick Tanner in town all week and suspected he was dealing with his own problems right now, and she even sent up a prayer or two for him.

She leaned back into her chair and studied the tall vase of red roses sitting on the corner of her desk. Jed had sent them to her as an early Valentine, and they had plans for dinner at his favorite Italian restaurant in Byron for Saturday night. At the moment, life seemed fairly calm and exceptionally good. Now if she could just finish her story covering Elizabeth's proposed plan for the Cultural Celebration this spring, she would turn off her computer and call it a week.

"Someone to see you," called Abigail on the intercom. By the lilt of her voice, Maggie suspected it to be a welcome visitor.

"Who is it?"

"Jeanette Reinhart."

It took Maggie a moment to recognize the full name of old Arnold Westerly's granddaughter. "You mean Jeanette is *here*?" she asked in surprise. "Or just on the phone?"

"She's here in person."

"Well, send her right in!"

Maggie got up to greet her visitor at the door. "What a great surprise, Jeanette. I had no idea you were in town."

Jeanette smiled. "We just arrived today, and hopefully, we're here to stay. I read the *Pine Cone* on the Internet this week, and decided it was time to come and see if I can purchase back Grandpa's farm."

Maggie nodded. "Of course. Well, I think your timing may be impeccable. But how did you come up with the money?"

"We had a family meeting and everyone, well almost, agreed to see if we could get the property back and share ownership, kind of like a corporation. And they chose me to manage it."

"That's great."

The two women visited briefly, Jeanette explaining how her boys had been reluctant, yet willing, to relocate. "I think the whole thing with their dad has made them a lot more sympathetic to me, and besides, they've always liked it over here. Plus they both enjoy snowboarding, and they don't get to go much where we live."

"Sounds perfect. We'll have to have you three over to my house sometime soon, and we can introduce your boys to my son, Spencer. And that reminds me, they might like to go to a dance at the high school tonight. It's for Valentine's Day, and my son's band is playing." Maggie gave her the details, as well as her home phone number so the boys could call Spencer, then the two women said goodbye, promising to get together for lunch the following week.

Maggie finished her story, then headed for home. She knew the kids were already at the high school, getting their sound equipment all set up, then taking time to warm up before the dance began, and her mother had gone over to Byron with Elizabeth to take in a new movie. So Maggie had the house to herself, which was perfectly fine with her. She made a nice fire and put in some classical CDs, then she decided to just kick back and relax. But just as she settled down with a good book, Jed phoned and asked her if he could come by, and of course she happily said "yes!"

"I thought maybe we could sneak over to the high school this evening and get a peek at the kids' band," he suggested as he joined her in the library.

She considered this, remembering how strongly he had reacted the last time he'd heard their style of music. "Are you sure you're up for that, Jed?"

He laughed. "You mean, am I feeling like a crotchety old coot tonight?"

"Yeah. I don't want to see your blood pressure go up unnecessarily."

"Well, I've heard the kids practicing a couple times and haven't gotten too upset. Plus, Leah assures me that they've adopted a completely different style."

"Hmmm..." Maggie studied him for a moment, then smiled slyly. "Can you promise me that we'll leave immediately, without you saying a word, if you find their music at all disturbing?"

He nodded and held up his hand. "I promise."

"Okay, then." She stood and smiled at him. "What are we waiting for?"

∽

The band was playing a somewhat mellow number when a teacher friend let Maggie and Jed slip in the backdoor. They leaned against the wall, not wanting to draw attention to themselves as they watched the kids finish up their song.

"See, that was pretty good," said Jed.

Then Daniel announced to the crowd that the band would take a short break, and in the meantime the kids could dance to a popular CD. Maggie and Jed stayed in the shadows, not necessarily wanting their kids to know they were there. Spencer and Daniel didn't even notice them as they headed straight for the refreshment table, and Taylor and Leah went for the dance floor and immediately began to slow dance. Maggie observed with some amusement how the two seemed quite comfortable with each other, and began to wonder if that relationship had been developing further, right under their noses, without any of them noticing. She glanced over at Jed to see if he had seen them too, and his gaze was directed their way, his face wearing a slightly perplexed expression.

"Well," she said, feeling uncomfortably like an undercover spy. "I suppose we could stand around and wait for the band to come back, or maybe you'd rather take me out for a piece of blackberry cobbler at the hotel."

He looked at her with a mixed expression of relief and frustration. "Sure, sounds good. Why not."

At the hotel, Maggie asked Jed if it bothered him to see Leah possibly getting romantically involved with Taylor.

"I don't know." He set down his coffee cup. "Taylor's a good boy and a hard worker and all. But I'm not sure that he's the best thing for Leah. Or at least, maybe not right now."

"And why's that?"

He shrugged. "I think I agree with your mom that Leah should go to college and see what's out there for her. I mean, selfishly, I'd like Leah to remain in Pine Mountain forever. But on the other hand..."

She nodded. "I understand completely. It's hard to know what's best, isn't it?"

"Yeah. And that's all I really want for Leah. Just what's best."

"Well, you know, it's her life, Jed. And she's pretty used to living it the way she wants to. I mean, let's face it, up until recently she's had very little parental influence of any kind."

"Yeah, at least not any good kind."

"And she's an independent young woman."

"I know, Maggie." He sighed in resignation. "And I know what you're trying to tell me. Even though you're trying to be quite tactful, I know you're telling me to keep my big nose out. Right?"

"Sort of. But not completely." She set down her fork. "I'm not sure that there are any easy answers to parenting our kids as they grow older. Maybe just to make sure they know we love them and only want what's best for them. But somehow we also need to convey that we trust them to make good decisions, and that they will suffer the consequences when they don't."

"And I suppose I worry that Leah might make some of the same mistakes her mom did."

"Leah's got a good head on her shoulders."

"Yeah. I believe that. I really do." He looked into Maggie's eyes. "Thanks for realizing what was going on there at the dance, and getting me away from there before I said something stupid and regrettable."

She smiled. "I thought something like that was possible. Maybe I know you better than I realized."

He chuckled, then reached across the table for her hand. "Sometimes I think you know me better than I know myself."

"Maybe in time."

"Say, how did your lunch with Amber go the other day?"

"Very nice. She fixed me this wonderful Asian salad, and I even got the recipe from her."

"I didn't really mean the food, Maggie."

"I know. But it was thoughtful of her to have me over to her home, especially since I was trying not to show my face around town this week."

Jed shook his head. "Yeah, what a week."

"Anyway, we had a very nice visit. And I really do like her, Jed. Although to be perfectly honest, sometimes I almost want to hate her because of this little green-eyed jealous monster that rises up within me." She smiled sheepishly. "But then before I know it, there I am talking with her and having a great time, and suddenly I realize that she's a really nice person."

"A really nice person who's had a rather sad life."

"She has, hasn't she?"

"But it was a life of her own choosing." Jed picked up his coffee cup. "Maybe thinking about that sort of thing adds to my concerns for Leah. I sure want her life to go better than, say, Amber's has gone."

"Well, I'd say Leah's already off to a better start. And I think she had a lot of her hard times earlier on. Maybe that will help some."

"Maybe. So, did Amber tell you anything about her plans for the—uh, future?"

Maggie studied Jed curiously. "Actually, she never talks about what she plans to do. It's almost as if she doesn't want to think about it. Just sort of living for the moment, I think. I suppose it's because she's still getting used to the changes she's made. It seems she has enough money to live on without being too concerned for work. But I would think she might like to do something just to keep herself occupied."

He shrugged. "I don't know."

"I know it would drive me nuts to live in a town this small and have nothing to keep me busy."

"You seem to thrive on busyness."

"Really?" She felt just slightly offended by this. "Do you really believe that?"

"Maybe not. But you must admit that wherever you go, action seems to follow."

She grinned. "Must be the reporter in me. If I can't find the news, I just make it myself."

He laughed. "I promise I'll keep that little tidbit to myself."

"Thanks, I appreciate it." Then she told him about how Jeanette had stopped by her office today.

"Hopefully, the property won't get all tied up with Greg's incarceration."

"I hadn't considered that. I sure hope not, for Jeanette's sake."

"I heard Rick Tanner went to visit his brother in Washington for a while." Jed pushed his empty dessert dish off to one side. "I think he's trying to lay low until things cool off around here."

"What a mess."

"Speaking of messes, I want you to come over and see the house tomorrow, if you can. I thought I'd pick you up early for dinner and we could walk through and make a few decisions and just leave from there."

"How's it going?"

"Slow but steady. It's a big help having Taylor around right now."

"Aha!" said Maggie.

"Aha?"

"Maybe *that's* part of the reason you don't want Leah getting overly involved with Taylor right now. You don't want her taking up too much of his valuable time."

"No wonder you make such a good reporter."

ᴓ

Later that night, Maggie waited up, as usual, for Spencer and Leah. She never liked going to bed without knowing they were safely home. And even if Daniel's car was supposed to be "safe as a tank," she knew there was still ice on the road and, well, you just never knew. But now it was past one in the morning, and they still weren't back. Of course, it would take them time to tear down the band equipment, but it seemed unusually late. Despite her worries, she felt reluctant to call and disturb Daniel's grandparents at this late hour.

She waited for another long hour before she began to feel panic set in. Should she call the sheriff? The hospital? Or just wait? Finally, she decided to simply pray. She wrapped herself up in a blanket on the couch and began to pray for their safety and for wisdom to know how to handle whatever might possibly be wrong, but it was almost three when she couldn't stand it another minute. She decided to call Jed and see if Taylor had seen them or had any idea of what was up.

She knew by his voice that she'd awakened him. "I'm so sorry to bother you, Jed," she said quickly, "but I wondered if Taylor is around?"

"Taylor?" he said sleepily.

"Yes, the kids aren't home yet and—"

"They're not home!" He sounded awake now. "But it's after three A.M.!"

"I know. And I've been waiting for hours and don't know what to do." She could hear his footsteps over the phone.

"I'm looking outside, and I don't see Taylor's car here," said Jed with worry in his voice. "Was he driving all of them?"

"I thought Daniel had picked up Leah and Spence, but I'm not sure. I could go wake my mom and see if she knows—"

"No. Don't do that. Let's think for a moment."

Just then, Maggie heard a car pull up. "That may be them, Jed." She listened as car doors opened and closed. "They're home." She looked out the window to see Leah and Spence coming up the steps. "It's Leah and Spence. Do you want to hang on until I find out what's up?"

"No. The important thing is that they're both safely home. I can wait until tomorrow, but I'd sure like to hear what kept them out so late."

"So would I. I suppose they might've had a flat tire or something." She could hear the kids coming in the front door, whispering and giggling. "I'll find out and let you know later," she said quietly. Then they both hung up.

She stepped out in the hallway to catch them both already trying to tiptoe upstairs. "Do you two know what time it is?" she asked.

They both turned to look at her, their eyes wide with surprise. Leah was the first to speak. "Oh, I'm so sorry, Maggie. We went over to a friend's house and the time just got away from us. We thought about calling, but it was so late—"

"Yeah," chimed in Spencer. "We didn't want to wake you up."

"I've been awake all night," she said coolly.

"I'm sorry, Mom."

He seemed truly sorry, and she wondered if she was overreacting. "Well, this had better not happen again. I was about to call the sheriff. Those roads are treacherous and I was really worried."

"Daniel's got snow tires, and he drives really carefully," said Leah.

"I'll bet his grandparents were frantic."

"He says they always go to bed early."

She made herself laugh. "That's probably when he's home with them. *Not* when he's out driving on these icy roads."

"I'm really sorry, Maggie."

"Me too, Mom. It won't happen again."

"Just make sure it doesn't. And if you're *ever* out and know you're going to be past curfew, just pick up a phone and call. It's not that difficult, you know."

"We will," promised Leah. "Now I've got to get to bed. I work in the morning."

Maggie was thankful *she* didn't work in the morning when she finally collapsed on her bed. But before she fell asleep, she remembered to thank God for the kids' safety. Still, something about the whole thing left her feeling uneasy.

Fourteen

Over a lovely Valentine's dinner, Maggie told Jed why Leah and Spence were out so late and how sorry they'd been. Somehow, it no longer seemed the big deal it had been the previous night. After some discussion, they chalked it up to the thrill of having performed for the school dance and the general irresponsibility of adolescence. In order to enjoy their evening out, they decided to forget about it for the time being. Besides, Maggie had reminded him, both Leah and Spence had promised it would never happen again.

The next couple weeks moved along fairly uneventfully. Spencer managed to make his curfew, and Leah began to date Taylor once or twice a week, sometimes staying out a little later than Maggie thought appropriate, but never so late as to worry her too greatly. She knew Jed was aware of this budding relationship, and she sensed he'd rather not talk about it, so she didn't bring it up. Life in town had been quiet too, with not much news to report on. Even the previous concerns of a white supremacy uprising had dwindled down to almost nothing after Randy Ebbert discontinued printing his "propaganda paper" as most had taken to calling it.

Though partially welcome, this small-town, humdrum period gave Maggie cause to reconsider her earlier idea of hiring on another writer. There seemed to be no urgent need at the moment, and Scott enjoyed covering what few interesting stories they seemed able to unearth.

Greg remained in jail, and according to Cherise he was both unable and unwilling to post his own rather expensive bail. Maybe it was for the best. The longer he stayed out of sight, the sooner the town might forget—if they would ever forget—the terrible thing he had almost done. In time he would come to trial and the court would decide his fate. At least he'd been taken off suicide watch. And he'd even allowed Michael to visit him, just once though. And no one, not even Jed or Barbara Harris, heard any details of the visit. But at lunch one day, Barbara had enthusiastically told Maggie that if *anyone* could help Greg to see the light, it was their devoted Michael.

Jeanette had rented a small house in town, and her boys seemed to be settling into school without too much trouble. Maggie had invited the three of them to dinner as promised, and Spencer had gone out of his way to make the boys feel at home. Jeanette didn't wait too long before she made Rick what she considered a fair offer on her grandfather's property. Actually rather generous, Maggie thought, especially considering what they'd done to old Arnold. But Jeanette had been determined to offer the same price that her grandfather had originally been paid. Besides the fact that Rick and Greg desperately needed the money right now, Rick had also seemed eager to have the whole ugly affair behind him. Maggie wondered if he'd even continue to live in Pine Mountain afterward.

By early March, Elizabeth had taken Maggie's suggestion and convinced Amber Feldman to join the Cultural Celebration committee. Maggie had thought Amber would appreciate having something to keep her busy, but when she met Amber for lunch at the hotel, she wondered if it had been such a good idea after all.

"I don't know why I ever agreed to do this," complained Amber as she picked at her spinach salad. "I'll probably ruin everything for everyone."

"Of course you won't." Maggie sipped her tea. "Just do the best you can. And remember this is only Pine Mountain. People here don't have great, huge expectations for these little community events. The purpose is mostly to generate good publicity for the local businesses, generate a little tourism, and in this case to show respect for people of all cultures." She then explained a little of their past with the racist group led by Randy Ebbert. "It's our way of standing up to them and saying we don't agree with that kind of ignorant thinking."

"Yes, I suppose you're right that I'm worrying too much about it. And I have managed to line up some rather interesting groups. So far, I've got a Celtic ensemble, Ukrainian dancers, a Mexican band, and a Native American who plays the most beautiful flute music I've ever heard." She smiled. "And that's just for starters."

"See, you're doing a great job, Amber. Just don't worry about it so much."

Her face clouded slightly. "It's hard not to."

Maggie studied her with curiosity. It amazed her how they had become so close over the past several weeks. But still, something about Amber troubled Maggie, and though she could never put her finger on exactly what it was, she felt sure it had nothing to do with Jed. In fact, Amber had just mentioned how little she'd seen of Jed over the past couple weeks.

"Is everything going okay with you, Amber?" Maggie set down her cup and looked into her friend's eyes. "Do you ever miss your old life? Are you still glad you moved back here?"

"I absolutely love it here. Why do you ask?"

"I don't know. Sometimes you seem sort of—well, sad, I guess."

Amber looked down at her plate without speaking.

"I don't mean to be nosy. But I just figured, since we're friends...and friends listen to each other's troubles, you know...good grief, I'm sure I've told you plenty of mine."

Amber played with the handle of her teacup. "I suppose I can be a bit of a private person sometimes...there are some things I tend to keep to myself..."

"It's not that I want to interfere. But if it would help to talk—"

"Maggie?" Her voice sounded urgent. "Can you keep a secret?"

She blinked. "Well, sure. What do you mean?"

"You're absolutely right." She sighed deeply. "I really *do* need to talk to someone. And I came very near to telling Jed about this whole thing, but then something stopped me. I mean, I told him part of it, and then I made him swear not to repeat a word. I guess I just didn't want him to—" she paused in mid-sentence.

"To what?" Maggie's voice grew quiet.

"I didn't want him to feel sorry for me."

"Oh."

Amber closed her eyes, then exhaled loudly. "It's a pretty long story. Are you sure you really want to hear?"

"Remember me?" Maggie tried to smile encouragingly. "I like long stories."

"Yes, I know. I think I'll try to give you the shortened version, for now anyway."

"Sure, whatever." Maggie waited, watching as Amber now played with her empty water glass, as if she were considering whether she really wanted to say anything more or not. Finally she spoke.

"I have cancer." The way she said the word seemed to say it all.

Maggie froze for a moment, and then nodded to show she understood. She waited quietly for Amber to continue, wanting her to further explain this bit of information she had so easily set upon the table, now resting like a live grenade between them. But then she noticed Amber's chin start to tremble slightly and the tears welling in her eyes. Maggie knew it was as serious as it sounded.

She finally spoke, just barely above a whisper. "I'm so sorry, Amber. How long have you known?"

"A while."

She nodded again, wishing for her mother's gentle abilities to graciously draw out the important information without sounding like a nosy reporter. But all she could be was who she was. "Are you undergoing treatment for it? I mean, you must realize how many of these cancers are completely curable these days—"

"Not mine."

"But how do you know for certain?" Maggie felt a wave of alarm run through her. "Are you absolutely sure? I mean, every day on the news you hear about some new wonder drug—"

"Not for me."

"But, how can you be so—"

"Because I *know*, Maggie! I *know* it's too late. I *know* it's only a matter of time now."

Maggie swallowed hard. "How long has it been since you were first diagnosed?"

"I was told at the end of last summer. The doctor recommended chemo, but told me I was so progressed that it only increased my chance of surviving by twenty percent. And the chemo made me so sick I began to wish I were dead. So I quit that."

"Oh, Amber, I don't know what to say. I'm just so sorry."

She nodded and wiped a tear with her napkin. "Me too. But I'm not telling you this to get your pity, Maggie. I couldn't stand that. I guess I just wanted someone here to know...in case..."

"How much does Jed know?"

"Only that I've been sick, and as a result had been reevaluating my life. That's why he brought Michael over to

see me. I never told him I had cancer or that it was terminal."
She shook her head. "I really *hate* that word."

"I know."

"I feel bad to have burdened you, Maggie."

"No, don't. Really, I'm honored you felt you could tell me. It makes me feel like our friendship is secure. I've felt something was wrong, but just couldn't figure it out."

"Yeah, I've almost told you a couple of times."

"Is there anything at all I can do to help?"

"Just one thing. I mean it, I don't want you to tell anyone. Not even Jed."

"But Jed is your friend—"

"I know. And that's why he can't know."

"I don't get it, Amber."

"Maybe that's the long part of the story."

Maggie glanced at her watch. It was already one, but it was Wednesday and the week's paper was out, and next week's seemed far away at the moment. "I have time."

She made a forced laugh. "So do I. But I'm not sure how much."

"Do you have any idea of—how long?"

"According to my doctor back in the city, I shouldn't be around much longer. Last fall he gave me six months."

"Oh." Maggie looked at Amber with new eyes. Suddenly she realized that what she'd taken for fashionably thin was probably just the result of a terrible disease. Even the shadows beneath her eyes began to make sense now. She wondered why she hadn't suspected an illness earlier. But then at the same time, Amber was so pretty and vivacious—and alive. "You hide the illness well."

This seemed to please her. "Thank you. I do my best not to wear my heart on my sleeve. And I'm taking some herbs that are supposed to help. I know it's unrealistic on my part, but I haven't completely given up yet."

"But why don't you want anyone to know?"

She set down her water glass and looked directly at Maggie. "Remember how I told you about my mom? From day one I was made painfully aware that she had cancer, always aware that she was dying. Each and every day I wondered, would this one be her last? And it just killed me, Maggie. And I absolutely hate to do that to *anyone*. Believe me, it disturbs me greatly to know that you know. I'm sorry—"

"Please, don't be. Like I said, I really appreciate that you told me." Maggie reached across the table and placed her hand on Amber's arm. "I mean, it totally breaks my heart to think I might not always have you around for my friend. But thank you for confiding in me."

"I just feel like someone here in town should be aware. In case, you know, well, something happens. For instance, what if I don't make it until the time of the Cultural Celebration—"

"Oh, don't worry about that silly thing, or anything else for that matter. I'm here to help you. In any way I can. Really. I mean it, Amber."

"I know you do. I knew from the first moment I met you that you were a person who could be trusted. Oh sure, I hated you at first because you had won Jed's heart. But after I got over that loss, I was really glad for Jed, and for you too. You are two very special people."

"You're special too. Jed and I both think so." Maggie hated to sound redundant, but she still wondered if Amber had gotten all the best medical attention available. "Are you absolutely sure there's nothing that can be done to stop this?"

"I'm positive. I even have a doctor in Byron now. I've had all my medical records sent to him, and he was surprised that I was still alive." She tried to laugh. "He's actually quite good, and not too hard to look at either." She smiled faintly. "He keeps searching the Internet for me, and well, wherever it is that doctors look for these days to find the latest medical discoveries. Anyway, I'm confident he'll let me know if he learns anything hopeful or new. In the meantime, he's prescribing some good pain meds, to use as I need them."

Maggie felt tears come into her eyes now, yet she wanted to remain strong for her friend. "I just wish I could *do* something—" her voice broke.

"You already have. You've become my good friend, Maggie. I wish I'd known you years ago. And honestly, your friendship is worth more to me than just about anything right now. That and knowing you'll keep my secret."

"Does your ex-husband know?"

She looked back down at her plate.

"Amber?"

Without looking up, she shook her head.

"He doesn't know?"

"Despite our differences, he's not a bad guy, and I couldn't let him suffer like that. I'm sure it would make him come running back to me, and I can't handle his pity right now. That's part of the reason I didn't tell Jed either. I hate pity."

"But, surely this isn't why you left—"

She looked up now. "No, our marriage was already in serious trouble. When I found out about this, it was just the final excuse I needed to call it quits."

Maggie still didn't quite understand. "But how would he feel if he knew that—"

"He *won't* know. At least, not until I'm gone."

"Oh, Amber, are you sure—"

Her eyes flashed. "I'm positive! No one is to know. I've entrusted you with this, please don't let me down."

"You have my word, Amber. But I just don't understand."

"That's because you haven't lived through this kind of loss before."

"I lost my husband."

"But you told me about it, Maggie. He was gone before you even knew he'd been shot."

"Yes, you're right. But..."

"But this is different."

"I suppose. But you realize that Jed knows enough to suspect something more anyway..."

She nodded. "I know. And I almost spilled the beans that time he brought Michael Abundi over to my house."

"But you didn't tell them."

"No. Since then, I have considered telling Michael a couple times, but for some reason I just couldn't. I've enjoyed talking to him, and he's a very dear man, but..." She paused. "I don't know. But, you never can tell, maybe when my time gets closer..." It sounded like she was trying to make her voice sound light and cheerful again. "Well, I might just tell him what's going on with me and ask him some questions about the hereafter. I must admit, he does seem quite sincere in his beliefs."

"Yes, Michael is amazingly wise about things like life and death and God." She studied Amber again, remembering how she hadn't noticed her in church the last week or two. "Are you still trying to understand things about God too?"

She shrugged. "I don't know. Sometimes it's all so confusing. Maybe it's better not to think about such things too much if you don't need to, but just wait and see what happens when it comes."

"You're a brave woman."

Amber's brow lifted. "What do you mean by that?"

"I mean facing this illness almost completely on your own and not leaning on God for strength. Even your willingness to face death without actually knowing *who* God is. I just think it's incredibly brave of you."

"What you really mean is, you think I'm incredibly stupid."

"No, Amber. Not at all. I just know I wouldn't be able to face what you're facing without God's help. I barely survived losing my husband. It was only God who got me through that."

Amber seemed to consider this. "Well, I haven't completely given up on God yet. You know, that's why I decided to stay in Pine Mountain in the first place. That and something else—"

"What's that?"

"I *needed* to be here."

"Is this where you intend to die?"

"It's where my mother died."

"How old was she?"

"Younger than me. Only thirty-nine."

"Did she believe in God?"

Amber thought for a moment. "We were never a church-going family. But right at the end, I remember my mom started reading an old family Bible that had belonged to my great grandparents. And I think she prayed sometimes, because I remember walking into her room and seeing her lips moving silently. But she never said a single word about her faith to me. So I'll never really know for sure what she was thinking. And I wasn't even there when she actually died."

For some reason this gave Maggie a small glimmer of hope. "I don't know why, Amber, but I feel sure your mom is with God."

Amber's brows came down. "I don't know how you can possibly be so certain."

Maggie smiled ever so slightly. "Well, just call it faith then."

ᔕ

For the next few days, Maggie had a hard time keeping this difficult news to herself. She longed to tell Jed the whole story so that they might both support Amber together as she walked through what must be the toughest season of her life. And several times, she almost slipped and told her mother because she knew Audrey might have some good counseling advice to share with her. But on top of all this, it disturbed Maggie greatly to think that Amber's ex-husband was totally in the dark about the whole thing. What if he still loved her? Or what if there was a chance they might be reconciled before it was too late? How hurt this poor man would be to find out that she was gone. But instead of telling anyone, Maggie kept her worries to herself, praying daily that God would lead and direct her in helping Amber.

The following week, Jed called to ask her to join him in town for lunch.

"I'm sorry, Jed," she explained. "I promised Amber that I'd come by her house for lunch today."

"Didn't you already have lunch with her *once* this week?"

"Yes." Maggie laughed. "Am I not allowed to have lunch with her more than *once* a week?"

"Well, now *I'm* starting to get jealous." His voice sounded only partially serious. "I'm starting to think you spend more time with Amber than you do with me."

She laughed. "Well, Amber needs a good friend right now."

"Hmm...Has she mentioned anything? Her plans for the future or anything?"

She could tell he was fishing, but knew she couldn't answer. "I don't think she thinks too much about the future." Now that was honest. "She's the kind of person who likes to just live for the day."

"Not a bad thing, really." The line grew quiet. "Well, why don't you see if you can schedule me in for a dinner date then? Say tomorrow night?"

She smiled. "All right. I'm looking forward to it."

"I guess I'll have to just eat in town by myself then."

"I suppose you could join me and Amber..."

"Nah, I don't want to sit and listen to a bunch of girl talk."

Maggie was relieved. She planned to broach the subject of Amber's ex-husband today, and hoped she could encourage her to at least consider notifying him of her condition.

◦

After a light lunch at Amber's, Maggie began her carefully thought-out little speech. "Amber, I know what you said about not wanting anyone to know about your illness—"

"You're not going to start in on me again." But Amber smiled, and Maggie knew she wasn't really too put out.

"Well, I just thought about what you'd said about how it was different when I lost my husband. Remember? How he was shot and killed before I ever even knew it."

Amber nodded, then refilled their cups with hot tea.

"Well, that was true. He was gone before I knew he was dead. But what you don't fully comprehend was that my husband was a *cop*—do you know what that means for a wife? He was a cop in Los Angeles County—where cops get hurt and killed on a startling regular basis. And so, almost every single day when I kissed him goodbye for work, I would wonder whether I'd see him again that evening. I know it sounds a little fatalistic, but it's the truth. Ask the wife of any law enforcement officer living within a large crime-ridden area, and she'll probably say the same—that is if she loves her husband. Now, do you sort of understand what I'm saying?"

"Maybe. Are you trying to convince me that you do understand a little of how I felt when my mom was dying of cancer?"

"In a way, I think I might."

"I suppose I can see the similarity. But what's your real point, Maggie?"

"Well, I was thinking, what if I hadn't known Phil was in danger? What if I'd just blithely told him goodbye every single morning, simply assuming I'd get to see him again at the end of the day? Then maybe I wouldn't have taken those extra moments to get out of bed, to look him in the eye, and to kiss him goodbye. You know what I mean?"

"I guess so."

"I'm not saying I liked feeling that I could lose him at any point in time. It was hard, especially with a child to raise. But on the other hand, it did make me cherish our times together. And even on the day he was shot, I could console myself that at least I had kissed him goodbye that morning."

Amber nodded. "I see..."

"Well, what I'm wondering is, doesn't your ex-husband deserve a chance like that too? A chance to say goodbye?"

Amber ran her fingers through her hair. "I don't know, Maggie."

She sensed her friend's frustration and didn't want to push her too far. "I know there aren't any easy, clear-cut answers, Amber. But maybe you could just give this some thought. Okay?"

"Okay." Amber's gaze seemed far away.

"And we're still friends?"

She looked back at Maggie. "Yes. Of course. I guess I'm just wondering how I could possibly go about it."

"What?"

"You know, giving Ben a chance to say goodbye. What do I do, just call him up and say: Hey, how ya doing, Ben? It sure is sunny today down here in Pine Mountain, and, oh, by the way, I'm dying." She closed her eyes tightly.

"I'm not exactly sure how you do it. Maybe the same way you told me. Just the simple, honest truth."

"And then just let the chips fall where they may?"

"I guess so."

"This isn't easy, Maggie."

"I know. But I wish you weren't so determined to keep this a secret. People are stronger than you think about these things. And some have a right to know."

"Like my ex?"

Maggie nodded. "And maybe Jed too."

Amber groaned. "I can't do this."

"Then just think about it a little. Consider how Ben might feel. And consider letting a few others in on what's happening with you. You'd be surprised at how many caring folks live in this sleepy old town. People who already like you and would love to help out, if only they knew. Just consider what I'm saying. Okay?"

"Okay, I'll think about it."

Fifteen

I know the locals would laugh at me," said Maggie as Jed pulled into her dark driveway, "but today I thought I could almost smell spring in the air."

Jed chuckled. "It is highly unusual, but I've seen signs of spring in early March before. Just once as I recall. It's probably a weather record for Pine Mountain. But who knows, this might be the year."

Maggie noticed several cars parked by the barn. "Looks like the band is practicing tonight."

"Yeah, Leah said they're getting ready for the local 'Battle of the Bands.'"

"That's right. Spence mentioned that a couple weeks ago."

Jed went around and opened her door, helping her out of the pickup. "Shall we go take a peek?"

"Sure."

As they neared the barn, Maggie noticed a couple of shadowy silhouettes standing just outside of the overhead light, but near the closed door. She said nothing to Jed, just continued walking toward them.

"Hey there," called Jed. "Is that you, Leah?"

"Oh—" She moved out into the beams coming from the barn light. "Hi, Dad. Hey, what're you guys doing here?"

"We thought we'd check out the music," said Maggie, feeling unexplainably uncomfortable, and suddenly smelling something besides spring in the air. Her nose caught the aroma of something smoky and sweet and reminiscent of something she'd almost forgotten.

"Hey," called Taylor, stepping forward and squinting into the brightness of the light. "We were just taking a break—getting some fresh air. But we're about to start back up again."

Jed opened the door, and all four of them walked into the brightly lit barn.

"It's about time," called Spencer from his drum set. "Hey, Mom and Jed, what're you guys doing here?" Maggie laughed uneasily. "Well, I happen to live here. Right next door, you know." She glanced at Leah and Taylor as they moved back toward their stage area, but something about them troubled her, yet she continued to speak. "Jed and I just got back from dinner, and we thought we'd pop in and hear what you're working on."

"Pull up a hay bale," said Daniel. "We've got a number you guys might like."

"Something for the old folks," teased Jed.

Maggie felt relieved that he didn't seem concerned about Leah and Taylor. And perhaps she was just imagining things. Just the same, she decided she would confront Leah face-to-face in private later tonight, just to make sure.

The band played a couple of songs, which Jed and Maggie enthusiastically clapped for and praised, then they said good night and returned to the house where she put on a pot of gourmet decaf.

"Jed?" she said after they were settled comfortably in the library. "Do you think Taylor might possibly smoke pot?"

Jed laughed. "No. Why do you ask?"

"Oh, I don't know…"

He looked at her curiously. "No, really, why did you ask?"

She knew she couldn't lie. "I just thought I could smell something like that when we were walking toward the barn."

"*Really?*"

She shrugged. "Well, I don't know for sure. I mean, it's not like I've smelled that smell for years. But I do have a faint memory of what it was like."

He looked at her slyly. "You mean, my sweet little Maggie used to smoke pot?"

She rolled her eyes. "Jed, I was a teenager once. Long, long ago. And, I'll admit I did try it one time, but I didn't inhale."

This made them both laugh.

"Seriously, I didn't inhale. And I didn't even like the idea of putting that stupid thing in my mouth. End of story, okay?"

He nodded. "Okay."

"But still, I wonder what I smelled out there tonight."

"Well, I didn't notice anything. And unfortunately that's a smell I should easily recognize—probably even more so than you."

"But I know I smelled something."

"They're doing slash burning in the woods," he suggested.

"Yeah, I suppose that could be it." Still, she wasn't entirely convinced.

"Taylor's a good kid, Maggie. A hard worker. I really don't think he'd be into pot. And I'm certain Leah wouldn't want anything to do with something like that."

"How can you be so sure?" She wasn't even certain that Spencer might not give it a try. She remembered the things Phil used to tell her about kids only eleven or twelve trying things like pot. Of course, that was in the city. Yet she no longer naively believed that just because they were remotely located that they were exempt from such problems as drugs and crime. They were part of today's culture.

"Well, I guess I just don't think Leah would do that. After all, she witnessed her mother make a complete mess of her life. Why would she repeat all that?"

"But remember how worried you were that she might repeat some of her mother's problems with men? Why would something like pot be any different?"

He put his arm around her shoulders. "I suppose I'm trying to think more positively. I remember how someone told me, more than once, that I can be pretty suspicious sometimes and that I should learn to think the best of people."

She blushed. "Good grief. It almost feels as if we're switching roles here."

He chuckled. "Well, that's okay as long as we keep balancing each other out."

Not long after Jed left, Maggie observed Daniel's car pull out, and then Spencer returned to the house.

"Hey, Mom," he called when he spotted her by the window that faced out toward the barn. "What'cha doing? Spying on the lovers?"

She turned, slightly embarrassed. "No. But to tell you the truth, I'm a little worried about Leah and Taylor."

He rolled his eyes. "Gee, Mom, aren't they like grownups? Why are you worrying about them? Can't they take care of themselves?"

"Yes. But when I came out to the barn tonight, I thought I smelled marijuana smoke."

He looked at her with raised brows. "How do *you* know what it smells like?"

"I know." She studied him curiously. "Do you?"

"Yeah, of course. What kid hasn't smelled it?"

"Really?"

He nodded. "Duh. It's everywhere, Mom."

She frowned. "Is there a lot of it here in Pine Mountain?"

"No, I wouldn't say a lot. At least, not like down in L.A. But it's here."

"I figured it was." She studied his face. "Do you know anyone who uses it?"

"Uses it?"

"You know what I mean. Smokes it? Whatever the current terminology is now days. Do you know anyone?"

He shrugged. "Sure. I'd have to, like, live under a rock not to."

"Do you smoke it?"

He didn't answer.

"Spencer?"

He shrugged again. "I have."

She took a deep breath, determined not to overreact. "I appreciate your honesty."

"Yeah, but you wish I'd said no, I've never done that." He started to head for the stairs, and she reached for his arm.

"No, that's not true. Well, not exactly." She gently pulled him back in front of her. "Sure, because I love you, I want to protect you from every single thing that I think is harmful. That's what moms do."

"Mom, you can't put me in a plastic bubble."

"I know." She felt tears building in her eyes. Suddenly, for the first time in ages, she longed for Phil to be around. Spencer needed his father right now. Then she wondered how Jed would handle this. He'd been awfully cool and laid back about things tonight. Maybe he'd actually do better than she.

"If it makes you feel any better, Mom, I'm not into that stuff now."

"Now?"

"Yeah, like, it was something I experimented with a little before we moved up here. Mostly cuz I was bored and stuff."

"And not since then?" She grew hopeful.

"Well, just a couple times."

"Oh…"

"See, every time I tell you the truth, you get all disappointed in me. Maybe I should just lie and say, 'No, Mom, I never smoked pot and I never will.' Would that make you feel better?"

She forced a smile. "It might make me *feel* better, but I'd rather hear the truth. I really do appreciate your honesty,

Spence." She reached out and hugged him. "That means more to me than feeling good." She looked into his eyes. "Do you know how much I love you?"

He rolled his eyes. "Yeah, Mom, I think so. Are you going to get all mushy now?"

She laughed. "What if I am?"

He sighed loudly. "So this is what I get for being honest."

She stepped back. "Okay, then can I please ask you one more thing?"

"Might as well, it's not like I can stop you."

"What made you decide to *not* do it anymore?"

He thought for a moment. "I guess it was something Jed said in church one time last summer. I kind of felt like it was God talking to me, you know, like he was telling me I didn't need that stuff anymore."

She smiled. "You don't know how good it is to hear that, Spence."

He shrugged. "Doesn't seem like such a big deal to me."

"Well, I guess that's good. But what do you think about others who smoke pot?"

"I figure it's their problem."

She nodded. "Do you think Leah and Taylor smoke pot?"

"Oh, Mom." He groaned dramatically and ran his hands over his face.

"Does that mean you think I'm way off base here?"

"No." He looked at her, his brow troubled. "Not exactly."

"But maybe that means you don't want to answer?"

His brows pulled together. "Nobody wants to be a narc."

"Okay, then I won't ask *you*." She looked back toward the window, wondering when Leah would decide to come inside. "I'll go directly to the source."

He made another moaning sound. "Good luck."

"You don't sound very hopeful."

"Well, you know how it is with these things."

"No, not exactly. What do you mean?"

"You know…" He looked at her like she should understand. "Like Grandma says, you can lead a horse to water, but you can't make him drink, or something like that."

"You mean, I can tell someone I think what they're doing is wrong, but I can't necessarily make them quit."

"Bingo."

She considered that. "Well, maybe not. But this is my property, Spence. And just like I told your old friend Ed—"

"He's NOT my friend."

"I know. But remember I told him he couldn't smoke in the barn. I also have the right to tell anyone they cannot smoke pot or do anything else illegal on my property. And if they don't like it, they can just go somewhere else."

He made a halfway smile. "Hey, you're turning into a real hard guy, Mom. You're starting to remind me of Dad."

"Is that good or bad?"

"I don't know. I guess you just do whatever you have to do, right?"

She nodded. "That's funny, I was thinking about your dad tonight too."

"He was a good guy, wasn't he?"

She looked into her son's eyes, almost surprised at how much she had to look up these days. "He was, Spence. And I can't believe how much you remind me of him."

"I do?"

"Of course. You always have. But it's even more so as you're getting older. He would be so proud of you."

"I like to think that maybe he can look down and see me sometimes."

"You know, I'll bet he can."

"And, I don't know if this is really true or not, but sometimes when I'm in a tough spot, I imagine that Dad's right there cheering me on to do the right thing."

Her eyes began to fill with tears. "I'm sure he is."

This time it was Spence who reached out to hug her. "You're doing a good job, Mom," he said in a husky voice.

"Thanks."

"Now, I'm going to bed."

"Goodnight, Spence," she called up behind him. "Love you!"

"Love you, Mom."

She prayed a silent prayer of thanksgiving as she resumed her spot by the window. But to her surprise, Taylor's car was no longer out by the barn. She walked outside and looked around, calling for Leah. But the yard was still and quiet with only the sound of the breeze whispering through the trees. She looked up at the starlit sky above her, so bright it seemed unreal. Then she prayed a prayer for Leah and Taylor—mostly for Leah—that she would hear God speak to her heart just as Spencer had.

She returned to the library and threw a couple more logs on the fire, then picked up a novel and found her place. She wanted to wait up for Leah and ask her the same questions she'd asked Spencer. But she fell asleep and when she awakened it was four in the morning, and the fire had burned down to dark ashes. She sat up in alarm. Was Leah still out with Taylor? And if so, what should she do?

Then she thought she heard a noise upstairs. She went up just in time to see a light go off inside Leah's room. Quietly, she tapped on the door, but received no answer. She pushed it open and whispered Leah's name. Still no answer. But she could tell by the shape of the quilt that Leah was beneath it. Partly relieved, and partly concerned, she closed the door. She would talk to her in the morning.

But when Maggie woke up, it was already after eight, and Leah was gone. Maggie marveled at the girl's ability to get up on time after keeping such late hours the night before. "Chalk it up to youth," she said out loud as she started a pot of coffee.

She decided to call Jed and see if she could come out and look at the progress of the house. Of course, he welcomed her company, and she offered to bring a lunch.

"That's even better," he said cheerfully.

"Say, did you happen to notice what time Taylor got in last night?"

"No. I don't really check up on him like that."

"I didn't expect that you would. After all, he's an adult."

"But now that you mention it, he hasn't been into the shop this morning. Not that he needs to. The kid already put in a full week, and I told him he doesn't have to work on weekends unless he wants to make extra money."

"Hmm...Well, I'll see you around noon, Jed."

She puttered around the house for a while, visited briefly with her mother without sharing her most recent concerns, then decided to go into town and talk directly to Leah about her suspicions. Perhaps she could save everyone a lot of trouble by hearing Leah's explanation of last night before she raised her concerns with Jed. It was possible that she was simply overreacting to an overactive imagination, although Spencer's slippery answer about not wanting to rat on his friends made her think otherwise. No matter what, the best thing seemed to be to bring the truth to light. Besides, she told herself, she was overdue for a workout at the fitness center (a good excuse to stop into town), and she wanted to check on Cherise too.

Sixteen

aggie decided to go to the fitness center first, hoping it might appear more casual to drop in and say hello to Leah after her workout. Just as she finished her last exercise, Amber came in. She knew that despite her illness Amber still worked out, convinced the exertion helped raise her endorphin levels and perhaps staved off the deadly cancer cells. She had lots of theories about such things. Maggie hoped she was right.

"Hi, Amber," she called as she climbed from the stepper machine. "I should have called you this morning. We could've coordinated our workouts."

"Oh, I doubt I can keep up with you," said Amber as she waved to Cherise. "But I wouldn't mind the company. Why don't we plan for next time?"

"How are you feeling?" asked Maggie as she approached her.

"I'm having a good day."

Maggie smiled, aware now of the difference between a good day or a bad day for Amber. "That's great. I'm having a sort of mixed-up day myself."

"What's wrong?" asked Amber.

Maggie glanced around the crowded room. "Too many ears," she said quietly. "Let's get together later. Are you doing anything this afternoon?"

Amber faked a bored yawn. "You know me, the woman of leisure, all the time in the world." She thought for a moment then smiled. "How about having afternoon tea at the hotel?"

"Sounds fun. Good thing I did a full workout. Now, maybe I can have a piece of Cindy's famous cherry cheese-cake."

"Say around four?"

"Sounds perfect."

Maggie chatted briefly with Cherise on her way out. Mostly she wanted to hear the latest on Greg. She knew that Cherise had visited him recently.

"There's really no news, Maggie. He's been doing a lot of reading and thinking. I took him some more books, ones he requested."

"So, he let you visit again?"

"He hasn't got too many visitors to choose from. Rick's still up in Washington, but he has seen Michael a couple of times now, and his lawyer has been keeping himself scarce lately."

"Probably knows Greg's low on cash."

"Oh, yeah, Greg said they're definitely selling that land back to Mr. Westerly's granddaughter. That was sure good to hear. And he's filing for bankruptcy." Cherise sighed in relief. "Because our divorce is final, I won't be wiped out right along with him."

"God works in strange ways sometimes."

"I'll say. But I'm sure glad he does."

"Is Greg—well, is he acting like he'd like to get back together with you, Cherise?"

She laughed. "No. Actually, I'd prepared myself for that possibility, as unlikely as it seems. And I was all ready to nicely tell him to forget it, thank you very much. But thankfully, he hasn't shown the least bit of interest. I'm pretty sure he and I are history."

"Poor Greg. It seems he's losing on every level these days."

"His own choices, Maggie." She smiled and waved as a customer left, then she turned and spoke quietly. "You know I'm not bitter against him, but I can't help but think what comes around goes around, if you know what I mean."

"It's a hard way to learn."

"But the only way for some people."

"You're probably right. I guess the important thing is that they learn." She told Cherise goodbye, and then headed over to Whitewater Works, rehearsing in her mind what she planned to say to Leah.

"Hey, Maggie," called Leah from behind the counter. "What's up?"

"I just got done working out and thought I'd stop in and say hello." She handed Leah a paper bag. "Here's a couple of carrot cake muffins that Mom whipped up and brought over."

"Mmm, thanks. I'm starved."

"Yeah, I missed seeing you this morning. Did you have a chance to get some breakfast?"

"Not really. Just some coffee from the kiosk by the market."

"I could pick you up some lunch."

"Oh, that's okay. I think these muffins will tide me over just fine. And I can put the sign on the door and pop out if I need to later. But thanks anyway."

Maggie decided to jump right in. "I waited up for you last night, Leah."

Leah's brows lifted with concern. "Oh, I'm sorry, Maggie. I suppose I got in pretty late."

She nodded. "You did. And that's not really such a big deal. I mean, you're older then Spencer, and it's not like I expect you to keep his curfews." Maggie realized that she and Leah had never really discussed a curfew before, had never needed to. And she didn't really want to discuss it now.

"But I should let you know when I'm going to be out late," Leah said contritely. "It's only polite. I'm sorry."

Maggie tried to smile. "Thanks, I appreciate it." She glanced around the shop, still not completely sure how to broach the next subject. "There's something else, Leah."

"Yeah?" She popped another piece of muffin in her mouth.

"I want to ask you something, and I want you to be honest. Okay?"

Leah set down the muffin and looked at Maggie. "What's wrong?"

"I want to know if you or Taylor have been smoking pot."

Leah's gaze dropped down to the counter. "Why do you ask that?"

"I thought I smelled marijuana last night."

Leah looked up at Maggie. "And *you* know what that smells like?"

"I was a kid once."

Leah shook her head and began wiping tiny crumbs from the counter and into her hand. "Well, I don't know what it was you smelled. Maybe it was just smoke from someone's chimney or something."

"I don't think so." She studied Leah closely as she focused her attention on cleaning the crumbs from the counter, and then continued by tidying up the pens and notepads next to the phone.

Finally Leah paused, then turned to her and shrugged. "I don't know why you're telling me this, Maggie. What do you want me to do?"

"Just be honest with me."

"Are you accusing me?"

"No. I just want to know what's going on. I have reason to think either you or Taylor or both may have been smoking pot, and I can't allow it. Not only for your sake, Leah, but because I have Spencer to think about too."

Leah's eyes narrowed. "Do you think I'd do anything to hurt him?"

She shook her head. "No. I honestly don't think you would."

"Look, I can't see any point in continuing this conversation. And I have work to do. I'm sorry for whatever it was you think may have happened. But you can trust me. Okay?"

Maggie nodded. "I know I can, Leah. And I do. I just don't want to see you getting into anything that wouldn't be good for you." She thought about Taylor again. Perhaps it was all his doing, and Leah was simply covering for him. "Say, have you given any more thought to taking some classes for spring term? It's not too late to sign up at the community college. But I'm sure you'd have to jump on it right now to get in."

Leah banged the pencil cup down on the counter. "Look, I've already told Dad and Audrey and even you that I don't want to take classes. Maybe I will *someday*, I don't know. But not right now. Why does everyone keep bugging me about it anyway?" She leaned forward and looked directly into Maggie's eyes. "It's because of Taylor, isn't it? Ever since he came into the picture, it's like all of you want to just ship me off to who knows where—maybe an all-girl boarding school or something. Well, I guess it's about time I let everyone know what's up. Just so you'll all understand that it's completely useless to push me like this." She paused for a breath. "It's like this—I think I'm in love with Taylor, Maggie. And right now I don't even care *who* knows."

Slightly hurt by Leah's tone, Maggie struggled for an appropriate response. "Well, I'm not really surprised, Leah. I'm sure we all suspected—"

"*Suspected?*" exploded Leah. "Why do you have to make it sound as if it's a crime or something?"

Maggie blinked. "I didn't mean it like that. I meant, it only seemed natural. Taylor's an awfully nice guy, and you two seemed to hit it off from the start."

Leah almost smiled now. "Yes. And everyone should be happy for us."

"I'm sure they will be, honey. But I hope you'll look at the bigger picture too. I mean, you're only eighteen—"

"Almost nineteen."

"Yes, that's right. And this is a great age to be looking ahead, to consider all there is to do with your life. There's college, career, travel—"

"What if I don't want any of that?"

"But how can you be so sure? How can you know if you haven't experienced some of those things?"

Leah sighed and folded her arms. "I've had a lot of experiences, Maggie. Many I would rather forget. Don't you think it's possible that I might know what's best for me? I mean, after all, this is my life, isn't it?"

"Of course it is. I guess we all just love you so much, Leah. We want what's best for you."

"Then you should trust me when I tell you I've found it."

Maggie knew she was in way over her head. And mostly she just wanted to end the conversation and get out of there. "Right. We do trust you. I guess all I'm asking is that you keep the communication doors open. And...that you be honest with me. Okay?"

Leah nodded briskly, as if she too were finished with this little chat. "I will."

"I'll let you get back to work then."

"Thanks for the muffins."

Maggie left the store feeling like her visit had been a total failure. She had accomplished absolutely nothing other than alienating Leah from her. Would she never get parenting a teenage girl right? She stopped by the deli to pick up some lunch for her and Jed. Rosa was at the counter.

"What's up, Maggie?" asked Rosa. "You look kind of glum."

She shrugged. "I was thinking how glad I am that I don't have to go through adolescence and young adulthood again."

Rosa laughed. "Teen troubles?"

"Sort of. I just talked with Leah. And I suspect I made her mad at me."

"Don't worry. She'll get over it."

Maggie considered asking her friend if she'd ever had problems with her kids smoking pot or anything like that, but because the deli was busy with the lunch crowd, she knew this wasn't the best time.

"Here you go, Maggie." She handed her a couple bags. "And don't let 'em get to you. Before you know it they're grown up and gone."

She nodded. "You're probably right."

"Tell Jed hello."

Maggie drove slowly to Jed's, trying to decide whether to tell him about her conversation with Leah or not. Last night, she'd felt certain he should know. In the light of day, she wasn't so sure. But when she pulled into his driveway, she considered how she might feel if the roles were reversed. She would certainly want to know if Jed suspected that Spencer was involved in anything potentially harmful. Besides, she and Jed would soon be married; they shouldn't have secrets from each other. By the time she knocked on the door, she knew she would tell him everything.

He gave her the complete tour, and they made some more decisions about some of the upcoming details. Then they sat in front of the big window, enjoying the early spring sunshine and their picnic-style lunch.

Maggie tossed the paper remnants into the fireplace and then turned to face Jed. "I need to tell you something, and it's not going to be easy."

His eyes widened. "Does it have to do with us?"

She smiled and slipped her arms around his waist. "Not like that. As far as I'm concerned, we are just fine, Mr. Whitewater."

"Good. You had me worried for a minute. Want to sit down to spill the beans? I'm guessing it has to do with the kids."

She nodded as they sat back down. "Yes."

"Does it have anything to do with what you thought you smelled last night?"

She nodded again. "It does. I asked Spencer about it and we had a good talk. He even confessed to me that he's smoked pot in the past, but doesn't anymore."

Jed's brow lifted with suspicion. "You're sure about that?"

"Yes. And I tried to get him to tell me if Taylor or Leah use pot, but he didn't want to say anything."

"That's natural."

"But he said enough to make me think they do."

"Smoke pot?"

"Yes. I think that Taylor or Leah or both of them have been smoking pot."

"Oh, Maggie, how can you be sure?"

"I talked to Leah this morning."

"Did she admit to it?"

"No. Actually, she didn't. But it was the *way* she didn't that got my attention."

"What do you mean?"

"She seemed to be evasive and unnecessarily defensive."

"Well, she was probably offended."

"It was more than that, Jed."

"Are you sure you're not blowing this whole thing up? How can you be so certain?"

"Oh, I don't know. Call it women's intuition, whatever. But I'm pretty sure that she and Taylor smoke pot. Or at the very least, Taylor does and Leah's covering for him."

"I don't think she'd do that."

"What if she were in love with him?"

Jed looked understandably perplexed and suddenly she felt sorry for dumping all this on him at once. He sighed deeply and looked out the window.

"I'm sorry, Jed. I didn't know how else to tell you. And just when I got to your house, I thought if it was Spence, I'd want you to tell me."

"But you said he's smoked pot too."

"Yes. But not anymore."

"So you're telling me that Spencer admits to smoking pot, but you don't think he does it now—whereas Leah says she doesn't, and you think she does?"

"Something like that."

"Does that seem fair, Maggie?"

"Fair?" She wondered what fair had to do with any of this.

"I mean, isn't it possible that Spencer, trying to deflect some negative attention from himself, has pointed the finger at someone else—"

"He did *not* point a finger at anyone!"

"You know what I mean."

"But, Jed!" She stood up, the indignation rising within her. She pressed her lips together, knowing she better not say too much.

"I'm not putting Spencer down. It's a perfectly natural reaction."

"It's not like that."

Jed stood now too, shoving his hands in his pockets. "Well, you've confronted Leah. She says you're wrong. What else is there to do?"

"I don't know."

"Maybe you should talk to Spencer—"

"This isn't about Spencer." She knew her voice was overly loud. But she didn't like the implication.

He stepped toward her and placed his hands on her shoulders. "Don't get upset, Maggie. It sounds like everything's under control. The important thing is that Spencer told you the truth. That's the first step."

She felt like a powder keg with a very short fuse. "Right," she said crisply, then looked at her watch. It was barely past two. "I just remembered I'm supposed to meet Amber. I better get going or I'll be late."

➴

She drove home, her fingers wrapped tightly around the steering wheel. She knew she shouldn't be so angry. It was silly, really. And Jed had meant no harm. But for some reason his insinuation against Spencer hurt her. She remembered that Spence had told her it was Jed's sermon last summer that had turned him around. Why hadn't she told Jed *that?*

Her mother was outside surveying the flower beds. "I see some daffodil greens starting to come up," she called cheerfully as Maggie approached the porch.

"That's great, Mom." She glanced over to see Daniel's car parked by the barn. "Are they doing music again?"

"They were. But now they're in the house playing video games."

Maggie considered telling her mother the whole story and asking her opinion. "What are you up to today?"

"I was getting ready to meet with Elizabeth. She has several boxes of books to donate to the library. And she's going to give me suggestions for the interior of the building."

"How's it coming?"

"Just great. You should stop in sometime and see the progress."

"I will. Maybe it's time for a follow-up article for the paper. I'll have Scott come and take some work-in-progress photos."

"Good idea. Maybe I can put out another plea for book and money donations. Elizabeth is going to approach the business association and see about having some proceeds from the Cultural Celebration being donated to the library."

"What a great idea." Maggie headed up the stairs. "Well, you two have fun."

Maggie could hear the sound effects of the video game coming from Spencer's room. Suddenly, she wondered if there might possibly be something going on behind that door besides a video game. She wondered if she caught them off guard—would she find them smoking pot? She tiptoed down the hallway, her steps covered by the loud game noises. Then she quickly knocked on the door and opened it. The boys were seated in chairs and never even turned around. Each held a control, immersed in a video game that looked like something from outer space.

"Hello?" she called, feeling guilty for her unfounded suspicions.

"Oh, hi, Mom," replied Spencer without looking back. "I didn't know you were home."

"Actually, I'm going to be leaving in a half hour or so. What are you guys up to today?"

"We were just about to head over to Daniel's—after I annihilate him, that is."

"Or I annihilate you," retorted Daniel as he punched his buttons repeatedly.

Maggie laughed. "You sure you guys will still be friends after this is finished?"

"Oh, Mom." Spencer used that exaggerated aggravation tone.

"I don't know," said Daniel. "I might make you ride Old Pete if you don't let up."

Spencer groaned. "Okay, okay, I'll let you win."

"So you guys are going to ride horses today?"

"Yeah, my grandpa's getting on my case to give 'em some exercise, and I talked Spencer into helping me out."

"He really had to twist my arm too."

"Well, be careful, Spence. And no more broken bones, you guys. Just have fun and enjoy the good weather. Jed says it won't last for long, and it's a beautiful day out there right now."

She smiled to herself as she shut the door. What did she have to worry about?

Seventeen

aggie drove back to town, satisfied that Spencer and Daniel seemed to be on a good track with wholesome activities to keep them occupied, and as far as she could see, no temptations to experiment with anything harmful. At least, she hoped not, although how could one know these things for absolute certain? But she didn't want to become paranoid either. Maybe the smartest move would be to just pray about it and then try to forget about the whole thing for now. But even so, she still felt slightly irritated at Jed for his insinuations against her son.

"Hi, Maggie," called Amber from the lobby of the hotel.

They were seated at the table, and Amber immediately pressed Maggie to explain what it was she couldn't discuss at the fitness center.

"It's probably silliness on my part," began Maggie, not really wanting to think about the whole thing anymore.

"Come on," urged Amber. "Goodness knows, you know all of my secrets by now."

So Maggie quickly explained her suspicions and how she had unsuccessfully confronted Leah, and then provoked Jed's reaction on top of that. "It just really made me mad that he treated it as though it was Spencer's problem."

Amber laughed. "Oh my, the fun is just beginning."

Maggie scowled. "What do you mean by *that?*"

She waved her hand. "I'm sorry, don't mind me. I probably sound like I'm gloating or wishing you sour grapes. I really didn't mean it. I just think that you guys may have a few bumps ahead. It's only normal when you blend two families. But the good thing is, you're both caring people, and you really do love each other. That will take you a long, long way."

Maggie nodded. "I hope so. But it infuriated me when Jed said that about Spence. I mean, here my son was being completely honest with me. And he even said he'd stopped smoking due to something Jed had said in church last summer, something that really helped straighten him out."

"Did you tell Jed that?"

"I was so upset at the time, I totally forgot about it until my drive home."

Amber shook her head. "Isn't that the way it goes. You think of everything you wish you'd said, you should've said...but then it's too late."

Maggie studied her for a moment, wondering if they were still talking about Spencer and Jed, or if they'd moved along to something altogether different. "Have you considered what we talked about the other day?"

Amber nodded. "I'm still considering it. But I'm just not sure what I think yet."

"That's okay. At least you're thinking about it."

"So, what are you going to do about these kids?"

Maggie shrugged. "I don't know what I can do."

"This is only a guess, but I suspect this young man, Taylor, has brought along some bad habits with him, and that he's introducing Leah to them."

"I didn't want to admit it, but I'm thinking the same thing."

"And it's a shame, because Taylor seems like such a nice young man. I really like him."

"So do I." Maggie set down her cup. "And what complicates things even more is that Leah told me she's in love with him."

"And so naturally, she'll cover for him."

Maggie nodded. "Yes, that's what worries me."

"There's more that should worry you."

"What do you mean?"

"Well…" Amber pushed her half-eaten dessert aside. "If Taylor gets Leah involved in pot, what might come next? I mean, think about it, Maggie, both of Leah's biological parents struggled with substance abuse and addiction. Sure, Jed cleaned up his act. But I believe there's something to be said for these genes that are passed down to us."

"I suppose…"

"I mean look at me. My mom gets cancer and dies. And then boom, like a time bomb…" She took a slow sip of tea. "Sorry, I didn't mean to go all maudlin on you."

"Oh, Amber, it's okay. That's what I appreciate about our friendship. We both feel free to say whatever we think without offending the other. And you make a good point about the genetic factor. To be honest, I've never even considered that before. I tend to forget about Jed's problems. But it does make me feel even more concerned for Leah's welfare. She really has become like a daughter to me. I want the best for her."

"Too bad Jed's in such denial about this whole thing. But give him time, Maggie. He can be awfully stubborn, but he always comes around eventually."

She smiled. "He does, doesn't he?"

"Yeah. You can always count on good old Jed to come around."

"But I wonder what I should do about Leah, if anything."

"Didn't you say your mom used to be a counselor?"

"Yes."

"And she and Leah get along pretty well?"

"Yes. I see where you're going with this."

"It'd probably alleviate the pressure in your relationship with Leah if your mom could intervene a little here."

"Yes, and it wouldn't hurt things between Jed and me, either."

Amber nodded. "My ex has a friend who had a teen daughter and married a woman with a teen son, and, let me tell you, it could get fairly complicated sometimes."

"I can imagine."

"Sometimes it helped to have an outside buffer, and that's where Ben would come in. He was pretty good at it too."

Maggie considered this. It seemed to catch her off guard sometimes to realize how Amber had lived a whole other life before coming to Pine Mountain. She treated her past so casually, so dismissively that, crazy as it seemed, Maggie often imagined her as only coming to existence when she relocated herself here. Maggie wondered what Ben was really like and what he'd think if he knew what was going on with Amber right now. "Ben sounds like a nice guy."

Amber stirred a teaspoon of sugar into her freshly poured cup of tea, watching it swirl round and round, then finally spoke. "He is."

"What went wrong in your marriage, Amber?"

Her brow creased as if she were struggling to remember something that happened very long ago. "You know, I can't even recall anything terribly specific or significant right now. Funny, isn't it? I guess a lot of little things sort of built up over time. For instance, we were both frustrated about not being able to have children. And then I wanted to adopt, but he didn't. So I threw myself into my work, which he didn't appreciate, and before long we were heading down two very separate roads. And then I kept suspecting that he was involved with someone else. But he always denied it, and I never found proof. Finally, when I heard the grim prognosis of my cancer, well, I didn't really have the emotional energy to deal with both that and a messed-up marriage. I just decided to call it quits."

"I see."

Half of Amber's mouth curved into a smile. "You see?"

Maggie shrugged. "Sort of. Although, I think it's a shame. And I still think Ben should know what's up with you."

Amber sipped her tea. "I know you do. And like I said, I'm giving it some thought."

"What about what you suggested to me?"

Amber set down her cup. "What's that?"

"Having someone to intervene for you?"

"Are you volunteering?"

Maggie brightened. "Sure."

She shook her head. "Thanks, but no thanks. I'm not ready for that. But, look, if I change my mind, you'll be the first to know. And, if it makes you feel any better, I've decided to write Ben a letter explaining everything. But only to be mailed afterward..."

"I guess that's better than nothing."

⌒

Maggie stopped by the soon-to-be-library on her way home. Audrey and Elizabeth were in their element, up to their knees in books.

"This is looking good, Mom," exclaimed Maggie as she looked over the freshly painted walls, the shelves still in process, and the many, many boxes of books. "I can't believe the progress you've made."

"Isn't it wonderful?" gushed Elizabeth. "I was just telling Audrey that she could probably open her doors by the end of the month if she keeps this pace up."

"Yes, and I've had so many offers from volunteers that I think it might actually happen."

"You're not worried about the competition, Elizabeth?" teased Maggie.

"Oh, pooh. I learned long ago that bookstores and libraries are two different animals entirely. You see, I make most of my money from the new bestsellers, periodicals, CDs, gifts, and, of course, coffee."

"And I won't have any of those things here," said Audrey as she slowly stood up and looked at her watch. "Goodness, Elizabeth, look at the time. It's nearly five. How about if I treat you to dinner for all your help in here today."

"Sounds like a good deal."

"You want to come too, honey?" Audrey asked Maggie.

Maggie considered it, then declined. She hoped she'd get to see Jed tonight. They usually did something on Saturday nights, although after the way she left him today, she wasn't so sure. "You two have fun. And don't stay out too late."

∽

She checked her answering machine at home and found that Jed had left a message. "Hi, Maggie. It's about three right now. A friend stopped by unexpectedly and invited me to come hear him play—he's a musician—and he's doing a gig over in Byron tonight. Anyway, call me if you'd like to come along. He plays classical guitar and he's quite good. I've invited Leah and Taylor and they're up for it. We'll leave here around five, get some dinner, and then go hear him."

Maggie wondered if it was too late. She quickly called Jed's house but only got his machine. Then she tried White-water Works and got that machine. There was no sign that Leah had been home, and she suspected that Jed and Taylor had picked her up in town on their way out.

"Phooey!" She clanked down the receiver, wishing Jed had thought to mention exactly where this musician friend was playing. She could've easily driven over to meet them there. And although she tried not to be angry at Taylor and Leah, this somehow seemed to be at least partially if not completely their fault. All because of that stupid pot-smoking thing last night, she and Jed had been thrown totally off balance today. And it just didn't seem fair. As a consolation, she decided to call her friend Rebecca down in L.A.

·"Hello?"

"Rebecca! I can't believe I actually caught you home on a Saturday night."

"Maggie?" She laughed. "Haven't I told you a zillion times that I'm not the party girl you think I am? I stay home almost every night. What's up with the mountain people?"

"Oh, I'm just sitting around here feeling sorry for myself, and I thought I'd give you a call."

"Why are you feeling sorry for yourself?"

Maggie went ahead and explained the whole Jed, Leah, and Taylor dilemma once again. She felt rather silly when she finished. "I know, I know…I'm probably blowing it way out of proportion. I'm sure that's what Jed thought."

"Oh, I think you just happen to care a lot about those kids. Nothing wrong with that. And these days you never know what might happen. But I'm sure you guys will work it all out. I can't imagine anything going too wrong in Pine Mountain." She sighed deeply. "Lately, I've caught myself daydreaming about moving up there."

"Seriously?"

"How serious are daydreams anyway? Aren't they kind of like those wispy clouds that blow away with the first stiff breeze?"

"I don't know. I started out by daydreaming myself and look where it got me."

"Hmm…It wasn't such a bad place for you to land, Mag. You live in a beautiful area, and you're engaged to a gorgeous man who also happens to be quite nice. Not a bad setup, I'd say."

Maggie laughed. "That's not exactly how I was seeing it just now. I guess it's a good thing I called you."

"Yeah, sure. Now you're all cheered up, and you're going to leave me feeling absolutely lousy."

"I'm sorry, Rebecca. But can't you do whatever you want with your life? I mean, you're single, childless, and goodness knows you've got plenty of money. I'll bet you could practice law anywhere your little heart desired."

"I suppose. But when the rubber hits the road, I start thinking how it's awfully comfortable down here. Like right now, I'm lounging out on my back deck in a little sheath dress, and it's a balmy eighty-one degrees. Can't beat that."

"No." Maggie tried to block out the longing for a hot balmy day. "Even though we're having an unseasonably warm day, it's still a breezy fifty degrees max outside, and cooling down fast. And it still freezes during the night."

"Brrrr."

"But the sky is perfectly blue. And the air is pure—"

"This is starting to sound like a battle of the climates. Let's knock it off, okay?"

"Okay." She smiled mischievously. "Are you and Barry still emailing each other?"

"As a matter of fact, we are. Which is nice, especially considering how a certain old best friend seems to be too busy to stay in touch anymore."

"I called you just now, didn't I?"

"Yeah, yeah..."

"And you're still coming for the wedding? My maid of honor?"

"Yeah, yeah...always a bridesmaid, never a bride."

Maggie chuckled. "Never heard you say *that* before. Sounds like you're changing your tune about marriage these days."

"Maybe I'm just getting old. A lot of different things are starting to appeal to me. Just yesterday I bought a pair of shoes simply because they were comfortable!"

Maggie laughed. "Sheesh, I've been doing that for ages."

"And what with this whole daydreaming thing about Pine Mountain, maybe I'll just stay on a couple weeks and really check the place out."

"Honestly?"

"Who knows?" She paused. "Oh, phooey, Mag, I hear someone knocking at my front door."

"I'll let you go then. It's probably Harrison Ford or Mel Gibson stopping by for cocktails."

"Yeah, sure. I think they're both happily married men. Now, you take care and don't worry about those kids too much. They'll be okay."

"Thanks, Rebecca."

ᴏ—

Maggie rambled around her quiet house, finally turning on the television for some noise and company, something she seldom did. Then she sat down with a magazine, absently flipping through pages and listening to the local news and the weatherman bragging about their "unseasonably warm weather." Obviously, he'd never lived in southern California. Then a community service ad came on about teens and drugs. She looked up and focused in on the celebrity who was encouraging parents to talk to their kids and get to know their friends, and finally they showed a scene where a parent was actually snooping through a teen's room. She picked up the remote and clicked it off in disgust.

"That's ridiculous," she said aloud. "Parents snooping in their kids' rooms. What a great way to build trust."

She stood up and stretched, then looked up toward the stairs and wondered. Was it a parental obligation to look through their kids' things? She wasn't so sure. It seemed something her father would've done, probably had done. But not her mother. Then she wondered what Phil would say. Of course, she knew. After all, he'd been an L.A. cop. He knew what could happen with teens and drugs. She was certain if he had reason to suspect anything he'd say "go ahead and look."

She crept up the stairs as if she were a criminal in her own home. Part of her was repulsed at the idea of snooping, while another part of her suddenly became quite curious. She opened Spencer's door, telling herself that she would only reassure herself of what she already felt certain of, and then she began to poke around. Careful not to move anything out of its place, she looked through messy drawers, under his bed (which was totally disgusting), and then in his closet. After about thirty minutes of finding dirty socks that looked to be growing live bacteria, an old pizza box, and a couple of encrusted ice cream bowls, she was convinced that no real contraband existed in his room, or else it was so well hidden that even the vice squad would be challenged to uncover it.

And now all she felt was an uncomfortable mixture of relief and guilt. What if Spencer knew what she'd done? Certainly, she wasn't supposed to tell him of this, was she? She stepped out and quietly shut the door, then looked across the hallway over to Leah's closed door.

Now, she reminded herself, Leah was *not* her daughter. Maybe she had no right to look through her things at all. But on the other hand, Leah lived under her roof, and right now it was Leah, or maybe Taylor, whom she most suspected. And to be fair, she should treat Leah no different than she treated Spencer. She walked into Leah's tidy room, convinced this wouldn't take long. All her drawers were neat as a pin, and her bed was made, impressive after getting only a few hours sleep! Maybe Maggie's fears were unfounded. She was just about to quit when she discovered a cigar box tucked way into a back corner of her closet beneath the old backpack that Leah had originally brought with her to Pine Mountain.

With foreboding, Maggie opened the box to see a small Ziploc bag filled with some shredded material that looked somewhat like tobacco, only more greenish in color. And, of course, she had no illusions as to what it was. Also in the box was a package of cigarette papers, and some matches. And then a note. Her heart pounding, she opened the note and read:

"To Leah, with love, T."

She snapped the lid back down and started to put the box back into its dark corner when she stopped herself. What was she doing? She couldn't leave this box in here! But to confiscate it was to admit to snooping. But then again, she had every right to snoop, for after all, this was her house. And as it turned out, she had found *something*. Something illegal. But finding this little box of horrors brought her no satisfaction at all, only a sick feeling of dread deep down in the pit of her stomach. Oh, what was she supposed to do with this thing now?

Somehow just holding that detestable cigar box in her hands filled her with anger and repulsion. And before she could even stop to consider her actions, she ran downstairs and shoved it in the fireplace. She quickly wadded up newspapers and struck a match, and then she watched grimly as the box and its evil contents flamed up and finally disappeared into a pile of white ashes. She worried for just a moment that someone outside might smell the odd smoke and wonder what was up. But then again, she had no neighbors as of yet. The Whispering Pines development was still in the early stages with little sign of the houses to come. For the moment, she felt thankful for the isolation of her home. As if personally responsible for her children's behavior, she didn't want anyone to know about this.

She paced the floor for some time, longing for Jed to come home, bringing Leah with him, so they could all sit down and discuss this whole thing calmly. Like the mature adults they were, they would surely come to some form of agreement, and that would be the end of it. Anyway, that's what she hoped.

Eighteen

aggie heard a car come into her driveway and looked out to see her mother pulling up in front of the carriage house. Grabbing a sweater, she ran out to meet her.

"Hey there," she called as her mother closed the car door.

"Howdy, neighbor," called out Audrey. "Want to come in and sit for a spell?"

"I was about to say the same to you, Mom. I just made a pot of Earl Grey tea. Do you have time for a visit?"

"Sure," Audrey peered at her in the light of the porch lamp. "Everything okay? I thought you'd be out with Jed tonight."

"I got home too late and missed out," she explained as she led her mother into the house. "And, no, everything is *not* okay."

Maggie spilled her concerns to her mother as she poured them both a cup of tea. Then they went into the library and sat before the fire as she finished her tale. "When I found that stuff in her closet, I went nuts and just threw everything into the fireplace."

"Can't say as I blame you. But now you don't have any evidence to confront Leah with."

"I know." Maggie shook her head. "I thought of that afterward. But to tell you the truth, I'm not sure I want to confront her."

"You really think you can just sweep something like this under the rug?"

Maggie shrugged. "I don't know. Maybe Leah doesn't really want that stuff in the first place. I'm hoping she'll be relieved to find that it's gone."

"And it won't bother her to know someone came into her room and took it?"

"I don't know. What exactly do you suggest, Mom?"

"I'm not sure. This is a tricky situation."

"That's what Amber insinuated."

"Amber?"

"Yes. I was so frustrated with Jed that I told Amber the whole story. Well, everything except about finding the pot, which I hadn't at the time. Actually, it was Amber's suggestion that I involve you. She realized how this stupid mess was playing havoc between Jed and me, sort of parent against parent, you know. And she thought you could be a good buffer for us."

"Well, I never would've thought Amber was the type to care. But she may be right about needing a buffer."

"There's a lot more to Amber than meets the eye." Suddenly she felt a weary kind of sadness. "I'm really starting to treasure my friendship with her."

"Well, that's wonderful, dear. Really good friends aren't always easy to come by." Audrey stared into the fire. "Now, let's see…what's the next best step here?"

"Do you mind getting involved in this, Mom?"

"Of course not. Goodness knows, I'm already involved. I mean, this is *my* family we're talking about here. You can't very well keep me out of it."

Maggie smiled weakly. "Thanks."

"First off, I think we need to talk to Leah as soon as possible."

"With Jed too?"

"Yes. He needs to hear this himself, and not secondhand this time."

"What about Taylor?"

"Hmm...that's tougher. On the one hand, he needs to be confronted too. But for starters I'd prefer to talk to Leah without him. Just in case he has a lot of influence on her. That way she won't be led by him, or feel the need to defend him. It'll just keep things simpler."

"Oh, yeah, I forgot to mention that she thinks she's in love with him."

"No surprises there. She's talked to me about him a lot already. She thinks he's Mr. Wonderful. She often compares him to her father."

Maggie winced. "Unfortunately, she's not too far off base on that account. Jed had problems with substance abuse in his young adulthood too."

Audrey nodded. "Poor Leah. Both her mother and father."

"That's what Amber said too. Do you think that makes it more likely that Leah could inherit the same troubles?"

"Not according to statistics or research. So far there's no biological hereditary connection to worry about. Of course, that's not to say that the underlying reasons might not be related, or that perhaps there's some other undiagnosed chemical imbalance or disorder like ADD. It's hard to say. A lot of this kind of research is still in the infantile stage."

"Do you ever miss your counseling practice, Mom?"

Audrey laughed. "Seems I still get plenty of opportunities with friends and family. Just the other day, Cherise cornered me in the supermarket with a question about our notorious Greg Snider. She read an article and seems to think he's bipolar now."

Maggie teasingly shook a finger. "Now, what about what you used to say about never practicing on family and friends?"

"Well, I don't charge for these consultations. I just consider it good, old-fashioned, friendly advice."

Maggie heard wheels crunching in the driveway again and got up to see Jed's pickup pulling up. "They're here, Mom. Should I go invite them in?"

"Do you think Taylor's with them?"

"Possibly."

"Well, do as you think best."

Maggie went out on the porch and waved. Jed, Leah, and Taylor all got out and came up to the house. "How was the music?" she asked brightly, hoping to disguise her emotions.

"Great," said Leah.

"I wish you could've come along." Jed gave her a hug.

"Yeah, he's one cool guitarist," added Taylor.

Without looking at Taylor, she opened the front door. "I really wanted to come, Jed, but I got home too late. Hey, do you guys want some coffee or cocoa or something?" She paused by the library. "Mom and I were just having some tea."

Leah and Taylor went into the kitchen to make cocoa, and Maggie ushered Jed into the library. "We need to talk," she said in quick, hushed tones. "I've already told Mom about what's going on and—"

"What is going on?" asked Jed. "You're not still all worried about that pot business, are you?"

"Jed!" she spoke with quiet urgency. "I found a stash in Leah's room."

His eyes opened wide. "Are you sure it was hers?"

She nodded. "And there was a note. Apparently it was given to her by Taylor."

"By Taylor?" Jed looked understandably perplexed. "But how did you find it?"

"Never mind. The important thing is to decide how to handle it." She looked over to Audrey for help. "Mom?"

"Well, I think we all need to sit down and talk to these kids about what's going on. Although I'm not sure how helpful it will be to have Taylor here."

"I *want* to have Taylor here," said Jed. "He's my employee, and I have a right to know what's going on."

"What's going on about what?" asked Leah suspiciously as she and Taylor walked in with three mugs of hot cocoa.

Maggie looked up in surprise. "Um, we need to talk—"

"Come in and sit," said Audrey warmly. "We have some concerns we need to discuss with—"

"This isn't that thing Maggie brought up this morning, is it?" asked Leah her voice growing sharper. "I thought we settled that."

"What's that?" asked Taylor as he sat on a footstool.

"Nothing," mumbled Leah, turning back toward the door.

"Leah," said Jed in a firm yet fatherly voice. "You and Taylor need to explain some things to us."

With everyone finally seated, Jed turned to Maggie. "Okay, go ahead and tell them what you told me."

Suddenly Maggie wished she could just forget the whole thing and vanish into the woodwork. She hated to admit that she'd gone through Leah's room. Taking a deep breath, she looked to her mom for support.

"Go on, honey. Just get it out into the open."

"Well..." she felt her voice quiver. "I found a cigar box in Leah's room—"

"You went through my room?" exploded Leah.

"I saw this public service ad on TV, and the guy said—"

"You went through my personal things?"

"Leah," said Jed gently. "Apparently, Maggie had cause to be concerned—"

"But I already told her I'm not doing anything like that!" Leah burst into tears. "Why can't she just believe me?"

Taylor put his arm around her. "Maybe we should go, Leah."

"Yeah, let's go, Taylor." She looked at the three adults with watery eyes. "I thought you guys were my family. I thought we all trusted each other."

"We want to, Leah," tried Maggie. "But we're concerned. We want to help—"

"If you wanted to help you shouldn't have snooped in my room," she snapped back.

"Uh, I don't have my car here, Jed," said Taylor, acting quite calm in spite of everything. "Do you mind driving us back?"

"Driving you where?" asked Jed, irritation showing in his jaw. "Leah lives here right now."

"Not anymore!" Leah stood defiantly.

"Leah," pleaded Maggie. "I don't want you to go. Not like this. I care about you, and I just want to find out what's going on. Can't we just talk—"

"What am I supposed to say, Maggie? It's obvious that you've already played judge and jury, and as far as you're concerned I'm already convicted."

"Wait a minute, Leah," said Audrey in a stern voice. She hadn't said much of anything until then, and they all turned to look at her. "That's not a fair accusation." She paused and looked evenly at everyone. "We all need to calm down now. And everyone needs their chance to speak. But, as of this moment, I'm taking over this family meeting. Blame it on my old age or whatever suits you. But I'm going to see that we get to the bottom of this." She stood up and faced Leah and Taylor. "Now, you two sit down."

They did as they were told, and Maggie marveled at her mother's authority as she began to conduct her little hearing.

"Leah, first of all, Maggie already told me how badly she felt when she decided to search Spencer's and your rooms. But she had a reason to be concerned. And as it turned out, her concerns were validated. Now," she paused for a breath, "please tell us why you had marijuana in your room."

Leah looked down at the floor. "I don't know," she muttered.

"Let me rephrase that," said Audrey. "How did the marijuana *get* in your room?"

Again Leah said, "I don't know."

"Okay, let's put it like this: Marijuana was found in your room. Did you put it there? Or did someone else put it there?"

"I did."

"Thank you for being honest. So, you put it in your room. Did you put it there because you planned to use it later?"

"No."

"Why did you put it there?"

"I didn't know what else to do with it."

"Where did you get the marijuana in the first place, Leah?"

Taylor stood up, his head held high. "This is all my fault—"

"It's okay, Taylor," said Leah quickly. "I'll handle this."

"No." He exhaled loudly then continued in a quiet voice. "I gave that box to Leah. It was stupid, okay. And I'm really sorry." He looked directly at Jed. "I know all about your zero tolerance policy, so I'll get ready to leave as soon as we get home."

"No!" exclaimed Leah.

"Let's go, Taylor," said Jed without any show of emotion.

"Wait, Dad!" Leah stood and grabbed Taylor's arm. "You can't blame all this on Taylor. I had a free choice here. I could've said no."

But Jed had already reached the front door. "Come on, Taylor."

"Let me go, Leah." Taylor looked at her with pleading eyes. "This is all my mess; let me clean it up."

She released his arm and turned to Maggie. "Can't you do something?"

Maggie shook her head in frustration. "What can I do? We need to let them go and sort this out."

"But—"

"She's right," said Taylor sadly. "See ya 'round."

As soon as the front door closed, Leah burst into tears again. "I know Dad will send him away, and I'll probably never see him again."

"Leah," said Audrey, "Jed's a reasonable guy."

Leah turned to face them both. "Not when it comes to stuff like this. I've heard him go on and on about it. He probably hates me now too."

"Jed doesn't hate anyone," said Maggie. "He's just upset."

"How can you know that? He's told me about his zero tolerance policy before, Maggie. He has specifically said he will not put up with substance abuse of any sort!" She threw herself onto the arm of the couch and continued to sob. "It's all my fault! I've ruined everything!"

Maggie and Audrey went over to her. Maggie stroked her hair while Audrey talked. "Leah, honey, it just feels like everything's ruined. But it's not. Actually, what happened in here tonight was a very good thing. It got our concerns out in the open. And both you and Taylor answered us honestly. Now we just need to wait until Jed and Taylor have had a chance to talk. Jed is a kind and gracious man, and he likes Taylor a lot. I'm sure they can work this all out."

Leah sat up and looked at them. "Do you really think so?"

"I'm sure of it." Audrey put her arm around Leah's shoulders. "We all care about you kids too much to let something like this just slip by."

Leah turned to Maggie. "I never really planned to smoke that stuff. I mean, I've done that kind of crap before, and I learned real quick that it's not for me. I watched my mom and her boyfriends get all strung out all the time. I saw what a mess they made of their lives. I don't want that. Not really."

Maggie nodded. "I didn't think you did. But what about Taylor? What does he want?"

Fresh tears began to trickle down Leah's cheeks. "Taylor's had a real tough time with this kind of stuff. He told me he'd gotten hooked on some of the hard crud about a year or so ago. But he'd decided it was a big waste, and he quit cold turkey. He got himself totally clean. But then he ran into someone in town who's into pot. And he said he was feeling kind of uptight one night, so he just thought he'd give it a try again. He said it helps him to relax."

Audrey sighed. "So does healthy food, exercise, and a good night's sleep."

"Speaking of sleep," said Maggie. "It's getting pretty late."

"Where's Spencer?" asked Leah.

"Spending the night at Daniel's."

"Spencer warned me to stay away from pot," said Leah quietly.

"He cares about you too." Maggie pushed a dark strand of hair from Leah's eyes. "We all do, Leah. We've adopted you into our hearts, and you can't expect us to stand by and say nothing when we're concerned about your welfare."

"I know."

Maggie cleared her throat. "And just for the record, I hated going through your rooms. I never want to do it again. It made me feel sick inside."

Leah nodded sadly.

"But you need to know that I would do it again in a heartbeat if I thought you two were getting into anything harmful. It's a mother's right to protect her kids."

Leah looked straight into her eyes. "I'm sorry, Maggie. I'm really, truly sorry. I knew it was stupid, and I felt so guilty for bringing something like that into your home—"

"*Our* home," corrected Maggie. "Remember, we're a family."

"Yeah. And I knew it was wrong, but I did it anyway. I just didn't want to hurt Tayor's feelings. He's really not bad, just a little mixed up, I think."

"But maybe Taylor needs you to stand up for what you believe," suggested Audrey. "If he's struggling with this, it might help to have someone he respects say no to pot or whatever, and then encourage him to do the same."

"Maybe..." Leah took in a ragged breath. "I just didn't want to lose him."

"I understand," said Audrey. "But can I tell you something it usually takes most people, including me, years to learn?"

Leah nodded.

"It is never, ever worthwhile to keep someone in your life by compromising yourself. Do you understand what I'm saying?"

"I think so. You mean I shouldn't give up what I believe just because I love Taylor."

"Exactly." Audrey smiled. "And if you can learn that now, you'll be one of the wisest young women I know."

"I think I understand it in my mind, but it's my heart that worries me."

"I'm not surprised," said Maggie. "But I honestly believe you can ask God to help you to *know* what's right, and then to strengthen you to *do* it."

"Yes," agreed Audrey. "When it comes to matters of the heart, we can all use a little outside help sometimes."

Leah hugged them both. "I love you guys so much. And I'm really sorry I hurt you." She turned to Maggie with pleading eyes. "But can you *please* call Jed and talk to him about Taylor? Ask him to go easy on him?"

Maggie glanced at her watch. "It's kind of late, but if it makes you feel better, I'll give him a call. Okay?"

"Thanks."

They all said goodnight, and Maggie went up to her room to use the phone. But once again, she only got Jed's machine. She suspected that he and Taylor might still be talking, and she didn't want to interrupt, so she left a brief message asking him to call her back even if it was late. Then she prayed that God would use everything that had happened tonight to help Leah to choose the right road, and that

Taylor would do likewise. She did appreciate how the young man had owned up to his mistake, and she hoped this might be a real turning point for him. Or if not, that Leah would somehow emerge unscathed, if that was possible.

Nineteen

The following morning, Maggie awoke to a gentle tapping on her door.

"It's just me, Maggie," said Leah.

Maggie pulled on her robe and opened the door. "What's up?" she asked blearily.

Leah's face was lined with worry. "Did you talk to Dad?"

Still struggling to emerge from sleep, Maggie remembered last night's confrontation. "I called him and left a message, but he didn't call back." She yawned. "I'll bet that he and Taylor talked way into the night, and then it was probably too late to call here."

Leah didn't look entirely convinced. "I sure hope so. I made a pot of coffee." She looked at Maggie hopefully.

Maggie glanced at the clock by her bed and saw that it was already past eight. "I must've been pretty tired, I didn't realize it was this late. I'll be down in a minute."

When she came into the kitchen, Leah had already poured juice and was now making toast. "I thought you might like a little breakfast. Do you want an egg?"

"No thanks, this looks just perfect." She sat down and watched Leah busily scurrying about the kitchen. "Did you even sleep last night, Leah?"

She set a cup of hot coffee before Maggie. "Not much. But I did do some thinking—and some praying too."

Maggie smiled. "Well, if you can't sleep, praying's probably about the best thing you can do."

Leah set a plate of whole wheat toast on the table, then sat down. "Anyway I feel pretty certain that God is going to work this whole mess out."

"I'm sure you're right."

"Because I just know that Taylor came to Pine Mountain for a reason."

"I think so too."

"And now that this whole thing's out in the open, I'll bet that he has decided he doesn't need pot or anything like that to make him feel good."

"I hope so." Maggie finished up her toast. "I'd better get ready for church now."

"Yes, I hoped we could get there early, so we can talk to Dad and Taylor before the service starts."

ᴓ

"There's Dad's pickup," said Leah happily as they pulled into the school parking lot a little while later. "I'll bet Taylor came with him to help set up chairs."

When they entered the school library, Maggie watched Leah searching the small crowd until she spotted Jed helping Michael unload a cart of folding chairs, but she didn't see Taylor. She followed Leah over to Jed.

"Where's Taylor?" asked Leah, not even bothering to say hello.

Jed looked up in surprise. "He left."

"He *left?*" Leah's brows pulled together.

Jed nodded. "Last night. He packed up and left."

Maggie saw tears fill Leah's eyes. "He left?" she repeated again, her voice quavering slightly. Then she turned and ran from the room.

"Didn't you talk to him, Jed?" asked Maggie.

"There wasn't much to say." He leaned a stack of chairs against the wall.

"What is wrong with Leah?" asked Michael with concern, leaving the unfolded chairs against the wall.

"She's upset about Taylor." Jed continued to unload another stack of chairs.

"What is wrong with Taylor?" asked Michael.

"He has a problem with drugs." Jed turned to face Michael. "And I told him I couldn't have him working with me anymore."

Michael nodded solemnly and then turned back to the chairs.

Maggie didn't know what to say. On the one hand, she wanted to probe and question Jed further about Taylor, and find out whether Jed had talked to him and given him another chance. But on the other hand, she felt worried about Leah. "I'm going to check on Leah," she finally said, then turned and left.

She went back to her car, expecting to find Leah sitting in the front seat, but she wasn't there. Maggie looked around the parking lot and didn't see her anywhere. Just then Audrey pulled in.

"What's up?" she asked as she parked next to Maggie's car.

"Leah's upset. Jed just told her that Taylor left. Apparently he left last night. And to tell you the truth, I'm feeling a little put out at Jed right now."

"That's too bad." Audrey shook her head. "I'm sure he's doing what he thinks is best."

"I know. But I hate seeing Leah hurt like this. She was so hopeful this morning, and she said she'd been really praying and everything..."

"Well, she probably just needs some time to work this thing out. I wouldn't worry about her."

"But she just took off on foot. Shouldn't I go look for her?"

Audrey shrugged. "If you think it will help."

"I don't think I could concentrate on Michael's sermon knowing Leah's wandering the streets of Pine Mountain with a broken heart." Maggie glanced across the parking lot that was slowly filling with cars. "Can you give Spencer a ride home? Daniel was supposed to bring him by here this morning."

"Of course. Do you want me to say anything to Jed?"

Maggie considered this. She could think of a couple things she'd like to say to Jed right now, but thought better of it. "Just tell him I'm with Leah."

⁔

Maggie drove all over town, but she didn't spot Leah anywhere. Finally, she headed for home, thinking she might find her walking back there. But she saw no sign of her on the road. Once home, she peeked into Leah's room, careful not to step past the door this time. But everything seemed in place. Perhaps her mother was right, maybe Leah just needed a chance to work this thing out herself. She knew the church service was half over by now, and besides, Maggie wasn't eager to see Jed just yet. She knew she'd need to carefully consider what she planned to say to him before that. Part of her understood his harsh stance on this—it came from his own personal background—but another part of her desperately wished that he'd extended a hand of grace toward Taylor.

She took the dogs for a walk out in the woods behind her house. The air had become quite cold and an icy breeze whipped through the tops of the pines. Overhead, the sky was filling with clouds, and although it was March, she knew that a snow shower was not an impossibility. When she got back home, Audrey's car was there.

She found Audrey and Spencer just starting to fix lunch in the kitchen. "Is Leah with you?" asked Audrey when Maggie walked in.

"No, I was hoping she might be with you." Maggie hung up her coat.

"Grandma told me about what happened last night," said Spencer as he ate a piece of cheese. "I guess I wasn't really surprised. But did you really go through her room?"

Maggie nodded and checked the answering machine to see if anyone had called. "Yes, and you might as well know I went through your room too."

"My room?" Spencer was indignant. "Why'd you go through *my* room?"

"I was just trying to be fair." She looked into his eyes. "I'm sorry, Spence, but I wanted to be able to tell Leah I was treating her like my own child."

"Gee, that must've made her feel real special," he said sarcastically.

Maggie shook her head. "Yeah, yeah...I know. But what was I supposed to do? And as it turned out, I had good reason to be suspicious."

"I guess so. But from now on if you want to snoop in my room, why don't you ask me first?"

Audrey laughed. "Then what would be the point of snooping?"

"Well, I might've straightened it up a little."

"I wasn't in there to give it the white glove test," said Maggie. "But now that you mention it, it wouldn't hurt to do a little cleaning—"

"I gotta hurry, Mom." Spencer grabbed the sandwich that Audrey had just made and flopped it on a plate. "I've got this book I need to read for homework today. There's a test tomorrow."

"Well, then how about after that?" she called as he scurried up the stairs.

"It's starting to snow out there," said Audrey as she stood at the sink.

Maggie glanced out the window. "I thought maybe it would. Can you believe it? It's snowing in March. And just when I thought spring was coming."

"Do you think Leah's out in it?"

Maggie shuddered, remembering another time when she'd found Leah nearly frozen. "I hope not. But maybe I should go out looking again. She wasn't dressed very warmly this morning."

"Well, here, take this with you," said Audrey, handing her another sandwich she'd just finished making. "And take your cell phone so I can call you if she shows up here."

Maggie started to reach for her coat again. "Maybe I should phone Scott and Chloe's first. She hangs out with Chloe sometimes."

"Have you already called Jed?"

Maggie paused, the phone in her hand. "No, I guess I should let him know."

"Yes. I told him that you were with Leah. But since that's not the case…"

She phoned Jed's number only to get his machine once again. She left a message telling him that she was out looking for Leah and to call Audrey for further details. Then she called Chloe and Scott's. Chloe hadn't seen Leah, but promised she'd have her call if she did.

Maggie pulled on her coat, a new sense of urgency pressing in. "I'll leave my phone on, Mom. And if you think of any other places I should look, let me know."

"I'm sure she's fine," reassured Audrey, though her eyes looked worried.

∾

As Maggie drove through town again, snowflakes were tumbling thickly down, even though they didn't appear to be sticking. Just the same, it was cold, and she hated the idea of Leah being out in such a mess. She stopped by the deli, but Sierra hadn't seen her, and then she went by several other places that seemed like possibilities. As she approached Whitewater Works for the second time, she was surprised to see Jed's pickup parked along the street there. The closed sign was still on the front door, but that didn't stop her this time. Of course, she thought, as she knocked loudly on the front door, Leah had a key to the shop. Maybe she'd been holed up in there this whole time. Maybe she was talking with Jed right now.

Finally, Jed opened the door. "What are you doing here?" His eyes lit up happily.

"Is Leah here?"

He gently pulled her in from the weather and brushed the snow from her hair. "I thought she was with you. Is anything wrong?"

"She's been missing since we saw you this morning."

Jed frowned. "But I thought you were with her."

"I went to look for her, but never found her. Then I went home for a while thinking she'd turn up. But she didn't. I've checked every place in town I can think of. I even stopped by Cherise's, and she offered to help look."

Jed glanced out at the weather, then exhaled loudly. "This is all my fault, isn't it?"

She didn't say anything.

"I didn't handle things right with Taylor."

She looked up at him. "What makes you think that?"

"You missed Michael's sermon this morning." He shoved his hands in his coat pockets and sadly shook his head. "I thought I was doing what was right. You know, being the tough boss, the firm dad—drawing my line in the sand and thinking no one would dare to step across—"

She reached out and put her hand on his arm. "I know you meant well, Jed. But it's never that simple, is it?"

"Michael talked about how God's grace doesn't mean much to people who think they're above making mistakes, but how it's the difference between life and death for those who know they make mistakes and are willing to admit it."

She nodded. "It's easy to forget that when we're dealing with our own kids, though. We get to thinking that we're supposed to be these great examples, the perfect adults who have it all together." She forced a laugh.

"Yeah. And we can totally forget that we were, at one time or another or maybe even still are, just as mixed up as they are."

Suddenly Maggie remembered her phone still out in the car. "Let me call Mom and see if she's been trying to reach me."

"No, honey," said Audrey. "Not a word. I was hoping that you had found her by now."

"Not yet, but I'll keep looking. We better get off the phone and keep the lines clear." Maggie hung up and turned back to Jed. She could feel tears building up in her eyes. "Oh, Jed, I'm starting to feel scared. Where do you think she is?"

"Why don't we both go out now in different directions," he suggested. "I'll go west. Maybe she's decided to hitchhike to the city in hopes of locating Taylor."

"Oh, no." Maggie's hand flew to her mouth. "But even if she made it over the pass, how would she know where to find him?"

He shook his head. "I don't know. I suspect he might try to get his old job back there. It's possible Leah might assume the same thing."

"Do you really think she'd do that? Just leave without saying anything?"

"I don't know. But I guess I wouldn't blame her. I've been pretty bullheaded about all this. Besides, young love can be pretty impulsive sometimes, not to mention just plain foolish."

"I suppose so." She watched him shove his arms into his coat, and then he walked her to the door.

They both ran through the quick-falling snow to their separate vehicles. Maggie decided to make one more run through town, just in case. As she drove down Amber's street, she remembered what Jed had said about "young love." Had he been referring to Amber? She wondered if Amber had once done something impulsive when they were young and together. Probably. Suddenly, she decided to stop in and check on her. She'd been keeping daily contact with

Amber these days, but what with her worries about Leah, she hadn't even thought of her today. And Amber was quite sensible at times—she might even have some idea about where Leah might have disappeared to.

"Hi, Maggie," said Amber warmly. "Come on inside here and get out of that messy weather. What happened to our spring?"

"Sorry to drop in like this. And I can't really stay—you see, Leah is missing, and I've got to go look, but I just wanted—"

"Slow down, Maggie." Amber patted her arm and smiled. "Why don't you take off your coat and stay a while."

"I would, but I've really got to keep looking—" Maggie stopped herself this time when she suddenly spied Leah sitting all warm and dry on Amber's couch. "Leah!" she cried joyfully, running over and throwing her arms around her. "What in the world are you doing here?"

"Just visiting," said Leah apologetically. "Is something wrong?"

Maggie laughed as she peeled off her soggy coat. "Not anymore. But, well, let's just say everyone was getting pretty concerned about you. We didn't know where you'd disappeared to."

"I'm sorry, Maggie. I didn't mean to—"

"It's my fault too," said Amber, draping Maggie's coat on a chair next to the fireplace. "We got to talking and time has just flown by."

"It's okay. But let me call Mom and let her know." She quickly phoned Audrey and explained that the search was over. Then she called the Galloways and Cherise to let them know Leah was safe and sound.

"Now, how about some tea?" asked Amber.

"I'd love it." Then Maggie remembered Jed. "Oh, no."

"What's wrong now?" asked Leah.

"Your dad just took off west, looking for you."

"West?" said Amber as she handed Maggie a hot cup of tea.

"Where's he going?" asked Leah.

Maggie smiled sheepishly. "He thought perhaps you'd decided to hitchhike over the pass and into the city to search for Taylor."

Leah's eyes opened wide. "Good grief! Does he think I'm totally nuts?"

"He said something about the folly of young love." She glanced uneasily at Amber, not wanting to stir up old memories.

But Amber simply started giggling, then broke into all-out laughter. "Poor Jed. He's probably remembering a crazy stunt *he* pulled once."

"What was it?" asked Leah eagerly.

"I probably shouldn't tell," said Amber. "It might embarrass him."

"Go ahead," said Maggie dryly.

"Well, it was just after I'd started college, and Jed wanted to borrow his dad's truck to come over and see me for a fall dance that weekend. But his dad wouldn't let him drive the truck because the tires were getting pretty bald, and there was already a lot of snow on the pass. And that's back when they didn't keep it plowed all the time."

"Oh, dear," said Maggie suddenly. "I'll bet there's a pile of snow on the pass right now. And I'm not sure how far Jed will drive before he comes back."

"Does he have his cell phone with him?" asked Leah with concern.

"I'm not sure. But I'd better try it, just in case," said Maggie. "Don't finish this story until I'm done." She went in the kitchen and dialed his number but was informed by a recording that his phone was currently out of range.

"No luck." She flopped down on the couch next to Leah. "Go ahead."

Amber continued her tale. "Anyway, Jed called and told me he couldn't drive the pickup, but not to worry because that wasn't going to stop him. So I assumed he meant he was going to get a ride with someone else. So, I waited and waited for him to get there, and finally, quite late that same night he called."

"What happened?" asked Leah.

"Seems he'd tried to hitchhike over the pass. And he got a lift with a friend up to the ski area, but after that, he couldn't get a ride. He stood out there until dark, and I guess there was absolutely no traffic, other than people heading back toward town after skiing. Finally, a worker from the ski area noticed him and drove over to where he was standing and asked what he was doing. Jed told him he was trying to get a ride, and the guy informed him that there had been a small avalanche several miles up ahead, and there were signs in town saying the highway up there was closed. No traffic was going through at all."

"Poor Jed," said Maggie.

"Yes, he might've stood up there all night with his frozen thumb sticking out."

"Did he get a ride back home then?" asked Leah.

Amber nodded, laughing. "Yes, but he was pretty embarrassed when he called me that night."

"The folly of young love," said Maggie.

"Man, I'm glad I'm not *that* dumb," said Leah, rolling her eyes.

The three visited some more, and then Leah explained to Maggie that Amber had shared some good advice about Taylor. "Amber said that if Taylor really loves me, then he won't let what Jed did keep him away. And I shouldn't worry about it. At least Taylor knows now that he needs to rethink how he's living if he wants to be involved in our family, whether it's with me or Dad."

Maggie smiled at Amber. "That sounds very wise."

"Not only that," said Leah as if making an announcement. "I've also decided to take some classes at the college in Byron next term if I can still get registered this coming week."

Maggie blinked in surprise. "Goodness, Amber, did you convince her to do that too?"

Leah firmly shook her head. "No, I was already thinking about it. You and Audrey have been encouraging me to look into school since last fall. But, like Amber said, I do need to find out who I really am, and not just who I think my dad wants me to be—or even who Taylor wants me to be, for that matter."

"That's great, Leah. I'm so glad for you." Maggie smiled. "I always knew you had a good head on your shoulders."

"I'm not sure Jed will be so happy," said Amber. "This might mean he'll have to hire someone besides his daughter to keep shop for him."

"Oh, I don't think he'll mind a bit," said Maggie, knowing how relieved he'd be to find out that Leah was thinking sensibly after all. She glanced over at Amber, who seemed to be fading now. She knew her stamina was deteriorating steadily. "Amber, we should probably get back home now in case Jed calls or stops by."

"I've really enjoyed having you both here," said Amber. She turned to Leah. "Maggie comes over quite a bit, you know, and I want you to feel free to drop in whenever you like too. Okay?"

"Sure." Leah stood and smiled. "It's funny. I just stormed off from church, and I didn't even know where I was going, and then I found myself walking down your street and thought, hey, I'll bet Amber would understand this."

Amber grinned. "And you were absolutely right."

Maggie hugged Amber and whispered a quiet "thanks."

"And you two don't have to mention anything to Jed about that frozen hitchhiker story," called Amber as they went out the door.

Leah laughed. "But it might do him good to remember he was young once too."

Amber waved while her visitors ran through the falling snow over to Maggie's car. "I think he's already remembering that," said Maggie as she started the engine. "Apparently Michael's sermon had a good message about something like that."

"Apparently? Weren't you there too?"

"No. I was out searching for a certain missing someone."

"I'm sorry, Maggie. I really didn't know it would create such a fuss. I should've called."

"It's okay. Actually, it might even do Jed some good to worry about this a little as he's driving up through the snowy pass. Or maybe he's even on his way back home by now."

"I hope so. I don't really want to worry him. And I know he means well with his fatherly concern. I just can't help but feel bad about Taylor."

"I know." Maggie considered her words. "I really care about Taylor. And I know Jed does too. But he tried to explain to me how he thought it was his responsibility to be firm and strong about his stance against drugs and everything. And as a result, he probably came across as unnecessarily harsh and condemning. But I know that's not how he feels underneath it all."

"I know that too, Maggie." Leah sighed deeply. "And, really, I do know that Dad loves me. And I'm sure he feels just as bad about this as I do."

"Probably worse."

Twenty

Jed didn't call until later that night, and Maggie immediately reassured him that Leah was home and fine and harbored no ill feelings against any of them. She even told him of Leah's plan to attend college next term. "She already went online to start the registration process."

"That's good to hear." Yet his voice sounded sad.

"Are you okay, Jed?"

"Just tired, I guess."

"I wish I could've reached you when I found her and saved you the unnecessary trip."

"It's okay. I needed to go. And I'm going to spend the night."

"Where?"

"I'm still in the city."

"You're kidding. What are you doing over there?"

"Looking for Taylor."

"Oh."

"You don't need to tell Leah that specifically. At this rate, I may not catch up with him anyway."

"Will you come home tomorrow then?"

"I hope so. But, who knows, I may just decide to stick around until I find him."

"Oh." She didn't know what to say. On the one hand, it was a sweet gesture, but what if Taylor didn't wish to be found?

"Don't worry, Maggie. Everything will be okay. I'll call tomorrow and let you know what's going on."

"Good. And make sure you get some rest tonight."

"I will."

"Do you want to talk to Leah?"

"No. You just give her my love, and tell her I'm sorry about all this. But don't mention anything about Taylor just yet."

"Okay. And I'll be praying for you and Taylor to connect."

"Appreciate it." Then they said goodnight and she hung up. She hoped he wasn't off on some fool's errand, trying to make up for something that wasn't really his fault in the first place. But then she hadn't quite known how to question him. And for all she knew, it might be important for him to find Taylor. Perhaps all she could do was pray.

∾

The next day, Jed showed up at the newspaper office just before closing. "I've been thinking about you all day!" she exclaimed in relief.

"Mind if I close the door?" he asked as he came into her office.

"Not at all." She smiled happily, thinking he was going to take her into his arms, but instead he sank down into the chair in front of her desk. She leaned forward against her desk and studied him. "What's up, Jed?"

"I need some advice."

"Sure. Is something wrong? Did you ever find Taylor?"

"Yeah, I found Taylor. And we had a nice, long talk. And, yes, something is wrong, but I don't really know what to do about it."

"Why don't you start by telling me."

"Well, I found Taylor this morning. And we did quite a bit of talking. He's really sorry about everything, and I honestly think he had been trying to turn over a new leaf. Apparently, he had been fairly involved in drug use until about a year ago when he had completely quit. But he said that living in the city, he'd often felt tempted to go back to his old ways, and so he'd thought moving here to Pine Mountain would help."

"And it didn't?"

Jed shook his head. "No, not that he's blaming Pine Mountain. He knows it was his own bad choice. But I guess it just caught him off guard."

"That's too bad."

"I wanted to find out just who in town is peddling this stuff. I know I'd like to see it stopped."

"So would I. Although, I doubt there's only one source."

He nodded. "Yes, but I figured it would be a start. So I pressured Taylor to tell me how he got it. And to tell you the truth, I think he was a little concerned that his connection might also be selling it to kids in high school. Which, as it turns out, is probably quite valid."

"So?" Maggie waited impatiently. "Where *did* he get it?"

"Well, he met this person through…" He paused as if thinking. "Actually, it's a kid who's new in town. And this kid, wanting to be real social and friendly and all, offered Taylor a joint at the Valentine's dance."

"Oh…"

"And here's another tough thing, Maggie." Jed grimaced. "After that, Taylor actually bought some more pot from this guy at *your* house."

"*My* house? What on earth do you mean?" She felt her voice grow louder. "Just what are you saying, Jed? You can't possibly mean Spencer?"

He held up his hands. "Slow down, Maggie. Let me finish."

She started to drum her fingers on her desk, waiting for him to tell her the rest. Surely, he wasn't suggesting…

"No, it wasn't Spence. And it wasn't Daniel or Leah either. It was Jeanette Reinhart's oldest boy, Brent."

"Brent?" Maggie was stupefied. She'd had them all out for dinner, but the whole idea of Brent Reinhart, old Arnold Westerly's great-grandson, selling pot seemed totally preposterous. "But he's such a nice, clean-cut young man. He's into sports."

Jed laughed ironically. "Now, don't start sounding like me."

"But I'm just stunned. Are you seriously telling me Brent Reinhart sells pot?"

"Well, I don't know how much of a regular deal this is for him. But apparently he sold some to Taylor, trying to earn money for a snowboard."

"Oh, good grief." She stood up and began to pace across her office. "Do you think Jeanette knows?"

"What do *you* think, Maggie?"

"Of course not. I'm sure she'd be just as shocked as I am." She turned and looked at him. "Oh, Jed, what are we going to do?"

"That's why I came to you." Jed stood and placed both hands on her shoulders. "I mean, we both know that I have a tendency to fly off the handle sometimes. I didn't want to do something we'd all regret later."

"What a mess. Well, we have to tell Jeanette. I don't know what else after that. I mean, I don't want Brent thinking he can go around town selling pot and getting away with it, but I don't want him going to jail either."

"And that could happen."

"Oh, dear. Why do I suddenly feel so responsible?"

"It's not your fault, Maggie. But maybe you can help Jeanette work this out."

"You know, she's told me lately that she's worried about the boys, especially Brent, because he was so upset about what his dad did."

"That might even be why he's doing this."

"I suppose. I just hate to see him get so messed up that he ruins his life. Not to mention those around him." She thought a moment. "Not that I blame him for Taylor, exactly. Everyone has to be responsible for their own choices. But if Brent is selling pot, he's clearly to blame for *that*. Although, it is interesting that in this situation, Taylor's the adult and Brent's the juvenile. I'm not even sure *how* I'd feel if the roles were reversed. Strange, isn't it?"

"Don't bother even thinking about it."

"I guess I'd better start by calling Jeanette." She looked up at Jed. "Will you go with me to talk to her?"

He nodded. "I hoped we could do it together."

"Did Taylor come back with you?"

"No. He's still trying to figure out what to do. He says he feels like a rat for telling on Brent. But I think I helped him to see that if Brent is not stopped, he might hurt others, not to mention himself. The good news is that for some reason, Taylor seemed fairly certain this wasn't a regular thing for Brent and he felt genuinely sorry for the kid."

"Well, let's hope it's *not* a regular thing. Still, we need to get to the bottom of this."

Maggie called, and Jeanette said to come on over, warning them that they still lived in cramped quarters with unpacked boxes all over the place.

It was as Jeanette described. Maybe worse. Maggie and Jed waded past packing boxes and found their way to a couch that was wedged between several other pieces of furniture. A family's life disrupted by divorce, relocation, and possibly drugs.

"Sorry about this." Jeanette waved her hands. "But hopefully, it won't be too long before we can get moved and settled into Grandpa's house."

Maggie cleared her throat. "Are your boys still here?"

She nodded. "They're playing some new computer game back in the bedroom."

Maggie glanced at Jed, anxious for help. "We need to talk to you about Brent," he began in a serious tone.

"Is something wrong?" Jeanette's voice grew strained.

"Maybe," said Maggie softly. "And we wanted to come to you first."

"Shall I call him out here?" asked Jeanette, her eyes growing wide.

"Why don't we explain first," said Jed kindly. Then he quickly began to retell what Taylor had told him. "We don't want to make accusations," he said. "But we need to find out what's going on."

Tears began to trickle down Jeanette's cheeks. "Oh, no. I've been worried about something like this. Brent seemed to have more money than he should lately—but only since we moved here. And whenever I ask him about it, he just says his dad sends it, and then Bradley covers for him too. Somehow I just didn't quite believe it…but I didn't know what to say. I never dreamed of anything like this. Oh, I feel so stupid, and so humiliated."

Maggie moved next to her and put her arm around Jeanette's quaking shoulders. "If it makes you feel any better, Jeanette, we do know something of how you feel. We've had to deal with Taylor and then Leah about a situation similar to this, and it wasn't easy. But believe it or not, it does help to get things out in the open."

"Brent!" called Jeanette suddenly. "Come out here. Bradley, you'd better come too."

Both boys came out and stood at the edge of the packed living room. "What's wrong, Mom?" asked Bradley, the fifteen-year-old.

"Mostly, I need to talk to Brent, but I want you to hear too." She stood up now and looked directly into Brent's eyes. "And I want you to tell me the truth, no matter how uncomfortable it makes you feel."

He nodded without saying anything. And Maggie felt sure by his expression that he knew exactly what was coming.

"Have you been selling marijuana?"

He looked down at the floor. Bradley looked at his brother in surprise, then spoke out defensively. "Aw, Mom, why d'ya think something like that—"

"Bradley, you be quiet," she said sternly. "I'm talking to Brent. And I want an answer. *Now!*"

Brent looked up, his chin out in defiance. "What are you going to do if I say yes? Send me back to my dad?"

"Just tell me the truth, Brent."

He said nothing, looking at all three adults as if this were all their fault. Finally, Jed spoke up. "Brent, I don't know if you're aware of this or not, but our state has some fairly tough drug laws, especially when it comes to selling on or near school grounds." He looked evenly at him. "And I happen to know one particular transaction was made at a school dance, on school grounds. And the second one was at Maggie's house." Jed paused. "And rather than going to the authorities, we have chosen to come directly to you. We understand that your parents' separation has been hard on you, and then moving here…I know it can't be easy."

Maggie's heart warmed toward Jed. And it looked as if Brent was softening a little too. "If it makes you feel any better," offered Maggie, "we've been dealing with our kids too. And everyone is trying to turn over a new leaf. So, we hope that you'll want to do the same."

Brent bit his lip, looked at all of them, then finally spoke quietly. "I just figured since everyone messed up my world, what did it matter if I messed up everyone else's."

Jeanette moved toward him. "Oh, Brent. You know how sorry I am about what happened with your dad. But you're not stupid, son, you've got to know that what you're doing won't help anything. Do you have any idea how much trouble you could be in if this was the police coming here instead of just Maggie and Jed?"

He shrugged. "I guess not."

"How old are you, Brent?" asked Jed.

"Seventeen."

"Do you know you can be tried as an adult for certain things at seventeen?"

He shrugged again. "I dunno. I suppose."

"Well, we need to sit down and talk to you," said Jed, more gently. "And we need to get to the bottom of this. Are you willing to do that, Brent, or would you rather deal with the authorities instead?"

Maggie glanced uneasily at Jed. But he kept his gaze on Brent, his countenance firm.

"I'd rather talk to you," said Brent.

Maggie sighed in relief as they all sat down on odd furniture and boxes and slowly untangled the tale of how Brent Reinhart managed to get hold of a fair amount of marijuana just before coming to Pine Mountain. He explained how a kid who was known for trouble back in his hometown had needed cash badly, and fast, and without knowing that Brent was moving, had talked him into taking the pot off his hands to sell. Brent, being mad at the world in general, had agreed, deciding he didn't care who he hurt, and even hoping he might embarrass his dad a little, although he assured them he never meant to hurt his mom or even Taylor.

"Did you sell it all?" asked Jeanette, her voice shaking, clearly in shock at his complete disclosure.

"No. Taylor's the only one I ever sold any to. And to be honest, I was pretty scared about that. But Spencer had introduced us at the dance, and I had brought some joints with me—I don't even know why. And all of a sudden I was just giving him one. Then later, Taylor and I made plans to do a deal at Spencer's house. Even then, I was pretty scared. I mean, I've heard stories of guys working for cops, and I thought that could've been the case with him."

"Where's the rest of the pot?" asked Jeanette, her eyes wide with fear.

"In my room."

Jeanette slumped back into the couch. "I can't believe it. I come to Pine Mountain and…I bring…all this with me…"

"I hid it really good, Mom."

She sat back up straight and glared at him. "Bring it out here, Brent."

He went back to his room, returning after a couple minutes with a backpack. Then he pulled out a number of full Ziploc bags.

Maggie tried not to gasp, astounded that a kid could get his hands on that much stuff. "Is this common?" she asked incredulously. "Do kids go around with their backpacks full of pot like that?"

Brent looked at her strangely. "Yeah. I suppose the ones who sell it might."

She felt sickened at the thought. "That's too bad."

He looked down at the pile, then nodded. "I know."

She felt some relief at his response, but still felt dismayed. "What are you going to do with it now?"

"Can we burn it in the woodstove?" asked Jeanette eagerly. "I want it out of my house now."

"I don't know why not," said Jed, moving some boxes out of the way. "There was a good stiff breeze blowing outside this afternoon, I'm sure the smoke will dissipate fairly quickly. No one should be the wiser."

As Brent handed the bags to Jed, Maggie felt certain she saw relief on the young man's face. Surely he'd gotten in way over his head and regretted this. But still she wondered if these consequences were enough to prevent this from happening again with him. Or did the adults have a responsibility to do something more? She just didn't know.

"You know, Brent," she began as they all watched Jed make a stack of kindling and paper. "I used to work for the *L.A. Times,* and I can remember some stories where drug dealers went out looking for guys who'd run out on them. Have you considered whether something like that might happen to you?"

Jeanette's hand flew to her mouth. "You mean they might hunt Brent down for their drug money?"

"It's possible." Maggie watched Brent for a reaction.

"I know." He shook his head sadly. "I've thought about it too. I guess if that happens I'll just have to go to the police and turn myself in. I'll tell them what I did, and who I took it from, and then just take the consequences."

Maggie felt a little relief. "And you're okay with that?"

"I guess so." He nodded, watching as Jed stuffed the bags into the hot flames and then tightly closed the door. "I know I did a really stupid thing." He turned to his mom. "And I know it doesn't change anything, Mom, but I am really sorry."

"Sheesh," said Bradley. "I never would've dreamed my brother was such an idiot!"

Brent didn't even react; he just looked down at the floor.

"We all make mistakes," said Jed. "Brent's fortunate that his ended up like this. It could've been a whole lot worse."

"I don't know how we can ever thank you," blurted Jeanette, her face still blotchy from all her crying.

Jed turned and looked once more at Brent. "I can think of a couple of things he can do. Are you willing, son?"

He nodded eagerly. "Yeah, just tell me."

"First off, how about if you and your family come and visit our church a time or two. We have a pretty good preacher there, and I hear he's getting ready to start up a youth group. He even wants to learn how to snowboard."

Maggie laughed. "Michael on a snowboard? Now that's something I've got to see."

"And then, this is only a suggestion," said Jed, "but I think you should donate the money you made from selling that pot to a worthy cause."

"I would, except I spent most of it."

"Then perhaps you could donate your time to something that will help the community," suggested Maggie.

"Like what?"

"Well, right now my mother is trying to get the new library set up in town. She could use a strong back to help move books and things."

Brent nodded. "I could do that."

"Great. I'll let her know that she'll be hearing from you."

"And about church," said Jeanette forcefully. "We've not been a churchgoing family. Buy we'll try it out, Jed. You can count on that." Then she profusely thanked them for coming directly to her. Brent shook Jed's hand and thanked him as well.

When Maggie and Jed left the house, she felt as if she were in partial shock as they walked toward his pickup. "Did that really happen?" she asked as he opened the door. "Or am I just having a really strange dream?"

He grinned at her. "It was real."

He drove her back to her car, still parked at the newspaper office. "Thanks, Jed," she said when he stopped. "I mean, thanks for the way you handled everything with Jeanette and Brent. You really surprised me."

He laughed. "Yeah, I'll bet. You probably expected me to go in there and read them the riot act, then call the sheriff in for backup."

"It was a pretty tough situation. I wasn't even sure what we were going to do myself."

"Are you going to cover the story in the paper?" He winked at her.

"Not exactly. But I do plan on having Scott do some follow-up investigative reporting on teens and drugs in this area, and perhaps list some things our community might do to prevent these things from happening."

"Like talking to our kids?"

She nodded. "And speaking of which, why don't you come on over for dinner and say hello to your daughter. I'm sure she'd be interested in hearing about Taylor, and maybe even this. I'm sure both she and Spence are aware of how and when Taylor got that pot."

He grinned. "I'll be there."

She shook her head. "To think this was all going on practically under our noses, and we didn't even know it."

He stretched over and kissed her on the nose. "Yours did, Maggie."

She smiled. "You're right, it did."

Twenty-One

As it turned out, Maggie was right. Spencer and Leah already knew about Brent's fledgling pot-selling business, but were still interested in the rest of the story.

"Yeah, I almost told you about it once, Mom," said Spencer casually. "But I didn't want to be a narc. Besides, I knew I'd get everyone into a whole lot of trouble."

"But couldn't you see that they were all getting themselves into trouble already?" asked Audrey as she passed the potatoes to Jed.

"Sort of. It was kind of complicated, I guess."

Maggie nodded. "I'll say. But from now on, if you guys know of anything that's going on in school or town, anything that's illegal or unsafe or whatever, would you *please* let the rest of us in on it?"

Leah set down the bottle of salad dressing. "Well, I know I have no intention of getting involved in *anything* like that again, myself. But I promise to let you know if I see anything *going down*, okay?" She grinned mischievously.

"Yeah, me too," said Spencer. "But I might need to seek political immunity or something like that. Do you guys offer any kind of witness protection programs?"

Jed laughed. "You really think you'd need it?"

"Possibly," said Spencer seriously. "You'd be surprised at the stuff a kid might see at school sometimes."

"Maybe you should just keep your eyes shut," suggested Leah.

"Maybe everyone needs to keep their eyes wide open," said Maggie. "And maybe this sleepy little town needs a wake-up call about what's really going on."

"Well, we better leave that one to you," said Audrey wryly.

After dinner, Jed and Leah talked privately about the situation with Taylor. Maggie knew he planned to reassure Leah that he would welcome Taylor back once he was relatively sure that he intended to remain drug-free. Leah later told Maggie that she thought that seemed fair, but she wasn't so sure it guaranteed that Taylor would return. Maggie could see the pain in her eyes, and, for Leah's sake, almost wished that Taylor would remain out of the picture indefinitely. Because even if he did come back there could be no real guarantees. Even if people tried to quit a bad habit, you just never knew for sure. And she didn't want to see Leah hurt again. Hadn't she suffered enough pain in her young life already? Maggie was so glad that Leah was finally showing interest in college and a possible life beyond Pine Mountain. She didn't want Taylor to return and mess any of that up.

᎒

The next morning, Maggie asked Scott to begin researching an article on kids and substance abuse in their town. He jokingly suggested that Sierra and Spencer might go undercover for him at the high school, and Maggie told him to forget it. "But you might ask Gavin some questions," she added. "He's had some experience with the drug elements around here—not that he's proud of it, but he's pretty open about discussing these things nowadays, especially when he thinks it'll help someone else."

"Yeah, I'll talk to him." Scott loaded some film in his camera. "He wants me to come out to Whispering Pines with him and get some shots of the first foundation going in today."

"Is that for the community building?" she asked. "I saw some equipment down there this morning."

"Yeah, the community building and the offices are just starting to go up. It's only a matter of time until that place really starts taking off."

She smiled. "It'll be fun to see. Almost makes me feel like an 'old-timer' to be able to say I moved out here even before Whispering Pines was a glimmer in Clyde's eye."

"What's in my eye?" asked Clyde, sticking his head into Scott's office.

She laughed and explained. "And I hear the lots are selling like crazy. I told my brother as well as a friend in L.A. that they better get up here and buy one while the price is still low, and they plan to give it some thought when they come for the wedding."

"Well, I hope they're not too picky," said Clyde. "Because there might not be that many good ones to choose from by then. Gavin and Stan Williams have done a first rate job of getting the word out." He looked at Maggie and Scott. "And that reminds me, I've been thinking there should be some sort of company discount for employees of the newspaper."

"Really?" asked Scott. "Chloe and I have been feeling pretty cramped in that little place of ours. We've even kicked around the idea of building a home."

Clyde winked at him. "You better go talk to Gavin then. Make sure he remembers the company discount."

Maggie followed Clyde out of Scott's office. "Is that for real, Clyde?" she asked suspiciously. "That company discount thing?"

"Sure. Why not? You might want to invest too."

She laughed. "I think I've got enough land out there already. But I'll keep it in mind."

Clyde came into her office. "Got a minute, Maggie?"

"Yeah, sure. Come on in."

He sat down across from her and folded then unfolded his hands in his lap without saying anything.

"Everything okay?" she asked.

"I reckon. But I need a little advice." He leaned over and pushed her door closed. "You see, I'm not as young as I used to be."

She nodded, trying to conceal her concern. "But you're pretty spry for your age, Clyde. Are you feeling all right?"

"Yeah, I'm feeling just fine. But what I want to ask you about has to do with women."

"Women?" Her brows raised slightly.

"Yep, and you're just about the best woman friend I've got at the moment."

She smiled. "Thanks, Clyde. I take that as a great compliment."

He waved his hand. "Well, you know, talking to you is almost like talking to one of the guys."

She laughed, certain that he meant it in the best way possible. "What's going on, Clyde?"

"Well, like I said, I'm not any spring chicken, Maggie. And I haven't had me a woman friend in years. Don't know that I ever really wanted to have one much after my wife passed on. Although I have gone out with a woman here and there, now and then. But not in the last ten years or so."

She could tell this was difficult for him. "And you've noticed someone you might be interested in?"

He nodded. "Don't know that she's noticed me though. But we have chatted upon occasion, just at the grocery store and the bakery and whatnot."

"I see." Well, that ruled out Abigail. He saw her on a nearly daily basis. "Have you known this woman for long?"

"Well, not really, but sort of."

"What did you have in mind? Have you considered asking her out for dinner? Maybe you could start it slow with coffee or something."

"That's what I was thinking, but I just wasn't sure which way to go. I figured if I asked her to dinner, she might think I was being too pushy. But I don't quite know how you ask a woman out for coffee. I mean, if you want coffee, don't you just go and get it? Doesn't seem all that special to me."

Suddenly she wondered if the mystery woman could possibly be her mother. And although Audrey liked Clyde well enough, Maggie knew she wouldn't think of him in this sort of way. She desperately hoped it was someone, anyone, else. "Maybe it would help if I knew who we're talking about here, Clyde. Because different women have different tastes, and if she's someone I know, maybe I can suggest something appropriate."

"Yes, that's what I was hoping. Well, you see, it's Barbara Harris." He leaned forward eagerly. "Now, what do you think of that, Maggie? You think I might have a chance with someone like her?"

Maggie smiled. "Of course you have a chance. And I happen to think Barbara is a wonderfully sweet woman."

Clyde sat up straighter. "She seems to have a good, kind heart."

"Yes..." Maggie studied Clyde in his old faded plaid shirt with the frayed cuffs of his thermal undershirt showing at the wrists. "And she's quite a lady too. I don't know if I've ever seen her go out anywhere without her pearls."

He nodded. "I think that's what got my attention, the way she carries herself like a real proper lady, and yet she's not pretentious at all. She seems to have a very genuine and caring sort of nature." He smiled.

"Yes. That describes her well." Maggie grew thoughtful. "I know, maybe you should invite her to have afternoon tea at the Pine Mountain Hotel. I know she enjoys that quite a bit."

"Tea?" He rubbed his chin. "Why, I never even thought of that. But I think you're right on the money. Tea would be a very good start." He stood up to go, then paused. "Say, Maggie, should I dress up a little for tea, do you s'pose?"

"Oh, yes, I definitely think so. You want to put your best foot forward for Barbara."

"Well, okay then." He grinned. "And I'd appreciate it if you kept this to yourself, Maggie, you know, for the time being."

"Of course. No use in starting any rumors yet. But you can be sure if anyone sees you having tea with Barbara they'll jump to their own conclusions."

"Oh, that's all right. I just don't want everyone flapping their gums about it *before* it happens. What if she turned me down cold? You know, a feller's got his pride even if he is getting up there in years."

"I won't say a word."

ᷓ

By the end of the week, Taylor returned to Pine Mountain. Jed hired him back with the understanding that he would remain "clean." Jed explained to Maggie that he'd told Taylor how being drug-free was critical to safety, especially considering all the power tools they used in making furniture. Taylor had promised to comply, and he even agreed to take random drug tests to further reassure Jed. Maggie tried to appear supportive of Jed's decision; after all, she had longed for him to give Taylor a second chance. But she felt even more protective of Leah now. What if having Taylor back caused further problems or brought more unnecessary pain into Leah's life?

Fortunately, Leah told Maggie she was taking Amber's most recent advice on the subject of Taylor. "Amber says I should just keep him at a safe distance for right now. I don't want him thinking he can just wrap me around his little finger. It's better to play hard to get. And taking classes in Byron will help put some space between us."

"Sounds like a good plan to me," agreed Maggie, wondering if she should send Amber flowers or chocolates or just go give her a great big hug.

Leah continued, "And Dad's going to have Taylor work in town at the shop too. He'll work on smaller projects and finish pieces in the back room, but he can also take care of the store while I'm at classes. We might have to hire someone else by summer, but for now this should work out pretty well." She smiled. "Dad says we'll keep Taylor so busy he won't have time to get into trouble."

On Saturday Maggie went to work out at the fitness center and discovered that Cherise had hired a high-school girl to help her out after school and on weekends. "It's about time," said Maggie, patting Cherise on the back. "I worry about you running yourself ragged over here."

Cherise laughed. "Oh, you know me, I like to keep going. But I got to thinking about something Michael said about not living for your work. I think that's what I've done for a long time. But now that I've got some free time, I don't hardly know what to do with myself."

Maggie glanced at her watch. It was after one, but she still hadn't eaten yet. "Want to go have lunch?"

"With you?" asked Cherise.

"Sure, unless you've got a better offer from someone else."

Cherise grinned. "I'd *love* to have lunch with you. Do you mind if I run up and change first?"

"Not at all. Maybe we should make this a really special event and go to the hotel."

"You know, I've never had lunch at the hotel before. I've always been working during the day, and if I run out for something, I try to get back real quick."

"Well, it's about time you went then. Shall I wait for you?"

"Sure, come on up. I'll just be a couple minutes."

Maggie hadn't been up to Cherise's little apartment since the day Greg had held them both hostage at gunpoint. As they reached the top of the stairs a little chill ran down her neck as she remembered that terrifying day. Yet as she slowly walked around the cheery apartment, the strange memory of it seemed to fade from her mind until it almost seemed like something that had happened to someone else. She glanced out the window and sighed in relief. She knew what had happened was real, and Greg was still spending real time in a real jail, but that feeling of horror seemed as distant as the clouds on the horizon. Cherise had mentioned to Maggie that he had decided he wanted to change his plea from "not guilty" to "guilty." Maggie was curious to hear what that was all about. Because despite everything that had happened and even what had gone on before, she did feel slightly sorry for him now. Michael's challenge to the congregation to pray for Greg had definitely changed her heart. Did that mean he should be free to roam the streets of Pine Mountain or anywhere else? She wasn't so sure about that, but she knew she wished him no harm, either.

At the hotel they were quickly seated next to a window, and Cindy handed them menus. Maggie suspected by Cindy's expression that she was surprised to see that she and Cherise were friends, out together to enjoy a nice lunch. And although Maggie liked Cindy well enough, she did get the impression, occasionally, that she perhaps looked down on certain kinds of people. To be honest, Maggie knew that she herself had been guilty of the exact same thing more times than she'd care to admit. But for some reason—maybe it had to do with Michael's sermons or God's own influence in her life—she had been trying to change her thinking. And, who knew, perhaps one day she'd even bring Dolly from the diner over here for afternoon tea. She could just imagine Cindy's expression over something like that!

"Tell me what's up with Greg," said Maggie after they placed their orders.

"Well, remember that magazine article I told you about, and how I asked your mom about bipolar disorder?"

Maggie nodded. "You were thinking maybe Greg could be manic depressive."

"Yes. And when I first told him about it, he just laughed at me. But then I made him listen to me, and I left the article with him. I went home and went onto the Internet to get more information, and the more I read, the more I thought maybe he really did have this thing." Her eyes grew bigger. "I mean, suddenly, just all sorts of stuff started making sense to me. Like the way he can get so over-the-top excited about something. You know, like that land development business, or whatever his most current interest might be, hunting, fishing, running the post office. And he can start acting like, well, like he owns the whole world, or at least Pine Mountain. I've seen him go on and on like he thinks he's next in line to God or something. He'll act as though nothing can stop him and nobody can hurt him. And then I've seen him at other times when he could be just totally the opposite, you know, like he's just certain that he's a useless, no-good nobody that no one appreciates and that he might as well be dead and gone. I don't know how many times I've tried to encourage him out of the blues like that, though maybe never to the point like at my apartment that day, when he was all suicidal and threatening to take us with him. That was pretty extreme, but he'd been drinking too."

Maggie considered all this. "I really don't know too much about the illness, Cherise, but what you're saying does make sense to me."

She nodded eagerly. "Yeah, even your mom thought it could be possible."

"And so what does Greg think now? Did he read all the things you left for him?"

"Yes. And he even asked if he could be examined by a psychiatrist."

"And can he?"

"He has an appointment for next week."

"Is that why he wants to change his plea?"

"Maybe. I suppose he thinks he can get off by way of an insanity plea. And it's not that I think he should get off, but I would like him to get help if he really does have a problem and can't help how he acts."

"The more I think about it, it does sound entirely possible that he's dealing with a real mental illness or some sort of chemical imbalance, but only a psychiatrist can make that diagnosis." She thought about Greg's strange and often erratic behavior in the short time she'd known him, and it suddenly seemed to fit together. "And if he really is bipolar and gets diagnosed, perhaps he'll get some form of treatment while he's incarcerated."

Cherise nodded. "I just can't help but think that's what caused all this, Maggie. Because, deep underneath all the rotten things he's done, I've always believed there was this basically good, though hurting, person hiding down there. I just couldn't ever figure out why he was like that. And it sure didn't take long for me to discover that I couldn't fix him either. So, I just tried to put up with it."

"Do you still love him?"

She shook her head. "I really don't think so. Not like I'd want to if I was to be married to him again or anything. But I think I do love him as a fellow human being. You know, the way God tells us to love our neighbors."

Maggie smiled. "Cherise, sometimes you totally amaze me."

She laughed. "*I* amaze you? Now, that's a good one."

"Yeah. It is."

As Maggie and Cherise were leaving the hotel, Clyde walked in wearing what looked to be a freshly cleaned suit, and he was proudly escorting Barbara Harris. They all paused to exchange greetings before going their separate ways. Maggie was afraid she couldn't suppress her childish giggles, but she waited until she and Cherise were safely out on the sidewalk before she burst into laughter.

"What is it?" asked Cherise, clearly puzzled.

"Clyde and Barbara," she gasped. "They were just so cute together."

"Are they going out like a couple now?"

"I guess so."

"Well, I happen to think they make a very handsome pair," noted Cherise. "And that Barbara Harris is just one of the sweetest little ladies I know. Why, she always talks to me at church and everything. And I'd say Clyde is pretty lucky to get someone like her."

"Can I quote you to Clyde on that?"

"You bet you can."

Twenty-Two

I was in to see Greg today," said Gavin as he sat down across from Maggie.

"Really?" Maggie saved her document and looked up. She'd asked him to stop by and give her some input on an ad that needed some editorial help.

"Yep. It was Michael who suggested it."

"Michael?"

"Yeah, he's been in to see Greg a couple times now, but just doesn't feel like he's connecting with him too well, and since he knew Greg and I *used* to be friends, he suggested I might go."

Maggie couldn't help but note the emphasis he'd put on the "used to be" part. "So, are you and Greg okay now? I remember how there were some pretty hard breaks in your friendship not that long ago. Are you over all that?"

He nodded. "I think so. You gotta forgive and forget and move on."

She smiled, thinking to herself what a long way Gavin Barnes had come from when she'd first met him nearly a year ago. "How's old Greg doing?"

"Certifiably crazy."

She blinked. "Are you serious?"

He chuckled. "Not completely. But he is. He says he's got some kind of bipolar disorder or something. Some shrink came to the jail and tested him, and sure enough, he's got it."

"Cherise told me about it, but I hadn't heard the final results."

Gavin frowned. "Yeah, that reminds me of something…"

"What's that?"

"Well, have you got an extra minute? I mean, I know you're busy, and we need to work on this ad, though I think I figured out an easy solution."

"Sure, I've got time, Gavin. What's up?"

"Well, it's kind of tricky…and I really don't know who to talk to. I know you and Cherise are…well…sort of friends…I suppose."

"Cherise and I *are* friends, Gavin." She grew somewhat defensive. "In fact, I happen to consider her to be a very good friend."

"Hey, I didn't mean anything—"

"I thought you liked her too." She studied him with growing irritation.

"Yeah, I think you're reading me all wrong here, Maggie. I do like her. I like her a lot! *That's* what the problem is."

Maggie leaned back in her chair and sighed. "I'm sorry, Gavin. It's just that some people in town act like Cherise is some sort of half-wit hillbilly or something, and it's really starting to bug me. Like just last night at the Cultural Celebration meeting, Cherise was being really helpful and everything, and then Elizabeth goes and treats her like she's the town idiot." Maggie made a growling sound. "Ooooh, It just made me so furious! And for Pete's sake, this whole cultural thing is about accepting people's differences."

"Hmmm…I can see I've touched a sore spot with you." He chuckled. "But I understand completely. In fact, I think I understand it from both ends. I've seen people do it to Cherise and others. And it's happened to me too."

Maggie nodded sadly, then remembered something humbling. "I'll bet I've even done it to you, Gavin, back when I first met you. And maybe I did it to Cherise too. People can be such fools sometimes."

"I'm sure we've all done it to someone."

"Yeah. But that's not what you wanted to talk about. You wanted to ask me something about Cherise." She smiled. "Go ahead."

"Yeah. Well, I feel that if I don't talk to someone, I might just explode, or implode, or something fairly disgusting. You see, I really do care about Cherise. We're not dating or anything, but I go to the fitness center to work out, and we talk, and I think she's really cool. She's so upbeat and easy going, and I find I just like being with her—a lot. But then there's this whole thing with Greg. She seems so sweet and understanding about him, and I know she really cares about him, and wants him to get better...and, now that I've visited him, I feel sort of pulled in two. I know she wants to hear how it went and all. Anyway, I'm just not sure what I should do." He paused and rolled his eyes. "Does this make any sense?"

She laughed. "Amazingly, it does. Let me play back what I think you said. You're interested in Cherise, but you think maybe she and Greg still have a shot at a relationship. And then you go and visit Greg, and you feel sort of guilty that you're interested in his ex-wife. Am I close?"

He grinned. "Dead on."

"What do you want from me?"

He ran his hand through his hair. "I don't know. Maybe just some friendly advice."

Maggie considered this. "Well, what I'm about to say is only my opinion and cannot be held against me in a court of law or otherwise. Okay?"

He nodded, his brow serious. "Sure."

"I've asked Cherise specifically about her and Greg. I've heard a lot from her about their relationship almost from when I first came here. Oddly enough, she confided in me. Anyway, their marriage was in trouble long, long ago."

He nodded. "I used to see the way he treated her."

"Cherise is very forgiving, and I think at one time she might have taken him back. To be perfectly honest, I'm almost positive Greg doesn't love her anymore. I wonder if he ever did. And from what she's told me, he doesn't seem to want her back even when he's rotting away in jail."

Gavin sighed. "Are you saying I should go for it?"

Maggie frowned. "Not really. That's not for me to say. As a friend, I'd say this: Yes, Cherise and Greg are probably history. And, yes, they're legally divorced. But I don't know what's supposed to happen with them. I mean, what if God wanted to do some miracle to bring them back together?" She noticed Gavin's face fall.

"That's what I was afraid of…"

"Well, I'd be pretty shocked if that happened, but who's to say?" She paused for a moment. "I'll tell you what I do think Cherise really needs right now."

"What's that?"

"Good friends." She smiled. "I honestly think the best thing you can offer her right now—and this is regardless of the direction your relationship may or may not take—is your friendship. I know that's what I wanted with Jed to start with. I wanted to get to know him as my good friend. I wanted someone I could talk with, laugh with, be quiet with, be comfortable with. I wanted someone who cared about me for who I am, and who wanted to understand my problems. And, quite frankly, someone who wasn't just looking for a good time."

Gavin nodded eagerly. "That's exactly what I want too!"

"Then, in that case, I'd say go for it! Be her friend."

He grinned. "Thanks. This has really been helpful."

She laughed. "Maybe I should start printing a 'Dear Maggie' column in the paper; you know, free advice for the lovelorn."

"Well, you might want to keep it anonymous, just in case anything backfired on you. But I promise not to hold you responsible for how things go with Cherise and me. Honestly, it's a relief to just think about it as a good friendship, at least for now. I think she'll appreciate that too. Takes some of the pressure off, if you know what I mean."

She nodded. "Believe me, I know."

ᴗ

Each time the paper reported anything on the upcoming Cultural Celebration, Maggie received an angry hate letter from Randy Ebbert. He had ceased publishing his radical paper, but he still seemed determined to at least try to stay in the limelight. Scott had tried to work up enough material to write another story about his group, but Maggie decided it just wasn't worthwhile, and after a short debate, Scott finally agreed. "I suppose it's just beating a dead horse, isn't it?" he finally admitted in defeat. "I mean, who really cares about Randy Ebbert?"

"I don't know, but I'd just as soon not give him the attention. But it's not your fault it's a no story. And maybe it's a good thing. Maybe it means that Randy and his kind really don't have anything to say that we haven't already heard. Perhaps if he's not breaking any laws, or making any threats, maybe it's just not worthwhile to give him any more exposure. I think our articles, as negative as they've been about him, just feed his ego and his warped sense of notoriety."

"Yeah, you're probably right. But I'll keep my eye on him, just in case anything new comes up."

"Good. Because, believe me, if he starts anything, I want our little paper to be right on top of it."

ᴗ

Maggie and Jed, both busy with work and other things, finally decided to relinquish all wedding plans to Audrey, Abigail, and Rosa, with Sierra, Leah, and Chloe all helping out as needed. They made their general requests known as far as colors, flowers, and whatnot, and then decided as long as they had a somewhat respectable ceremony, got officially hitched, and everyone had a reasonably good time at the reception, it would be just fine and dandy with them. Of course, the "weddin' women" as they'd taken to calling their little group were thrilled with this kind of freedom, and occasionally Maggie wondered what she'd gotten herself into. But mostly she distracted herself with work at the paper, her novel, which was finally coming along quite well, her family, and of course, Jed. All in all, it seemed a good way to live.

By the end of April, everyone in town was longing for warm spring weather in the same way they had longed for snow last winter. When would it come? Would it ever come? Did it really need to snow in April? Jed soothed Maggie with the promise of honeymooning somewhere warmer, but he kept the location a secret. She trusted him with the details, but made a special trip to Byron for a new swimsuit just in case it involved a beach somewhere. She had yet to find the perfect wedding dress, and in fact did not even know what that might be. She knew she didn't want anything frilly or silly or outrageously expensive. She tended to lean toward classic two-piece suits in raw white silk, but Jed thought they looked too matronly. She had to remind herself that this was, in fact, Jed's first wedding, his first bride, the whole bit. More than ever, she wanted it to be special for him. But each time she tried to question him on her dress, he didn't seem to have an opinion, other than what he didn't like. Finally, she asked him what he would like to wear to the wedding. At first he hedged, saying he'd wear whatever she wanted him to wear.

"That's not good enough," she said stubbornly. "Okay, think of it like this. Pretend we're both supposed to come up with our own outfits for the wedding. And we don't get to know what the other one is wearing. Okay? Are you with me?"

He nodded. "Yeah. So I have to show up at the wedding wearing something I *think* will go with your dress, right?"

"Not quite. I mean, you have to show up at the wedding wearing whatever it is you'd most like to wear, even if it's nothing but a leather loin cloth." She giggled, her cheeks growing warm. "Now, that might not be so bad if it were just you and me."

He grinned. "Too bad it's been so cold lately."

"Okay, let's get serious. What would you most like to wear—regardless of what you think I might be wearing. You have good taste, Jed. I honestly think you have a better sense of style than I do. Come on, what would it be?" He grew quiet and thoughtful, then finally spoke. "Oh, I don't know, Maggie. Probably something comfortable."

"Well, that's a big help. But maybe it rules out a tux."

"I don't want you to rule out anything, Maggie. You just decide what you want to do and I'll play along. It's only a day. You can dress me however you like. I have the rest of our lives to wear whatever I want. Right?"

She smiled. "Of course."

"But you better get it figured out soon, or I might have to wear that loin cloth."

She laughed. "And I suppose I'd have to wear something compatible, maybe something in tiger or zebra? Something with one strap and a bone in my hair?"

"Now, this is starting to sound like fun."

"Can you imagine the reaction we'd get from our guests?" She laughed. "I can just see Elizabeth Rodgers or Barbara Harris fainting in shock."

"So you think we'd better go with something a little more traditional then?"

"I suppose we should keep up appearances just for the sake of our guests."

He laughed and stuck out a tall leather moccasin. "Then you better select the wedding garments, my dear bride, because everyone in town knows I don't give a hoot about what other people think of my appearance."

She wrapped her arms around his neck. "You know, that's one of the first things I noticed about you, Jed White-water, and I liked it right from the start!"

"Do you know what my first impression of you was, Maggie?" He chuckled.

She remembered the moment clearly. She was still new from L.A., dressed like a city slicker, and appearing to look down on his rustic furnishings, although that hadn't really been her intent. "No, and I'm not even sure I want to know."

"You looked like a lost little girl, just waiting for someone to find you."

"Really? And here I thought I was this self-assured newspaper woman coming to teach this small town some new tricks."

He smiled. "I think we've all learned a thing or two from each other."

"Okay, not to change the subject, but I want to be perfectly clear here. Are you saying you'll agree to wear whatever I decide upon for the wedding?"

"Yes, but you'd better get busy. Do you realize our wedding date is less than a month away?"

"I can't believe it. And to tell you the truth, it makes me a little nervous. Do you ever wish we could just slip away and get married quietly?"

He smiled slyly. "Yeah, how about tonight?"

"No, I mean *seriously*."

"Actually, I kind of like the idea of an old-fashioned ceremony with all our friends and family gathered around. I missed out on a lot of that stuff as a kid. I think it's important to be part of a family, a community, connected, you know. That's one of the things I noticed right off about you. You seemed to have this ability, this desire, to be right in the middle of things. And not just a spectator either, but a real participant."

"But you've always seemed connected to this community, Jed. When I first came you were leading the church and everything."

"Well, those things don't come naturally to me. And if left to my own devices, I might turn into a hermit. Not that it would make me happy. It wouldn't at all. I need to be around others, to exchange ideas, to give and receive, and all kinds of good stuff. And you help me to do that."

She sighed happily. "I think God knew what he was doing when he brought us together, Jed."

"You think so?"

"I know so."

Twenty-Three

For the past couple weeks, Maggie had visited Amber almost every single day at lunch time. She usually brought lunch with her, either from home or something she'd picked up in town. And occasionally Amber would have the strength and energy to fix a little meal for both of them. But Maggie knew that Amber was growing weaker with each passing day. Her condition worried Maggie. But so far, she'd managed to keep Amber's secret, and no one else in town knew she was dying. Amber had told her few friends that she'd been suffering from a bad case of flu and was having a hard time shaking it, but Maggie couldn't believe that people didn't wonder if it was something more. And yet, Amber was the master of disguise when she wanted to be. She could dress up in her designer clothes, apply perfect makeup, and smile as though she were the happiest woman in the world. It was only Maggie who saw beneath the pretty veneer.

Today, Maggie saw her at her worst. Amber hadn't answered the door when she'd knocked, so she let herself in as she had on numerous other occasions, calling out Amber's name as she walked through the quiet house, always afraid of finding Amber unconscious, or worse. Today she was in bed, propped up with pillows, but lifeless and pale as a ghost.

"Sorry, Maggie," she whispered.

Maggie went over and took Amber's hand in hers. It was cold. "Are you all right?"

"Just tired."

Maggie looked at her silky pajamas. "Have you been up today?"

"No. Too weak."

"Have you eaten anything?"

"No appetite."

"But you need to keep up your strength." Even as she spoke the words, she wondered about the answer herself, but Amber provided it for her.

"Why?"

"Because we love you, Amber. We're not ready to lose you. And I don't think you're ready to go." She knew Amber had still not made her peace with God. They discussed this a lot, but Amber had a stubborn streak in her. And often, Maggie wondered if Jed might be the one who could get through. But she knew she couldn't get him over here without betraying Amber's trust and breaking her promise.

"Amber," she began. "You've kept your secret longer than I would've thought possible. But don't you suppose you're being just a little bit selfish? I mean, there are people who would love to be involved with you right now, but they're staying away, just thinking you're sick."

"I am sick."

"You know what I mean." Maggie picked up a glass of water from the bedside table cluttered with various prescription bottles and handed it to her. "Have you had anything to drink lately?"

She took a small sip. "I can't remember."

"See?" Maggie shook her head. "You need help, and there are people all over town who would love to help you. Can't you let them? Or shall I quit working at the paper and come over here and do it all myself?" Her unexpected firmness surprised her.

"Oh, poor Maggie." Amber's words sounded sincere. "I guess I haven't really considered how hard this is on you. I'm so sorry."

"No, no, I didn't mean it like that." Maggie closed her eyes, longing for the perfect words of persuasion. "I would gladly do that for you, Amber. And I could bring my laptop over and work from here even. But I think you're denying others the chance to help too. Just the other day, Jed and I were talking about how important it is to be connected to friends, family, and community. And you are so isolated right now."

Amber seemed to consider this. "I guess I am. I don't know, it's almost like I don't know what to do anymore. Maybe you're right. But how do I change? And then again, I still don't want everyone feeling sorry for me. And I don't want them worrying. Like Leah for instance. She calls me once in a while. I just hate the thought of hurting her."

Maggie frowned. "Well, you should have considered that before you allowed her to *love* you. Now, she will be hurt one way or another. And quite honestly, I think it will hurt her a whole lot more to discover that you shut her out when you really needed a friend. And Jed too. He would want to talk to you, Amber. I know it. He really cares about you."

A tear slipped down Amber's cheek. "Maybe you're right, Maggie. I'm starting to feel like I really don't know anything about anything anymore. Maybe you're right."

Maggie gently squeezed her hand. "I really believe I am. Can you trust me with this?"

Amber nodded.

Maggie sighed with relief. "Now, I've got some soup from Dolly's Diner, and don't worry, it's not floating in grease. I'm going to warm it up a little, and I want you to eat some, okay?"

In the kitchen, Maggie called her mother. She knew she'd be at the library today because they were very close to opening. Thankfully, a library board had been established, complete with a full list of active volunteers, and all had been helping out. She waited for the phone to ring as the soup warmed, and then told her mother the whole sorry story about Amber. Relief washed over her as Audrey jumped right in with a multitude of ideas and suggestions.

"Why don't you bring her over to your house?" suggested Audrey. "Do you think she would do that?"

"I'm not sure. She may want to be in her own home. But I'll ask."

"Yes, I suppose she might feel more comfortable in her own home. And we could take turns coming over and bringing food and things."

"I'll talk to her and see what she'd like best."

Maggie put the soup and some crackers on a tray and went back to Amber's bedroom. She sat with her, making small talk and watching to see that she actually ate.

"Amber," she began. "I called Mom, and she really wants to help out. She wondered if you might like to come stay with us for a while. You know how huge my house is. We have plenty of room, and I'd love to have you."

"I don't know, Maggie." Amber looked around the room. "I like being here."

Maggie nodded. "I understand. But maybe just think about it."

"I will. And I appreciate the offer." She took another spoonful of soup. "This isn't bad."

Maggie smiled. "Dolly's Diner might not have the best menu in town, but she's got some good soup recipes."

Maggie helped Amber get up, then scurried about straightening and cleaning while Amber took a quick shower and got dressed. She even took a few minutes to go outside and snip several daffodils and a few sprigs of cherry blossoms to put in a vase. Then she called her mother to let her know that Amber wanted to remain at home for now.

"That's not surprising," said Audrey. "And I have a plan. I need to do some phoning and whatnot, but I'll let you know all about it when you come home tonight."

When Amber emerged from the bedroom with makeup on and hair in place, she could've almost fooled Maggie as to the state of her health...except for the dark shadows beneath her eyes.

"You look great," said Maggie.

Amber glanced around the kitchen. "Thanks for cleaning up, Maggie. I wanted to do it, but I just didn't have an ounce of energy. And the flowers are a lovely touch." Her voice broke, then she walked over and threw her arms around Maggie. "You have no idea how much I appreciate you."

Maggie held her for a long moment, surprised at how fragile she felt as she heaved with sobs, just skin and bones. Her heart gave a sharp twist at the fresh realization of how little time this poor woman might actually have. "Amber," she spoke softly, "I'm here for you. And so is everyone else. We all want to help however we can. We all love you."

"I know," she sobbed. "I know."

They sat on the sofa and Maggie explained that Audrey was already cooking up some plan. "You know how my mother can be; she just loves to roll up her sleeves and get involved, and her work at the library is about to come to an end. But I want you to feel free to tell her what you want too. Don't let her take over. And, believe me, she'll understand."

"I think Audrey is wonderful." Amber sighed. "And, you know, I already feel like a bit of the weight has been lifted off my shoulders."

"Oh, I'm so glad. I really don't believe you were meant to carry this thing all by yourself, Amber. This is exactly what friends are for."

She nodded. "I guess you're right."

"Thanks for letting me take this next step," said Maggie. She wanted to ask her about her ex-husband, but didn't want to push too much all at once. Besides, she reasoned, perhaps it was something she could do on her own. She'd ask Jed for advice.

Amber glanced at her watch. "I know you need to get back to the office..."

"Yes. And it sounds like my mom's coming by this afternoon. So you might want to rest a little until then." Suddenly, Maggie felt alarmed. Earlier, she had noticed all the bottles of pills on Amber's bedside table. "Amber?" she began uncertainly.

"Yes?"

"Well, I don't know quite how to ask this, but I need to know something, okay?"

"Sure, what is it?"

"You wouldn't do anything, would you? To hurry things along...I mean, I noticed a lot of medications by your bed."

Amber looked down into her lap, and Maggie spied another tear streaking down her cheek. "Oh, Maggie. I don't know. I'll be honest with you, yes, I was thinking that might be an easy way out."

"I can understand how you might feel that way. But easy isn't always best. Sometimes God has a reason for doing things the hard way. I know it seems unfair at the time, but when it's all said and done it makes sense."

Amber shook her head. "I don't know. Nothing really makes much sense to me."

"Well, have you heard the story about the cocoon? This kid sees a butterfly struggle to get out of a cocoon, so the kid decides to help. He carefully cuts the cocoon open with a razor blade, and presto the butterfly comes out."

Amber looked at her curiously. "And?"

"And then the butterfly dies."

"Gee, that's a cheerful story, Maggie. Tell me another."

Maggie smiled. "I'm sorry. But the point is, the butterfly needed that struggle to develop his stamina in order to survive. And as difficult as it seemed to the casual observer, there was a purpose to the butterfly's pain. You know what I mean?"

A deep sigh. "Maybe."

"Amber, would you mind very much if I put those meds away for you? I could just leave out what you need."

"Go ahead." She sounded defeated.

"It's just that I don't want you going before it's time. I really like having you around. And you never know what God might be up to."

Amber said nothing, just remained on the sofa, her hands in her lap. Maggie went back to the bedroom, read the prescriptions, and put out enough pills to get Amber through the afternoon. The rest she put in her purse. She would give them to her mom and let her figure out something. Maggie stopped by the sofa again, and put her arm around Amber's shoulders. "I know this is hard for you. And I really do wish I could make it all go away, but maybe there's a reason for all this. Maybe it's an opportunity for everyone to show how much we really care about you."

Amber nodded without looking up. "Maybe."

As soon as Maggie got to her car, she called her mom again. "Mom, you've got to get over here soon, if you can. I'm really worried about her." Then she explained about the pills and how depressed Amber seemed.

"Everything's under control here," laughed Audrey. "In fact, I'm sure they'll be quite glad to be rid of me. I'm on my way now. So, don't you worry. But you might say a little prayer."

Maggie smiled. Her mother had never put too much stock in prayer before. But things were changing. Next she called Jed.

Taylor answered. She told him it was fairly urgent, and she needed Jed to call her back at the newspaper office. Taylor said he'd tell him and then hung up.

Nearly an hour passed, and Jed still hadn't called. Then she heard a quiet knock on her door, it opened, and Jed came in. His face looked worried. "What's wrong?" he asked with concern. "Taylor said to call, but I needed to come to town, so I thought I'd just stop in."

She rose from her desk and went over to him. "Oh, Jed, it's just so sad. I've been wanting to tell you, but—"

"What?" he demanded.

"It's Amber."

His face seemed to relax a little. "Oh, I thought it was you, or Leah, or—"

"I'm sorry. I guess I'm just feeling upset. But now that she's willing to let everything out in the open, I guess I should be relieved."

"Maggie, why don't you sit down and begin at the beginning."

She sat down and explained everything, and by the time she finished his face began to look strained again and his brow became creased. "So that's why she came back here," he finally said. "Poor Amber."

"She doesn't want our pity, Jed."

"Oh, I know. But I feel so bad now. I've treated her—well, pretty harshly—If I'd known…"

"If you'd known, you would've felt sorry for her, and that's just what she didn't want."

He nodded. "I know. And I guess she was right too. But what made her change her mind?"

"I don't think she has much time." Maggie swallowed against the lump in her throat. "She's so weak. And I think she'd just like to end it all now."

He sadly shook his head. "Poor Amber. I feel so bad for her. What can we do?"

"Just be there for her. She needs friends, and she needs them badly. Mom is over there right now. She's trying to put a plan together to help with her care. But there's something else, Jed. I need your advice."

"Sure, anything, what is it?"

"Amber hasn't told her ex-husband."

"Oh."

"And I get the impression that Ben's really a decent guy."

"He probably is. Even though I used to hate the sound of that name, I just can't imagine that Amber would've married a jerk."

"No. I think they loved each other. And I just think he'd want to know about this. I mean, how's he going to feel once she's gone?"

"He needs to know," said Jed with urgency. "Do you have his number?"

"No, but I doubt it would be hard to get."

"Do you want me to call him?"

"I don't know, Jed. I mean, how would that make him feel to have her old boyfriend calling from her hometown, telling him that she was dying?"

"You're right. Do you mind? It seems Amber has relied on you for a lot of things; you seem like the right person to do this."

Maggie nodded. "Yes. I just wasn't sure if it was the right thing to do or not. I wanted your opinion."

"Of course it's right. Even if Amber thinks she wants to keep it from him, I think she'll be glad in the end. And I'm sure you'll sound him out. If he seems uncaring, just don't tell him everything."

"Yes. That's what I'll do."

"Do you think it'd be okay if I stop by Amber's before I head back home?"

"Of course. I think it would be good. Just be gentle with her, Jed. She seems really fragile to me right now."

He reached over and pulled her into his arms. "I can't believe you, Maggie. Here you are, all this time, helping my old girlfriend, being such a trooper. How'd I ever get so lucky?"

She smiled up at him. "It's a two-way street, Jed. And, just for the record, Amber might be your old girlfriend, but she's been a wonderful friend to me. And I love her for who she is." Maggie felt her eyes filling with tears. "I'm going to miss her."

He tenderly kissed her forehead. "I know you will."

She lingered in his arms for a few moments before pulling away. "You'd better go now. I know it'll be good for her to see you. And maybe you can get her to talk more. I know she has something inside her that she can't quite get out. I think it has to do with her mother's death, and, perhaps as a result, her understanding of God. But I know there's something holding her back."

"Maggie, do you know how much I love you?"

She blinked back the tears and hugged him again "I think I do."

Twenty-Four

It wasn't long until Abigail located Ben Feldman's phone number. But he wasn't home when Maggie called, so she left a brief message explaining that she was a friend of Amber's and needed to talk to him as soon as possible. She left both her work and home numbers and then hung up, dismayed that she hadn't spoken to him personally. After that she called several friends, including Cherise and Rosa, to let them know about Amber's condition. She asked that they not bombard her with visits right at first, but suggested perhaps they could talk to Audrey about ways they might help or work together on a schedule. As she'd predicted, everyone was very concerned and more than willing to lend a hand.

When she finally went home, she felt emotionally drained. But she'd barely stepped in the door when Ben Feldman returned her call. She quickly explained her connection to Amber, apologizing for disturbing him, still wary as to how he would receive the call. "I just wondered if you might have some concern for your ex-wife's welfare, or perhaps you two have just gone your separate—"

"Of course I have concern for Amber's welfare!" he interrupted hotly. "Is something wrong?"

"Well...actually there is something wrong."

"Please tell me." His voice grew quieter. "Is she okay?"

Maggie sensed that his concern was sincere and decided she had no choice but to tell him the whole story, or at least all she knew. "Amber was trying so hard to keep all this to herself," she began, hardly knowing where to start. "She's a very strong woman. But unfortunately she has cancer—"

She heard him take in a sharp breath. "Is it bad?"

"Yes."

"Please...tell me everything."

She told him what Amber had told her, as well as her own elevated concern for Amber today. "She almost seems to be giving up."

"I've got to come to her—" His voice broke. "Oh, blast! I don't know why we were both so stubborn. I never quit loving her. Never! It was all about pride, that's all. It just got in the way—for both of us. But if I'd known about this, I would've done something..." He paused and Maggie waited, unsure of how to respond. "I'm sorry to go on like this," he continued. "It's just...well, I guess I'm in shock."

"I'm so sorry to tell you all this, Ben. But I felt you should know. I thought you'd want to. And Jed thought so too."

"No, no, don't worry about me. You have no idea how much I appreciate knowing. It's just that...oh, I don't know... But I'll leave as soon as I can, first thing in the morning. Do you suppose it will upset her much to see me?"

"What do you think?"

"I think I know Amber well enough to handle this right." He made a choking sound. "If only I'd known sooner."

Maggie tried her best to comfort him, but her words sounded flat and empty even to her. Finally she told him that perhaps it would be best if he came to her office first, and then she could take him over to Amber's and sort of break the ice for them, if that would be helpful. He gladly agreed and promised to let her know his arrival time, then thanked her again and hung up.

"Was that the ex?" asked Audrey from the kitchen.

"Yes," groaned Maggie. "What an excruciating conversation!"

"But aren't you relieved to at least have it while Amber's still with us?"

"Of course. I can't even imagine how his heart would've been broken to hear about it after it was too late. He sounds completely crushed as it is." She filled a glass with water and sighed. "How was Amber when you left her, Mom? Do you think I should go back over there for the evening?"

Audrey smiled. "We have another sweet angel staying with her tonight."

"Who?"

"Leah. I told her all about it, and she wanted to spend the night."

"Dear Leah."

"Yes. And she suggested she might even stay on there for a while if it's okay with Amber."

"I bet Amber would like that." Maggie sighed. "Thanks for your help, Mom. This was getting too heavy for me to carry alone."

"And you've known all this time?"

"Not from the start. But long enough to begin feeling overwhelmed."

Audrey hugged her. "You've been a good friend, honey. Amber really appreciates you and all you've done."

"Did Jed come by?"

"Yes." Audrey rinsed a head of lettuce. "I think they had a really good talk. I tried not to eavesdrop, but I couldn't help but hear a few things. They were reminiscing about when they were kids and how they felt when they lost their mothers. Amber was talking a lot. I think it was good for her. I can't help but feel she has some old ghosts or something haunting her."

"I know. I've had the same thought."

"Well, I think Jed was good medicine. And just about the time he left, Leah arrived. So everything's working smoothly so far. I told Leah where I hid the meds you gave me. That was wise on your part, Maggie, to put them away for now."

"She just seemed so discouraged and depressed. I didn't know what she might do."

ᴥ

Ben arrived late the following afternoon, stopping by the newspaper office just before closing time. He still seemed fairly upset and shaken by the devastating news, but Maggie couldn't help but like the tall, well-dressed, gray-haired man as he firmly shook her hand while looking directly into her eyes. "I want to thank you again for calling me," he said soberly.

"I'm so glad you could come. I was just finishing up here, and we can go right over to Amber's now." Maggie shut off her computer and got her coat. "I took the liberty to hint to her that I'd notified you when we had lunch together today. It was funny. She sort of ignored me about the whole thing, didn't even respond. But I know she heard me and understood what I was saying. To tell you the truth, I think she may actually be relieved. My mom's been staying with her this afternoon, and she may have talked with her about how you were coming as well. So, she may be more prepared to see you than we'd expected."

"I hope so. I've been replaying the past through my head over and over during my trip. I realize now just how many times I've let her down...how stupid I've been...if only I could turn back the clock and change some things."

Audrey opened the door at Amber's and let them in. "She's been having a nap the last hour, but I think I heard her stir just a bit ago. Let me go check."

Maggie hung up their coats and invited Ben into the living room. "Have you ever been here before?" she asked as they sat down.

"No, but it's as I imagined. I've seen old snapshots from Amber's childhood, before her mother died. I don't know that her father took many photos after that. Things were rather sad for the two of them."

"That's right, I forgot you knew her father too."

He nodded, rubbing his hands together, and looking very much like a nervous young man about to have his first date. "I hope my coming here doesn't upset her."

"Well, hello there," called Amber from the hallway. "Don't worry, Ben, I already know that you're there, and I'm not going to yell and scream or throw anything. So everyone can just relax."

Ben and Maggie rose and watched as Amber came into the room. Maggie thought she looked amazingly well, especially compared to yesterday, and suddenly she wondered if Ben might think she'd made this whole thing up. But he went immediately to her and, to everyone's surprised relief, gathered her into his arms and held her while both of them began to sob quietly. Maggie glanced at her mother, feeling as if they should leave them alone for this emotional reunion. Audrey, as if reading her thoughts, darted her eyes toward the door; and in a flash they both quickly gathered their coats and made a silent exit.

"Wow," whispered Maggie on the porch. "That went better than expected."

"Let's hope it continues to go that way." Audrey glanced nervously over her shoulder. "Maybe we should go tip Leah off before she comes over here after work and interrupts them."

"Good thinking. And maybe we should stick around in town a little while, just in case."

They stopped by Whitewater Works and told Leah what was going on over at Amber's, and Leah said that was fortunate as she had some things to finish up anyway. Then Maggie and Audrey went over to the Window Seat to visit with Elizabeth and have a cup of coffee before returning to check on Amber and Ben.

"Hello, ladies," called Elizabeth cheerily, looking up from where she was dusting a low bookshelf. "What can I do for you?"

"Mostly we just want to kill some time, and this seemed a good place to land," said Maggie. "But I'll have a café mocha while we wait."

"Make that two," added Audrey.

"How's it going with Amber?" asked Elizabeth with a slight frown. "You know, I still can't get over the news. Good grief, she's such a vibrant young woman."

"You just never know," offered Audrey, pulling up one of the high counter stools and sitting down.

"But she's just in her prime, poor thing, with so much to offer…" Elizabeth made a tsk-tsk sound. "It just doesn't seem fair."

"That's life," said Audrey, taking her coffee. "And *fair* is just the place you go at the end of summer for a good time."

Maggie pulled a stool up to the counter too. "Elizabeth, did you know that Amber is worried about letting you down on the Cultural Celebration?"

"Pish posh." Elizabeth waved her hand. "Amber has already done far more than her share. And she's a wonder, really. Even more amazing now that I realize what she was dealing with. But it's like that sometimes. Often we can forget about our troubles by throwing ourselves into our work."

Maggie studied the older woman more carefully. Could she be describing her own life? She'd never considered Elizabeth to be the type to have problems of any sort. So self-assured and capable, she seemed to walk above the everyday troubles of life. And yet, who really knew?

"How are *you* doing, Elizabeth?" asked Maggie with sincerity.

"I guess I'm okay for an old lady like me." Elizabeth laughed lightly.

"Well, do you need any more help for the celebration?"

"Are you offering?"

"I'll do what I can."

Audrey chuckled. "Goodness, Maggie, don't you have enough on your plate already? Taking care of Amber, running a newspaper, not to mention planning for your upcoming wedding."

"You and your little crew are planning my wedding. I hardly give it a thought these days. And now that everyone is helping out with Amber...why, I have all the time in the world."

Elizabeth chuckled. "Well, if I get really good and desperate, Maggie, I'll give you a call. As it is, the publicity you're giving us in the paper is really great help. I've even had some out-of-state calls from folks who've read about us on the Internet. I'm expecting a good turnout."

Maggie and Audrey finished their coffee and went back to see how things were going at Amber's house.

"Come on in, you two," called Amber as she opened the door. "What's the deal about sneaking off like that anyway?"

"I think I must've scared them away," said Ben apologetically.

"We just thought you might need some time to yourselves," said Audrey. "And we'll both be on our way now if you—"

"Not so quick," said Amber. "Can't you stay a moment?"

"Sure," said Maggie. "Anything we can help with?"

"Well, I'm in something of a quandary," began Amber as they all sat down in the living room again. "You see, Ben is being really sweet and all. Now he wants to take me back home with him." She reached over and patted Ben's knee.

"I hate to leave her, and yet I have to attend to some loose ends back home," he explained. "Actually, some fairly urgent things need to be taken care of. But once they're all wrapped up, which shouldn't take but a day or two, I can have as much time off as I need."

"And I'm torn," said Amber, "because I really feel so at home here in Pine Mountain, but I hate to be a burden to you—"

"Don't even think that," Maggie spoke firmly. "We're your friends, Amber. There is no such thing as a burden. Do you understand that?"

"I guess so." She turned and looked back to Ben, and for the first time ever, Maggie thought Amber almost looked truly happy. "I think I should stay put, Ben, if you don't mind."

He nodded, though clearly disappointed. "I understand. I just wish I didn't have to go back—"

"It's okay, honey. I know how it is—"

"Well, I'll wrap it all up and be back in four—" he paused, "no, make that three days, max." He looked into her eyes. "That is if you really want me, Amber. I don't want to force myself on—"

"Ben," she said quietly. "We've already gone over this, haven't we?"

He sighed. "I just hate to leave you again, sweetheart. I'd do anything not to, but there are a lot of people back at the business who would be seriously messed up if I didn't attend to things first."

"It's okay. I'll be here when you get back."

"Promise?"

She nodded, then turned back to Maggie and Audrey. "I guess it's all settled. You guys are stuck with me until Ben gets back."

"And if I can catch a flight out later this evening, I might be able to get back here that much sooner."

"Then we'll go and let you two have some more time to yourselves," said Maggie. "Oh, I just remembered, Leah will be over after she closes the shop. Do you want me to tell her to wait until later?"

"No, I want Ben to meet her." Amber's eyes glowed. "I sometimes pretend Leah is my daughter, you know, the one I never had—" She stopped herself and looked at Maggie with alarm. "Oh, I didn't mean to sound like—I hope that's okay."

Maggie laughed. "Of course it's okay. It's wonderful. You know, Leah's not my real daughter either, but I like to pretend the same thing."

"Leah's a very lucky girl," said Audrey. "She's got all kinds of mothers around to love her."

Twenty-Five

*F*or the next couple of days, Amber seemed better than ever and Maggie began telling herself that perhaps the cancer wasn't as progressed as Amber's doctor had suggested. Perhaps Amber had lots of time left. And maybe she'd even beat this. Those things happened occasionally. She'd read articles and seen television specials where someone survived an impossible prognosis. Besides, lots of people were praying for Amber right now, including Michael Abundi—and he believed in miracles!

Ben returned after three days, relieving Leah of her night shift. It wasn't long before they were all glad to see Ben around. He seemed to be just what Amber needed. After several days, Amber privately told Maggie how much she appreciated how she'd intervened and informed Ben of her condition. "I was being pretty stupid and stubborn. I'm so glad I had a friend step in who's wiser than me."

Maggie laughed. "I don't know about wiser. But it just seemed that Ben should know. And Jed thought so too."

"Speaking of Jed, we thought it would be fun to have dinner with you two. I have hardly been out of this house all week. But since I'm feeling so much better, do you think we could all meet at the hotel on Saturday? I really do want Ben and Jed to get acquainted."

"Sounds great." Maggie was aware that Jed felt a little uncertain about getting to know Ben, but she knew he'd do it for Amber's sake. It would probably be good for all of them. "I'll check with him and get back to you. I'm planning to do some die-hard wedding dress shopping on Saturday."

"You mean you don't have your dress yet?"

"No, and I'm getting a little worried. My maid of honor keeps bugging me about what she's supposed to wear, and Jed said it was completely up to me to decide what he is going to wear. The only thing I could get out of him is that he wants to be comfortable. I have all his measurements and everything, but that's as far as I've gotten."

"Is it because of me?" asked Amber. "Have I taken too much of your time?"

"Goodness, no! It's because of *me*. I just don't know what I want to wear. I suppose I might just go with a nice two-piece dress or something classic like that."

"That sounds lovely."

"But Jed thinks it will look too matronly. And I realize this is his first, and hopefully, only wedding. I know he wants it to be special. And so do I, of course. But I just don't know what that would take. The problem is that I don't want to walk down the aisle looking like Cinderella on prom night. Most of the dresses I see either look too youngish or too spectacular." Maggie sighed. "I don't know what to do."

"You know, Maggie, I have this really strange idea. I mean it's probably totally absurd. To tell the truth, I'm even a little embarrassed to mention it to you."

"What?" she asked eagerly. "What is it? I want to hear."

"Oh, it seems too silly."

This only increased her curiosity. "Come on, Amber, I want to hear it. Really I do."

"Well, a long time ago, back in high school when Jed and I were dating, I was up at his house one time. He had gone out to chop some firewood for his dad, and Mr. Whitewater and I were just talking, looking at old photos and stuff, and he was reminiscing about his wife. I was really quite interested."

"Yes, Jed's shown me some of those old photos too. His mother looked a bit like Leah."

"Yes. Anyway, Mr. Whitewater opened up this old cedar-lined trunk and took out a box. And in it was a beautiful white leather dress, Native American, you know, all fringed and beaded. It was gorgeous. But that was back in the days when we were into all that kind of stuff—you know, beads and fringe and earthy things."

"You mean the hippie days?" Maggie winked. "I was still just a little kid back then."

Amber laughed. "Yes, well, you should have seen us. We wore the long hair, beads, headbands, the whole nine yards."

"So are you thinking I might actually wear that dress? I mean, if it still exists?"

"Like I said, it's probably just a crazy idea."

"No..." She considered this. "It's not so crazy. But what are the odds that something like that would even fit me? Or that it would be wearable?"

"It was in surprisingly good condition back then even though it was pretty old. I think perhaps her mother or grandmother had worn it before her."

"Really?"

"It was absolutely beautiful, Maggie. And the leather was so soft, just like butter."

"I want to see it."

"Wouldn't it be something if you could use it?"

"I wonder what Jed would think..."

"He'd love it, Maggie."

She wasn't sure. But she knew she wanted to look into this further. "Maybe I can slip over there and take a look at it without him knowing what I'm up to. It would be so fun to surprise him."

"It's worth a try." Amber smiled. "I just hope I haven't sent you off on some wild goose chase."

"Not at all. If anything, you've reminded me I need to get this whole wedding clothing business nailed down. And I'd love to see that dress anyway." She hugged Amber and thanked her for the idea, then said goodbye. "I'll let you know about dinner on Saturday," she called as she left.

⟶

The next day was Friday and Maggie, caught up with everything at the paper, decided to take the afternoon off. After lunch, she drove over to Jed's place to check on the progress of the remodeling. At least that was her pretense. But to her relief, he was gone and only Taylor was working. She wasn't sure exactly what she was looking for or even if it might still be in the cabin, but after a while, she discovered what looked like an old wooden trunk. It was wedged into a corner and nearly buried with boxes and things. She moved everything away from its top and slowly opened it. The lining was of fragrant, pink-colored cedar. She carefully removed numerous items of memorabilia, controlling her compulsion to examine everything, until she finally came to an old cardboard box. She took out the box and gingerly removed its lid. There was the leather garment, exactly as Amber had described. Maggie's heart began to pound, and suddenly she felt certain Jed would walk in and discover her at any moment. She quickly replaced everything except for the precious box and piled the other things back on the trunk just as they'd been. Then she slipped out the backdoor without even saying goodbye to Taylor, put the box in her car, and feeling very much like a thief, drove directly to her house.

At home, although no one was there to hear her, she tiptoed upstairs. Once she was safe in the privacy of her room, she opened the box again. She gingerly removed the soft dress, taking time now to hold it up and examine it more carefully. The garment was heavy with its long fringe and glass beadwork, but just as Amber had said, the leather was as soft as butter and about the thickness of a fine velveteen. She held it up to her and stood before the mirror. The fringe on the bottom came just above her ankles. With her eye she estimated the size of the garment and it seemed about right. Then she noticed a few places where beadwork appeared to be coming loose, and some places where the leather lacing was broken or worn thin. Oh, maybe this was a crazy idea. Perhaps this dress belonged in a museum somewhere. She studied her reflection again, imagining herself in Jed's eyes as she fingered a loose piece of beadwork, careful to keep the beads from slipping off. Maybe it wasn't so crazy.

She gently laid the dress across her bed. Weren't there people who could mend such things? She pulled out the phone book and searched until she found the number for a leather shop in Byron. After a brief conversation she was given the name and number of someone named Lottie Smith who was supposedly an expert at restoring historical garments of this sort. She called the number, and what sounded like the voice of a very old woman answered. Maggie introduced herself and explained why she was calling.

"Yes, I can help you," said the woman.

Maggie took down the address and directions and told the woman she could be there within the hour if that was agreeable.

"I'm not going anywhere," said Lottie. "Just watch out for my llamas when you come through the gate. Don't let any of 'em get out."

Maggie smiled in amusement. "Yes, of course, I'll be very careful."

⌒

Several longhaired brown llamas came closer, curious about their visitor, as Maggie opened the gate and moved her car inside. She quickly got out to close the gate, careful not to let any of these big-eyed creatures out. At the end of the dusty driveway she spied an old single-wide mobile home, nearly obscured by plants and trees, with a lean-to building attached on one side. Maggie went up the steps of the rickety porch and knocked on the door, unsure of what she might be getting herself into, but feeling a sense of adventure just the same.

"Hello?" said a short, dark woman who appeared to be of Native American descent.

"I'm Maggie. I called about the dress."

"Yes, yes. Come on in. Don't mind the cats. They think they own the place."

Maggie stepped inside, quickly taking in the room crowded with old furnishings, several cats, and all sorts of various bead and leather projects in various stages. She held out the box. "This is the dress I told you about."

The little woman set the box on the table and removed the lid, then almost reverently lifted the garment out and studied it, making little noises with her tongue. Finally, she spoke. "This is beautiful."

Maggie nodded. "Yes. I've never seen anything like it."

Lottie's brows drew together as she studied Maggie with what appeared to be suspicion. "Where did you get this?"

"It belonged to my fiancé's mother. You see, he's Native American. I think it may go back several generations. He doesn't know I have it—"

"Why not?" asked the woman sharply.

Maggie laughed lightly. "Well, I was considering wearing it as a wedding gown. Our wedding is only a few weeks away, and I just can't find a dress." She looked down at Lottie. "I'm not sure if that's an acceptable thing to do or not. I realize I'm not Native American, but then he is, and it's his first marriage, and, oh well, I just think it would mean so much to him, and…" suddenly she felt very foolish.

"You think if you wear this dress you are becoming like him?"

"I…I guess so. I don't know. Is that bad?"

Lottie smiled. "No. It is good." She walked over to a group of framed photos on a crowded end table, picking up one of a man in uniform. "This was my husband. He wasn't Indian. But we loved each other. We were married for over fifty years. He only died a year ago."

"I'm sorry." Maggie studied the photo of the smiling fair-haired young man. "He was handsome."

Lottie nodded. "Yes. We were happy." Then she turned to look at Maggie, the dress still in her hands. "Have you tried it on?"

"No. I just got it today, and I was a little worried that I might damage it further by trying it on."

"So you don't know that it will even fit?"

Maggie shook her head. "But regardless, I think it should be mended. Don't you?"

"Yes, but let's have you try it on first." Lottie pointed to a door at one end of the long room. "You may change back there."

Maggie went back to a small but neat bedroom. A full-sized bed with what looked to be an old handmade quilt was in the center of the room. "I may need some help," she called as she got ready to put on the dress. "I don't want to break any more of these laces or anything."

"Yes, yes," called Lottie, "I'm coming."

She loosened some laces and moved some pieces around, then helped slip the garment over Maggie's head. She adjusted the laces again, pulled it here and there and then finally said, "Look in the mirror."

Maggie moved over to where a full-length mirror was mounted on the closet door and looked. "Oh, my…"

"It is beautiful," said Lottie.

Maggie turned from side to side, watching as the long fringe swished gracefully and the beading caught the light and reflected it back. "It's beautiful." She felt tears coming to her eyes. "It's perfect. Jed will love this."

"If he doesn't, he's not worth having."

"Oh, believe me, he's worth having."

"Good." Lottie smiled, then began pinching and pulling at the garment again. "I think I can make this fit better by adjusting these laces, and I'll fix this right here." She turned Maggie around again, nodding in what seemed satisfaction. "Yes, this dress is happy with you."

"Happy?"

"Yes, I can tell if it's not. It will not hang right or move right. But this dress is happy for you to wear it."

Maggie smiled. "Well, I know I'm happy in it."

Lottie helped her remove the dress, then took it back to the living room. When Maggie joined her, she had her bead box out and was already matching colors.

"I'm not sure what I should wear with it," said Maggie. "Like on my feet, for instance."

"Oh, I'll help you with that. I have a friend who makes wonderful leather goods, moccasins, shirts, pants…whatever. We'll have him make moccasins to match this."

Suddenly, Maggie remembered she was supposed to choose Jed's clothing as well. "Do you think he could help me with my fiancé's wedding outfit too? I know we don't have much time."

Lottie handed her a business card. "His shop is in Byron. He carries quite a few pieces to choose from, and he custom makes others. You go see him and ask if he has time. Tell him Lottie sent you."

"Lottie, you're a lifesaver. Only yesterday I didn't even know what we were going to wear. And now I feel as though it's all falling into place. Thank you so much." Maggie suppressed the urge to hug the woman, not wanting to make her uncomfortable.

"Thank you," said Lottie. "It is a pleasure to see such a beautiful garment again."

"How long will it take to repair it?"

"Come back in one week, I think. If not, I will call you."

⟶

Maggie went to the leather shop the following day. As it turned out, it was the same one she'd called earlier. She met Lottie's friend Pete and explained what she was trying to do.

"I sort of want it to be a surprise," she told him. "My fiancé asked me to choose his wedding outfit, and he agreed to wear anything I selected."

Pete looked slightly skeptical. "I hope you're right. You know some guys wouldn't want to wear something like this to their wedding. And I can't take returns on any custom or specialty orders."

Maggie nodded. "I totally understand. But if you knew Jed, you would know there's no need to worry."

His brow lifted. "Jed *Whitewater*?"

"Yes!"

Pete smiled. "So Jed's getting married?"

"Yes. You know him?"

"Not really well. But he's been a regular customer in here for years." Pete reached out and shook her hand. "You must be quite a gal to hook ol' Jed Whitewater. He's one nice fellow."

She smiled. "He sure is."

He rubbed his hands together. "This is going to be fun!"

In less than an hour they had it all worked out. Pete suggested buckskin pants and a shirt designed to complement Maggie's dress. He would handle the moccasins as well. "How about a headband for you?" he asked.

She was unsure. "I don't know. What do you think?"

"Well, come over here and have a look." He led her to a glass case filled with beaded pieces.

"The dress has quite a few blue beads," said Maggie. She pointed to a band with beads of a similar color and design. "Maybe that one?"

He lifted it out. "My favorite." He directed her toward a mirror on the wall. "You'd better take your hair out of that ponytail," he suggested.

She shook her hair free and let it fall loosely over her shoulders as he tied the beaded band across her forehead. At first she giggled, feeling like she was playing dress up, but then she looked more closely at her reflection. With her long dark hair and slightly olive complexion, it was rather believable. "I like it," she said in surprise. "I think it looks kind of pretty."

Pete nodded. "It's beautiful. I think Jed will love it."

"Well, you're going to have to come to our wedding, Pete," she said before she left. "And Lottie too."

"I'd be honored."

"Oh, yeah," she remembered. "If Jed happens to come by before then, mum's the word about all this, okay?"

"You bet."

⟿

Maggie told Audrey about the wedding garments, making her promise not to tell anyone else, not even Leah or Spencer. "The only reason I'm telling you is so that you can help make sure the flowers and decorations sort of go with this look. We've already said we want everything to be sort of natural, so it shouldn't be much of a problem."

"Not at all. But that does give me another idea. You know that Native American musician who's coming for the Cultural Celebration the week before your wedding?"

"Yes?"

"I know Spence and Leah are doing some music, but why not see if this guy could play something for the wedding too?"

"That's a great idea, Mom."

"And Spence and Leah wanted to know what they should wear. Maybe I can encourage them toward something complementary. Leah has that brown silk dress that looks so pretty on her. It looks almost Native American."

That night at dinner, Maggie couldn't help but smile as she thought about how pleased Jed would be with their unusual wedding garments. And although she had sworn Audrey to secrecy, she knew she had to share this happy news with Amber because she'd been the inspiration behind the whole thing in the first place. So when they went to the ladies' room together she quickly explained how it had all worked out.

"That's wonderful, Maggie." Amber's eyes shone happily, then flickered briefly with a trace of sadness. "I sure hope I'm still around to see it."

Maggie reached for her hand. "Of course you'll be here. You're doing great, Amber. Why, just look at you. You look absolutely fantastic. And you've been eating better, and sleeping more…"

Amber smiled. "Yes. I am feeling better. It's good to have Ben here."

"And isn't it great that Ben and Jed really seem to like each other?" asked Maggie cheerfully.

"Yes. I always suspected they would."

The women went back out to join the men, and everyone continued visiting and getting along as if they'd been friends for years. Maggie had to remind herself that some of them had.

Maggie tried to push away the words Amber had spoken in the rest room. The wedding was only three weeks away, surely Amber would still be around. How could she not? She glanced at Amber across the table, laughing at an old story that Ben was telling about the time the airline lost their luggage, and they traipsed around Paris one evening wearing some horrible clothes the hotel manager had scrounged up for them. Amber's eyes sparkled and she looked the picture of health. Yes, Maggie decided, Amber was definitely making a comeback. With good food, rest, and medicine, she would be getting better with each day. And in time, she would prove those doctors wrong!

Twenty-Six

The following two weeks passed in a blur for Maggie. Between preparing for the upcoming Cultural Celebration, visiting Amber, and last-minute details for her wedding, it seemed that there just wasn't enough time in the day. And consequently it had been a little while since she'd been up to see the progress on the remodeling project at Jed's place.

"That's okay," he said as they ate lunch at a picnic table outside the crowded deli. "I've decided I don't want you to see it until after the wedding."

"Why's that?"

His eyes twinkled mischievously. "I want it to be a surprise."

"Well, I happen to know how busy you and Taylor have been lately with orders. Leah keeps me informed, you know. So, are you sure it's not that you just don't want me to know that we'll be living amid a pile of lumber and ladders and a house that's still unfinished?"

"Would that change anything?"

She firmly shook her head. "No way, mister. Don't you start thinking you can get out of marrying me that easily."

He reached for her hand. "You wouldn't mind living in the middle of a construction site? I mean, as long as we're still together."

She smiled. "Sure, but don't forget that there's always my house. We could live there for a while."

He laughed. "Covering all your bases, aren't you?"

She nodded. "But seriously, are you really saying I can't see the house until *after* the wedding?"

"That's what I'm saying. I want it to be a surprise."

"Does that mean I have to wait until after the honeymoon too?"

"That's right. But I expect you'll have your mind on other things during that week."

"And you still won't tell me where we're going?"

"I want to surprise you."

"So many surprises." She grinned as she remembered their wedding clothes, still her secret. "And you never know, I might have a few surprises up my sleeve too."

"I was hoping you would."

She laughed. "Speaking of surprises, I'm not supposed to know this, but Cherise is throwing me a surprise bridal shower tonight."

He frowned. "How'd you find out? I know it wasn't from me."

"Poor Amber let it slip. She felt so bad that I promised her I'd act totally shocked about the whole thing."

"How is she anyway? I've been so busy this week I haven't even been able to stop by."

"It's hard to say. Some days, I can almost fool myself into believing she's perfectly fine. But on other days, she seems pretty bad off."

"Michael told me she allowed him to pray for her."

"Yes, she told me that too. She said after he prayed she instantly began to feel better and almost believed that God had really healed her."

"It could happen, you know."

"I know. I really do believe that, Jed. I've been praying too for her to be healed. I just can't bear to lose her."

"You two have gotten so close this spring."

"The only consolation I have, when I think about all this, is how she seems to have reached a place of peace about everything."

"Yes. Michael told me that she's completely trusting God for the outcome now."

"Yeah, I suppose that's what makes me believe that she could actually be healed. That and what Michael said at church last week—about how God likes to walk us through the darkness just so we can really appreciate his light."

"His light reaches far beyond this earthly life, Maggie."

"Yeah, I suppose you're right."

⌒

That evening Maggie walked into Cherise's apartment and pretended to be totally stunned by the group of women who had gathered for the bridal shower.

"Oh, Cherise!" said Maggie. "I can't believe you did this!"

Cherise giggled as she hugged her. "I had everyone park their cars on side streets just so you wouldn't guess."

"You thought of everything."

"And here's one more thing," announced Cherise as she motioned to someone in the kitchen. "Your maid of honor is here."

"Hey there, girlfriend!" called Rebecca as she came out of the kitchen.

"I can't believe it!" The two women hugged. "And you told me you couldn't come until next week."

Rebecca grinned. "I lied."

"Hey, now you'll get to be here for the Cultural Celebration."

Most of the women already knew Rebecca from her Christmas visit, but Amber hadn't met her yet. Maggie took her straight over to where Amber and Audrey were seated on the couch and quietly visiting.

"Okay, I want two of my very best friends to meet," said Maggie as she introduced the women. "In fact, you remind me a lot of each other—you're both positive and outgoing, not to mention beautiful, women."

"Wow, thanks," said Amber. "Shall I pay you now or later?"

"I'm serious. Right off the bat, when I first met you, you reminded me of my old buddy Rebecca."

Audrey nodded vigorously. "You know, I'd thought the same thing, but hadn't wanted to mention it in light of the whole 'other girlfriend' thing."

Maggie sat down between Amber and Rebecca. "Okay, now I'm just about perfectly happy."

"Well, don't get too comfortable, Maggie," warned Cherise, "we've still got to play games."

Cherise led them through a series of games and refreshments and then finally the opening of the gifts.

"We decided that between you and Jed, you probably didn't need a thing for your home," explained Cherise, her blue eyes sparkling with excitement. "But we thought you might need a few things for the honeymoon."

The women joked and laughed as Maggie opened up package after package of pretty nighties and personal items she was certain both she and Jed would enjoy.

"You guys are all too much!" she finally exclaimed as the last gift was passed around. "This has been such fun tonight, and though I don't want to be a party pooper, I do realize most of you will be getting up early to get ready for the Cultural Celebration, so I don't mind if anyone wants to call it an early night."

"Yes," agreed Elizabeth. "I've still got to work on my Tanzanian exhibit. I finally unearthed the box of my safari souvenirs from my trip there last year."

One by one, they began to leave. But before she went, Amber pulled Maggie aside and hugged her firmly. "I just wanted to take a minute to tell you, once again, in private, how very glad I am for you and Jed."

"I know you are, Amber."

Her eyes were moist with tears as she continued. "I think you guys are two of the most special people I've ever known. And it's absolutely wonderful how God brought your lives together."

"Well, in a way, you've had something to do with that." Amber smiled. "Oh, the old 'I broke his heart' theory."

"Yeah, if not for you, he might have married someone else." Maggie glanced at Kate just heading out the door. "He certainly had enough chances."

"God was saving him for you, Maggie."

They hugged again. "Thanks, Amber, I appreciate that."

⟿

The following day Maggie took Rebecca to see the Cultural Celebration. Audrey and Spencer were already there running the Italian booth; it had been Audrey's idea and somehow she'd managed to persuade her grandson to help. Leah was working at Whitewater Works, where Jed, when pressed by Elizabeth, had offered to be the area that honored Native Americans, and he'd even dug around to find a few things to display. Maggie had been worried he'd notice the missing garment that had been his mother's, but to her relief it hadn't been mentioned.

As they walked through the crowded town, bright colored banners hanging from the lampposts flapped in the breeze. It almost seemed as though the spruced-up town sparkled and shone for this special two-day event. Even the weather seemed cooperative, with blue skies and sunshine and high temperatures in the seventies. In fact, the only shadow that preceded the event was the short-lived protest from Randy Ebbert and some of his hate-mongers who marched through the street the day before, but fortunately they were stopped by the sheriff for not having a parade permit. Luckily it was late enough in the afternoon that the city's offices were closed until Monday, which meant the rabble rousers wouldn't be able to secure a real permit in time to disrupt the weekend event. The sheriff, when pressed by Elizabeth Rodgers, even promised that any other attempts to protest would result in arrests. So as Rebecca and Maggie strolled through town that morning, it all appeared to be going off without a hitch.

"This is absolutely wonderful," gushed Rebecca for what must've been the third time. "What a great idea."

Maggie smiled. "Yes, we small-town people sure know how to throw a bash, don't we?"

"I'll say. And I must admit the idea of moving up here grows more appealing by the moment."

"Hey, that's Ben's booth," said Maggie, pointing across the street. "He's Amber's husband, and Elizabeth talked him into doing a booth on Hebrew culture."

"There's Amber. Let's stop and say hi."

An Israeli flag hung overhead, and Amber was dressed in what might pass for some sort of Middle Eastern costume. "Hi, you guys," she called. "Isn't it nice that I could just show up in my bathrobe?"

"Might as well be comfy," said Maggie as she examined the menorah and a few other things. "Are these all from Ben's family?"

"Yeah, some are pretty old, but his mother didn't mind sending them down for this."

"Are you manning the booth all by yourself?" asked Maggie.

"Just for a few minutes. Ben went over to Scandinavia to get some goodies for us."

"How are you feeling, Amber?" asked Rebecca. Maggie had explained Amber's condition to her already.

"Pretty good." She smiled brightly. "I might just hang around here all day." Then she laughed. "Although I'm a poor one to answer any questions regarding Judaism. I never did convert to Ben's faith. And to tell the truth, he's been rather neglectful. But he was raised in a very religious family, and we both have great respect for their beliefs."

"The way I see it, Jesus was Jewish," said Maggie, "and since I believe in him, I figure we must have a lot in common."

"That's just what Michael said the other day. He's been to visit a lot lately, and Ben's quite impressed with that young man's wisdom."

"I haven't seen his booth yet," said Maggie. "I guess we'd better keep moving on. I see Ben heading back this way with what looks like some delicious pastries."

"I think *we* should stop by the Scandinavian booth next," suggested Rebecca.

Maggie and Rebecca slowly made their way through the many exhibits, taking time to have lunch with Jed and Leah at noon, then heading back home to relax during the afternoon. There would be a concert in the park that evening, and the festival would continue into Sunday. Maggie had been pleased with all the media coverage in town today. All her press releases seemed to be paying off. Not only that, but Pine Mountain was packed with tourists.

"It's hard to believe what this town was like just a year ago," said Maggie as they sipped iced tea in the quiet shade of the porch.

"I still remember your first reports," commented Rebecca. "Seems to me you called it a ghost town."

Maggie laughed. "Can't say that anymore."

"And that Whispering Pines development looks like it's going to be fantastic. I'm thinking that whether I move up here in the near future or not, I'd better buy a lot while I can still get one."

"Yes, the price will only go up with time."

The two women chatted until they started preparing dinner for Audrey, Spencer, Leah, and Jed, who would be joining them shortly.

After dinner, everyone headed back into town to enjoy the musical celebration that had been carefully prearranged by Amber. To everyone's pleasure, Amber introduced each musical group herself with energy and flare. And Maggie marveled how, even though ill, Amber still had such a spark and wit to her.

The following day, the festival continued with just as many tourists as the previous day. Maggie and Rebecca offered to help relieve several locals who were slightly worn out from the day before, including her mother and Spencer. But by midafternoon Maggie decided to head home and start getting things ready for dinner. Rebecca would stay on with Audrey. On her way out, Maggie noticed that Amber wasn't in the booth with Ben. "Did yesterday tire Amber out?" she asked.

"Yes. I encouraged her to take it easy today," said Ben, glancing at his watch. "But she said she'd come during the afternoon. She had such fun here yesterday."

"And she was totally marvelous last night," said Maggie.

"Yes, she was pretty pleased with the whole thing." He smiled.

"Do you want me to stop by and check on her?" asked Maggie, feeling mildly concerned by Amber's absence.

"I'd appreciate that. I brought my cell phone, but the stupid battery went dead on me. And I get a little worried when I'm away from her for too long."

Maggie nodded. "I understand. She's been doing so well lately, I almost forget she's sick." Just then several kids came up and began looking at things in Ben's booth. Maggie waved and headed to her car.

She knocked several times on Amber's door, then suspecting she might be asleep, Maggie let herself in. The house was cool and still, with everything clean and in order. It was a welcome change after the hot noisy festival.

"Amber?" she called her name quietly, not wanting to disturb her friend, then went down the hallway toward her bedroom. The door was open, and Maggie stuck her head in. "Amber?" she whispered, "are you asleep?"

The room was still. Too still. Maggie stepped closer to the bed and looked down on her friend lying completely motionless there. Amber's face was the color of alabaster, and her pale lips were slightly parted. Maggie knew without a doubt that she was dead.

Her knees collapsed beneath her and she knelt on the hard floor at the side of the bed and sobbed. "Please, God, no! Don't take her away yet. Please!" Then common sense pressed its way into her consciousness, and she grabbed the phone and punched 911. Perhaps it wasn't too late, she hoped desperately. Hadn't people been revived before? With one hand, she held Amber's cool one, praying for help, for a miracle, for anything. Yet, all the while, somewhere deep inside her, she knew it was too late.

Ben arrived only minutes after the ambulance. "I heard the siren," he gasped as he met Maggie in the hallway. "And I knew—how is she?"

"Oh, Ben!" Maggie's voice broke. "It's too late. I'm so sorry. She was already gone. I didn't know what else to do."

"Can I see her?"

"Of course. The paramedics already said there was no hope of reviving her. They estimate she's been gone for at least an hour or more."

He nodded and continued down the hallway, explaining to the paramedics that he was the husband, and he'd take care of everything. Then the paramedics gathered their things and left Ben to have some time alone in the bedroom.

Maggie answered the paramedics' questions in the living room, her eyes darting down the hallway every few seconds. Finally they packed everything up and went on their way, this time with no lights or sirens.

Maggie called Whitewater Works and told Leah the sad news, asking her to let the others know as well. Then Jed got on the phone. "I'm so sorry, Maggie," he spoke softly. "I know you loved her too. I'm coming right over."

Then in the cool silence of Amber's living room, Maggie broke down and cried with abandon. She cried for her own loss, and she cried for Ben. And then she cried for Amber, so full of life and love only yesterday, and today, gone. It made no sense. And although Maggie longed desperately to entrust God with her loss, she still felt it was entirely unfair.

Twenty-Seven

The funeral was held on Wednesday, and Maggie wished the skies didn't have to be so darned blue. Why couldn't it have rained, or at least been cloudy and overcast?

But perhaps it was a good thing, for Amber had requested that the memorial service be held out-of-doors, in the cemetery, at the grave site, right next to where her mother was buried. It seemed Amber had worked out all these details ahead of time with Michael, who was officiating. But one thing Amber had not counted on was the large crowd of people who gathered to remember her. The small cemetery became quite crowded before the service began.

"Did Amber really know all these people?" whispered Ben, as several more cars pulled up and parked nearby.

Maggie looked over the crowd, all of whom were friends of hers as well, then nodded. "Yes, Amber made friends easily."

"And some of these people are old-timers," added Jed as he slipped his hand around Maggie's. "They remember Amber and her family from when she was a child here in Pine Mountain."

"Last night, Michael showed me a letter that Amber had shared with him," said Ben. "I wanted you two to read it too, but I agreed that Michael should read it here today first. It was written by her mother shortly before her death. It's helped me to understand a few things."

Just then the sound of bagpipes began to fill the air, and everyone turned to see the Scottish bagpipe band that had performed at the music festival only days ago.

"Amber loved them," Ben whispered. "I thought she'd appreciate this."

They played "Amazing Grace" on the pipes, and then Michael Abundi stepped up to the small podium that Jed had arranged at the head of the open grave site. He began to pray: "Dear Father God, we come here today to say goodbye to our dear friend Amber Feldman. And although it is exceedingly difficult for us to part with our beloved friend, we know that you, Lord Most High, have decided to take her home to be with you. And so we ask that you might help our hearts to be willing to let her go."

Michael briefly shared Amber's history, facts he must've gleaned from her or Ben earlier, then he spoke of her searching heart, and how during the past several months in Pine Mountain she'd been seeking answers. "I still remember when I first met Amber. She very nicely told me that she respected my beliefs, but that she had absolutely no interest in them for herself." Michael laughed lightly. "But within the very same week, she called me up and took it all back. And that was the beginning of our many wonderful conversations. Conversations where I learned as much from her as she learned from me. I, too, will greatly miss our friend." Then he read several verses about life after death and the hope of the Resurrection.

"Now I am going to share with you from a letter that Amber shared with me only last week shortly after she found it hidden in some of her mother's old things. Why this letter did not make it to Amber sooner is a mystery, but she was thankful to find it when she did. And it was her desire that I read it to you all today." He looked out upon the crowd, his dark eyes glowing with warm compassion. "Yes, she knew her time was coming soon. In fact, she told me she felt she was living on borrowed time."

He cleared his throat. "The following was written by her mother, on the very day of her death: 'Dear Amber, if you are reading this, then I am gone. And for that I am sorry. For it means I shall miss all the wonderful events in your life. Your first date, your graduation, your wedding, the births of your children. But I know you will make me proud, my dear. And I know that I will be watching. Because now, for the first time ever, I feel completely assured that I will be watching you from heaven. And the reason I know this is because today I placed my life and my heart into God's very own hands. I accepted his Son as my savior, and I have no doubt that I will spend eternity in his care. How do I know this with such assurance? I simply do. I think it's called faith, and it's hard to explain. And so, my dear child, until we meet again on the other side, know that I am with God and that I am up there praying for you, watching over you, and waiting for you to join me. All my love, your mother.'"

Maggie wiped her eyes and smiled. It was just the type of reassurance that Amber had been looking for. And to think she found it within days of her own death. But as if that wasn't enough, Michael invited members of the audience to share their own memories of Amber. To Maggie's pleased astonishment, she heard testimony after testimony of people who's lives had been touched one way or another by Amber. Her own Spencer, then Leah, and even her mother shared some special words. There were several who shared who'd only met her at the Cultural Celebration. One young man took the microphone, his hands shaking as he spoke. "Yeah, I'd stopped by the Jewish booth last weekend just because I always thought it might be kind of interesting to become Jewish. But then this pretty redheaded lady started telling me about how Jesus was Jewish too and how he came to be the Messiah for the Jews, and, well, it just kind of blew my mind. For some reason it all made sense. But I was real sad to hear that she died the next day. Now I'm more determined than ever to find out more about this whole thing."

Maggie felt Jed tense up beside her several times, as if he was about to rise and speak, but something seemed to be holding him back. Then Ben stood up and began to share. "I have to confess that my head is still spinning over all that's taken place these last few weeks. It was such a shock to learn of Amber's illness, but then I learned that she'd been adopted by the wonderful caring community of Pine Mountain." He shook his head. "I still can't quite figure it all out. But thanks to many of you here, Amber lived her last days beautifully. And I was invited back into her life and allowed to share them with her—" His voice broke and he could no longer speak.

Jed rose and went to stand next to Ben. Putting his arm around his shoulders, he took the microphone. "I wasn't going to speak today because I felt fairly certain that I wouldn't be able to keep it together either." He glanced at Ben and tried to smile. "As Ben knows, Amber and I go way back. She was in all actuality my very first best friend. She helped me when I needed it, and I'd like to think I helped her too. She was truly one in a million, and there was even a time in my life when I thought I'd never recover from her breaking my heart." He smiled over at Maggie and then back at Ben. "But thankfully, God had other plans for both our lives." Then Jed looked up to the blue sky overhead. "And I'd like to think you're looking down on us right now, Amber. And I'll bet you're laughing with delight, wondering what this big fuss is all about. It's just that we miss you, girl. We weren't quite ready to let you go. But you can be a good reminder to all of us that this life down here is only temporary, isn't it? And it won't be all that long until we start joining you. Until then, Amber, know that you are much loved and greatly missed."

Michael said a few more things, although Maggie had difficulty paying attention because her mind was fixed on what Jed had just said about all of them joining Amber in heaven someday. And for the first time, heaven seemed very real and true to Maggie. She thought about Phil, and how good it would be to see him again. Perhaps he and Amber were chatting together right now. Suddenly the whole thing just didn't seem so heartbreakingly sad.

Many of Amber's closer friends gathered at her house after the memorial service ended. Despite Audrey's protests, Ben had hired the Pine Mountain Hotel to cater the event, and Maggie was relieved as it was now only a week before the wedding. She and Jed had suggested to Ben that they would postpone the ceremony out of respect for Amber, but he wouldn't hear of it. "How do you think that would make her feel?" he demanded. "No, you must go on as planned. She would want it that way."

Maggie had known he was right, and now more than ever she felt certain Amber would witness their vows from her seat on high. And she'd probably chuckle over the strange wedding attire she had inspired Maggie to utilize.

"What are your plans for this lovely house?" asked Audrey as Ben refilled her punch glass. "Will you put it on the market?"

"No, I think I'd like to keep it, and maybe I'll actually retire over here." He looked at them curiously. "That is, if I'd be welcome."

Maggie patted him on the back. "Welcome? You'd be like family."

He smiled. "You know, that's what it feels like here. Like one big family."

"I know exactly what you mean, Ben," said Audrey.

"Maybe you just needed Amber to bring you home," offered Maggie.

Then Ben lifted his glass, and they all followed him as he made a toast. "To Amber," he said with emotion. "To a life not only well lived, but also well ended."

"To one in a million," added Jed. But when the toast was over he turned and whispered into Maggie's ear, "You're my one in a *billion*."

Twenty-Eight

Just one day before the day Maggie had been anxiously and joyfully awaiting, the skies turned a dark slate color and the wind began to howl like demons. She had gone into work that morning only planning to stay until noon, but by ten o'clock was so restless because of the weather that she thought she might as well go home. The plan for the wedding was to hold the ceremony in her house, and then to proceed outside for the reception. But not if this continued. She stood and stared at the dark skies, noticing flashes of lightning not far off, then turned on the radio hoping to catch a recent update of the local weather forecast.

"Get a load of that weather," said Clyde when she went out into the reception area.

"Yeah," she said dismally. "I was hoping for a little sunshine on my wedding day."

"This could all be gone by tomorrow," he said with a hopeful smile.

"Or else we could tell the guests to bring raincoats for the outside reception my mom has planned."

"Speaking of wedding clothes." Clyde's brows drew together. "You sure you really want me to wear that old rawhide vest and everything?"

Maggie put a forefinger over her lip. "Yes, but remember I said it's a surprise. And don't worry, you'll go right along with the rest of us." She looked out the window again. "I just hope this all blows over soon."

"Don't you worry," called Abigail. "Your house is plenty big enough to pack everyone into if it decides to keep this up."

Maggie frowned. "But who wants to get married on a day like this? Why, even for Amber's funeral last week it was a beautiful day."

Abigail sighed. "And what a beautiful service too."

The phone rang while Maggie started to open up her umbrella. She waved goodbye to Abigail.

"Just a minute, Maggie," called Abigail. "What did you say, Audrey?"

Maggie recognized the alarm in Abigail's voice, and putting down the umbrella approached her desk, her heart beginning to pound with anxiety. "What is it?"

"Hang on, Audrey," said Abigail. She looked up at Maggie with a strange expression. "Um...it seems a tree just fell on your house."

"*What?*"

Abigail nodded with wide eyes. "Your mother says one of the pines around the back just fell onto your house."

"Oh, my—" Maggie gasped. "Is everyone okay?"

"Yes. They're fine. But your house may need some help."

"Oh, blast it," exclaimed Clyde. "I always meant to cut that old pine down. I knew it was getting way too tall to be safe."

Maggie reached for the phone receiver. "Mom, are you okay?"

"Sure, honey. Actually, I was at my house when I heard the boom, and Rebecca had just left to pick up her dress in Byron. The noise was so loud, it sounded like a bomb going off. Then I looked out my window, and there was that old tree broken in half, with the top half hanging right through your roof."

"Oh, no!"

"I'm afraid to go in—"

"No, of course not, Mom, stay out. Oh, dear, I wonder what you do when a tree falls on your house."

"Call the fire department," ordered Abigail from behind her desk.

"Really?" Maggie considered this. "Abigail says to call the fire department. So stay put, Mom. I'll call them and then meet you there. Good thing no one was home. I hope the dogs are okay."

"Don't worry. Bart's with me, and, as usual, Lizzie went to work with Leah this morning."

"I'm on my way, Mom." Maggie hung up and turned to Abigail. "Can you call the fire department?"

"You bet. They'll need to check for broken electrical wires and the structural safety and whatnot before any of you go in."

"I feel like this is all my fault," said Clyde. "I'm gonna drive out there too." He turned to Abigail. "Tell Gavin I won't be able to meet him for lunch today."

Although Maggie was relieved that no one was hurt, she felt worried that her beautiful wedding dress, which she now knew to be extremely valuable, might have been damaged by the falling tree. And if so, how would she ever explain this to Jed?

But she was pleasantly surprised that the situation didn't look quite as bad as she'd imagined when she pulled up. For some reason she'd envisioned her house smashed clear to the ground. As it was, it looked like the tree had only punctured the roof, then stopped at the third floor, although who knew what kind of unseen structural damage might result from that. She picked up her cell phone to call Jed just as the fire engine pulled up.

"Guess what?" she said loudly to hear herself as heavy raindrops pelted down on the roof of her car.

"What is it? Are you calling to tell me how many hours it is until we're officially wed?"

"Not exactly. I'm calling to tell you a tree just fell on my house."

"You're kidding."

"I wish I were. But I'm sitting here seeing it with my own eyes."

"Is everyone okay?"

"Yes. No one was home. But the roof looks pretty bad."

"Well, you were going to need a new roof before too long anyway."

"And the third floor doesn't look too hot, at least the back half."

"Well, at least it's unfinished up there."

"But what about the wedding tomorrow?"

Jed exhaled loudly. "Hmm...I suppose we could move it over to the church building. It's not very pretty in there. It's in the middle of the drywall stage."

"Oh, Jed!" Maggie felt the tears building in her eyes. "Why did this have to happen today of all days? I mean, just last week we lost Amber—" Her voice choked. "And now this."

"It's going to be okay, honey. Just calm down. I have an idea."

She sniffed. "What?"

"How many people are coming?"

"Mom's been estimating about a hundred, although I doubt that it'll be that many."

"Let's get married up here."

She blinked. "At *your* house?"

"Don't you mean *our* house?" She could hear the smile in his voice.

"But is it finished?"

"Oh, it's coming along okay."

"Jed?"

"Just trust me, Maggie. It'll be fine. I promise."

"But you said I couldn't see it until after we were married."

"Guess I'll just have to make an exception."

"What about Mom and all their stuff and the decorations and everything?"

"Tell them to come on up whenever they like. But I'm warning you—you had better not show up until tomorrow just before the wedding."

"Oh my, you sound very threatening."

He laughed. "Well, I just want to save part of the surprise."

"Okay. I'd better go now, Jed. I see one of the firemen waving my way, and my poor mom's been peering out her window every thirty seconds. I have to go hear what the verdict is."

She hung up and got out of her car in time to see Clyde's old truck pulling up. She waved over to her mom as she ran up to the protection of the front porch and then breathlessly asked the fireman how it looked.

"The trunk of the tree busted right through the third floor and part way into one of the back bedrooms. The roof is a disaster. You need to get some big equipment in here to remove the weight of the tree, then get some tarps up to stop the water damage. We've shut down your water and electricity, and of course you don't have gas to worry about out here."

"What a mess," said Clyde as he stomped up the steps. "I just spoke to Gavin, and he suggested having his heavy equipment guys come down from the development and give a hand over here."

"That'd be great," said the fireman. "The sooner we get that tree off, the better."

"Looks like we won't be able to have a wedding here then," said Maggie, still hoping for a miracle.

The fireman laughed. "Not anywhere in the near future."

"Can I go in?"

"Not yet. And maybe not at all. We're still checking out the structural integrity of the building. You may have to stay out until some things get fixed."

"But I'm getting married tomorrow. My things are in there!"

He frowned. "We'll do the best we can. Maybe if we escort you in, it might be okay."

"There are just a few things in my bedroom I've got to get to," she pleaded.

"Why don't you tell me what they are and where they are, and I'll bring them to you."

"Thanks." She carefully described exactly where everything was, either in boxes or hanging in her closet protected by garment bags. "I appreciate this so much."

By the time the fireman returned with her precious things, they had received yet another call for a fallen tree on another house. With Clyde's help, she carried the garments over to her mother's house and laid them out on her mom's bed.

Clyde explained to Audrey what they'd learned as Maggie carefully examined the clothing. Everything seemed to be perfectly fine.

"We'll get that tree off there this afternoon," said Clyde. "Then we'll see if it's structurally sound enough for you people to stay there." He turned to Maggie. "How many you got staying with you?"

"Barry!" exclaimed Maggie, looking at her mom. "He'll be arriving any minute."

"He'll be fine," said Audrey calmly. "And someone can stay with me. But besides Barry, you've got Rebecca, Leah and Spence, and you, of course."

"Well, anyone's welcome at my place" offered Clyde. "Maybe your brother would like it—"

"Barry would love it," said Maggie. "It would be a real treat."

"And Leah and Spence can stay here with me," suggested Audrey. "Maybe you and Rebecca should stay at the hotel tonight." Then her face grew grim. "But what about your wedding, honey? Have you thought about that?"

Maggie smiled brightly. "Jed said we can have it out there. And he said for you and your wedding ladies to come out whenever you like to set it up." She paused. "I know that's going to mean a lot more work for you, Mom."

"We'll make it work. I just hope we can get to the freezer." She nodded over to her living room crowded with various kinds of preparations. "Fortunately I've got most of the decorations over here."

Maggie threw her arms around her mother. "What would I ever do without you?"

"Well, leave all the house business to me for now," instructed Clyde. "Gavin's going to meet me here pretty soon. I'll bet we can sort it all out."

"What about insurance?" asked Maggie. "Should I call?"

"Give me the number and I'll take care of it," said Clyde.

Now she threw her arms around him. "Clyde, what would I do without you?" Then she stepped back and grinned. "You know, you got me into this whole thing in the first place."

He winked. "And aren't you glad I did?"

"You better believe it."

"Now, why don't you head on over to the hotel?" suggested Audrey. "Get a room and try to relax a little. I'll let Rebecca know. Maybe we could all meet there for dinner tonight. See if Cindy can take us."

"But I should stay here and help—"

"No thanks, honey. You look stressed out already, and we don't need the bride falling to pieces tomorrow."

"Well, since you seem to have everything all under control..."

"Don't you worry, these things tend to all work out."

⌒

Maggie tried not to imagine all that could possibly go wrong with her wedding tomorrow. When it was all said and done, what would really matter anyway? Simply that she and Jed had repeated their vows before family and friends. The rest of it was just the icing on the cake. In fact, the more she thought about it, she actually envied the way his ancestors had probably gotten married in previous centuries—perhaps standing together in the woods while solemn words were spoken. So simple, so beautiful. And even if Jed's house was still filled with lumber and ladders, what difference would it really make?

She checked into the hotel and explained the whole thing to Cindy. She decided to reserve the whole banquet room because she really wasn't sure how many people they'd have. "Sorry to sound so flaky," she apologized, "but Mom was taking care of this, and now everything's been turned upside down."

"Don't worry," said Cindy. "That's what we're here for. Have you let all the guests know about the change of location for the wedding yet?"

Maggie smacked her hand on her forehead. "I hadn't even thought of that."

She dashed through the rain down to the deli to get a sandwich and have a quick word with Rosa before she returned to her room to begin phoning.

"I heard the news," exclaimed Rosa before Maggie could even say "hi."

"You're kidding! How?"

"Jed called Sam. He wanted him to go have a look at your house."

"That was good of him. Did he tell you about relocating the wedding?"

Rosa nodded. "I've always wanted to see a wedding up there. It'll be beautiful."

"I hope so. Although, right now, I mostly just want it to be over and done."

"I understand."

Maggie ordered a sandwich to go. "I've got to get back and start phoning everyone about the change in location."

Rosa laughed. "Not so fast. Chloe was just in here and she's doing that, and then Kate upped and offered to take half the list for her."

Maggie blinked. "Oh, then I guess I don't have to worry about that."

"No. In fact, what you really need to do is head over to the fitness center. Cherise has been looking for you. Do you have time to stop in?"

"I guess so. It looks like everything else is under control."

Rosa handed her the sandwich in a bag and smiled. "See, Maggie, this is what it's like to live in a small town surrounded by friends who love you."

Maggie shook her head. "Amazing."

She called her mom from the hotel to let her know she'd be over at the fitness center for a while. "Tell Rebecca she can either meet me there or at the hotel later."

"Oh, good. Cherise has been trying to reach you."

"Is everything okay there?"

"Everything is under control. Gavin and his crew are at your house right now. And even Sam and a couple of his guys showed up."

"I'm starting to feel pretty dispensable here."

"Just enjoy it."

When Maggie got to the fitness center, Cherise swooped her upstairs. "I want to give you the whole beauty treatment," she explained, showing where she had all her spa and beauty products laid out. "You're always doing things for other people, and now it's your turn for someone to do something for you. So, you just better cooperate with me, missy," commanded Cherise with a bright smile.

"I'll do as you say," said Maggie. "Actually, I'm starting to enjoy having everyone ordering me around. It gives me a chance to rest my brain."

"Well, good. You just let that noggin of yours have a nice little break."

By the time Cherise finished with all the exfoliating, herbal wrapping, manicure, pedicure, facial mask, and a few things Maggie couldn't even remember, she felt totally relaxed and refreshed. She hugged Cherise. "Thanks so much. I really do feel great."

Cherise smiled proudly. "And you look great too!"

Maggie got back to the hotel in time to have a short nap before Rebecca came and knocked on her door. "Hi, sweetie," said Rebecca sympathetically. "I heard all about it. How terrible, and right before your wedding day. You must feel absolutely awful."

Maggie smiled. "Actually, I feel great." Then she explained how everyone was being so kind and helpful. "I feel like a queen." She laughed. "Or maybe it's Cinderella. But I'm worried the magic will all end at midnight, and then I'll be back in my fallen-down house wearing a broken glass slipper."

"No such thing. We'll have a good dinner, you'll sleep here tonight, and tomorrow you'll ride off into the sunset with Prince Charming."

"You make it sound so wonderful." Maggie looked at the plastic-covered garment in her hand. "Is that your dress?"

Rebecca grinned. "I sure hope it's the right one. The lady said it's the one you picked out, but it's pretty strange looking."

Maggie peeled off the plastic to reveal a long fringed and beaded silk dress in a soft shade of blue. "I know it's really different, but believe me, it's perfect."

"It's your wedding, Maggie. And I must admit it's better than pink chiffon. I mean, I could actually wear this down in L.A. again—it'd have to be sort of a southwest function, but I could do it."

Maggie looked down at her own outfit, just some old working clothes she'd thrown on earlier that morning to go in for a half day. "I wish I could've grabbed something a little more festive to wear for tonight, but the fireman wouldn't let me in the house until we know it's safe. Mom says maybe by tomorrow morning it'll be okay. Otherwise I might have to do some shopping on my honeymoon."

Rebecca's brows lifted. "Well, you might be in luck. I found a few other things while I was out today. I left them in the car. Maybe you could borrow something for tonight."

"The Fairy Godmother strikes again," laughed Maggie.

Sure enough, Rebecca pulled out a pretty new sweater set that she loaned to Maggie to wear with her jeans. Feeling festive and relaxed, they both went down to the banquet room to meet the other guests for dinner. Barry had arrived safely and took up with Rebecca right where they'd left off back at Christmastime. Clyde brought Barbara Harris as his date, and the two of them were already chatting happily with Ben and Michael. Ben had decided to stick around for the wedding (for Amber's sake, he said) but Maggie hoped it was more than that. All of the Galloways were there, Sam being Jed's best man and all. And of course, Leah and Spence and Audrey, not to mention a few others.

Despite all of the turmoil of the day, everyone was in good spirits, and no one appeared particularly concerned about the inconveniences or the change in wedding plans. For the umpteenth time, Jed prodded Maggie for any information he could get about their wedding outfits, but she managed to fend off his questions with wit and good humor, reminding him that he too was holding out on her about the condition of his house. "We'll both just have to be patient and wait until tomorrow," she said glibly, glancing at her watch. "Only about sixteen more hours, since I'll be out there around twelve."

"Showdown at high noon then?"

She laughed. "Something like that."

"Well, I'll be there," he whispered, "even if all I have to wear is my loin cloth."

"Don't worry, we'll save *that* for the honeymoon."

Twenty-Nine

The next morning, Audrey called Maggie and told her the house had been reinforced and they could now go in to get their things for the wedding.

"We'll be right over," said Maggie eagerly. She hung up and gently nudged Rebecca to wake up. "I'm heading over to the house now. Looks like I won't have to go shopping on my honeymoon after all."

"Too bad," said Rebecca sleepily. "If you ask me, any excuse to shop is a good excuse."

"You want to come?"

"Nah, I think I'll sleep in a little more."

"Okay. Mom said Barry's already there helping her to pack up a bunch of stuff to take over to Jed's."

Rebecca sat right up. "On second thought, I'll bet your mom could use another set of hands."

Maggie grinned. "Yeah, I'll bet she could."

"I'll drive so we can fill up my car too. Good thing I got that mid-sized rental instead of that little pea-sized car they tried to pawn off on me."

Once at her mom's, Maggie left them all to their own devices as she went into her house to gather her things. The electricity was still off, so it was dark and quiet, but fortunately the sun was beginning to stream through the windows. And as Clyde predicted, the storm had come and gone in less than six hours, and today promised to be nice.

She went down the hallway to peek at the bedroom that had been damaged. Fortunately it was the one Barry would've stayed in, so no personal belongings were lost. But the room itself was a disaster. She closed the door and turned away. No need to think about that now.

She got her bag, already packed for her honeymoon with warm-weather clothes as Jed suggested. Then she picked up several more personal items and finally knew it was time to go. For some reason, she felt touched by the whole thing. Maybe it was the quiet semi-darkness of the house. Maybe it was because she was leaving this home that had been so good to her. Or the fact that only a week ago, she had lost a good friend. Or maybe it was simply that in a few hours she would become Jed's wife and enter a whole different chapter of her life. She just wasn't sure. But somehow it moved her.

She got down on her knees next to her bed and bowed her head, but the words just wouldn't come. Why was it her fingers could fly like the wind across her keyboard, but sometimes she just couldn't find the right words to pray?

"Thank you, God," she finally whispered. "Thank you for all you've done in my life this past year. For all you've done for all of us. Thank you, God. From the bottom of my heart, I thank you!" Then she stayed there for some time, just meditating on all that had happened since she'd relocated her life to Pine Mountain. It seemed unbelievable, even to her. But it was real. And how thankful she was for it.

Spencer, always eager to put his learner's permit to use, drove her out to Jed's house. He'd already loaded the music equipment into the back of the Volvo. And now he was acting quite grown up and mature, sitting in the driver's seat. "Are you nervous, Mom?" he asked, quickly glancing her way and then back to the road.

She smiled. "I guess a little. But not nearly as much as I thought I might be. I mostly feel kind of quiet and peaceful inside."

"That's good." He took in a deep breath, as if preparing to say something important. "You know, Mom, I've told you before that I like Jed."

She nodded absently, then a small trickle of alarm ran through her. Surely he wasn't going to express some concern now?

"To tell you the truth, I've always liked him. But I remember for a while I acted like I didn't. I guess I was kind of jealous—like who's this guy think he is trying to take my mom away?"

She chuckled. "I remember that."

"But even then, I really liked him. It was weird. It was like he felt familiar to me, as if I'd known him all my life. I just always felt comfortable around him. When we worked together on the house, I'd even get mad at myself sometimes, 'cause I'd be thinking, this should be my dad working with me, but it's not—and at the same time I really liked him. You know what I mean?"

"Completely. It's as though loving someone else was betraying your dad."

"Yeah. But you know what I think now, Mom?"

"No. What?"

"I think Dad's just really glad we've got a great guy like Jed in our lives."

She smiled, trying hard not to tear up. "I think you're right, Spence." She reached over and touched his arm. "And I think you're becoming a man right before my very eyes."

"Aw, Mom!" But he was smiling.

ᘐ

She walked into the house and nearly dropped the precious garment bags she was carrying. Literally gasping, she looked all around. "Oh, my goodness!" she cried. "I can't believe it!"

"Shoot," said Jed. "I wanted to see your face—" He stopped, then laughed. "Although, I think I'm getting the picture."

"Oh, Jed! How did you do this? It's like a miracle. Everything looks completely finished. It's beautiful."

He put his arms around her. "To tell you the truth, there are still a few things to finish up, but it's mostly done." He looked around the big room proudly.

"Hey, the bride's here," called Taylor as he came in from the backdoor. "Do you like our work?"

"I'm in shock." She continued looking around. "It's more beautiful than I'd ever imagined." She held out the garment bags. "Can I go put these down and then have the complete tour?"

"Sure," said Jed, eyeing the well-concealed coverings. "Are any of those for me?"

"Later," said Maggie. "First, I've *got* to see this house."

After an amazing tour, Maggie went into the master bedroom where Jed had told her to make herself at home and began to unpack the wedding clothes. Then she sneaked downstairs where all her friends were chattering, decorating, and preparing for the wedding and slipped the groom's outfit into Jed's room. Thankfully, he was nowhere in sight. Then on her way back upstairs, she told everyone not to allow Jed to come upstairs under *any* circumstances.

"What if there's a fire, Mom?" asked Spence as he fiddled with the sound equipment in the corner.

"I think it's pretty doubtful we'd have a tree fall on our house one day and a fire the next," said Leah sensibly. Then she turned to Maggie. "Does that mean no one can come up, or just Dad?"

Maggie smiled. "You can come up, Leah. And you too, if you like, Spence."

"No way, that's girl stuff. I'll wait down here with the rest of the men."

"How about me?" called Audrey from the kitchen.

"Of course, Mom. I expect you to come up. You're the mother of the bride."

"That's good to know. I was starting to feel like the hired help."

"Can you use a hand in there?" asked Maggie, coming around the corner, ready to be useful.

"Not on your life," warned Rosa. "You march yourself upstairs right now."

"But it's almost two hours until the ceremony."

"Well, then go fix your hair," suggested Chloe.

"But I'm not really fixing it."

"Then go take a nap or a shower or something," commanded Abigail. "We don't want to see you again until you come marching down those stairs in your wedding gown."

Maggie giggled at the word "gown." "Okay, I'm going. Will you guys tell Rebecca she can get changed upstairs with me? It might get lonely up there."

Actually, Maggie enjoyed having a few moments to herself in the beautiful master bedroom. She went over each detail, from the hand-tiled jet tub in the bathroom to the cedar-lined shelves of the walk-in closet. And the room had never been used. She and Jed would be the first ones to spend a night here.

Rebecca arrived just an hour before the wedding, all breathless. "I'm sorry I'm late. Barry and I had to run back to the house for some things your mother forgot."

"It's okay. There's no hurry. It's not like one of those weddings where I have to put on layer after layer of frills. And I'm going fairly natural with makeup. So I'm just hanging out and enjoying this room."

"It's beautiful," gushed Rebecca. "The whole house is fantastic. I thought it was still in the finishing stages, but it looks perfect to me."

"That was Jed's surprise."

They chatted a while longer, reminiscing of days gone by and dreaming of ones yet to come. Maggie felt pretty certain that Barry and Rebecca were becoming something more than just friends, but didn't dwell on it. All in good time. And then, suddenly it was time to get ready.

Rebecca got into her own dress and then helped Maggie into hers, exclaiming over and over at the incredible beauty of the unusual garment. "It's totally amazing, Maggie! I swear, it's the prettiest wedding dress I've ever seen, and I'm not kidding."

Before long, Leah and Audrey came up. And once again she received the same reaction. Leah even began to cry, hugging Maggie tightly as she sobbed. "It's just like you're my own real mother, Maggie. I mean you even look like Jed and me with your hair like that. Way more than my mom ever looked." She stepped back and wiped her tears. "Do you think I can wear it too, if I ever get married, I mean?"

Maggie grinned. "Of course, I hoped that you would want to. It's a one of a kind piece. And we may need to get it insured or something. It's pretty valuable."

"It could be in a museum," said Audrey, wiping her eyes with a handkerchief. "I've never felt more proud of you, Maggie, than I do right now."

"Why?" asked Maggie.

"Choosing to show your love for Jed like this," her voice choked. "Why, it's just so, so sweet and wonderful."

"Oh, dear," said Maggie. "You guys are going to have me crying too if you keep this up. And I'd really like to make it through this without having red, puffy eyes."

They all laughed. Then Leah excused herself to join the band for the music. "And don't worry, Maggie," she reassured. "We're only doing the quiet stuff." Then she grinned. "Well, at least until the reception. Then we want to *get down and boogy*. Isn't that what you guys used to call it back in your day?"

"Away with you, young thing!" scolded Rebecca good-naturedly.

⌒

Finally, the moment arrived. Rebecca had already gone out the door and was proceeding down the big log staircase. Clyde, dressed as requested in his old-timer shirt and rawhide vest, complete with bolo tie and dark pants, was at Maggie's side. She turned and smiled. "Clyde, if I could've handpicked a dad, he would've been just like you."

Clyde grinned. "Same back at you, Maggie girl. But no more stalling now, you got a good man down there waiting fer ya."

They proceeded to the stairs to the sound of Native American flute music played beautifully by the same musician Amber had located for the Cultural Celebration. The notes floated on the air like wonderful, living, breathing things as Maggie and Clyde walked slowly down the stairs. She felt very much like an Indian princess about to wed her handsome prince. When she saw Jed's eyes on her, she knew her choice of wedding garments was no mistake, and she silently blessed her friend Amber. She smiled as she took him in. His buckskin outfit suited him well, and he looked more handsome than ever. Suddenly it seemed as if they were both acting out some sort of wonderful old folk tale. But it was real. Very real.

Then all she wanted was to get down there quickly, to feel the solid touch of his hand wrapped around hers, but the pace of the sweet flute music forced her to move slowly, gracefully, acutely aware of the silence of the crowd of onlookers as they all looked directly her way. But then she realized that they too were smiling.

She could hardly recall the ceremony when it was all said and done, and to her surprise it passed rather quickly, too quickly perhaps. All she remembered was the feeling of strength and protection as Jed stood next to her, and his hand holding hers. And when it was over—the kiss. Ah, such a kiss!

And the next thing, they were surrounded by friends and congratulations. Doors were opened and the sunshine poured in. The music grew livelier, and she and Jed slipped off to the sidelines for a quiet moment.

"I couldn't believe it when I saw the clothing you'd picked for me to wear," he began. "And I don't know why I never guessed what you might be wearing." He fingered the soft fringe lovingly.

"It was okay then?"

He laughed. "Far better than okay. It was like a dream. A miracle. Beyond my best imaginings." He pulled her close and kissed her again.

"So we both liked our surprises."

He smiled. "I totally loved mine."

"Me too."

"Thanks, Maggie. I'll never forget this day."

She relaxed in his arms, suddenly ready for all the celebrating to be over, for it to just be the two of them alone for an extended time. "How about telling me about the next surprise, Jed?"

"Hmm?" He ran his hand down her cheek with a happy grin.

"You know, like where are we going for our honeymoon?"

He threw back his head and laughed. "Not on your life!"

"Hey, you lovebirds over there in the corner," called Spencer, using the microphone to reach them. "This dance is for you!"

Jed led Maggie over to where they had cleared the chairs for a small dance floor, and the two began to slowly dance to the music. And just as the dance came to an end, Jed whispered in her ear, "Okay, darling, you win."

"What's that?" she murmured.

"Tahiti." He laughed. "We're going to Tahiti."

She laughed and kissed him, then in a quiet voice said, "There's just one place I need to stop by first."

"Your wish is my command."

On their way to the airport, they stopped by the cemetery. Maggie, now changed from the beautiful leather dress into more practical traveling clothes, found her way to a fresh grave site with Jed just a step behind. In her hand was her beautiful wedding bouquet, which she had managed to slip away without actually throwing. Abigail, thinking she meant to keep it as a keepsake, had provided another "throwing" bouquet, which she had joyfully tossed, aiming carefully to Rebecca, who's hand had reached far above the rest to snatch it in midair. But *this* bouquet, her wedding bouquet, she laid upon Amber's grave with a smile.

"Thank you, sweet sister," she whispered. "I hope you were watching."

And in the next moment, Jed gathered her into his arms once again, and their tears mingled together in a mixture of precious gladness and sweet sorrow. Then, hand in hand, they made their way back to his pickup, now ready to embark on their new life together.

About the Author

Melody Carlson is an award-winning author of more than 60 books, from novels to children's stories, including *Homeward* and *King of the Stable*. When not writing, she enjoys skiing, hiking, and boating. Melody lives in Oregon with her husband and their two sons.